ESCAPE
From
RICHMOND

Mary Lu Warstler

IN LOVING MEMORY of:

My Grandmother, Eleanor Dooley Coleman;
My Mother, Mary Coleman Pennock;
My Uncle, James Emmet Coleman.

A Word from the Author

Escape from Richmond is based on family history. Like many oral traditions, there were at least three different versions of the story from my mother, my grandmother and my uncle. Even though their narratives varied, the main points were the same. One of my great…grandmothers left Richmond just before the beginning of the Civil War with a wagon train of women and children. Her husband, both a minister and a doctor, refused to fight in any way. He and several of his friends were imprisoned because of their refusal to join the *Richmond Volunteers* and later the Confederate Army. My great…grandmother invited his friends' wives to travel with her to the Kanawha Valley in northwestern Virginia – now known as West Virginia.

A slave woman from one of the plantations heard about the journey north through the special communication system of the slaves. She waited at the side of the road for the wagon train as the women left Richmond and gave her baby to my great…grandmother, asking her to take him to freedom. The baby's name was Charles. I have a family picture of Charles as an adult with family members who lived in what is now the Charleston, West Virginia area.

On their journey, the women encountered both Confederate and Union soldiers. Each gave them permission to travel unharmed through their territory. The women settled in the Kanawha Valley where some of my family still lives. Oral tradition says my great…grandfather lost his vision either in prison or during his flight when he escaped. Somehow, he and his friends found their way to the women months later.

While I used some family names for fictitious characters, embellished the truth and filled in gaps, I have tried to stay true to the history of the time. Based on research of the Civil War, the areas of Richmond and Charleston and the battles that took place there, I have written the story as I think it could have happened. Throughout my research there were stories of brothers who fought on opposite sides of the war – some even fought against each other in battle. Maverick soldiers often raided small towns and farms, hiding in the thick forests of western Virginia. Many of the places named in the story are real, but I have used poetic license to place them closer together or farther apart for the sake of the story. I also added places that exist only in my imagination.

During the bicentennial celebrations in 2006, I rode in a covered wagon for a day just to experience the feel of riding in a wagon pulled by mules and to develop some idea as to how far a covered wagon full of supplies and people could travel in a day's time. The person driving the wagon shared a lot of information with me about mules. They are better than horses for that particular job because they are stronger and can work harder and longer with less food and water.

While some things might seem impossible, truth is sometimes stranger than fiction. After I had finished one of the many edits, I talked to the Captain of a sternwheeler. He told me of a time when covered wagons were taken by barge up the Ohio River so the settlers could move West. No one had gone before to prepare roads of any kind.

I did most of my research in our local library in Cambridge, Ohio. The historical department was extremely helpful, supplying maps and helping with addresses where I could find more information. I am especially grateful for the help of Tom Snyder, a young airline pilot from the church I attended in Cambridge, Ohio. Tom is a Civil War buff and spent hours helping me to understand the filing system, looking through maps and books and supplying me with information.

The internet provided another source of information from Richmond newspapers of the 1850's and 60's to stories and books written at the time. Pictures and descriptions of homes, furniture and social affairs are available also. One story that one of the characters in the story read was *Peter Parley's Story of the Trapper* by Samuel Goodrich, Boston, 1830. I found it on www.merrycoz.org/books/trapper/TRAPPER HTM.

I could not have even begun to tell the story without the stories from my now deceased, grandmother, mother and uncle. And of course, I am thankful to all my faithful editors – my friend Don Shilling, my husband, Rodney, my son Tim, my daughter Martha and my daughter-in-law Sandra– all who gave their time in editing for the mechanics of writing – plot, structure, grammar, and punctuation. While not editing my work, my daughter Liz gives me invaluable help with medical knowledge and my son Jim's technical computer skills keep my writing tools operable.

Always I am humbled and encouraged by faithful readers who

keep asking for more. My aim is to help the reader to see God at work in our world – even in those times when people discriminate against one another, destroy peace of mind and forget that God created each one of us. My hope is that the reader can find courage, as well as enjoyment, for his/her own life's journey.

Book I

OLIVIA'S PROMISE

Richmond
1859-1861

Prologue   Harpers Ferry

Except for the rumors of war, Sunday, October 16, 1859 in Richmond was an ordinary, Indian summer day. Lone riders, horse-drawn carriages and wagons as well as many families who walked gathered for the evening services at the little white frame Community Church. Reverend William Brunner greeted folks while his wife, Olivia met with her friends before heading for the second pew from the front.

"Wasn't today a beautiful day?" Olivia shooed the twins ahead of her while she paused to greet her friends.

"It was," said Jeannette, "until we met the mayor."

"I suppose he had to try again to recruit Joe," said Olivia. "He's so certain there will be a war that he's going out of his way to talk to Will. He wants both of them in his *Volunteers.*"

"He said something about hearing news that would guarantee a war and he wanted Joe and Will – now."

"What kind of news?" Claudia and Corinne turned to listen.

"I don't know. I don't like that kind of talk. I don't listen," said Jeannette.

"Robert said he heard something about John Brown moving toward Virginia expecting to recruit several hundred slaves for an uprising," said Maggie.

Claudia looked as if Maggie had said the sky is falling. "Ha!" she said. "That's ridiculous. He would have to be crazy to think he could accomplish that."

"Maybe," said Olivia, "but that wouldn't prevent him from trying. And it certainly would create the war the mayor is hoping for."

"Well, I think it's all just talk," said Jeannette. "There will be no war. And I don't think this John Brown even exists. The mayor is just trying to scare us." Jeannette clamped her mouth shut, took two-year old Sarah's hand and shoved Joey ahead of her to the pew where she normally sat.

"That's going to be one surprised woman someday," said Maggie. "I hope she's right, but…"

"Well, I think she's right," said Claudia. "John Brown, if he exists, has nothing to do with us here in Richmond."

"Claudia," broke in Tillie who had been listening, "everything anyone does causes reactions throughout the universe. If John Brown acts on this plan to involve the slaves, whether he wins or loses, we will feel the effects."

Claudia gave her a sneering look and followed Corinne to the pew where their children were already creating a disturbance.

"I hope she's wrong," said Olivia.

"So do I," said Maggie, "but…"

Grandma Ethel Cooper hit the first chord on the piano ending their conversation. As she played "Rock of Ages, Cleft for Me," the worshipers found their seats and Will moved toward the pulpit.

Maybe this newest report is more scare tactics on the mayor's part, as Jeannette said. Olivia. Even if John Brown moves tonight, it won't mean Richmond will be involved, will it? But then…Tillie is probably right.

The pleasant Indian summer day ended in Richmond with folks raising their voices in praise while nature raised her voice in thunder and lightning. An unusual storm was blowing in from the north.

***

Meanwhile, to the north of Richmond, John Brown led a group of 21 men across the Potomac River from Maryland to Virginia. Within hours, they would raid the cache of weapons stored at the U. S. Arsenal at Harpers Ferry.

"Slash those telegraph wires," Brown called to two men. "Make sure you get them all. We want to cut off the town from the outside world. I'm not ready for everyone to know what we're doing – not until I get my reinforcements from the slaves."

The men slashed the wires and moved on to take the arsenal.

"Spread out and round up the townspeople. We don't want them to get away and warn anyone," Brown's voice rose in excitement as he issued orders.

By the time the B & O Railroad train arrived for its regular stop, they had 60 hostages.

"Take them to the fire engine house," Brown called and watched his men herd surprised hostages to the designated place. Then he strolled over to talk to the engineer of the train as it stopped, releasing a rush of steam.

"Got a problem here?" asked the engineer, craning his neck to see what was happening.

"No, just having a community-wide surprise party for the mayor," said Brown. "Everything's all right. You have a good trip."

"Sure will," said the engineer giving the signal for the train to begin moving.

"What'd you let him go for?" asked one of the men who came to see if Brown needed help. "We shoulda held the crew too."

"We don't have enough men to hold everyone in the country," said Brown, his excitement turning to irritability and anxiety. "My reinforcements should be here by now. I planned on at least 200 slaves or more. Where are they?"

"Looks like they ain't coming, but that train sure will send U. S. troops back here." The man turned and stomped away leaving Brown glaring after him.

***

While Brown and his men held the hostages and looked for reinforcements, the train reached Baltimore. The engineer, sensing something was not right at Harpers Ferry raised the alarm. Federal troops arrived in Harpers Ferry, Monday evening.

Four of Brown's men escaped, but the federal troops seriously wounded Brown. They killed ten others and took six more into custody. In Charles Town, the courts tried and convicted Brown of treason against the commonwealth of Virginia. They would hang him on December 2, 1859.

1   *The Promise*

Fall slipped silently into winter – October to November and now to December. Olivia watched Will walk toward Richmond for the evening *Enquirer,* a habit of many years. She felt tension in the air – more than just the coming of Christmas. With the eerie sixth sense she had inherited from her grandmother, she knew there would be trouble. *I'll have to begin working on the Christmas pageant soon.* She shook her head and turned back to dinner preparation with Rosy.

"You is worried 'bout something, Miz Olivia," said Rosy, her dark eyes round, her brown face glistening from sweat as she closed the oven door.

"Not really, Rosy. I just feel uneasy." Olivia pushed her red-gold tendrils from her face and laughed. "Must be Grandma Poff's gift warning me of a change in the weather."

"Your Grandma had the gift sure 'nuff," laughed Rosy. "But she didn't ever foretell the weather."

"Well, whatever is happening," said Olivia, "God is here and we will handle it."

"You got that right," said Rosy.

***

Will reached Richmond and made his way to blind Noah's newsstand. Noah was just opening the stack of papers, so Will helped him sort them and prepare for selling.

"What the headline say, Master Will?" asked Noah.

Will hesitated, the sighed deeply and read, "John Brown Hanged for Treason."

"That be bad," said Noah. "That be real bad. Do I hear sounds of celebration?"

"Maybe… Nelson must have received a message from his outside informants," said Will. "You do hear the sound of celebration, Noah. Toward the courthouse, people are pouring out of buildings into the streets – singing, drinking and laughing. Looks like they're moving toward the outskirts of town. I need to get home and let Olivia know what's happening."

"Yes, sir, Master Will. You take care, sir."

"I will, Noah. You too." He paused and looked around. "Where's David?"

"Here I am, Master Brunner," answered the boyish voice from behind him. David, Noah's thirteen-year-old grandson helped him with the paper stand in the evenings.

"If those rowdies start sounding too nasty, you get your grandfather out of here."

"Yes, sir, Master Brunner. I'll take care of him."

Even amidst the chilling revelry, Noah laughed. "That's my grandson," he said with a proud lilt to his voice. "The good Lord gave him to me when He took my son."

"I'll see you tomorrow," said Will then made his way through the drunken mobs toward home. Above the din of merrymaking, he heard Mayor John Nelson call to him.

"Doctor Brunner. Doctor Brunner."

Will ignored him and continued walking with long even strides until he felt a tap on the shoulder. He stopped and turned to face the mayor and his aide, Matthew Parker. The smile across the mayor's face spoke volumes. *He's pleased with news that has brought on the air of festivity, even if it means a man's death.*

"Quite some news there," said Nelson glancing at the newspaper folded in Will's hand.

Will nodded. "Haven't read it yet," he said.

"But you know what it says," continued Nelson.

"Won't be long 'til we have us an out and out war," said Parker.

"Thought anymore about joining the *Volunteers*?" Mayor Nelson glared at him with a forced smile on his face.

"No."

"Someday you won't have a choice, Brunner." Nelson's eyes narrowed, the smile faded. "You *are* a doctor. We need you."

"I am also a minister and my church and family need me."

"You'll join us Brunner. One way or another, we'll have you in our service." Mayor Nelson continued to glare at him. Parker said nothing, but stared. Will could almost feel his searing hatred.

"Good day, Mayor." Will tipped his hat to the mayor, ignored Parker and walked away. He didn't want to worry Olivia, but he knew they would have to have a serious talk – soon

***

"The biscuits are done," said Rosy. "Shall we keep them warm until...?" Blackie began barking and the twins ran across the back

17

porch. "Never mind," she said, a smile spreading across her face. "Sounds like Master Will is home."

The back door flew open. Corey and Michael ran into the kitchen pitching gloves and hats at the rack in the corner.

"It's snowing," said Michael.

"And Blackie is now Whitey," said Corey. Both boys giggled.

"Dad's home," said Michael.

"He looks worried," said Corey.

"Boys," Olivia stopped them. "Hang up your outdoor things and go tell Betsy and James to wash for dinner."

They started giggling and ran toward the hallway. Olivia called after them. "You wash for dinner, too."

They laughed and called out as they disappeared down the hall. "Betsy, James, Mom said…" Their voices faded and Olivia turned to Will, who followed the boys in. He closed the door behind him and hung up his coat and hat.

He does look worried. We'll need to talk later.

***

Later that night when the children were in bed and Rosy was home with Samuel, Will and Olivia occupied the two rockers beside the kitchen hearth. The fire crackled, sending puffs of smoke up the chimney. Will unfolded the newspaper and Olivia picked up the socks from her knitting basket.

Will shook his head, sighed and began to read, "On October 16, John Brown led 21 men in a raid on Harpers Ferry. The U. S. troops seriously wounded Brown and quickly captured him. They took him to Charleston. A brief trial convicted him of treason. Friday, December 2, Brown was hanged for his treasonous act."

Olivia watched Will's carefully controlled expressions. *Something other than the news is worrying him. He'll tell me in his own time.* She continued knitting, waiting for Will to speak again.

"People were dancing in the streets, drinking as if they were having a special party."

"They were celebrating a man's death?"

"They hope it will bring us to war. I saw Mayor Nelson. He's working harder to get his *Volunteers* ready. He's more sure than ever there will be a war and he wants me and Joe."

"But…"

"I'm concerned, Olivia. I don't want to fight, but I don't want to cause trouble for you and the children, either. Nelson's not going to leave me in peace."

"Will, I know your convictions. You would never fight, nor would I want you to go against your beliefs – war or no war. You know I will support you in whatever decision you make."

"I know you will, Olivia. I won't fight but I'm concerned about you and the children if Nelson should..."

"What Will? What could he do?"

"He can't make me fight, but he could put me in prison – or worse."

"Worse? What could be worse than prison?"

"He could charge me with treason."

"But...they shoot...or hang..."

Uncommon tears welled in his eyes. He blinked them back. "Olivia...promise me..." His voice caught. The words were hardly more than a whisper. He took a deep breath and tried again. "Promise me... that if war comes to Richmond you'll take our children out of here to a safer place."

"You mean leave you here and..." Olivia's hands held tightly to her knitting. She stared into the flames hoping for an omen or oracle. Her thoughts went back to the summer of 1847.

***

Martin Jones, one of the church elders, had introduced Will as the new minister. He was also apprenticing with Doctor Watkins. She was only seventeen, but she told her friends, "I'm going to marry him." On December 24, of that same year – her eighteenth birthday, she married Will over her mother's protest, but with her father's blessing. Matthew Parker had expected to marry her. He was livid. A vengeful man, he would bide his time and make Olivia's life miserable.

***

Olivia wondered if Matthew Parker was somehow behind the harassment to get Will in the *Volunteers*. Olivia shook her head, laid aside her knitting and said with a trembling voice, "Will, surely it won't come to that. You can..." Something in his eyes made her stop. Fear? Will had never shown fear of anything or anyone. She repressed the shiver that followed a sudden chill and changed directions of her words.

"Will, you know I'll do everything in my power to keep our children safe. If they force you into the army, I'll take them North to Uncle George's in the Kanawha Valley until you can join us."

Olivia saw the tension ease from Will's face as he reached for her hand. "That's all I ask," he said. "Just a promise that you will do what you can if I'm not around. I know you're strong and can do it, but I wanted to hear you say so."

Is Will over-reacting? Maybe, but at least my words seemed to give him some relief from his worries. But...leave Richmond? Without Will? Surely, I will never have to keep that promise. It's too...too unthinkable.

***

Olivia pushed her promise to the back of her mind. Talk of the war, while not disappearing completely, dried up somewhat. Olivia had other things to think about.

The following October she was expecting another baby. Talk of war once again dominated conversations everywhere – this time with much more passion. Most of her friends and neighbors agreed with the headlines: "If Lincoln is elected – War Will Follow."

Election Day was only two weeks away.

2   Threat of Things to Come

Shading her eyes against the bright sunlight, Olivia stood on the church porch. Children chased one another around trees and through the connecting cemetery as if it were July instead of the end of October. Dust rose and settled on the ground and various bushes as horse-drawn wagons and carriages clip-clopped away from the church.

Olivia turned as she heard Grandma Cooper's cane-jabbing walk. Although she was Robert's grandmother, everyone claimed her because she was the oldest member of Will's church. Fiercely independent, she allowed Maggie, Robert's wife, to walk with her as long as she didn't try to lead her. They stopped beside Olivia.

"Beautiful day," said Maggie.

Neither Maggie, nor Grandma Cooper commented about Olivia's obvious condition. They knew she never let her pregnancies keep her from her tasks – especially supporting Will on Sunday mornings. People could say what they would, Olivia would do what she believed was right.

Olivia glanced at the clear blue sky and smiled. "A true Indian summer day."

"It might be beautiful now," said Grandma Cooper, "but it'll rain afore nightfall. I feel it in my bones." She laughed – a soft chuckle – and started toward the steps, her cane clicking on the cement floor with each step.

Maggie laughed and followed to give her an arm down the steps. "You take care, Olivia," she said over her shoulder. "Looks like you better rest if you plan to be back here tonight."

Olivia smiled at her friend. "I will," she said.

Jeannette, with Sarah and Joey in tow, followed her husband, Joe out the door. He stopped to speak to Olivia, but Jeannette hurried around him trying to protect the children from seeing Olivia's bulging mid-section. Olivia heard her mutter to herself – something like, "should stay home…disgraceful…"

Joe shrugged and shook his head. Everyone knew how strict and fearful Jeannette was – about everything. "Are you all right, Olivia?

Send Samuel for me if Will needs help when the time comes," he said.

"Thanks, Joe. I'm fine and I am so grateful that you are Will's partner."

Joe ran to catch up with Jeannette and the children. He helped them into their buggy and soon it rolled out of the parking area trailed by a small puff of dust. Several horses still waited, snorting and pawing at the ground as if anxious to leave with the rest.

Olivia pushed back red-gold tendrils that crept from beneath her bonnet to her forehead. At age thirty, friends often told her she was still a very pretty woman. She sighed and leaned against a white column that gleamed in the early afternoon sun. Today she felt tired and old. Pressing her hands into the small of her back, a vague cramp should have concerned her. However, a small dot growing on the horizon toward Richmond caught her attention. The blue sky was cloudless, so what she saw couldn't possibly be a storm approaching. But it was growing. *Maybe it's a small brush fire.* The odor of singed leaves hung in the air and rain had been sparse.

Olivia shielded her eyes with both hands to get a better view. *That's no rain cloud, nor is it smoke. Whatever it is, it's not good.* She pulled her gray wool cape close around her to hide the involuntary shudder.

Turning her eyes from the possible trouble, she looked for her children as she descended the three steps from the church porch. Corey and Michael sometimes acted older, but today they were only five-year-old twins playing tag among the trees between the churchyard and the cemetery. Walking with the clumsy gait of her near-term pregnancy, Olivia crossed the gravel parking area to the wagon where Betsy waited like a proper little lady of ten, fidgeting with the yellow ribbon ties to her brown bonnet. Between her fingers, she twisted the strands of red-gold curls so much like her mother's.

Olivia rubbed her back once more and glanced toward James, her oldest son. He waved to his friends then grabbed each of the twins by an arm and started toward the wagon. At almost twelve, he already matched her height of five feet six inches. Dark hair, like his father's, tumbled over his forehead almost hiding his hazel eyes.

"Tom said his older brothers left for Pennsylvania yesterday," said James with his slow drawl that cracked occasionally. "They're going to work for their uncle in Pittsburgh."

"Their mother mentioned that to me," said Olivia, glancing once more toward the horizon. *That has to be dust stirred up by riders in a hurry.* She forced her attention back to her son.

"Tom says they're really going up there so they can join the Northern army when we have a war."

"James…"

"I know." He grinned and lifted Michael into the back of the wagon. "We don't talk about war."

"Well, not until there *is* a war, anyway," said Olivia. "We hope and pray it's all just talk."

"There's a lot of that – talk that is," said James, swinging Corey up beside his brother and glancing back at the church. "Looks like Dad's ready to go. Shall I help you aboard?"

"Thank you James."

Olivia steadied herself with a hand on her son's shoulder and then climbed with difficulty onto the wagon seat. As if drawn my some magnetic force, her eyes immediately sought that cloud approaching from Richmond. James joined his brothers and sister in the back of the wagon.

Olivia's thoughts wandered. *Ever since John Brown's execution almost a year ago, Mayor Nelson, has been convinced war will follow. He intends to have Will and Joe in his Volunteers. But, today is Sunday. Surely, he wouldn't…*

She let her thoughts dangle and shook her head to erase the uncomfortable direction they had taken. Instead, she turned her attention to Will who was closing the church door. He was as tall, slim and as handsome as he was they day they met. She watched him amble toward the wagon, with a smile for his family. *If he's aware of any danger or tension in the air, he doesn't show it.*

She glanced upward – still no clouds – no breeze. That faint odor of burned leaves was too weak to be a new fire. Dust from the departing worshippers rose and settled for lack of wind to move it. And yet, that cloud from Richmond rolled on like an ominous thundercloud. Olivia pulled her cape tighter around her shoulders as Will stopped beside the wagon.

"Are you all right, 'Livia?" he asked and climbed up beside her. He touched her forehead with the back of his hand.

"I'm fine," she said, forcing a smile.

He took her hand and gazed into her eyes. "Maybe we ought to go home and send our regrets to your parents. With the baby due…"

"Lucy's not due for another week." She knew she answered too quickly, but countered the sharpness with a smile. "I'll be all right," she said. But, try as she might, she was unable to keep her gaze from returning to that rolling cloud or to expel a growing sense of anxiety that had nothing to do with the expected baby.

"Will, that cloud toward Richmond…"

He shielded his eyes with his hand to see better and looked at the moving shadow. "Looks like some kids out racing their mounts," he said. He looked back at her. "'Livia, I know your mother is expecting us, but if you don't feel up to the trip…"

Olivia shook her head. "I'll be all right," she repeated as if saying it again would make it so. "Daddy has some new toy for the twins – some kind of mouth organ, or harp or something like that. They would be disappointed."

"We'll cut our visit short and…"

Suddenly that ominous cloud was no longer moving toward them. It was upon them. Pounding hooves silenced his words, as a great boom of thunder would do. Two uniformed men on horseback reined to a stop before them. One led a third horse with an empty saddle. Swirls of dust like miniature cyclones surrounded the wagon. The younger of the two riders pulled his horse up too quickly, causing it to rear. He gripped the reins with one hand and the saddle with the other to stay on the animal's back.

Betsy and the twins screamed. James pulled them to the floor of the wagon and covered them with his body. Olivia pressed the back of her hand to her mouth to keep her own screams silent. The other hand went protectively across her unborn baby. Will fought to control his own team of horses that reacted to the excited animals before them by tossing their heads, prancing in place and complaining loudly.

The young officer looked hardly old enough to be away from home, much less in an officer's uniform. He continued to struggle to stay in his saddle. The other man looked older and more experienced with horses. He settled his own and the one with an empty saddle with only a word and gentle touch.

Not waiting for his mount to settle, the irritated young officer spoke harshly, "William Brunner?"

"Yes?" Will gripped the reins to keep his team of horses under control. Olivia knew he was also trying to check his temper.

"We have orders to transport you to City Hall."

"Now? Sunday afternoon?" Will sounded more surprised than worried.

The young officer, still fighting his excited mount, said, "Sergeant Parker wants to talk to you."

"*Sergeant* Parker?" asked Olivia, anger replacing her fear. She knew it wasn't proper for a woman to question men in any situation much less a *Volunteer,* but she had never been one for proper formality. Will took her hand. She stared at the young man on the horse until he squirmed. Her anger began to ebb somewhat.

The young man, keeping his eyes on Will, refused to acknowledge Olivia. "Mayor Nelson appointed Matthew Parker as Chief of Recruitment for the *Richmond Volunteers* and gave him the rank of Sergeant."

Before Olivia could say more, Will squeezed her hand and asked, "Can't this wait until tomorrow? Jefferson Dooley is expecting us this afternoon."

Olivia felt Will's muscles tense as he squeezed her hand tighter. She knew he was fighting to keep his own anger under control as well as warn her to do the same.

"I don't care if the president is expecting you," snarled the young man. "Sergeant Parker said to bring you in – now."

"Will?" Olivia, brow furrowed with anxiety, looked up to his troubled face.

"It'll be all right, 'Livia." Will frowned and turned to his oldest son. "James, you drive the team to your grandfather's." He glanced at Olivia's pale face then back to James, who was climbing over the seat back. "Take it slow and easy. I'll be there in a couple of hours."

"I wouldn't count on that," said the young man in charge. The other man, closer to the age of Will, stared at the sky and held the reins of the extra horse. He shifted in his saddle and turned his head to release a flow of tobacco juice across the yard.

"And who do you think you are that you can order my husband around like that?" Olivia stared at the young man. He glared, apparently not used to anyone questioning him – especially a woman. Her hands tensed into fists. She felt Will's eyes upon her as he left the wagon, but she could not ignore this affront to her from Parker – and she knew it was to hurt her as much as it was to harass Will.

"Not that it's any of *your* business, ma'am, I'm Corporal Fredrick Stevens."

Proper behavior for a woman or not, Parker knew Olivia well enough to expect a response from her and she would not disappoint him. "Well, Corporal Fredrick Stevens," said Olivia, words clipped with cold, controlled anger. "You give *Sergeant* Matthew Parker a message from *me* – *Olivia* Brunner. I expect my husband to be at my parents' plantation within two hours' time – or I will personally drive into Richmond and speak to him."

"But…"

"You tell him." Olivia fixed her eyes on the man's face until it turned scarlet. Will, long used to his wife's outspokenness, smiled, kissed her then mounted the extra horse.

"Tie his hands, Private Roberts," barked Corporal Stevens. "We don't want him getting away from us."

"Yes, *sir*," said Roberts. He took a piece of rope from his saddlebag and put it around Will's wrists.

"Behind his back." Stevens' voice cracked again.

"Don't be stupid – *sir*," said Roberts. "You want him to fall off the horse? Sergeant won't like that."

"Well, all right," said Stevens, "but make it tight."

"Sure," said Roberts as he secured Will's hands with a loose knot.

James, from his father's place on the wagon seat, flinched and moved as if to jump at the man with the rope. Olivia placed a restraining hand on his arm.

"It'll be all right, James," she said. "Matthew Parker owes your grandfather too much to risk any trouble with him."

The three men turned toward Richmond. Olivia forced a tight smile for the benefit of her children, but her heart pounded so hard against her chest she was afraid she would have a heart attack before she had a baby. She clasped her hands together to hide their shaking. No matter what she said, she was worried and she knew Will was too. *Can they force him into the Volunteers? Can they keep him from his family, his church and his medical practice?*

3 Taken to Richmond

Will, more concerned about Olivia than his own discomfort, forced his gaze to stay on the road ahead of him. He was afraid if he looked back, Olivia would know how worried he was. He knew she was upset and he couldn't bear to see her concern. *Surely, Parker is just flexing his political muscles. He knows he can't force me into the Volunteers now, or the army later if the nation goes to war. My faith and will power are stronger than his desire for revenge.*

The three horses pounded their way back to Richmond, sending a cloud of dust into the air like an exploding giant puffball. Will clenched his teeth as Corporal Stevens kicked his horse, slapped its sides to force his steed to gallop ahead. *He probably thinks Parker will give him a big promotion for bringing me in. If I know Parker, that young man will be mighty disappointed.*

Holding tightly to the saddle, Will glanced at Roberts. Will had known Carl Roberts for several years. The man was a heavy drinker and gambler. *Probably ended up as a Private in Parker's Army because he lost one card game too many.* In the same line of thinking, Will couldn't help a small lift in the corner of his lips as he thought of Parker losing his bid for Olivia's hand in marriage.

He must be getting desperate. I need to have a serious talk with Olivia soon – remind her of her promise if Parker succeeds in keeping me from my family. Looks like he's getting more serious. Hard to tell what he'll try next.

Richmond came into view with its many buildings and wooden sidewalks. Stevens didn't slow down until they were almost to City Hall that housed the mayor's and other government offices. The horses slowed to a quieter clip-clop.

Not much activity here on a Sunday afternoon, which is probably why Parker chose this time of the week. No witnesses around.

Roberts dismounted before his horse hardly stopped moving and gave Will a hand. Stevens glared at him.

"Thanks," said Will. He was sure Stevens intended to humiliate him in some way.

Roberts nodded. Stevens threw his reins at the Private. As if commanding his dog to sit, he said, "Tend to the horses."

"Yes, *sir*," said Roberts. He led the three horses away – Will assumed to the community stable behind City Hall.

Corporal Stevens grasped Will by his coat sleeve and shoved him toward the main entrance. Will tripped on the step to the sidewalk, but managed to right himself without falling. Stevens jerked him toward the over-sized, wooden double doors. Still holding Will's arm, he rapped twice. Matthew Parker opened the door as if he had been standing on the other side waiting for them. Corporal Stevens pushed Will inside the expansive, empty waiting area of City Hall and kicked the door shut behind them.

"Doctor Brunner," said Matthew Parker. "My office is this way." He nodded his head toward the row of doors then led the way across the dark, gray-carpeted floor. Will couldn't help looking down on Parker's smaller frame from his own six-foot stance. Parker was older and much heavier. Thinning strands of gray/black hair tried without success to cover the balding pate.

Parker stopped at the door, raised his arm and polished his nameplate with his coat sleeve. "Pretty impressive, don't you think?"

Will said nothing.

Parker shrugged, opened the door and stepped inside, motioning for Will to follow.

"Let's cut the artificial niceties, Parker. What was the idea of sending that man charging at us in the churchyard? And why drag me off like a common criminal with my family watching?"

Corporal Stevens followed them into the room uninvited. He knocked Will onto a chair and backhanded him, the heavy ring on his finger leaving a slow trickle of blood making its way down Will's face.

"That's *Sergeant* Parker to you," Stevens said.

"That's enough, Corporal," said Parker frowning at the man. "I asked Doctor Brunner here to talk, not fight."

"But sir, he…"

"I said that's enough. Learn to control that temper of yours, Corporal, or you'll be mucking out stables the rest of your enlistment."

"Yes sir." The reply was sullen.

"And why are his hands tied? Take those ropes off."

"We didn't want him to get away."

Parker's face turned scarlet. He glowered at Corporal Stevens. "Doctor Brunner is a man of honor. I want *him* in my army. I can get along quite well without Corporals who have ambitions of taking my place. Now get that rope off him and wait in the reception room."

"But…"

"Now – and we'll talk about your careless attitude with a young family later."

"Yes sir." Corporal Stevens' face mottled with anger. He removed the rope and stalked out of the room.

"Now, Doctor Brunner, let's talk about deals."

"We have nothing to talk about," said Will, massaging his wrists. "I told the mayor before I'm not interested in deals."

"Oh, but now we can make it well worth your while. Whatever your income is from both your medical practice and your church, we'll double it. I'm sure you want Olivia to have nice things like she had before she married you."

Will smiled to himself at the man's envious expression and obvious attempt to make him feel guilty. "Olivia is happy with things the way they are. She doesn't want more."

"Of course she would tell you that, but the truth is, she's a woman. All women want wealth. She was raised with it. I'm sure she misses it."

Will stared. There was no point in arguing with the man who still carried a grudge against him and a torch for his wife.

"We have other methods of convincing you, Brunner. One way or another we'll get you into the *Volunteers*. Mayor Nelson has given me a free hand – and funds to back it. I've recruited help from South Carolina. They're working on another plan even as we speak."

4   At the Plantation

Olivia felt James giving her sideways glances from the corner of his eye while he drove the wagon as carefully as he could. She turned to him and forced a smile. "It will be all right, James," she said. "Your father can take care of himself."

He nodded and she fell back into her troublesome thoughts. She knew James also was lost in thoughts too complicated and frightening for children. She dared not look back at Betsy and the twins, but they were unusually quiet, especially for the twins.

They passed white rail fences surrounding a pasture still green and vibrant. Two frisky colts played a game of tag, running and nipping at each other. Above them a hawk, wings stretched to full width, sailed in circles looking for dinner. Suddenly he swooped, silent and swift. Without disturbing so much as a blade of grass, the hawk's huge talons wrapped around a small rodent then he flew back to the trees to enjoy his meal. A large, gray cat that had been stalking that rodent swished her tail and ran back across the field toward a barn on the hill. Olivia heard Betsy sigh and the twins giggle. She was glad that they were still children enjoying antics of nature.

As they rounded the bend that brought the Dooley Plantation into sight, Olivia smiled in spite of her worry. Her parents' three story white mansion with its white columns gleaming in the sun stood majestically on a hill overlooking River Road. Beyond the mansion, the blue sky and forest's display of fall color framed the plantation's array of buildings – barns, outhouses and slave dwellings. Threat of war and Parker's revenge seemed too incongruent on such a picture perfect day.

With almost as much skill as his father, James pulled the wagon around the half-moon drive of the mansion. Jefferson Dooley and one of his slaves awaited them on the verandah. Olivia always thought her father was a handsome man – tall and broad-shouldered. Even now, with a half-ring of hair, streaked with more white than red, brushing his ears and neck, he looked younger than his sixty some years. She had inherited his red-gold hair and sapphire blue eyes.

"Whoa, there," said James drawing the wagon to a stop. Jefferson's smile turned to a frown as he reached to give his daughter a hand down.

"Olivia? Did Will have an emergency? He shouldn't have let you come alone in your condition."

Before his mother could answer, James said, "Mr. Parker sent two men after him when we were leaving the church." The red circles on his cheeks told them he was still angry over his father's treatment.

"Matthew Parker? Today? For what?"

Olivia nodded and kissed her father's cheek. "The mayor made Matthew a sergeant and put him in charge of recruitment. I guess he decided today was as good as any other to talk Will into joining."

"Matthew knows better than to pull a stunt like that," said Jefferson. He turned to the tall, thin black man, who waited beside the horses. "Moses, saddle Prince. I'll go have a word with our friend, Matthew Parker."

"Yes sir, Master Jefferson."

"Moses, bring Beauty, too," said James. "I'm going with you," he said turning to his grandfather.

Jefferson gave his grandson a half-amused, patronizing look. "Sorry, James, you're too young…"

Blood rushed to the boy's face adding more color to his already red cheeks. Holding his clenched fists close to his side, he said, "I'm not a little boy. I'm almost twelve and that man has my father." His voice cracked, but he paid no attention. He stared at his grandfather, eyes flashing.

Surprised, Jefferson stared back at his grandson, who had never talked back to him – or anyone else – before. Then he threw back his head, laughed and slapped James on the back. "By golly, boy, you might look like your father, but that sure sounded like a Dooley speaking. Moses, take the wagon and saddle both horses."

Moses jumped on the wagon. "Second thought," he said, "we'll ride with you. Be quicker that way. Olivia, tell your mother we'll be back as soon as possible. Don't wait dinner on us. Come on James."

"Yes sir," said James. He turned to Olivia. "Don't worry, Mom. We'll bring him back." He ran after the moving wagon and threw himself on the back.

Afraid she would embarrass her son if she tried to speak around the lump in her throat, Olivia nodded. She watched them leave then followed Betsy and the twins as a young slave girl led them into the house.

5   The Rescue

As if glad for the chance to run, Prince and Beauty thundered down the path to the road to Richmond. Their riders, both experienced, let the animals have their way. The pounding hooves made talking impossible, but both man and boy were too lost in worrisome thoughts to talk anyway.

James is only a boy, but I can see worry and anger on his face. I understand his anger. What is Parker trying to prove anyway? Does he really think he can pull a King David and get Will killed in some far off battle so he can have Olivia? We aren't even in war yet – unless he knows more about the rumors than most of us know. What will happen to Olivia if Will doesn't come home? She's too stubborn to come live with us. Jefferson nudged Prince in the side and sent him running faster. James followed his grandfather's lead.

Reaching the city limits, they reined the horses to a trot and were finally able to speak. "Do you know where they are?" James looked at his grandfather with hope and anticipation as they turned down Main Street.

Jefferson nodded. "Probably at City Hall – where the mayor's office is. I expect Nelson put Parker next to him so he could keep an eye on him."

They continued in silence until they reached the government building. Jefferson dismounted. James slid down beside him. "Shall I take the horses to the town stable?"

"We shouldn't be here that long. We'll just hitch them to the post. Moses will give them a good rub down when we get back. Henrietta will be hopping mad as it is because she has to hold dinner."

"But you told Mom…"

Jefferson slapped the boy on the back and laughed. "Now, you don't really think your grandmother will listen, do you?"

James grinned.

"Let's find your father and get back to the plantation."

Jefferson stomped up to the door. Fist doubled, he pounded, waited a few seconds and raised his fist for another round of assault.

The door flew open and Corporal Stevens jumped back to avoid Jefferson's fist from falling toward the space where the door had been.

"Today's Sunday," he said. "These offices aren't open to the public."

"We came to get my dad," said James pushing under his grandfather's raised arm into the room.

"I don't know what you're talking about kid. You can't come in here."

"You took him and…" James leaped at the man, fists doubled. Jefferson grabbed his arm and pulled him back.

"Hold on there, boy. We don't want any violence – yet." He stared at the soldier and nodded for James to check the names on the doors. "You brought Will Brunner in to see Matthew Parker. Where are they?"

"I don't know what you're…"

"Kid, if you expect to live long enough to become more than a corporal, you better refresh your memory – real quick. I don't want to tear all those doors off their hinges one by one to find him."

"You don't scare me. Sergeant Parker can…"

"Can what Corporal?"

Jefferson and Stevens stood in the doorway arguing. The corporal seemed to have forgotten the boy behind him, who was moving from door to door, checking names. He stopped and turned to face the arguing duo.

"Grandfather, over here."

Jefferson pushed Stevens aside and started toward James. The corporal grabbed his arm. "Let go of my sleeve, young man," said Jefferson with a low growl. Bright red color crept up the corporal's face, but he held on and pulled. "I warned you," said Jefferson and swung his other arm around clipping the young officer's jaw. He let go of the sleeve and fell onto a chair. Before he could regain his stance, James turned the knob on Parker's office door, pushed it open and rushed in to kneel beside his father.

"You all right, Dad?"

Parker jumped from his chair, tipping it over. "Get out of here, kid. Corporal! Corporal, come in here and…" James turned and glared at Parker as Jefferson appeared in the doorway.

"He's on the chair out there nursing his chin," said Jefferson.

James turned back to his father, pulled his handkerchief from his pocket and dabbed at the cut on Will's cheek. "Looks like you might have a shiner by morning," he said.

"It's only a superficial cut," said Will trying not to smile and ruin his son's heroic action. "Nothing serious. How's your mother?"

Jefferson had Parker under control, so father and son ignored Parker's sputtering.

"She's all right," said James. "They're all with Grandmother."

"Did you think I needed help?"

"No, I just didn't want Mom to worry…Besides," he added then grinned, "I didn't want to miss any of the action."

Parker started for the door calling for Corporal Stevens again, but Jefferson Dooley put his arm across the doorway to stop him. "I don't think I would leave just yet," he said.

"You can't barge in here and…"

Jefferson said nothing, but took a step forward, towering over Parker who had to take two steps backward to avoid the older man from knocking him over. Jefferson took another and another until he had Parker backed behind his desk.

Parker picked up his fallen chair, dropped onto it, pulled a large white handkerchief from his coat pocket and wiped his brow.

While James talked with his father, Jefferson leaned on Parker's desk and glared at him. Parker shrank back into his high-backed chair.

"Have you lost your senses, man?" With Jefferson's deep bass voice, he didn't need to raise the volume. Parker winced. "You can't abduct a pastor from his church in front of his family like a common criminal just to fill the ranks of your *Volunteers*!"

"Stay out of it, Dooley. You know we want him for his medical knowledge, not his preaching."

"I'll not stay out of it," Jefferson said through clenched teeth. "I can't help it that Olivia chose Will over you. That's all in the past. He's her husband now and my son-in-law, so I'll not stay out of it."

"He's a doctor. We need him and we'll have him." A scarlet color rose up Parker's neck all the way to the tip of his ears and on to his face.

"He's also a preacher and his family and congregation need him. Is this the way you get all your recruits? Does Nelson know your methods?"

Parker's already red face took on a darker shade approaching a purplish color. "Nelson told me to do whatever it took to get Brunner and Phillips in the *Volunteers*."

"Including scaring his wife, who is expecting a baby any day? You better pray that shock doesn't make her lose the baby."

Parker stood, straightened his coat and smoothed his hair.

"Corporal Stevens is young and eager. He might have gotten a little carried away. No harm done. I'll see that he's disciplined." He turned to Will, keeping his tightened fists at his side. "Get out of here, Brunner, but don't think you've heard the last of me."

"I'm sure I haven't," said Will.

Jefferson shook his finger at Parker as if he were reprimanding a naughty child. "Remember what I said, Matthew. I won't stand by and let you destroy my daughter."

He turned abruptly and stalked out of the room. "Let's go boys," he said. "Elizabeth is holding dinner for us."

6　*Grandma Elizabeth*

Mattie, not much older than the twins, led Olivia and the children to the parlor. Corey, too impatient to follow her, ran ahead and threw open the door. Elizabeth Dooley sat beside the partially open window, waving a fan back and forth, as if it were July instead of October.

Elizabeth was shorter than her daughter and a little on the plump side, but she knew how to use fashion to look her best. Her navy dress with a white lace collar and cuffs and tiny pearl buttons up the sleeves and down the back, made her look pounds thinner. Through years of practice, she could sit straight with the multiple hoops and so many petticoats that she lost count when putting them on. She raised her head and held the fan mid-wave as Corey burst into the room, Olivia, Mattie, Michael and Betsy following.

Arching her eyebrows in question, Elizabeth glanced at the children then Olivia and asked, "Where are Will and James? Is something wrong?"

Olivia, aware of her own dark maroon dress minus the frills of lace, fancy buttons and hoops surrounded by many petticoats, paused inside the door. The breeze from the open window carried her mother's familiar scent of lavender across the room. She opened her mouth to answer, but the twins ran to their grandmother, dropped to their knees on either side of her chair and as they often did, told their grandmother what happened speaking as though the words were one thought.

"Grandma," said Corey, "we were leaving the church…"

Michael picked up the thought mid-sentence, "…two men rode up on giant horses…"

"… and one reared…"

"…and almost made the man fall off…"

"…but he didn't…"

"…and he yelled at Dad…"

"…and the other tied him up and…"

Betsy, at a more lady-like pace, followed her brothers, gave her grandmother a kiss then punched her brothers on the arm and said, "Corey! Michael! Where are your manners? Say hello to Grandma."

She scolded the boys as if she were their mother instead of a sister only a few years older. Olivia smiled and Elizabeth had difficulty keeping a straight face.

"Sorry," said the twins together.

"Hi, Grandma," said Corey. His familiar giggle followed his words.

"Good afternoon, Grandmother," said Michael, scowling at his brother and bowing to his grandmother.

Elizabeth wrapped an arm around each of them and said in her soft, deep southern drawl that she had never lost since moving from Georgia to Virginia as a child. "Now, what were you saying about giant horses tying up your father and dragging him off?"

They giggled. "The horses didn't tie him up," said Corey.

"And they didn't drag him away," said Michael.

With Betsy's help and clarification, they retold the story. Elizabeth looked to Olivia for confirmation.

"They told it pretty well, Mother. Daddy took James with him to Richmond to see what he could do. He said not to wait dinner."

Elizabeth brought her brow into a frown then glanced at the children. Letting the frown slip away, she smiled at them and reached for the pull. "Thank you, children, for informing me. I'm sure your brother and grandfather will take care of the problem. We'll wait dinner for them, of course, but I'll send yours to the nursery right away. You must be hungry."

"Yes, ma'am," said Betsy, punching Corey in the arm before he could speak, "but if you don't mind we'll wait until the men return." Corey and Michael glared at their sister.

"Very well, Betsy," said Elizabeth, "I'll send some crackers and milk in case you need a snack before they return for dinner."

"Thank you, Grandmother," said Betsy.

"Thanks, Grandma," said the twins.

Mattie tumbled into the room. Although she tried, she had too much energy for her tiny body and seemed to always trip over her own feet. Eyes like saucers and a toothless grin across her shining black face made it impossible to scold her.

"Mattie, take the children to the play rooms, then tell Henrietta dinner will be delayed until Master Jefferson returns – two hours at the most."

"Yes ma'am," she answered and followed the children from the room.

Elizabeth waited until they were gone then turned to her daughter, who had seated herself in the opposite wing-backed chair. Olivia sat on the edge of the seat, ignoring the vague cramping in her back.

"Now, Olivia, tell me why those men would take your husband?" Elizabeth's brown eyes narrowed watching her daughter's face.

"Mayor Nelson put Matthew in charge of the *Volunteers*. They want Will." Olivia didn't intend to cover the truth, nor did she intend to let her mother know how worried she was.

"Matthew Parker? Surely he…"

"I know, Mother, he knows better."

"But he used to…I mean he wanted to…"

"Marry me? I can't help but believe that's part of…"

"Surely he wouldn't hold that against you after all these years."

"I hope not, but…"

The two women sat silently watching each other. Elizabeth glanced away, looking out the window. She bit her lip then said, "Everyone knows Will's view of war and slavery isn't very popular."

"I know that," answered Olivia with a note of defense in her voice, "but he has his convictions and Matthew Parker is not going to change him."

Elizabeth waved a hand as if shooing a fly. They both knew better than to argue, it would only lead to more friction. Olivia had her father's temper and her mother's stubbornness. "Well," said Elizabeth changing the subject, "like I told the children, I'm sure the men will get it settled."

"I hope so."

Both fell into their own world of thought. What could they talk about? Nothing about the war, or even the possibility of it. That wasn't polite conversation for ladies. The weather? How much could they discuss a beautiful day?

Elizabeth sounded more concerned about her daughter than the weather, or even Will's problems with Matthew Parker, for that matter. "Olivia, you look pale. Why don't you lie down until the men return? It's getting too close to time for that baby for you to worry so much. I wish you would consider staying…"

"Don't start, Mother. You know I won't stay here."

"But, we have far more room and help to…"

"I know you mean well and I appreciate your willingness to help, but I have Will and Rosy. That's all I need."

Elizabeth smiled. "I'm surprised Rosy is still with you after you…well, you know…"

"Freed her?" Olivia smiled too, remembering when her mother

had given Rosy and her husband Samuel to her when she and Will were married. She freed both of them as a Christmas gift. Both had chosen to stay with Olivia as paid help.

"How is Rosy?"

"Bossy as ever," said Olivia. She smiled glad to have the focus off her and her coming baby.

Finally, after a few more periods of silence followed by attempts at conversation, Olivia cocked her head to one side and said, "I think I hear the men returning."

7 Where's Corey?

The parlor door opened and James ran into the room ahead of his father and grandfather. "Sorry we're late, Grandmother," he said going down on one knee beside her chair to give her a kiss on the cheek. "I'm sure Corey and Michael told you where we went…in great detail."

Elizabeth smiled at her oldest grandson. "I don't think they left anything out." She placed a cool hand on the boy's flushed cheeks. James pushed his damp hair from his sweaty face.

"Olivia, when did this boy become such a nice looking young man?" James blushed and she continued, "If you're man enough to accompany your grandfather on such an important mission, perhaps it's time you join the adults at the dinner table."

Olivia's eyebrows rose and she blinked with surprise. Her mother had always insisted that the children eat in the nursery. When Olivia had tried to include them in the family mealtime, Elizabeth said repeatedly, "Mealtime is for adult conversation."

A deeper shade of red spread across James' cheeks as he refused his grandmother's invitation. "Thank you for the offer, Grandmother," he said, "but Betsy and the twins need me. They'll be worried. Dad and Grandfather can fill you in on what the twins didn't know, but I need to let them know Dad's all right."

"Very well," said Elizabeth, her own eyebrows arched. "Maybe next time."

While James talked with his grandmother, Jefferson kissed his daughter's cheek and Will knelt beside her. Olivia laid one hand on the side of Will's face and took her father's hand in the other. A frown crossed her brow as she touched the cut.

"It's only a scratch," Will said and kissed her on the other cheek. James left the room and Will turned to greet his mother-in-law.

Jefferson squeezed his daughter's hand and she glanced up at him. "Daddy?"

"Like he said, Olivia, it's only a scratch. Parker's just flexing political muscles. Will can tell you about it later."

Elizabeth arched her eyebrows at her husband. "Jefferson Dooley," she said, "you will not wait until later. You will tell us now. We've worried about you for the last two hours. We'll not allow you to breeze in here as if it were nothing."

"Mother's right," said Olivia. "Henrietta has waited two hours. What are a few more minutes?"

"All right," said Jefferson, throwing his hands up in mock surrender, "but why don't we talk while we eat?"

"Very well," said Elizabeth. "I expect the children are hungry. They refused to eat until they knew their father was all right."

Will's eyes widened in surprise as he helped Olivia to her feet.

"Betsy's decision," she said and smiled. "You know how bossy she can be with the twins."

Elizabeth rang for Mattie. "Tell Henrietta we're ready for dinner to be served." Then she took Jefferson's arm and led them to the dining room as if she were leading a large dinner party.

***

Adhering to the old customs, Olivia and her mother returned to the south parlor after the meal, while Will and her father went to the library. Olivia looked longingly after the men as they closed the door. "Mother, couldn't we all sit together today? It's not like this is a big dinner party."

Elizabeth looked as if she were lost in thought. "Maybe next time," she answered. "I'm sure Will and your father need to talk about what happened today."

"I know you're probably right," said Olivia. "It's just that…"

"You were frightened and need to be near him?"

Olivia was surprised. "You know, Mother," she said, "I never thought you understood me, but…"

Elizabeth chuckled. "Olivia, do mothers and daughters ever really understand one another? I don't understand you sometimes, but woman to woman we have the same fears where our men are concerned."

"I guess you're right," said Olivia. They fell into more small talk about the weather, life on the plantation and the children until Olivia felt another twinge in her lower back, stronger than the earlier ones.

Trying not to show any concern, she leaned forward as if to stand. "If you don't mind, Mother, Will has another church service tonight and it's been a rather harrowing afternoon for all of us. I think we ought to leave now."

Elizabeth, not so easily fooled, narrowed her eyes at her daughter.

"Olivia, I know the baby's not due for another week, but…"

"I know, Mother. Babies have minds of their own when it comes to being born." Olivia pushed herself from the chair with obvious difficulty.

"Maybe you should stay. Will is here and Henrietta and…"

"I want to be home."

"But, what if…"

"You and Daddy taught me not to live by *what ifs*." Olivia moved with more determination toward the door as she spoke. "I'll be fine."

"Olivia, you don't want her to be born in the wagon on the way home."

"No, I don't." Olivia smiled at her mother's use of *her*. "I want to be in my own home with Will and Rosy to watch over me."

Mattie waited, looking from Elizabeth to Olivia and back as each spoke. Olivia smiled at the little girl. "Mattie, please tell the children and Master Brunner we need to leave now. Then ask Moses to bring our wagon around."

"Yes'em." She made a clumsy curtsy and ran before anyone could scold her.

"Olivia, please reconsider…" Elizabeth followed, laying a hand on her daughter's arm as if to hold her back.

Olivia gently pulled away and continued to the verandah where she glanced around for Will and the children. *Mattie probably couldn't get the men's attention.* Betsy, James and Michael were on the verandah, but…

"Where is Corey?"

James shielded his eyes with his hand and looked toward the wooded path to the river. "He took one of the horses for a ride. He should've been back by now. Do you want me to find him?"

Typical of late October, the earlier clear sky had become cloudy and the Indian summer day was slipping into fall temperatures. A brisk breeze blew steadily from the west bringing with it the moist smell of the river. Olivia nodded to James and pulled her cape closer to her, even though she knew the breeze did not cause her chill.

James gave her a concerned glance. "You all right, Mom?"

"Yes, James," she said, "but, please hurry."

"I'll have him back here as quick as I can," James called over his shoulder as he ran toward the stables.

Olivia began pacing. It was still early, but she was sure now that the cramps in her back were the beginning of labor. Since this was her fourth pregnancy, the time of birth could be much shorter from the onset of contractions. She didn't want to give birth at the plantation – or worse, yet, as her mother suggested, in the wagon on the way home. That all concerned her, but an even greater fear lurked at the edge of her consciousness – something she had read.

A tiny article buried in the pages of *The Richmond Enquirer* at least a week ago…*Something about kidnapping children in South Carolina and forcing them into military service, or…using them to force their fathers into service, or…*She couldn't remember it exactly. South Carolina had seemed so far away at the time and had nothing to do with Richmond. Now, it not only seemed important, but crucial, for her to remember. Someone had kidnapped children. Irrational fear for Corey gripped her harder than the real fear of having a baby in the wrong place.

"Olivia, why don't you come and sit down?" Elizabeth motioned to the rocking chair.

"What…?" Her mother's voice startled her. Lost in the clutches of her fears, Olivia had almost forgotten where she was. "I'm sorry, Mother. I was…I was thinking. No, I can't sit. I need to move around."

"Olivia, you can be so stubborn…"

Olivia said nothing but walked to the edge of the verandah, leaned against the white column and watched for her sons' return.

Elizabeth tried again. "I think…"

Olivia whirled around. "I'm fine, Mother. Please, just leave me alone!"

Elizabeth looked startled then hurt at the sharpness of her daughter's voice. Betsy and Michael stared with wide eyes. Even Olivia was stunned. She had never used that tone of voice with anyone and especially never to her parents.

Olivia clenched her teeth as another contraction caught her back. When that wave of pain passed, she sighed, her cheeks warm with embarrassment and fear. "I'm sorry, Mother. I'm worried about Corey, but that doesn't give me the right to speak to you that way."

Elizabeth nodded. "I understand," she said. "Betsy why don't you and Michael come here and tell me what you're learning. Your mother will let us know if she needs anything."

Olivia wasn't sure if her mother was being helpful or sarcastic, but she was glad to have the children occupied.

Elizabeth sat in a rocker while Betsy and Michael sat on the edge of the porch on either side of her. Betsy began telling her grandmother about school and Michael told her about books Betsy was teaching him to read. From the corner of her eye, Olivia could see her mother watching her. That both irritated and pleased her but she was more concerned about Corey than her mother's possessiveness. Where was Corey?

8 Kidnapped

James ran, stumbled, righted himself and raced into the stable. Moses, hitching the team to the Brunner wagon, turned. "Slow down there, Master James. I'm hitchin' the team fast as I can. Yo' mama must be in a big hurry."

"She is, but…have you seen Corey? I got to find him."

"Said he was goin' to watch the river. Beauty still got her bridle. Want a saddle?" Moses started toward the horse to help, but James already had the black mare out of her stall.

"I'll take her the way she is." James said and hopped on the stall gate then to Beauty's back. He took off, not waiting for further comment from Moses.

"The river's a good mile the other side of the woods," James muttered to himself as he ducked into the woods and followed the well-worn path. "Wait 'til I get my hands on that kid. I told him to skip the ride today. He's probably sitting on a boulder by the river, lost in his own little world."

James leaned close to Beauty's neck to avoid a low hanging limb. Blue jays screeched in the trees above him and a chipmunk scurried across the path barely missing the thundering hooves. The wooded tunnel of bright colored leaves fanned out into a short clearing that divided the forest from the river. The smell of fall mingled with river smells – burned leaves, coming rain, crops harvested, ground prepared to rest for spring planting and the odor of fish and river water.

James broke through the last of the brush. "There's the mare tied to a tree, nibbling at the grass around her, but no sign of Corey…and, what's that?"

About a hundred yards downriver, a small riverboat bounced and bobbed against the river current. James stared. "Why is a riverboat anchored out here in the middle of nowhere – and on Grandfather's property? Just the thing to draw Corey's attention."

James slid off Beauty's back, tied her beside Corey's mare and ran toward the riverboat. A man in a gray military shirt with a red bandana around his neck glanced up as James approached the boat.

"Hey there," called James.

The man ignored him and returned to his task of pulling in the gangplank.

James moved closer. "Did you see a little red-haired boy around here? That's his horse over there." He nodded toward the path.

The man kept working but mumbled an answer. "Seems I seen a kid like that take off through the woods over yonder. Looked like he was chasing a squirrel or something."

"Sounds like Corey," said James. "He's real curious. Could he have turned back to check out your boat?"

"Possible, I guess. Didn't see him get on, but come on aboard and have a look for yourself if you want."

"Thanks. I guess I will."

The man shrugged and bent to shove the gangplank back to the shore. James tried not to stare at the man's many scars that stretched white across his upper arm muscles. Other scars on his face drew his right eye downward and the corner of his mouth upward.

"Thanks, mister," said James, trotting up the gangplank to the deck. "I won't be long. Corey likes anything that moves."

"Look all you want, kid." The scarred man turned back to his task of preparing the boat to move out.

What looked like a large upside down square box took up most of the forward area of the deck. James couldn't see around it to the other side, so he ran between the railing and the box-like cabin, calling to his brother.

"Corey. Corey, are you on this boat? You better come out if you are. We gotta go, so don't be playing games."

An uneasy feeling gripped the pit of his stomach. *Something's not right. Corey would never leave his horse tied to a tree like that for very long. He can get in more trouble than any five-year old I know, but he's also considerate and thoughtful of others. He knows how to care for animals and he knew Mom wanted to leave early.*

Behind him, a squeaking and squawking like a henhouse invaded by a hungry fox sent a chill down his back. James whirled around. The man with all the scars was turning a crank drawing the anchor from the river. It hung precariously above the end of the boat, dripping water onto a coil of rope, while the man secured the crank.

He's getting ready to leave before I'm off the boat. James glanced back to where he had boarded the boat. *The gangplank is gone. The boat is moving. That man is going to kidnap me!*

"Hey, how am I supposed to get back to shore?" James tried to keep the panic from his voice.

"You ain't. Hey, Mike, we got us another one. Come and get him."

"Another what? Where's my brother?" James turned to look for Corey. He caught the smell of something that almost made him gag – a cross between strong body odor and wet fur. Even Blackie didn't smell that bad on the hottest days of August when they threw water on him to cool him off.

"This the kid you talking about?" A big, burly, man twice the size of the first one came around the corner. His hairy hand covered Corey's mouth, while Corey wiggled and squirmed under his arm like a caught bass.

James looked up at the giant of a man who seemed to be covered – head, face, arms and hands – with thick black hair. Now he knew where the smell came from. The man had to be a cross between a giant and a bear.

The boat lurched and picked up speed. *He shouldn't be moving so fast.* The movement threw him off balance. James grabbed the top rail to steady himself, keeping his eyes on his brother.

Mike also caught off guard, staggered and pitched toward the rail. Grabbing it, he bellowed at his partner. "Hey, you trying to throw us all overboard?"

A cackle-like laugh from the captain's deck answered. Mike shot back some words the boys knew existed, but had never heard. Corey took advantage of Mike's distraction, clamped his teeth into a finger and kicked a leg. The big burley man roared like the angry bear he resembled. He yelled more words the boys had never heard and dropped Corey, who backed away like a startled crayfish.

Scar Face, as James had dubbed the other man, ran unsteadily back to help Mike, who roared and beat the air trying to grab the boys. James and Corey ducked, avoiding his flailing arms.

"Corey, quick! Under the rail," James yelled. Corey jumped to his feet and dived between the rails. Both men moved in on James. With heart pounding, James listened for Corey to hit the water. When he heard the splash, he slipped over the side and followed him. Angry shouts from the boat faded as it continued downriver.

The retreating boat left rippling waves rocking the boys against the riverbank. Corey hauled himself out of the cold water, sat on the bank and took long, gulps of air. Throwing himself to the bank beside his brother, James caught his breath and together they watched the boat disappear.

Corey gasped for air between chattering teeth. He pushed his wet, red hair back from his face and looked up at his brother with wide eyes. His familiar giggle was missing, but the twinkle in his eyes said he had enjoyed the thrill of the adventure – now that it was over and he was safe. "Thanks, James. I was really scared 'til I heard your voice."

"Corey, you're going to be the death of me yet." James shook his head spraying his brother with river water. He slapped Corey on the back. "We better get back. Mom needs to go home. I think the baby is going to be early. She don't need two cases of pneumonia on top of it." James stood and reached for his brother's hand.

"I didn't mean to be gone so long," said Corey running beside James. He gasped for breath as he tried to run and talk at the same time. "I…just wanted to watch the water…The boat…man invited me to come…and see…"

"Better run and talk later," said James, "That riverboat took us about a half mile from the horses. Let me do the talking when we get back."

Corey nodded and they ran faster until they were back at the path to the plantation. James picked Corey up and pitched him onto his horse, then stepped on a log to boost himself onto Beauty's back. They sped up the path, galloped through the woods and into in the meadow.

"Looks like Mom is watching for us," said James.

"Is she mad?"

"I think she's more worried than mad. Better ride on up to the house. Moses can take care of the horses."

9 Corey's Story

Olivia heard rumbling like far-off thunder before she saw the mounted horses emerge from the woods and race across the meadow. She sucked in her breath – in part because of pain, but more in relief that there were two riders. Corey was safe. But even from that the verandah, she could tell something was wrong. Mother's intuition? The gate of the horses?

The horses galloped across the meadow and the boys reined them to a stop in front of Olivia. They slid from their horses' backs, still wet from the river water. Corey's wide-eyed expressions told her she was right. *There is trouble.*

"James? Corey?"

"Sorry, Mom," said Corey.

"He fell in and I had to go in after him," offered James. Olivia raised her eyebrows and gave James a quizzical look. She knew both boys were good swimmers.

"There has to be more to the story," she said. She knew Corey couldn't have just fallen into the river. "But for now, we need to get both of you to Henrietta. The air is becoming colder and I don't need two sick boys on my hands."

She turned to Moses, who had been waiting with them beside the wagon. "Take care of the horses, Moses. I'll take the boys to Henrietta. Michael, find out what's keeping your father. Mattie probably couldn't get their attention. Betsy, stay with the wagon. Don't let the horses wander off."

Elizabeth rose and moved toward the door. "Michael, you stay with Betsy," she said. "I'll get your father."

Olivia was aware her mother had changed her orders, but she was more concerned with getting everyone, including herself, home safely – soon if possible. Whatever the reason, the boys were soaked and needed to get warm and dry. Henrietta could handle that better than she could under the circumstances.

***

Will and Jefferson, still involved in speculations about the possibilities of war, forgot the time and Mattie's message. The sudden knock at the door – much more forceful than Mattie's – broke into their conversation. Elizabeth opened the door and stood glaring at the men.

"Elizabeth? Where's Mattie? You should have…"

"She came once. Apparently, you didn't pay much attention to her. Corey was missing. James went after him. They both returned soaking wet. Olivia took them to Henrietta. She wants to leave."

"Is she all right? Are the boys…?" Will asked, putting on his suit jacket.

"She says everything is fine, but she's not acting like it is. I think the baby is on its way. Jefferson, you should talk to her. She won't listen to me. Make her stay…"

"Mother Dooley, Olivia has made it clear she wants to be home when she has this baby."

"I think it's coming sooner than she planned. You better talk to her."

"Well, we can't talk to her if we stand here arguing the point," said Jefferson. "Let's go."

***

Taking each boy by an arm, Olivia hurried to the back entrance. Henrietta, a tall, slim black woman in her later years, had been with the Dooley's most of her life. She laid aside the broom when Olivia pushed the door open and burst into the kitchen with James and Corey shivering in wet clothes. Henrietta shook her head and hurried to the stove to move the water from the back warmer to the hotter front area.

"In the pantry," she ordered pointing the way for James and Corey. "Strip those wet things off. They's blankets on the bottom shelf. Wrap yo'selves and get out here by the fire. What yo' mean goin' down in the river this time of year?"

While she scolded the boys, Henrietta set pans of hot water beside the fireplace and threw another log on the fire sending more heat along with the smell of burning wood into the kitchen.

Olivia waited, foot tapping until the boys settled beside the fire wrapped in their blankets, feet in pans of hot water. While Henrietta hung their clothes around the room to dry, Olivia looked first at Corey, then James.

"Well?"

James took a deep breath and explained how he followed the trail to the river where he found the riverboat.

"Riverboat?" Olivia's thoughts raced back to the kidnapping

article in *The Enquirer*.

"Yes ma'am," said James. "I thought they might be poachers, but they had Corey and didn't seem to have any hunting or fishing equipment."

Olivia felt the blood drain from her face. She gasped, but nodded to James. "Go on," she said.

"We jumped overboard when the boat started toward Richmond. That's about it," he said. "We hurried back as quick as we could."

"Corey, what did they want?" Olivia looked at her younger son. She could always count on him for some kind of mischief.

"I don't know exactly. They said something about using me to make Dad join the *Volunteers*."

A chill added to her tension. She was afraid to ask, but had to know the truth. "Where were they from?"

"One of the men wore some kind of uniform – sort of like the *Richmond Volunteers*. I heard him say something about this being easier than South Carolina."

Olivia's heart skipped a beat. She would have a talk with Will later, but for now, she had another, more urgent concern. The boys were safe, but she had a baby coming early. "Stay here and get warm and dry. Moses will bring you home later. I can't wait for you."

"We'll be all right, Mom. I won't let him out of my sight." James glared at his brother.

10   Lucy

Will and Jefferson hurried to the verandah, Elizabeth right behind them. Michael and Betsy waited in the wagon where Elizabeth had left them. Michael held the reins, keeping the horses steady.

"Where's your mother and brothers?" Will asked.

"Mom took James and Corey to Henrietta 'cause they were all wet," said Michael.

"We were ready to go and Corey wasn't here. Mom sent James after him. James said Corey fell in and he had to go in after him." Betsy said eyes wide with concern.

"James had to go in after Corey?" Will asked. *Something's wrong. Corey has been able to swim like a fish since he was three.*

"Stay put, we'll be back in a minute," he said and started toward the back of the house, almost colliding with Olivia as she came around the corner.

"Olivia?"

"It's all right, Will. Henrietta is taking care of the boys. Moses will bring them home later. I'll explain on the way."

"Maybe we should…"

"No, Will. I need to leave. *Now*." When Olivia used that tone of voice, something was wrong and he knew she wouldn't talk about it until they were alone.

Will gave her a startled look, but took her arm and helped her back to the wagon. Michael climbed over to the back beside Betsy and Will helped Olivia to the seat. Elizabeth stood beside it wringing her hands and shaking her head.

"Jefferson, will you talk some sense into her?"

"Olivia, your mother's right. Maybe you should stay here tonight. It's been a hard day."

Olivia settled on the wagon seat beside Will and said, "Thank you, Daddy, but I really want to go home." She clamped her mouth tightly shut. Will knew that look. If they opposed her much more she would burst into tears. The wagon started to move forward and she turned back to her father.

"You need to talk to the boys before you send them home, Daddy."

Jefferson gave his daughter a curious look. "More trouble?"

She nodded and turned her face homeward. Will frowned, but snapped the reins. Olivia was pale and her face drawn with more than just worry about the boys. Once out of earshot of her parents, Will asked, "Are we having a baby when we get home?"

Olivia tried to smile, but clenched her teeth and took a deep breath. "Maybe before," she said when that wave of pain had receded.

Will gave her a horrified look. "Olivia! We should have stayed…"

"Just drive, Will. We'll make it home," she said, then added under her breath, "At least I hope so."

As soon as they were out of view of the plantation, Will stopped the wagon. He jumped down, ran around to the back of the wagon and pulled cushions from the benches to the floor. He insisted that Olivia lie on the makeshift bed.

"Betsy, sit with your mother. Tell me if she needs me to stop. Michael, come up here with me in case you need to hold the reins."

"Okay," Betsy answered. She folded her legs under her, sat on the floor and removed Olivia's bonnet. Olivia lay with her head on Betsy's lap.

Pulling her handkerchief from her pocket, Betsy daubed at the sweat forming on her mother's brow. Michael scrambled over the seatback and sat close to his father, eyes wide and staring ahead, hands folded in his lap.

Will urged the horses on with as much speed as he dared on the rough dirt road. At least with the election only weeks away, politicians had given the road some attention. He knew her jaws must ache from clenching her teeth. Not wanting to worry the children, she would hold back any cry of pain.

With a final slap of the reins on their rumps, the horses galloped into their backyard. Blackie came running around the house to greet them, yapping excitedly.

"Whoa there," said Will pulling on the reins and reaching for the hand brake. He set it, hardly waiting for the wagon to stop moving. He jumped down, issuing orders as he ran to the back of the wagon.

"Betsy, get some water on to boil. Michael, fetch Rosy then draw more water from the well. Samuel will take care of the horses."

He picked Olivia up and carried her into the house, down the hall and into their bedroom.

***

Samuel sat in their porch swing and Rosy in the rocker enjoying the October Sunday afternoon. Rosy, never one to be idle, stitched some baby clothes for Olivia while she rocked. Samuel whittled a new whistle for one of the twins. A cool breeze began to blow across the porch caressing Rosy's chocolate colored skin that glistened in the fading heat of the Indian summer day.

"That sure felt good," said Rosy. "I hope that rain comes soon."

Samuel grinned. He and Rosy had been married for as long as they could remember, but never had any children of their own. The Brunners were their family. "Might be best if it held off till the folks get home," he said.

Rosy chuckled and nodded in agreement. Blackie, who had been sleeping at Samuel's feet raised his ears and cocked his head as if listening to a distant sound. He jumped to his feet and looked toward the main house, twitching with excitement. With the sound of hooves pounding into the backyard, Blackie flew off the porch and ran. Rosy lifted her overweight body out of the rocker and started down the steps, Samuel right behind her.

"Sounds like Master Will's in a mighty big hurry," said Samuel.

"Must be Miz Olivia," said Rosy lifting her skirts and running toward the house. "He don't drive that fast – not with the kids in the wagon and her in that condition."

At the corner of the house, they collided with Michael. Samuel threw his arms around the boy before they both fell. "Easy there boy. You don't want to knock us all down."

Rosy paused long enough to ask, "Your mama need help?"

"Yes ma'am," said Michael "Dad said to come quick. I'm to get more water for Betsy."

Rosy picked up her skirts and ran much faster than her weight should have allowed her to do. Samuel grabbed Michael's hand and followed.

***

Betsy ran into the kitchen, threw her cape and bonnet on a chair and grabbed some kindling from the box in the corner. She lifted one of the front plates on the stove and threw the shreds of wood onto the bed of hot coals. Without waiting for it to catch and burn stronger, she reached for the kettle of water on the back burner and pulled it forward to another front plate. The kindling had caught, so she carefully placed several small logs crossways so they'd have enough air to burn then pulled the plate over the hole.

Rosy followed her into the kitchen and reached for more pans to

54

help. "Daddy wants you back there," Betsy said, nodding toward the bedroom at the end of the hall.

"Um, um, um," muttered Rosy shaking her head as she ran down the hall. "I just knowed this was gonna to happen. She shouldn't oughta been out in her condition."

Betsy moved the plate on the stove, poked the fire, added another small log and re-covered the hole. Soon the heat and aroma of burning wood filled the room. Water that was still warm from sitting on the back burner began to bubble. Rosy hurried out several times to get some of it and returned to the bedroom without saying a word. Betsy filled several more pots and set them on the stove.

***

Samuel took the horses and wagon to the barn, while Michael ran into the kitchen, grabbed two empty buckets and ran back to the pump in the clearing between the main house and the cabin around back. Filling them as full as he could carry, he returned, sloshing water along the way. Back in the kitchen, he grabbed the mop and cleaned up the spills. Waiting for another bucket that needed filled, he sat in one of the rockers, eyes wide and hands folded in his lap. Betsy put on a pot of coffee then sat beside her brother in the rocker. He slipped his hand into hers and Betsy put one arm around him and squeezed his hand with her free hand.

"It's all right, Michael," she said trying to sound very grownup. "Women have babies all the time."

"I know," said Michael, "but she looked so…so…scared."

"That's because those men took Daddy away after church this morning, then she thought Corey was lost this afternoon. They're both back, so Mom's all right."

"Oh. But…" Before Michael could finish his thought, the lusty cry of a newborn infant came from the bedroom.

Betsy grinned. "See?"

"Why is it crying?"

"Babies always cry when they're born 'cause now they have to breathe air and wear clothes and stuff."

"Oh. But, I'll feel better when Dad…"

"When Dad what?" Will slipped into the kitchen and dropped onto a chair where he could lean his elbows on the table. Betsy and Michael jumped up. Michael ran to his father and Betsy reached for the coffee pot.

"I made some coffee for you, Daddy," said Betsy handing him a cup with steam rising in great swirls above it. Strong coffee aroma filled the air.

"Is Mom all right? We heard the baby cry." Michael pressed against his father who wrapped an arm around his son.

"Your mother and the baby are both just fine, Michael. Thank you, Betsy." Will took the coffee, set it on the table and put his other arm around his daughter. "Rosy's cleaning up your new sister, Lucinda Marie."

A grin spread across their faces. "Now Betsy has a sister, too – born on her birthday," said Michael. "Course James and Corey and me have two sisters."

"You both have been a great help. Thank you."

"We'll help take care of her, won't we, Betsy?" Michael looked up at his sister, who smiled back at him and nodded.

***

Olivia, exhausted, but content, sat propped up with pillows, the little bundle beside her. The door opened and Betsy stuck her head around it. "Are you sleeping?" she asked.

"No, Betsy. Come in and see your little sister."

"Me too?" Michael slipped in holding onto Betsy's hand.

"Of course, you too," said Olivia. "Your father told me what a good job you both did helping him. Thank you."

"Betsy did most of it," said Michael. "I just carried water. I didn't slosh much. Betsy built the fire and boiled the water and made coffee for Daddy and…"

"Michael," said Betsy, "that's built, not builded." Her cheeks were cherry red with embarrassment and pleasure.

"We get the picture, Michael," said Olivia. "Sit here on the side of the bed and you can hold Lucy for a minute."

"Really? Me too?" Michael's eyes widened.

"You have to be really careful and gentle," said Betsy. She helped her brother hold the baby, under the watchful eyes of mother, father and Rosy.

Olivia allowed herself a few tears of pride as she watched her children. Although she had pushed thoughts of war and fear far into the background of her consciousness, that nagging sixth sense warned her they were still near.

Lucinda Marie was a healthy baby and had a good set of lungs. Betsy handed her back to her mother. "I think she's hungry," she said. "I'll go help Rosy fix our men some supper."

Olivia smiled as Betsy and Michael left with Rosy. Lucy began sucking her nourishment. For the moment, she had not forgotten

Corey's worrisome adventures, but had tucked them away in her memory until a later time.

***

Later that evening Will announced to a full congregation the arrival of their new daughter, Lucinda Marie Brunner. The men, however, were more interested in hearing about his experience of the afternoon. They talked longer than usual after the service that night.

11 Pre-election Speculations

Olivia stared out the kitchen window. She pulled her gray, woolen shawl around her shoulders, holding the ends together close to her breast. Two weeks ago, the weather had been almost summer-like. Today, only the heated protests, arguments and speculations on the coming election, warmed the wintry air. Olivia knew in her bones – the way her Grandmother Poff had known things unknowable – that this election, would bring disaster for everyone.

Behind her, Rosy hummed while preparing for the day's baking. "Now, Miz Olivia," she said, abandoning her humming for her *Mammy lecture* tone. "You ain't gonna make the cold go away or the political situation any different by stewing about it."

Olivia turned her gaze from the window. Even though the warm kitchen turned away the cold wind, she shivered. "Rosy, are you a mind reader?"

"No, ma'am. Don't take no mind reader to know you is upset. Don't think it's the weather that makes you shiver neither."

"You're right, of course," said Olivia, watching Rosy place the ingredients on the table. *Such a normal action in an upside down world.*

"I remember *helping* you bake bread when I was just a toddler."

Rosy chuckled. "You was my baby – my responsibility. I didn't do nothing you couldn't do with me."

"We've been through a lot together, Rosy. I just hope this war talk…"

"Miz Olivia, you just stop that right now. We ain't in no war yet and if we do get in one – well, the good Lord ain't gonna abandon us. Besides that, you shouldn't oughta be up working so early this morning – worrying about things you can't fix no way. That little angel ain't even two weeks old." Rosy scolded as she began mixing her bread dough.

"I'm not working hard, Rosy. I only packed lunches for Betsy and James. You don't want them to go to school hungry do you?"

Rosy shook her head and muttered to herself, a smile softening the gentle rebuke even more. Olivia laughed. Flour dusted Rosy's face, apron front and her arms up to her elbows. She kneaded the dough – pushed, pounded and shaped it into loaves that would be fresh bread by suppertime. Already the yeasty aroma filled the room.

Olivia glanced toward the hallway door as Corey and Michael ran into the kitchen. Olivia noticed their hair fell over their faces as they giggled and poked each other. *I need to cut their hair.*

They stopped at the table, one on either side of Rosy.

"What you doing, Rosy? Can we help?" Corey giggled and poked a lump of dough. "Hey, Michael, look. It bounces back." He reached to poke again.

"Corey Jefferson Brunner, you keep them dirty fingers outa my bread dough. It don't need no help from you." Rosy slapped at his hand sending a cloud of flour into the air.

Corey giggled and ducked under Rosy's arm, popped up on the other side of her and reached for the dough again. Michael stepped back to watch.

"Corey," said Olivia, "that's not a game. Leave Rosy alone."

"I just want to play. Rosy don't mind, do you, Rosy?" Corey lifted his wide blue eyes to Rosy and grinned impishly at her.

"You just go on off and play somewhere else if you want bread for this week." Rosy shooed at him with her hands sending more flour into the air.

Michael leaned his elbows on the table and lifted his hazel eyes to Olivia. *He's so different from his twin, more sensitive.*

"Mom, we haven't been to Worthington's for a long, long time. Can we go get a book today?" Michael gave her a pleading look.

"Let me think about it. Why don't you two go see if Samuel needs some help?"

"Okay," they answered together, grabbing their coats and running out the door. Laughter and playful punching each other continued as they ran across the porch.

Olivia smiled and began helping Rosy clean up and prepare for lunch. "Remember when school started last fall? The twins wanted to go to with Betsy and James, but they were too young."

Rosy chuckled. "I remember. James and Betsy didn't hardly get in the door 'til those two jumped them."

Olivia laughed. "Corey said, 'I don't know why we can't go to school.'"

"And Michael said, 'Yeah, we want to learn to read and write, too.'"

Betsy tried to reason with them, but those two don't take to reason. She reminded them they were only five and they couldn't go to school until they were six." Olivia paused. "I'm glad they worked out a compromise. James and Betsy have been teaching them at home in the evenings."

"They's good boys, Miz Olivia, and smart too. They'll learn a lot."

"Both boys can already write all the family's names and the letters of the alphabet. They can read simple books and add and subtract small numbers."

Someone ran across the back porch. The door flew open. "Did you think about it yet? Will you take us to Worthington's?"

"Close the door," said Olivia, feeling Rosy's disapproval boring into her back. She knew without even looking that her head was shaking. She heard Rosy muttering, "Um, um, um." *Rosy is right this time. It's too soon after giving birth to walk a mile to the bookstore and back, but the boys needed some attention, too.* She smiled at Michael who waited for an answer.

"Maybe you can go with your father when he goes for a newspaper in a little while. With the election so near, there'll be extra editions and he'll want to see them."

"Okay, we'll go wait for him." They ran back outside

Minutes later, she heard Blackie yapping and the boys' laughter. Once more, the door flew open sending another blast of cold air across the kitchen. This time they closed it quickly before Olivia said anything.

"Dad said we could go with him," said Michael.

"We'll be back for lunch," said Corey.

The door opened and closed so quickly there was hardly a breath of cold air. Suddenly the room was in silence. Both Rosy and Olivia sighed and enjoyed the moment. Then Rosy laughed and set her dough to rise. Olivia went to feed Lucy.

When Olivia returned to the kitchen, it was almost noon. She lifted the lid from the pot of vegetable soup. Its tantalizing aroma filled the kitchen.

"Smells good Rosy," she said. "Will and the boys should be back soon. Why don't you dish up some for you and Samuel? I'll dish it up for the boys and Will when they get home."

"Yes ma'am, Miz Olivia." Rosy had her coat on ready to leave when the door burst open again. Michael and Corey rushed in ahead of their father.

"Mom," the twins called together and ran to her. Olivia put a finger to her lips reminding them that Lucy was sleeping.

"We each got a new book," said Michael lowering his voice.

"We almost didn't get any," said Corey putting his book on the table to remove his coat. Olivia turned sharply. Will followed the boys in and hung his coat on the hook by the door. Olivia gave him a questioning look but turned back to the twins.

"Did you boys give your father a hard time?"

"No, ma'am," said Michael.

"That Stevens man tried to take Dad again," said Corey.

"Will?"

"I wouldn't go with him and leave my boys alone downtown," he said tousling Corey's hair. "Is lunch ready?" Olivia knew she would get no more information from him until later. Rosy had waited to hear what happened. When Will refused to say anything more, she left, shaking her head.

"All but dishing it up," Olivia said. "Wash your hands, boys. You can read after lunch."

***

After the boys left the table, Olivia poured Will another cup of coffee. She raised her eyebrows and waited. Will cradled his cup in both hands and stared into his cup. Finally, he sighed, took a sip and said, "Like I said, Olivia, I refused to go with Stevens and he knew better than to push it with so many people milling about. He'll be back. Parker won't give up."

Olivia clasped her hands around her own cup, wanting to know more. But what more was there to know? "What's in the paper? Does it have much to say about the election?"

"There are several articles, editorials and letters to the editor with varied opinions. Some express anger, some argue over a view expressed by the editor and some blast the editor for seeming to side with the Union. This one says, 'Virginia is for the Union, but only as long as the status quo remains unchanged.'"

"What does all this mean?" Olivia held her cup to her lips, enjoying the aroma as well as the flavor. "It sounds like Virginia will agree with the Union as long as they don't make any changes. How can we have progress without change?"

"We can't," said Will, "but you're right. Virginia is against any change that refuses them the right to own slaves."

"Will," Olivia spoke with quiet concern, "what do you think? Will there *really* be a war? And if there is, will it last long? Will our children…?" She couldn't finish her thought. War and children in the same breath were too incomprehensible.

"Olivia, I'm not God. I don't know what will happen. Nobody does. But, I truly believe that if the country elects Mr. Lincoln President of the United States, war will not be far behind – not that he wants war, but what he stands for is too incompatible with southern views. How long will it last? More than the few weeks or months that most are predicting – more likely years."

"I don't want to believe this…" She reached for his hand. "Help me to be strong if it really happens."

"Olivia, you are a very strong woman, but you might have to be stronger than you ever believed possible." He squeezed her hand and looked into her eyes with a longing she had never seen before. "Just remember your promise to protect our children – if they… if I…" He stopped, his eyes clouded.

"If they what?" She waited, not wanting to hear, sensing the fear in him.

"Never mind," he said. "I hear our baby fussing and I need to get to my office." He rose, kissed her and went to his waiting patients.

Olivia forced a smile. She wouldn't let him know she sensed his fear. That would only cause him more pain. She shivered with Grandma Poff's foresight and felt the future rushing toward them like a sudden violent thunderstorm.

12 Prophecy of Things to Come

Bare trees stretched skyward in search of light and warmth in the November chill. The rising sun sent a rainbow of color across the dusting of frost. Silently October had fled the coming winter, leaving November to bridge the gap.

Sunday morning dawned – two days before the big Election Day. Olivia was already dressed for church and helped Rosy put breakfast on the table for the children, who gathered around the table trying to keep their church clothes clean. She had eaten earlier with Will who liked to get to the church before people started arriving.

"Miz Olivia, you shouldn't oughta be taking that baby out. She's too young. You ain't well yet."

"Rosy, I'm fine. I'll bundle Lucy up good. Will needs me."

"Um, um, um. That election gonna be the death of us yet."

Olivia thought her words sounded more like prophecy than grumbling. "Rumor has it that folks on both sides are spouting off in angry threats. I've got to be there to support Will – whether people stay away or come in droves." She paused. "Tell Samuel we'll be ready in about ten minutes."

"Yes'em," said Rosy slipping into her coat and tying her scarf around her head.

"He can bring back the smaller buggy that Will took earlier so you and Samuel can get to your church."

***

Most attendees that morning hardly noticed the chill in the air as members, friends and more visitors than usual flocked up the stairs to the church. Olivia hurried in with the rest. Although it was still early, the church was nearly full. Olivia wasn't concerned about a place to sit. She knew her regular pew at the front of the church would be open.

She paused inside the door for a moment and glanced around the familiar room. Like most small churches, it was only one room and a basement. The pot-bellied stove in the center of the room had folks removing their coats, even with the cold wind blowing outside.

Olivia raised her gaze to the cross on the altar in the center of the raised chancel and breathed a prayer for Will. Grandma Cooper was at the upright piano turning pages in the hymnbook. *Looking for appropriate music for the morning.*

Behind her Will greeted visitors, avoiding comments and questions concerning the coming election. She nudged the boys and started toward the front of the church, pausing to speak to the Maggie, Tillie and Jeannette who stood at the back corner.

"Isn't Lucy a little young to be out?" asked Jeannette. Olivia looked from Maggie to Tillie, who stood relaxed as opposed to Jeannette's poker straight demeanor. Jeannette looked older than the rest, but was younger and more naive.

"She's two weeks old already, Jeannette," said Olivia, "She still sleeps a lot. She'll be all right."

"But…how will you…I mean…" Jeannette's face turned scarlet. Olivia smiled. Maggie turned her smile toward the window. Tillie didn't bother to hide her grin. All the women understood that Jeannette's strict upbringing would never allow her to speak of anything that even *seemed* unusual, or that would draw attention to the woman's body – especially a nursing infant.

"She shouldn't be hungry until church is over," said Olivia. "I'll be up front with my back to everyone. If she does need to nurse before church is over, I'll cover her with her blanket."

"Oh. Well, come on Sarah." Jeanette took her three year-old daughter's hand and nodded for Joey to follow her. She sat several rows behind where Olivia would sit. Tillie chuckled and went to join John. Maggie winked at Olivia and joined her family.

Olivia smiled again. She knew Jeannette would not take a chance that her children might get even a sideways glance of her nursing Lucy, if she should have to do that. "Children," she said, "we need to get seated."

Grandma Cooper hit the first chord of "O God Our Help in Ages Past" and people began moving to their places, whispering the last of their conversations.

Olivia nodded appreciatively to Ethel as she gathered her family in the second pew from the front. She knew that was one of Ethel's favorite hymns, but it was also a subtle way of calling the people to prayer for the coming days of uncertainty. Lucy slept in her arms, the twins squirmed on either side of her and Betsy and James sat on the other side of each twin.

With a sense of pride, as well as apprehension, Olivia watched Will walk to the front of the church. He paused, knelt at the altar for a moment then stepped to the pulpit with determination. She knew he was concerned about the future and not everyone in his congregation agreed with his beliefs about war – or slavery. So, new baby or not, she had to be there for moral support for him.

When it was time for the message of the morning, Will moved from the pulpit to the center aisle. With Bible in hand and all the fervor and enthusiasm of one who felt the touch of the Almighty's hand upon him he began to speak.

Olivia turned slightly so she could see Will as well as some of the congregation. Most were always attentive, but today they seemed even more attuned to his words. She noticed several strangers on the far side of the room. *Looks like visitors from the mayor's office. Wonder if they are hoping for fuel to spread the fire of patriotism?* She turned her attention back to Will.

"My friends," he was saying, "God called me to preach the Gospel of Good News. You called me to preach to this congregation. Difficult times lie ahead of us. The Good News today is that, with God's help, we will face them together."

Will paced in front of the congregation as if his steps were drawing out words from his reservoir of knowledge and beliefs – words that people needed to hear, but were reluctant to accept.

"Our world is changing," he said, "changing faster than the rolling clouds of a winter storm. As surely as I see you sitting before me this morning, I can see that storm approaching on the horizon of time. Like the prophets of old, I stand before you, my friends and fellow Christians, to warn you. The end of an era, as we know it, is upon us. Can you feel the winds of change?"

Murmurs and undertones of both approval and disapproval rippled across the room. A few bass voices shouted, "Amen, brother." Some – those Olivia could see – met Will's flashing eyes with stony silence and half-closed eyes that hid wrinkles of frowns and glares. Olivia tensed. Would they interrupt Will's message to disagree?

"We live in perilous times," Will pressed on, ignoring both the negative and positive responses. "Brother will rise up against brother, father against son. God did not put us here to wring our hands and wail with self-pity. God gives us the ability to make choices – choices between good and evil, right and wrong. Our United States government gives us the right to vote. You know my views on slavery. You know what I believe about war. I'm not here to tell you *how* to vote, but I firmly believe that Tuesday's election will decide the fate of our country, be it peace or war. If we don't vote, we throw away our choice."

Olivia listened, her back straight. *If this election has the potential to bring about war, then why don't I and all the other women, have a say in it? War will destroy our lives as much as it will the men's.*

Lucy squirmed and whimpered. Olivia felt the tenseness in her arms. Forcing her muscles to relax, she shifted the position of the infant in her arms. *Oh Lord, only You know what is to come. I can't vote, but with Your help I can be strong enough to stand with Will – come what may.*

At length, a rustle of pages accompanied the shuffle of feet as the congregation stood for the closing hymn. Betsy and James helped the twins find the page and follow the words. Olivia was surprised at how quickly they had learned to read the words of the hymns. Had she been able to look into the future, she would have seen how much more quickly they would learn things other children their ages may never learn.

Following the benediction, the congregation visited with one another while they gathered belongings and donned coats and hats. Hardly a man refrained from commenting to Will as he greeted them at the door. Although she was too far from the door to hear what the men said, she heard bits and pieces from raised voices while she bundled Lucy for outside and Betsy and James got the twins ready to leave.

"…mighty fine sermon…."

"…keep your nose out of politics..."

"If…go to war… show …Yankees…"

"Will gave us a mighty fine sermon today, Olivia," said Grandma Cooper. Her voice startled Olivia, bringing her attention back to the women who had gathered around her, trying to ignore talk of war from the men who clustered in the far corner of the room.

"Too much talk about war and trouble," said Jeannette.

"You just might have to hear about war talk whether you want to or not," said Grandma Cooper, shaking a thin, boney finger at Jeannette. "If Mayor Nelson has his way, he'll have all our men in his *Richmond Volunteers* – and our boys, too."

Maggie Cooper smiled and laid a hand on the older woman's arm. "Grandmother Cooper," she said, "I think we need to go. It looks like a storm is brewing."

Grandma Cooper laughed her soft cackle. "In here or out there?"

Maggie laughed with her and said, "Maybe both." Maggie was the opposite of Jeannette. She had learned to bend with the blows of life and accept her responsibilities of caring for her children and her grandmother-in-law.

The women, having admired the baby began to move away. Most pretended to have neither heard, nor understood, Will's words. With sudden insight, Olivia saw through their facades of calm to fear and anxiety. *They are scared to death and have no one with whom to talk about their fears.*

In most of their homes, women didn't talk about war and politics even with their husbands. Only the Coopers and Tillie seemed to understand the severity of the situation.

13   Election Day

Tuesday dawned looking like any other November day in Richmond. From his fence post, Old Bill called the sun to come forth. The sky was clear, the air nippy, frost coated the ground. In opposition to the forecast of a beautiful day, tension hung in the air like a storm cloud ready to burst. Although Olivia tried to ignore it, she knew Will was anxious. Even the children seemed to know something was different about this day.

Before Betsy had hardly finished breakfast, James took his last swallow of milk and started gathering his books and homework. "Come on Betsy," he said nudging her with his elbow. "We don't want to be late."

"We have lots of time James," she answered as she set her glass down. "What's your hurry?"

"Mr. Mullins' friend from *The Enquirer* will be in our class today to talk to us about the election."

"What's so special about today?" Betsy asked as she tied her bonnet. "It's just another Tuesday."

"Betsy," James grabbed his jacket from the hook by the door, "today isn't just any Tuesday. It's Election Day. Today the country votes for a new president. We're going to have a mock election in history class."

"Does everyone vote?"

"All adults do, or at least they should."

Olivia raised her eyebrows, but said nothing. James looked sheepish and added, "Well, all *men* do. Women aren't allowed to vote – yet. But they will soon. Mr. Mullins said although women can't vote, he will let the girls in the class vote anyway."

Olivia glanced at Rosy who stood with her hands on her hips. James blushed. "Well, I guess black folks don't have a vote either. But they will too, some day."

"Didn't we ever have an election before?"

"Sure, every four years, but this one's important because it might mean we'll have a war. There are a lot…" James continued to lecture his sister as they went out the door on the way to school.

Will had been listening as he finished his coffee. He put on his coat and hat and smiled. "I'll walk with them, go vote then stay around town for a while to listen to some of the comments before I come back to the office."

"Will, be careful…and…let me know what's happening."

"I will," he said, kissed his wife and followed James and Betsy out the door.

"That Master James is some teacher, Miz Olivia," said Rosy as the door closed behind Will.

"Yes, he is Rosy. He has some good insights. Makes one wonder how history will record this day."

"That's too far for me to see," said Rosy. She chuckled, picked up the broom and started cleaning the kitchen floor.

Olivia stood by the window a little longer, watching Will, James and Betsy until they were out of sight. Blackie had trotted along beside them, but ran back home when they turned the corner.

Betsy had said, 'it's only another Tuesday' and yet why does my stomach churn as if the world is slowly tipping upside down and I'm holding on by a thread as thin as a spider's silk? Olivia forced the knot of fear and foreboding into the recesses of her mind and turned away from the window. *We need to do the chores – Election Day or not.* With a deep sigh, she sat in the rocking chair and pulled her basket of mending close to her.

"How do those boys manage to get so many holes in their socks?" She wasn't necessarily talking to anyone, but Rosy laughed.

"They's boys and boys always wear out their clothes faster'n girls do," said Rosy placing the irons on the stove to heat while she set up the ironing board.

"Maybe you're right. I guess I need to start knitting some more."

A soft kitten-like sound from the bedroom reminded them that Lucy's schedule didn't include fears and daydreaming.

"I'll get her, Miz Olivia," said Rosy.

"Thank you, Rosy." Olivia laid aside the sock she was darning and prepared to nurse Lucy. She could hear Rosy talking to the baby and the twins at the end of the hall.

"She's all nice and dry and ready for her mama," said Rosy as she cradled the infant next to her ample bosom. She placed Lucy in Olivia's arms, beaming at mother and infant. The twins followed Rosy into the kitchen, reached for their coats on the hook by the door and slipped arms into dangling sleeves, giggling and punching each other.

"We're going to see if Samuel needs some help," said Michael.

"Rosy said he was calling us," said Corey.

Olivia raised her eyebrows at Rosy. She hadn't heard Samuel calling them. She smiled because the boys understood that Rosy was teasing and just wanted them to go outside for a while. Both boys giggled and ran out the door. Rosy laughed her soft chuckle and reached for the hot iron on the stove.

Sitting in her grandmother's rocker beside the blazing fire, Lucy in her arms nursing, for a few brief moments Olivia felt content. When Lucy had finished nursing, Olivia cuddled the infant, enjoying the pop and crackle and the aroma of the wood burning in the hearth. At that moment, all was well with the world. There was no war – or threat of war.

Then she heard Blackie barking and moments later Will scraping his feet on the back porch mat and her contentment began to fade like the morning mist. The real world pressed in as Will brought news of the election. Pulling the blanket over Lucy in anticipation of the cold air that would accompany the open door; she wished she could pull a blanket of protection from the coming storm of change over her family.

Will saw her in the rocker and quickly closed the door. Grasping the special election issue of *The Enquirer* in one hand, he reached for the second rocker with the other and pulled it close to her. Rosy handed him a cup of coffee.

"Thanks, Rosy," he said.

"What does it say?" Olivia asked nodding to the paper in his hand. "Surely there can't be any news of the election yet."

"No results," he said, "but, *The Enquirer* urges men to vote." He held the paper so he could read the front page. "The headline says: Election Day – Vote." He continued to read, "The importance…involves patriots and friends of the Union. The hope of the nation rests upon the results… We appeal to you to stand by your flag, candidates, principles and country."

"What about the men downtown? What are they saying? Do they still look for war if Mr. Lincoln is elected?"

Will hesitated then nodded. "They sound like they're not only expecting war, but are eager for it. We'll talk more after we get preliminary results tonight."

Will kissed her and Lucy then set his cup in the sink. "I need to get to my patients," he said and went to his office at the back of the house. Olivia watched men parade past the kitchen window all afternoon.

"Is there an outbreak of some dread disease, Miz Olivia?" Rosy nodded toward the window and the intermittent flow of pedestrian traffic.

Olivia smiled. "Not unless we count *election fever* as a dread disease," she answered.

Rosy chuckled. "They probably got more rumors and guesses from the streets of Richmond than they have aches and complaints."

"I think you might be right," said Olivia turning from the widow to help Rosy begin preparations for supper. "Will wants to go to town after supper and wait for the election results."

"Ain't gonna make no difference in the outcome."

"I know, but we'll know sooner what we have to deal with."

The last of the visitors walked with Will as far as the back porch where they separated – Will to go in for supper, the visitor to return to his affairs.

14   Gathering at the Newsstand

Dinner over, Betsy and James began clearing the table. "Sounds like Mr. Phillips is here," said James. He glanced out the window. "Can't see in the dark for sure, but it sounds like his squeaky wheels and looks like him in the lantern light on the wagon post."

Will took his coat from the hook by the door and kissed Olivia. She held the coat while he slipped his arms into it. "I'll be late, so don't wait up for me."

"Will, you know I won't sleep until you get home."

He smiled and gave her another kiss. "You children be good and don't give your mother a hard time." He cast a deliberate glance at Corey and Michael.

"We won't," said the twins together then giggled.

"We'll make them mind," said James. Betsy nodded.

Will closed the door softly behind him as if that would soften the news which would bring trouble to the world.

***

Joe waited until Will had seated himself on the wagon bench then said, "I don't suppose Olivia was upset because you'll be late."

"No, she understands our need to know what's happening."

"I wish Jeannette was more like Olivia."

Will laughed and slapped his friend on the back. "Joe, there *is* no one else like Olivia. She is one of a kind. Jeannette was raised differently, but she cares as much for you as Olivia does for me."

"I know you're right, Will, but sometimes I worry about her. No, worry is too mild. I'm scared for her. If Parker ever gets to us, I don't know what she'll do."

"She'll adjust. I've asked Olivia to promise me that she will take our children north to the Kanawha Valley if war comes and I'm unable to provide for her. She has relatives up there."

"Will she go – alone I mean – without you?"

"Yes. When Olivia makes a promise it is as good as done."

"Maybe I'll have a talk with Jeannette – get her to promise to go with Olivia. Do you think Olivia would mind?"

"I think she would be glad for the company." Will nodded to the crowd gathering ahead of them. "We're nearly to the newsstand. Why don't we park the wagon here and walk the rest of the way?"

"Good idea. There's Robert and John talking to Noah," said Joe.

"And here comes Kenny and George," said Will. "Looks like the gang's all here."

Joe laughed as they disembarked from the wagon and waited for Kenny Jones and George Walsh to catch up with them. Then they joined Robert Cooper and John Rayburn at the newsstand. *The gang* was indeed all there – six men who had been friends for years and had the same faith and belief in God and their country. As they had done since they were children, they would stand together in any battle – physical or spiritual.

"Evening Noah," Will called as they approached the blind man.

Noah raised his head and gave them a wide grin. "Evening Master Will. Sounds like all the gang is here. I hear your voices."

"We're here," said Robert.

"Had to come and help you with all the extras you'll have," said John.

"Looks like all of Richmond is out tonight," said Kenny.

"It sure do, Master Kenny. Everybody's waiting for election news."

"You heard anything yet?" George asked.

"No. Too early. Won't really know anything for days – maybe weeks. But that makes words on paper and that's what I sells." Noah laughed and the men laughed with him.

"Where's David tonight?" asked Will

Noah grinned again. "I sent him home to stay with his mama. He'll come back later and help me."

"He's a good boy, Noah," said Joe, "and a good worker."

"Yes sir, he is. When God took my son, he done blessed me with that grandson. I sure hope the war don't take him away from me."

"How old is he, Noah?" asked George.

"He be thirteen soon. We get in a war, maybe his lame leg will save him."

"We hope there is no war, Noah, but if there is we'll pray for David's safety."

"Thank you Master Will. I 'preciates that."

A rumbling noise, followed by a clanging of metal over the rough street, sent a look of fear across Noah's face. Will turned to see what was happening. "It's all right, Noah," he said. "Someone just turned a barrel over and rolled it to the middle of the street. They're building a fire in it so men can warm themselves while they wait. It's only a wood fire for warmth."

Noah sighed and swiped the back of his hand across his sweating brow. "Thanks Master Will. For a minute I was afraid…"

"I know, Noah. This time it's all right." The others murmured their comfort to Noah as well. They all knew his blindness was no accident. When his master gave him his freedom, a vengeful mob deliberately took his sight.

"I hear the news wagon coming," said Noah recovering from his fear.

"Hey, Noah," called the man on the newspaper delivery wagon. "How you doing?"

"Fine Jim. Real fine. You got lots of papers for me tonight? I's got a crowd here waiting."

"I see that, Noah. I'll leave you two bundles this time."

"Thank you, Jim. Just drop them here. The boys'll help me."

"Here you go," said his friend as he threw two bundles of papers on Noah's counter. "You take care now and have a good night."

"Sure will, Jim. Sure will."

Men started moving in closer and grabbing at the papers before Noah could cut the cords that held the bundles.

"Hold it," said Will lifting his voice. "Give Noah a chance to get the papers ready and take your money. We've waited this long, we can wait a few more minutes."

Someone in the crowd yelled back, "Who appointed you the protector of the newspaper, Brunner?" Others took up the chant and started to move closer. The six friends positioned themselves around the newsstand – feet apart, arms crossed over their chests, daring anyone to touch Noah or his newspapers before he was ready.

"No one appointed me protector any more than they appointed you the leader of a vigilante mob to take the law in your own hands. Now back off."

The man stared at Will then sheepishly moved back.

"Thank you Master Will. What do the headline say?"

"It says: Lincoln Elected. The article says, 'It would seem from the messages coming across the wires that Lincoln has won. More news will follow in the next few days.'"

Will handed Noah the coins for papers for himself and his five friends then stepped aside for the others to get their papers.

"Looks like our war is coming." The familiar voice broke into the circle of friends.

"What do you want Stevens?" John Rayburn – a big, lumberjack size man – towered over the corporal.

"That's *Corporal* Stevens. And you men had just better get used to the idea of war. It's coming whether you like it or not and you will *all* be in our army."

"I wouldn't count on that if I were you," said Robert.

"You'll be there," said Corporal Stevens as he strutted away.

"He's not going to leave us alone," said George.

"You each have to make up your own mind," said Will. "I can't and won't fight."

"We're with you Will," said Joe and the rest nodded in agreement. "Olivia has promised Will that she'll take their children north to the Kanawha Valley if they put him in prison – or whatever. I'm going to push Jeannette to go with her."

"That's a great idea," said Robert.

Each agreed and parted knowing Stevens would hound them until they either gave up or died in prison. That day would come sooner that any of them expected.

Joe dropped Will off and continued on his way home. A soft glow of candlelight poured from the kitchen window. Will knew Olivia waited up for him.

15   Waiting for News

Even though Olivia knew Will would be late, she paced from window to door, from front room to kitchen while she waited up for him. Finally, the mantel clock in the living room struck eleven and she forced herself to sit by the kitchen fireplace and pick up her knitting. With each pull of the wool between her fingers, a feeling of foreboding twisted itself around her heart the way the yarn wrapped around her needles.

Rocking and knitting brought memories of playing on the floor while her Grandmother Poff rocked and knitted in that same chair. She could almost hear her grandmother's soft southern drawl, "Honey, sometimes I just know things without understanding what I know, or why I should know it. It's a blessing and curse – a blessing if it helps change something for good; a curse when you know something is going to happen and you can't stop it, or change it."

Olivia ceased the back and forth motion. The needles crossed, waiting for the next knit one, purl two. That ominous foreboding again. Fear squeezed her heart as she thought about what the outcome of this election would be. She knew – as her grandmother had known impossible things – that her family, as well as her country, was on the brink of change so radical that no one could possibly predict it.

Vaguely through her jumbled thoughts, Olivia heard the first chime of the midnight hour. Another half hour slowly crept by before Joe's wagon pulled into the backyard and Olivia heard Blackie greet Will. Relief pushed aside her sense of foreboding and apprehension. Will was home and that was all that mattered – at least for this night. With him beside her, she could weather any storm.

"'Livia," Will hardly waited to close the door behind him. He waved the special edition of the paper. Olivia put her finger to her lips to remind him the children were sleeping.

"Sorry," he whispered. "He was elected. Abe Lincoln was elected."

Olivia slipped into his arms and lifted her face for a kiss. Will obliged her before sharing the news. After a lingering kiss and the comfort of his heart beating against hers, she removed herself from his embrace.

"Now, tell me about the election. How did *The Enquirer* receive word so soon? Is it good news or bad news that Mr. Lincoln will be our new President?"

"Probably both good news and bad," he answered, hanging his coat by the door. "I wish I could say otherwise. I believe Abe Lincoln is a good man, but I wonder if our country will need more than just a good man in the years to come."

"Are they sure? Don't they have to count…?"

"I don't know much about the process of gathering information, but *The Enquirer* said it received *estimated results* from the telegraph wire from different areas – enough that they feel certain of their results. Of course it might be weeks before we have definite proof, but…"

Olivia set a cup of coffee and piece of chocolate cake before him. Will took a large bite of cake and sighed with contentment as the chocolate melted on his tongue. He sipped the coffee, then said, "The truth is, the estimate is close enough that people are willing to accept it as final. I'm afraid there'll be many conflicts," he said. "Too many of our southern neighbors are opposed to Lincoln and his ideas on slavery and just as many of our northern neighbors are thrilled with the idea of going to war to defend their ideals. I'm not sure Mr. Lincoln wants war, or…" He sighed. "Anyway, I'm really afraid for our country, 'Livia."

"Maybe, he'll be able to pull us together." Olivia spoke with more hope than conviction. Will believed war was imminent and she hoped with all her heart he was wrong, but somehow – with her grandmother's inherited sixth sense – she knew he was right.

"Maybe," said Will, "but I doubt it. Do you mind if we invite Joe and his family over after prayer meeting tomorrow evening?"

"I know you need to talk with Joe and I don't mind. I only wish Jeannette felt the same so we could all talk together." Olivia made a face, then smiled and reached a hand to Will, who returned her smile and squeezed her hand. They both knew Jeannette had so many fears it was impossible for her to enjoy any conversation other than safe, woman talk.

Olivia stood and kissed his cheek. "Jeannette won't come without a formal invitation, so I'll send Samuel and the twins over in the morning to invite her. And it happens to be morning already."

Will rose with her and they moved hand in hand to the room they had shared since their wedding night.

No matter what the future holds, I'll always have Will at my side. Won't I? A shiver ran across her shoulder and she sent the foreboding feeling into the far recesses of her mind. *I won't think about them now.*

16   Prayer Meeting

Wednesday evening the parking lot began to fill early. Some had already left their buggies and wagons at the side of the road. Samuel had taken Will in early, so James could drive their wagon with Olivia and the children.

"Looks like we'll have to stop here and walk," said James. "Will that be all right, Mom? I can take you up closer then come back and park the wagon."

"This will be fine, James."

James held the lantern high, spreading a circle of light around her and Betsy. Michael and Corey unconcerned about tripping ran ahead, but Betsy stayed close to her mother's side. Even though the doors were open, spreading light across the top steps, James continued to hold the lantern until Olivia reached the top. Then he extinguished the light and placed his lantern at the side of the steps with the others.

Men's voices rose and fell carrying snatches of conversation out the door. Some sounded angry, some resigned. Olivia listened, but knew she would not hear Will. He would neither raise his voice, nor argue the points of war with anyone within the walls of the church. As she started through the door, Albert Johnson, a lay assistant, was saying, "Looks like we need to have an election more often."

Robert Cooper reached a steadying hand out to help Olivia and laughed with Albert. "Good evening, Olivia," said Robert then turned back to Albert, "We haven't had a crowd like this for prayer meeting since the last election."

"Evening, Miz Brunner," said Albert. "How's the little one tonight?"

"She's doing just fine, Mr. Johnson. Thank you for asking."

"We gonna sit up front?" Corey glanced toward the door. "Looks like our pew is taken. Maybe there's no room and we'll have to go home."

James playfully punched his arm. "Sorry Corey but there's plenty of room yet. We won't go home and it's too cold and dark for you to go outside."

"Oh." Corey glared at his brother.

"Why are so many people here tonight?" Michael looked up to James.

"Probably to try for an argument about the election," said James. Again, Corey's eyes lit up with hope.

"We're here for prayer meeting and your father won't let them turn it into a political circus." Olivia smiled and Corey sighed.

James nudged his brothers. "There's room in the next to the last row beside the window aisle in front of Mrs. Jones. Corey, you and Michael climb over Mrs. Phillips and get it before someone else takes it while Mom is going around."

Olivia nodded her thanks to James and moved toward the outer aisle. As Olivia slid into the pew, Claudia leaned forward to speak to her. Before she could answer, a stranger to their congregation, dressed much more elegantly than most of their group, caught everyone's attention with his loud, authoritative voice.

"*Pastor, w*hat did you think of...?"

Will gave the man no chance to finish his question. He stood, glanced around the room and spoke. "It's good to see so many of you here for this Wednesday evening prayer meeting and Bible study. Let us begin our evening by inviting God's presence to be with us." Without waiting for the murmur across the room to recede, Will began to pray. Talking ceased. Prayer meeting had begun and Olivia knew Will would hold them to the agenda for the evening.

Olivia, two rows behind the stranger, watched a scarlet color creep up the back of the man's neck to his ears. He muttered undertones of disagreement as Will continued with the Bible study. Those sitting nearest to him, glared. Tillie Rayburn, who sat behind him, tapped him on the shoulder and shook her finger at him as if he were a naughty child. He turned and glared, but sat quietly for a few minutes. Then he tried again.

Raising his voice, he said, "We don't want to hear about all that stuff that happened centuries ago. That doesn't have anything to do with what's happening in our world now. We want to talk about the election."

An uneasy half-silence fell across the room – feet shuffled, papers crackled, a few cleared their throats and whispers like a soft breeze swept across the room.

Will faced the man. "I'm sorry, sir," he said. "We are in the Lord's house tonight for prayer meeting and Bible study. If you want to talk about the election, there will be a political rally tomorrow evening in Richmond. If you have a need to talk tonight, I'm sure some of the men will be glad to wait around and talk with you outside after the service ."

Without waiting for an answer, Will returned to the passage from Luke that they were studying. The man stood and plopped his hat on his head. His coat sleeve slapped Olivia's face as he shrugged into his coat while stomping down the outer aisle. James half rose out of his seat to go after him, but Olivia placed a hand on his arm and shook her head. He sat back and glared after the man. Olivia felt a chill. *That was George Beecham, Mayor Nelson's right hand man. Why was he here tonight, except to cause trouble for Will?*

The rest of the service proceeded without further incident. When the last amen faded, men began to gather in clusters. Olivia couldn't hear everything they said, but she heard enough bits and pieces to know they weren't discussing the Bible study.

Women gathered around Olivia to talk – but not about the election or the man who tried to cause a disturbance. They would rather talk about Lucy, their latest recipe or the newest fashions for the coming winter – anything to keep the world of war at bay.

Lucy began fussing, so Olivia excused herself and turned to the children. "James, Betsy, help the boys with their coats. We'll have to leave now. Your father will come with Mr. Phillips."

Olivia then turned to Jeannette. "The men are going to be awhile," she said. "I'm taking the children home in the buckboard. Do you want to ride with us?"

"No, thank you," said Jeannette. "I better wait for Joe."

"Do you want Sarah and Joey to go with us?"

"They better stay with me."

No one paid much attention to what seemed like a snub from Jeannette. Everyone knew she was too fearful to get very far from Joe and certainly, she would never let her children out of her sight.

17 *Friends*

Mixed aromas of boiling coffee and fresh baked cookies hung in the air as Olivia watched the Phillips' wagon pull into the backyard. Will and Joe continued to talk while Jeannette and the children walked around to the front door.

Olivia smiled as she hurried to the front of the house and reached for the door. Friend or not, Jeannette would no more come to the back door than she would break any of the rules of her strict up-bringing.

"I'm so glad you could come tonight," said Olivia taking Jeannette's cape. Even though they both had just left the same church meeting, as far as Jeannette was concerned, this was a social affair, not an extension of church. The two could never be considered equal.

"Thank you," said Jeannette in her whiney southern drawl. "I guess the men couldn't wait for the niceties. Them and their war talk. All that political stuff makes me nervous." She looked around the room. "Where's Rosy tonight? Shouldn't she…?"

The thought was left hanging. Jeannette blushed. Olivia knew her friend never understood her view of slavery in general or her friendship with Rosy and Samuel in particular.

"She and Samuel went to their church tonight. Their services are usually longer than ours."

"Oh."

Olivia couldn't help smiling as she turned away to take care of the coats. Jeannette was several years younger than Olivia, but the way she pulled her brown hair into a severe, tight knot at the back of her head, she looked years older. However, in many ways, Jeanette seemed younger than Betsy, who hurried in with the twins to greet Joey and Sarah.

"Come on, Joey," said Corey reaching for his arm. "We got some new books."

"I can't read," said Joey. "I'm only five." He was smaller than the twins and while only a few months younger, seemed years younger to Olivia.

"That's all right. Betsy and James have been teaching me and

Corey. We'll read to you," said Michael.

"I wants to read too," screeched Sarah.

"You can't read. You're too young," said Joey as he gave his sister a shove.

"Am not! I three!" She shoved back.

"Would you like to rock my baby doll?" Betsy reached for Sarah's hand.

"No! Want to rock real baby." Sarah stamped her foot and stuck out her lower lip.

"You can't rock Lucy," said Betsy with an air of adult wisdom. "Mom has to feed her."

"Oh." Sarah's lower lip curled into a larger pout, as if she would throw a tantrum.

"Sarah, go with Betsy. Maybe she'll read you a story." Jeannette looked both pleased and relieved when Sarah started toward the hall with Betsy without further complaint. At the same moment, Joe followed Will from the kitchen into the living room. Jeannette scowled at Joe for using the back door.

Joe, a small man, who seemed even shorter when he walked beside Will, ignored his wife's displeasure and said, "It's good of you to have us over, Olivia. Looks like Lucy is really growing."

"Yes, she is." Olivia smiled at her husband's best friend. She didn't think Joe was near as handsome as her Will, but he had a pleasing smile and personality that drew people to him.

"If you folks will excuse me," Olivia said, "I do have to nurse Lucy and put her to bed. You can come with me if you want to, Jeannette, or you can sit here with the men."

"I'll sit here," she answered. Olivia knew Jeannette would never dream of going into someone else's bedroom, nor would she have approved of Olivia nursing the baby in their presence. Olivia left Jeannette sitting rigidly on the edge of her chair, hands folded in her lap, lips drawn into a tight pucker.

When she returned after caring for Lucy, Jeannette's stance had not changed except that she had twisted her fingers together so tightly that Olivia was sure she would have bruises by morning. A bluish tinge circled her tightly pursed lips. Children's laughter drifted down the hall into the adult conversation and Jeannette's head turned from one direction to the other trying to listen to both children and the men's conversation.

"I wasn't surprised," Joe was saying, seemingly oblivious of Jeannette's presence.

Olivia glanced at the men then at Jeannette *Joe is so used to bantering and arguing with Will that he simply doesn't notice or understand Jeannette's discomfort.*

"We can both expect Parker to step up his attempts to get us into the *Volunteers*," Joe continued as he glanced toward Olivia when she slipped into the room.

"Well, he can just keep trying," said Will. "He should know by now that we aren't interested."

"I don't think it matters to Parker whether we're interested or not."

"You're probably right," said Will. "He wants us and that's all that matters to him."

Joe nodded. "Some places will try to exempt clergy, but physicians won't be so lucky."

"I don't think even clergy will be overlooked when we really get into a war," said Will.

Olivia was more interested in the conversation between Will and Joe than anything she and Jeannette could possibly say to one another. She would rather stay and listen, but she could see Jeannette was on the verge of a mild hysteria and the men didn't seem to notice.

"If you men will excuse us," she said, "Jeannette and I will go pour the coffee and set out the cookies Rosy and I baked this afternoon. You don't mind helping me, do you Jeannette?" Olivia smiled as Jeannette's face relaxed and her fingers became disentangled. She followed Olivia to the kitchen like an obedient puppy seeking a promised a treat.

Olivia poured the coffee while Jeannette set the cookies on the table. "Shall we take some to the children in the back room, or bring them in here to eat?" Olivia was sure of Jeannette's answer before she even asked and it had nothing to do with the gift of her Grandmother Poff's foresight.

"Oh, I think they should be in here. I'm afraid Sarah might choke. These cookies don't have nuts in them do they?"

"No. They are simple sugar cookies. Why don't you get the children and I'll take a plate to the men. They can continue their conversation while we entertain the children." Jeannette didn't seem to notice the sarcasm in Olivia's voice.

***

It was almost midnight when Will poured another cup of coffee and sat in the rocker opposite Olivia. All the noise and excitement of the Phillips leaving had awakened Lucy early, so Olivia was nursing her again, hoping she would sleep the rest of the night. Will turned his cup in his hands repeatedly and stared at the flames leaping toward the chimney. Olivia waited for him to speak, knowing he was sorting out his thoughts and reflecting on the visit with Joe. A log fell. Sparks shot up the chimney. A trickle of smoke crossed the room, tickling Olivia's nose. She sneezed. Will glanced toward her with a startled look then smiled.

"Sorry, 'Livia. Guess I was lost in my thoughts." He took another sip of coffee. "Joe is as concerned about his family as I am about mine. We can almost feel the tension in the air. Parker will step up his efforts and one day he will push too far."

"Is that why Beecham was at church tonight?" Olivia watched Will's face.

"You noticed. Yes, I suppose he thought he could start a riot of some kind and blame me. Then he would have reason to arrest me and make a deal – jail or *Volunteers.*"

"Did Joe recognize him?"

Will nodded. "I doubt if Jeannette did. Joe won't say anything."

"Too bad Jeannette doesn't share his concern."

"He's tried," said Will, "but Jeannette is just too fearful. She throws her hands over her ears and declares she doesn't want to talk, or even think, about war – or trouble of any kind for that matter."

"What will she do when *real* trouble comes? She has no family to help her."

"You're right, 'Livia. Joe has asked her to go with you when you take the children north. Maybe…maybe you can help her."

Olivia raised her eyebrows. She noticed he said *when* not *if.* She let it go for now. "Will, I'm not God. I can't perform miracles. I'll do what I can, but Jeanette has to want my help."

Will looked even more serious. "I'm sure you'll do more than anyone else when it comes to protecting our family and helping our friends. I just hope it doesn't come to that."

Olivia felt that familiar chill and the hovering spirit of her grandmother.

18   The Beginning of the End

Feeling the outdoor chill even from the warmth of her kitchen, Olivia watched the sudden swirl of snowflakes blow against the window. Down the hall, the twins laughed and giggled. An occasional thump told her they were jumping off some makeshift, pretend mountain. Behind her the soft whoosh, tap, whoosh, tap, told her Rosy was cutting out biscuits. Rosy opened the oven door to slide the pan in, but instead of feeling its warmth, Olivia shivered as if the oven had released cold air, not warm.

"Miz Olivia, you all right?"

Startled by the sound of a voice, Olivia shook her head and turned. "I'm…fine, Rosy," she said, "just lost in the flurry of snowflakes. They reminded me that Christmas will soon be upon us." She sighed deeply. "How can we even think of *Peace on Earth* when rumors of war swirl faster than those snowflakes and blow colder than the December wind? Hardly a day passes without someone from the *Volunteers* harassing Will and Joe."

"Now, Miz Olivia, we be in hard times, but the good Lord, He watches over us."

"I know, Rosy. It's just that sometimes I…"

Blackie's yapping interrupted her. "Sounds like Will is back with the afternoon *Enquirer.*" She looked out the window again to see the black dog bounce around in the snow as Will gave him some attention. He said something to Blackie and the little dog bounded around the corner of the house.

Olivia turned back to the stove. Lifting the lid to the pot of the stew, she released the aroma of chicken with all its special spices. Will stomped his feet as he crossed the porch, then the door opened, sending a blast of cold air into the room. He quickly closed it, and removed his coat.

"What smells so good in here?" He asked as he lifted his nose and sniffed the air. "Has to be chicken stew and Rosy's biscuits."

Olivia whirled around, aware of tension in his voice. She held the spoon above the pot and gave him a searching look. *He's forcing himself to sound cheerful. Why?*

"Will?"

A sheepish smile played at the corner of his mouth. He shrugged and held the newspaper up. "I should know by now, I can't hide anything from you."

Olivia said nothing; she waited. She felt the heat from the oven as Rosy checked the biscuits behind her. He sighed, unfolded the paper to page one and read the headline to her with a tremble in his voice. "South Carolina Secedes."

Olivia laid aside the spoon and took the paper he handed to her. She read it aloud for Rosy to hear. "Yesterday – that was December 20 – South Carolina called a convention of the people and passed an ordinance of secession." She felt the blood drain from her face and Will's arm slip around her shoulders. *What will it all mean? What is happening to our world?*

Rosy lifted the steaming pan of biscuits from the oven, sending the fresh-baked aroma through the kitchen. She picked up Olivia's spoon and stirred the stew – even if it didn't need stirring. Olivia continued to read, "We wonder why our friends to the south would take such action without consulting her surrounding neighbors. The answer is clear. The time for talk has passed us by. The time for action is upon us. Should we follow our sister's action?" She stopped reading and looked at Will with horror. Rosy turned to stare at her.

"It's the beginning, 'Livia," he said. "It won't be long until others follow."

"What about Virginia? It sounds like *The Enquirer* is urging us to follow South Carolina. Do you think Virginia will secede?" She paused then asked the question that was foremost in her mind, "Can they make you go into the army?"

"We won't worry about it, now," said Will as he squeezed her shoulders. The words were brave enough, but his tone didn't sound very convincing. "We'll continue to pray for guidance and know that God won't forsake us whatever comes our way." He held her close to him until sounds of laughter told them the children were on their way to supper.

"Of course you're right," she said with as much bravado as possible. "With God's help we'll make it." She left his comforting embrace and took the spoon from Rosy, who turned to dish up the biscuits. Olivia couldn't let the children, or Will, see her anxiety. She would force it to the back of her mind, but she couldn't erase the fear she saw and felt in her husband.

Will grabbed the twins, one in each arm, and turned around like a top with them. They giggled and called for, "more, more." Instead, he picked up Betsy and swung her around with a little less exuberance than her brothers. James, too big for that kind of horseplay, laughed as Will tousled his hair and slapped him on the back. "James, you're getting taller every day. Soon you'll be taking over my job as head of the house."

James laughed again and took his place at the table, but Olivia felt her heart sink. She bit her tongue to keep from crying out. Many fathers said similar words to their sons every day and even Will had said them to James more than once, but this time was different. *Is he trying to prepare our children for a time when he will no longer be with us?*

With the turmoil of things to come brewing in the back of her mind, Olivia tried to keep the family time normal – whatever that might mean. As he always did, Will bowed his head and gave thanks to God for the food set before them. He added a prayer of guidance for President-elect Lincoln in the coming months and for men and women who would have difficult decisions to make.

They passed the food around the table and the conversation turned to school. All the children loved books and Betsy and James both enjoyed school. They talked about today's classes and tomorrow's school play. Since the older children had been teaching the twins to read and write, Corey and Michael were happier staying home. They had come to believe they had the best of both worlds – play time at home as well as learning to read. They filled their brother and sister in on their latest escapades. Finally, talk turned to Christmas.

"Are we going to the plantation for Christmas Day this year?" James asked.

'Course we are," said Corey.

"We always go to Grandma and Grandpa's for Christmas," said Michael sounding as if James had uttered a blasphemy or said some forbidden words.

"I know that," said James. "I was just bringing up the subject."

"Oh," said both boys together.

"Grandma will have lots of presents for us," said Corey.

"Corey, that's not what Christmas is all about," scolded Betsy.

"Betsy is right," said Olivia. "Your grandparents enjoy giving you gifts. Just don't learn to depend on them or expect gifts every time we visit them. Of course, we'll go, but not for the entire day. Lucy will need her rest. I think a couple of hours before dinner and an hour afterward should be sufficient. What do you think, Will?"

"I think that's an excellent idea," he said. "Now, what do you say we help your mother clean up the kitchen? Then I have a new book to begin reading to you tonight."

"What is it, Dad?" James' eyes shone with anticipation.

"I just picked up a copy of *Woodworth's Youth Cabinet* at Worthington's this afternoon. *The Arabian Nights* is one of the stories. I think you'll like it."

Olivia was glad they wouldn't discuss the possibility of secession. She didn't want to think about it anymore.

***

The Brunner family – and every other family of the church – would remember Christmas 1860 as the year that Corey, Michael and Joey portrayed the Three Wise Kings. Joey, as somber as his mother, hardly smiled or said a word throughout the pageant. Corey and Michael, however, were a different story. They made camels out of some broomsticks and old cloth. Their entrance brought a roar of laughter from all but Jeanette, who pursed her lips tightly and commented about people allowing their children to blaspheme a holy event.

Threat of war continued to loom high on the horizon, but the holiday was relatively worry-free. With the approach of a new year, Olivia pondered the fate of their lives in 1861.

19   New Year – New Hope

December 31, 1860, brought with it a new blanket of snow. Huge fluffy snowflakes began to fall mid-afternoon, adding an air of festivity to the farewell of 1860 and the greeting of 1861. Prancing horses pulled polished and decorated sleighs across snow packed streets. Sleigh bells jangled to the beat of the horses' hooves like drums in a parade. War and seceding states were, if not forgotten, at least pushed aside to celebrate the New Year.

Elizabeth Dooley's New Year's Eve Ball was the most important event of the social season in Richmond. Everyone who was *any*one sought an invitation. Elizabeth prided herself on the list of attendees.

Eighteen-sixty would soon fade into memory. Only the pages of history or family Bibles would reveal the highlights of the year. Eighteen-sixty-one spread into the future with hope for new challenges without the old fears.

Olivia hated fancy social events, but felt trapped. The New Year's Eve Ball was more important to her mother than even Christmas. Elizabeth would be disappointed if her only daughter didn't attend. Olivia's sense of frugality didn't permit her to buy a fancy ball dress for a once a year occasion, nor did her pride allow her to accept help from her parents.

She lifted her green velvet gown from the hook where Rosy had hung it after pressing away the wrinkles and mending a ripped seam or two. She loved the dress, but had to admit that fourteen years was a long life for a ball dress. It had been her wedding frock on Christmas Eve fourteen years earlier.

Olivia sighed and began to dress. *At least it still fits, even after five children. Even though Samuel and Rosy are staying with the children, as a nursing mother, I'll have a legitimate excuse for leaving early.* She stared at her reflection in the mirror on her dresser, lost in her thoughts until she was suddenly aware of Will standing behind her.

"Olivia, my darling," Will's soft baritone voice pulled her from her reflections as he whispered in her ear and caressed her bare shoulders. "You will be the most beautiful woman at the ball, tonight."

Olivia twisted her head so their lips met. With reluctance, she turned back to the dresser and picked up her grandmother's pearls, the only real jewelry she owned other than her wedding ring.

"Let me get that," he said.

"Will, I know you don't like these parties any more than I do, but it is important to Mother. We'll leave as early as possible." She smiled at her husband's reflection in the mirror.

"'Livia, we'll be all right. As I said, you will be the most beautiful woman there."

Olivia laughed then stood and faced him. "Do you remember when I first wore this dress?"

"Of course, I do. You were beautiful then and still more beautiful now."

"Will, look at it. It's not fancy with a lot of lace and satin. The style isn't right. The nap is worn off the velvet around the hem."

"Darling, I don't know much about style, but that emerald green turns your hair to gold and makes your eyes sparkle. And if another man dares to look any lower than your chin, to your lovely neck and soft white shoulders, I'll forget I'm a gentleman."

A soft, rosy pink color crept into Olivia's cheeks. "Will Brunner, after all these years and five children, you still make me blush. Shame on you."

He laughed a soft chuckle she loved to hear and kissed her shoulder.

"Will, thank you for the compliments, but you know Mother will take one look at me and say what she says every year, 'Olivia Brunner whatever were you thinking wearing such a faded frock to the most important ball of the year?'" They both laughed at her imitation.

"You're probably right. I'm sorry I can't give you beautiful things you were used to having."

For a fleeting second Olivia saw a hint of regret in her husband's eyes. *Is he remembering Parker's deal when he was detained in the fall?*

"Will Brunner, don't you dare go down that road. If I wanted baubles and things, I would have married that man – what was his name? Oh, yes, Matthew Parker, now *Sergeant* Matthew Parker." She made a face then put her arms around his neck. "Will, you are far more important to me than all the *things* in the world. You and the children make me happier than riches could ever do." Olivia stood on her tiptoes and kissed her husband, who pulled her closer into his embrace.

"'Livia, what did I ever do to deserve a gem like you?"

"I'm not sure which of us got the better deal." With a sigh, she backed out of his embrace. "I think I hear Daddy's sleigh arriving. It wouldn't do for us to arrive in our beat-up old buckboard." She laughed at his sour expression. "We'd better get moving."

***

"Looks like Mother has outdone herself," said Olivia as Moses drove her father's team of prancing horses around the curved drive. "The mansion looks as if the house itself has become a giant candle shinning in the night. Every window reflects a red-orange glow on the snow – almost as if the entire house is ablaze." Olivia squeezed Will's hand and for a split second saw the house in flames. Premonition, or imagination?

Will nodded. "Your mother probably bought every available candle in the state of Virginia," he said and laughed.

Olivia shook her head and groaned. "And every surrounding state, too," she added.

Moses stopped and jumped down from the sleigh, assisted Will and Olivia then got back in the driver's seat to take the sleigh to the barn.

Will and Olivia walked hand in hand into the house. As they entered the foyer, the smell of warm candle wax greeted them. A blast of cold air sent the hundreds of candles flickering. Tiny glass chimneys covered the candles on the teardrop glass chandelier that hung high above the entryway. Tiny prisms of color bounced around the walls and floors. Kerosene lamps along the walls added more flickering light.

Elizabeth, on her way to the stairs, stopped and waited for Will and Olivia.

"It looks like you went all out again this year, Mother," said Olivia, giving her a peck on the cheek. "Is there anyone who wasn't invited?"

Elizabeth tittered like a child, took her daughter's arm in hers and together they sauntered up the circular red-carpeted stairs to the ballroom. Will followed behind them. At the top, more candles and oil lamps lit the room.

An orchestra, elevated on a stage built especially for them at the far end of the room, played an old familiar waltz by Strauss. Already several couples danced around the floor. Will wrapped his fingers around Olivia's hand. "Excuse us, Mother Dooley. I believe Olivia promised me this dance."

Without waiting for an answer, he led his wife to join the other dancing couples. That waltz ended and another began. Jefferson tapped Will's shoulder. "May I have this dance with my beautiful daughter?"

Will nodded and stepped aside. Jefferson took Olivia's hand and guided her across the floor with perfection. "You look very pretty tonight, Olivia."

"Thank you, Daddy." She grinned at him. They both knew her fourteen-year old green velvet wedding dress was out of style. Neither of them cared.

"Is Parker still after Will?"

Olivia nodded.

"I'll run interference as much as I can – tonight anyway. I don't know what's wrong with that man."

Olivia laughed. "I think we both know what's wrong with him, but I'm sure there's more to it than just disappointed love. He has to prove something to someone – if only to himself. With Virginia gearing up to follow South Carolina, he can't have anti-slavery talk – especially from men of influence."

"Olivia, where did you get so smart about…men talk?" Jefferson winked at his daughter. They both knew she learned it early from him. "But, you're probably right. And Will is almost as stubborn as you are."

"Not stubborn, Daddy, just full of conviction."

That waltz ended and Olivia went back to Will. After several dances, Will wandered over to the corner where men gathered. Olivia and her mother sipped punch, watched the dancers and chatted with other women.

"Olivia, darling, what an…unusual dress." Carolyn Parker Moore – Matthew's sister – had been one of Olivia's childhood friends. After her marriage to Will, most of her friends, who moved in the higher financial circles of society, seemed to have forgotten her. Carolyn spoke to her, but just barely.

"Thank you, Carolyn," said Olivia pretending the words were a compliment. "It's the dress I was married in. Will likes to see me in it." Olivia was amused to see the expression on her ex-friend's face. She knew Carolyn could no more wear her wedding dress than she could answer Olivia's veiled insult.

"Humph!" She changed the subject. "Don't the *Volunteers* look handsome in their uniforms?"

Susan Rice, another used-to-be friend, fanned herself and drawled, "Even Matthew is almost handsome in his sergeant's uniform." She nudged Carolyn, covered her mouth and tittered.

"There's more to being in the *Volunteers* than having good looks," said Olivia. "Will doesn't need a uniform or the *Volunteers* to make him handsome."

Carolyn and Susan glared at her as if she'd said something unpatriotic. She smiled and said, "Excuse me, I think I need to go home. I feel like I need to nurse my baby."

Elizabeth smiled and nodded at her daughter. Neither of them missed the gasps and looks of shock from the other women who turned away to follow the dancers. "Olivia, that wasn't very lady-like. Maybe you owe her an apology."

"Do you really think so, Mother?" Olivia turned to face her, knowing her mother was only teasing. "Maybe I was a little vague. What I should have said was something more like, 'I'm sorry to see you've added so many pounds to your already fat behind that you can't wear your wedding dress.' Or maybe, I should have been more specific about nursing Lucy."

"Olivia!" Elizabeth covered her mouth with her fan to hide her smile. "Sounds like the men are having a heated discussion," she said glancing toward the boisterous group near the window. "Will looks a little uncomfortable. Wouldn't hurt to pull him away from Matthew."

Olivia returned her mother's smile. "I think you might be right, Mother." She strolled toward the men who seemed oblivious of the party around them. Women didn't join in the men's conversation, but as her mother had said, Will looked uncomfortable, which meant Parker was pressuring him again. Will wouldn't make a scene at Elizabeth's party, but Matthew had no such qualms. His voice rose in anger. Clenched fists hung at his side.

"Now, you listen to me, William Brunner. You are treading on mighty thin ice with talk like that. Folks around here don't cotton to talk against owning slaves. No one, not even the president of the United States, is going to tell us we can't keep our property."

"I'm sorry we disagree," said Will, "but I'm not saying you can't keep your property. And what the president-elect does is his business. I've got all I can do to keep up with my church and my medical practice."

"*Mister* Brunner," Sergeant Parker's face turned bright scarlet, "you mark my word, there's going to be a rebellion. South Carolina already withdrew because of Lincoln and Virginia will come to her senses soon. And when she does, you *will* serve in our army, whether you like it or not. We need doctors and you won't get out of doing your duty."

"I'm sorry," Will's voice was even and controlled but Olivia could see the anger flashing in his eyes, "I will not be bullied into betraying my beliefs." He glanced toward Olivia as she approached. She slipped in beside him and he placed an arm around her waist. "Excuse me, gentlemen, but I believe my wife needs my attention." Will nodded to his father-in-law, turned and walked away with her.

Moses was waiting for them and soon had them home. Matthew Parker's words haunted Olivia. Would war come? Would Will have to leave her? How would she live without him?

20   More Secessions

Short, gray days of early January trudged along, moving the year toward February. Peaceful resolutions to the talk of war seemed as far away as spring with all its sunshine and warmth. Small boys on the street corners shouted headlines. Blind Noah, added his memorized shouts, while his grandson, David joined the boys on the corners. News hungry men gathered to read and discuss the happenings.

Corey and Michael accompanied Will to get the late afternoon paper. "We brought our marbles," said Corey.

"Can we clear a spot over there out of the way?" asked Michael.

"Share with some of the others who don't have theirs – and no playing for keeps!"

"Okay," said the twins and ran over to some other boys while Will approached Noah's stand.

"Evening, Noah," he said. "Weather's been a little erratic."

"Yes sir. Rain one day, snow the next. Soon be spring and be all rain and wet." Noah laughed.

"You could be right," said Will.

"Things is getting mighty tense, Master Will," said Noah. "Did I hear the boys with you?"

"Yes. They like to come and play marbles with the other boys if they can find a spot with no snow or mud," said Will glancing at Corey and Michael who were involved in clearing a spot off to the side where they could play without being in the way of the men.

"Not much of that this time of year," said Noah then laughed.

"They're inventive," said Will. "They're making a spot."

"They's just like their daddy," said Noah. "Don't let stumbling blocks make them stumble." Noah paused then added in a more serious tone, "We's livin' in real bad times, Master Will," he said.

"Yes, we are," answered Will. "And I'm afraid they're going to get a lot worse."

"Don't you let that Stevens fellow take you away, neither. He's a bad'un." He nodded toward the street across from the newsstand as if he could see Corporal Stevens leaning against the lamppost.

"I'll oppose him, Noah, but I am frightened for my family."

"Don't you worry none 'bout them neither. That Miz Olivia will fight like an angry she-bear to protect them younguns."

"I'm sure she will," said Will. He smiled at Noah's words, but felt a chill. He knew Corporal Stevens watched, arms folded across his chest, a scowl on his face.

"And 'sides that, Master Will, the Good Lord ain't gonna let you down. Why, He'll send a whole flock of eagles to carry Miz Olivia and them little ones to safety if He has to."

Surprised at the insight of a blind, former slave, Will laid a hand on the man's shoulder. "Thanks Noah. I needed to hear that."

"You knows it, Master Will, but God tells me to say it anyway." He paused, cocked his head and listened. "Here comes the papers." David moved in beside his grandfather to help him sort them.

Will hadn't heard anything, but sure enough, the clip-clop of the horse and jangle of the bells on *The Richmond Enquirer's* delivery wagon told him what Noah had already heard. The deliveryman threw the papers at the newsstand and moved on. Will helped David pick them up and put them on Noah's counter.

"What's the headlines say, Master Will?"

Will read, "Star of the West Fired On! More States Secede!" Then he gave Noah a short reading of other front-page articles. "Confederate soldiers fired shots at the unarmed Star of the West as it was attempting to reinforce Fort Sumter, forcing the ship to withdraw and return to New York."

While Will read to Noah, a confrontation erupted in the crowd. "Hey, who do you think you're pushing," shouted a man waiting in line to get a paper.

"Watch it," shouted another. "That's my foot."

"You ain't got no right to move ahead of the rest of us. Wait at the end of the line like we all do."

Will stopped reading and looked first to see if the boys were all right, then turned to the crowd. He laid a hand on Noah's trembling arm. "It's all right, Noah," he said. "It's just Stevens pushing his way through the men waiting for their papers."

"Ain't he go no manners at all?" said Noah.

"Shut up old man or I'll see that you never sell another paper." The harsh words crept around the sneer on Steven's face.

"You touch him and…" David moved to protect his grandfather.

"And what?" Stevens laughed, an evil sound.

"You'll have to deal with all of us," said a large man in the crowd.

"That's right," said the rest as they moved to surround the newspaper stand and protect Noah and David.

Stevens glanced at the men and apparently decided not to take on the crowd alone. He turned to Will. "Don't matter," he said, "It's him I want, not some old blind Nigger."

Will clenched his teeth to keep back the words he wanted to say. Balled fists hung at his side itching to fly into the face of the corporal. "What do you want?" he asked, "As if I didn't know."

"Parker wants to see you – now," said Stevens. A low rumbling murmur moved through the crowd. Stevens looked uneasy, but held his ground.

"Sorry," said Will. "I have to take my boys home."

"I'll see that they get home. You come with me."

Stevens and Will stood face-to-face – as much as possible. Stevens had to lean backward to look up into Will's grim face.

"You so much as speak to one of my boys," said Will through his still clenched teeth, "and you will have trouble speaking at all."

"You can't threaten a government official like that, Brunner."

"I thought we lived in a country where the government doesn't harass honest citizens," answered Will.

"We're getting ready for a *new* government."

"Then I want no part of your *new* government. Now go harass someone else. I need to take my boys home."

Stevens looked as if he would try to force Will, but Will walked around him and the others surrounded the corporal so he couldn't move.

"Come on boys," called Will. Corey and Michael picked up their marbles, put them in their pockets and ran to catch up with their father.

Behind them, Will heard the men begin to talk to David. Noah began to call out, "Extra! Extra! Star of the West fired on! More states secede."

As Will and the boys turned toward home, he heard a harsh laugh from Stevens, whose words flew after him. "We'll get you yet, Brunner."

Will shook his head and ignored the man. The twins each took one of his hands and pretended they didn't hear. Will decided to share the headlines with Olivia and Rosy while they finished cooking dinner. Later he and Olivia would read the paper more thoroughly and discuss events. Then he would tell her about Stevens – if the boys didn't do it first.

21   *The House Call*

Will and Olivia had tried to keep talk of the war away from the children – especially at mealtime. However, that night as they sat around the supper table, James surprised them.

"Mr. Mullins said a supply ship to Fort Sumter was fired on and Florida, Alabama, Georgia, Mississippi and Louisiana all seceded."

"How did he learn that?" Will held a fork full of dumplings to his mouth. "*The Enquirer* only published it late this afternoon."

"Mr. Mullins' reporter friend stopped by the school at lunch time today," James said. "He said when war comes to Virginia, the farmers and plantation owners will have to give up their animals and maybe even their homes."

"Sally said Sergeant Parker made her dad join the *Volunteers*," said Betsy. She frowned and looked expectantly at her father, her blue eyes wide with uncertainty. "How can Sergeant Parker make a person be a volunteer? I thought a volunteer was someone who offered to do something because he wants to."

Olivia smiled and Will chuckled. "You're right, Betsy," Will answered, "but it seems Sergeant Parker is pushing his power button."

"Oh." Betsy frowned, but before she could ask more questions there was a sudden, persistent hammering at the front door.

"I'll get it," said James. "Probably one of dad's patients." He jumped from the table and hurried to the front door. Voices drifted back to the kitchen, words unclear. Will stood, took his last swallow of coffee and reached for his coat.

"An emergency?" Olivia gave Will a questioning look.

"Probably someone wants to get married. James would have come back for me quicker if it were an emergency. I'll take them around to my office to talk." He smiled and moved to the doorway as James returned, a frown wrinkling his forehead.

"It's Mr. Beecham from the mayor's office," he said. "He has Mr. Phillips with him and wants Dad to go to City Hall with them."

"Will? Can't you finish your supper first?" Olivia asked. She wasn't as concerned over missed dessert as she was the summons at this hour of the day – and the reason for it. "Surely they could have waited until morning."

"I'm finished," said Will, buttoning his coat. "Save my dessert for me. I won't be gone long." He kissed her forehead, squeezed her shoulders and left the room.

Olivia heard the front door close and called to Samuel, knowing he would've heard Beecham's sleigh and would be hovering nearby in case he were needed. The back door opened.

"Yes'em, Miz Olivia?"

"Take one of the horses and follow them. Bring me word about what's happening if they don't let him return."

"Yes'em." He bowed the way he'd been taught as a child and went out the back door. Olivia knew she could trust him to stay hidden and find out what she needed to know.

"Are they going to make Daddy join the *Volunteers,* too?" Betsy was pale.

"Dad's not like Sally's father," said James. "He won't let them force him into it."

"Your brother's right Betsy. Your father won't fight." Olivia smiled at her children, but every nerve fiber in her body twitched like a nervous cat's tail. Why would they come and drag a man away from his family at mealtime? She was as confused as Betsy but tried to continue through the evening as if Will had been called out for a medical emergency. Surely, he would be home soon. But, bedtime came and Will still wasn't back.

22   Locked Up

Joe and Will rode in silence to the mayor's office. Will's sharp sense of hearing picked up the sound of a lone horseman behind them. *Must be Samuel? Not many people in town this time of evening. Mostly men going from bar to bar seeking someone to talk to.*

Beecham's driver – one of Mayor Nelson's slaves – pulled the buggy to a stop in front of the City Hall building. "This where they brought you last fall?" asked Joe. He sounded cheerful enough, but Will knew his friend well enough to know he was trying desperately to mask his fear.

"Yeah, like Jefferson said, Parker's office is close to the mayor's so he can keep an eye on the new sergeant."

"Keep your mouths shut," said Beecham, "until the mayor tells you to talk."

"Yes *sir*," said Will and Joe together. They grinned when Beecham glowered.

Following Beecham into the mayor's office, Will wasn't surprised to see Parker standing beside the mayor's desk with a pleased expression on his face. Corporal Stevens stood at the window with his back to the room.

"Well, Doctor Brunner, have you further considered our offer?" Sergeant Parker, hands in his pocket, rocked on his heels and smiled as if he had finally hauled in a prize fish.

"The answer is still the same," said Will

Stevens turned and glared at Will. *He's probably angry that he doesn't get credit for bringing me in.* Stevens moved and Will saw a slight movement outside the window. He would have missed it had he not known what to watch for. Samuel would report to Olivia if Parker locked him up.

"Both of you can sign up together and we'll guarantee you'll stay together." Mayor Nelson picked up the enlistment forms and held them out for Will and Joe.

"No thanks," said Will. Joe shook his head and held up his hands in refusal.

Corporal Stevens spoke with a snarl. "Maybe a few days in Libby will help you change your minds. I'm sure your wives will miss you."

Joe looked startled, which seemed to please Stevens. Everyone knew about Libby Prison – a cold, drafty warehouse converted to a prison. Will clenched his fists at his side and clamped his jaws firmly shut lest he say something to make the situation worse. He knew Olivia could handle whatever came her way, but he wasn't so sure about Jeannette. He glanced at Joe, who had recovered from his surprise and waited with resolve. They would stand together, or die together.

Parker glared at Stevens then back at Will and Joe. "Lock them up," he said nodding to Stevens. "When you are ready to sign up, we'll release you," he said.

"Exchange one prison for another?" Will said.

Parker raised his fist to strike Will, but seemed to think better of it when the mayor cleared his throat, reminding them that it was his office and he was in charge.

***

"Take them away," said Nelson.

A guard took Will and Joe from the room. Samuel turned to go, but stopped when he heard Parker's voice again. "Maybe when they find their friends in there they'll all change their minds."

"What friends?" asked Mayor Nelson frowning.

"Jones and Walsh. We stopped them this morning. Jones gave us a hard time, so we had to rough him up a little."

"You should have told me," said the mayor.

"The whole point is to get all of them," said Parker. "We have four. Tomorrow we'll grab the other two – Rayburn and Cooper."

"We'll wait," said Mayor Nelson. "Give these four a chance to give in. We'll get the others soon enough if this doesn't work.

"Maybe Olivia will make him join now," said Parker.

Samuel moved quietly away from the window wondering if the wives of Kenneth Jones and George Walsh knew where they were. *Better swing by and let them know. They ain't far from Miz Phillips' place.*

***

The guard shoved Will and Joe into a large, dark, damp, cold room. A small candle did its best to push aside the larger darkness. Two other men huddled in a far corner – away from the open window six feet above the floor.

"Will? Joe?"

102

"George? Who's that with you?"

"It's me, Kenny."

"They beat him when he resisted," said George.

"Let's have a look," said Will. "We don't have any equipment but we'll do what we can."

"Don't think it's too bad," said Kenny. "Jaw is sore – leg where he kicked me."

Will ran his hand over Kenny's leg and jaw. "Don't feel any broken bones," he said. "What do you think, Joe?"

Joe gave him the once over. "I think you're right. Don't pay to fight them, Kenny."

"Yeah, so I learned."

"How long…?"

"They took me this morning as I was walking to work," said George. "They brought Kenny in around noon."

"It's me they want," said Will. "Maybe…"

"Don't even think that way," said Kenny. "Sure they want you, but they want all of us in the *Volunteers*, so they aren't about to let us alone even if you give in."

"He's right, Will. We're all here because of our faith and belief. We'll stand together as long as we can and separately when we can't."

"Thanks friends," said Will. "Now let us get down to some serious prayer for our women and children. I'm sure that Samuel was outside listening. He'll let Olivia and Jeannette know where we are and I'm sure he'll find a way to contact us tomorrow."

"Our wives don't even know we're alive," said Kenny. "Wish there was some way to let Corinne know."

"We do need to pray," said Joe. "I'm not sure how Jeannette will handle this."

They knelt on the cold, stone floor and prayed.

23 *Waiting for Word*

James returned to the kitchen after getting his brothers settled in bed. Olivia sat in the rocker staring into the embers of the burned logs, knitting needles motionless in her hands. She was aware of his presence, but couldn't speak.

"Are you all right, Mom? I mean…do you think…? Will Dad…?"

Olivia looked at him for a brief moment feeling like a bewildered child, herself. "Thank you for helping your brothers, James. Would you like to read to me for a while?" She couldn't have explained her feelings if James had asked, but a lump of fear in the pit of her stomach sent chills over her shoulders and down her back. She didn't want to be alone with her thoughts while she waited for word from Will.

"I got a new book from Worthington's on the way home today. I'll get it." James went to his room that he shared with his brothers and returned with his book.

"Why don't you throw another log on the fire? We might have a long wait." She said, glad her oldest son was perceptive enough that she didn't have to explain her need, or her fear.

James picked up the heavy iron poker and jabbed at the coals and ashes until tiny flames licked the charred logs. Then he added another log and watched the flames grow and leap around it like a hungry animal licking the bones of its prey. Heat and warmth penetrated the kitchen, but couldn't dispel her anxiety. James pulled the other rocking chair near the fire and faced his mother.

"What's the name of your book?" Olivia picked up her needles and let the red wool slip through her fingers, over and around the clacking needles in a soothing rhythm.

"It's called *Peter Parley's Story of the Trapper* by Samuel Goodrich." He began reading, "I suppose you have heard of Lake Superior…" James continued to read until the chiming of the mantel clock in the living room startled them.

"My goodness, James," said Olivia. "It's eleven o'clock. You must be tired and you have school tomorrow. You read so well, I lost track of time."

"It is a good book, don't you think? I didn't know it was so late either." James paused giving his mother a serious look. They both knew she'd heard little of the story. "Mom, can they make Dad join the *Volunteers*? Will they put him in jail, if he don't join?"

"If he *doesn't* join," she corrected him.

James grinned at the correction then turned serious again. "But, will they?"

"James, you're too young to worry about such things, but I can't lie to you. Everything will be all right, because God is with us, but that doesn't mean things will be the way we want them to be. I don't know what will happen with your father, except that he won't join the *Richmond Volunteers*. He…"

Suddenly Blackie began barking. The sound of a horse's hooves thundered into the back yard.

"Samuel?" James asked, glancing at the door.

"Probably."

The sound of footsteps across the porch then three short taps at the door followed. "It is Samuel," said James. He jumped up and was at the door before Olivia could set her knitting aside. She stood with heart pounding as Samuel stumbled into the room, covered with snow.

"Get him a cup of hot coffee from the stove," Olivia said to James.

Samuel shook the snow from his head and stood by the door where the snow dripped on the mud-rug. He accepted the hot liquid and said, "They put Master Will in jail, Miz Olivia – him and Master Joe. I hid in the bushes outside the mayor's window. That Sergeant Parker was there – and that Stevens man. The mayor tried to make them sign some papers. They refused and Stevens said that maybe some time in a cell would make them change their minds. The sergeant agreed and told him to lock them up."

"Did he say how long he plans to keep them?" Olivia would be strong for her children, regardless what happened to Will. It's what he wanted, but her inner world twirled like the snowstorm blowing outside.

"They made Master Will and Master Joe think they would have to stay 'til they changed their minds, but after the corporal took them out, the mayor said he would keep them for two days then see what they had to say. I started to leave then I heard Parker say something about others, so I listened more. Seems they took Master Kenny and Master George this morning. Sergeant Parker suggested maybe you could make him change his mind."

"Claudia and Corinne must be worried sick and Jeannette is probably in a state of panic."

"Since the three of them live near each other, I stopped and told them. Thought you might want me to do that."

"Thank you, Samuel. I'm sure Corinne and Claudia are upset, but they can handle the worry. What about Jeannette? Was she all right?"

"She was crying, but at least now she knows he won't be home for a couple of nights. The other two were worried because they had no way to find out where their men were. Like you says, they'll be okay."

Olivia exhaled a long slow breath. "It's not good, but not as bad as it could be. Maybe Matthew will realize Will won't change his mind. Thank you for your help, Samuel. You better get some sleep. I'm sure Rosy is worried. I'll need you to check on Will tomorrow."

She smiled and offered her hand to Samuel, who still refused after all his years of freedom to be that familiar with Olivia. He bowed and hurried out to care for the horse then go to his own cabin. Olivia locked the door behind him and stood silently staring at it, as if she could will it to open and bring her husband rushing into her arms.

"Mom?"

Olivia whirled around. For a moment, she'd forgotten James was still there. Understanding her son's concern, she answered his unasked questions, "It's all right, for now, James. The prison is not a nice place to be, but your father, Joe, Kenny and George are together and it won't be for long. I just wish they knew that, so they wouldn't worry."

"Maybe if I go down there tomorrow," said James, "they'll let me see him and…"

"That's a good idea, James, but I'm afraid Matthew Parker wouldn't allow you in. Samuel can probably find a way to get to them. We'll let him try first. You better get some sleep and James…"

"Yes ma'am?"

"Thank you for keeping me company and reading to me tonight." She smiled at her son who blushed with pleasure.

"Sure," he said and went to join his brothers.

Olivia turned off the lamp and went to the bed she and Will had shared for fourteen years. For the first time since her marriage, she would sleep alone. When she finally fell into that twilight between waking and deep sleep, scenes of battles, dungeons and crying children dominated her dreams.

24 Olivia's Threat

Old Bill flew to the fence to announce a new day – a day Olivia was anxious to greet and at the same time dreaded its arrival. She dragged herself out of bed. Tired, aching bones suggested she had not slept at all. Action of any kind was better than the sleeplessness of the night. Already the aroma of coffee and bacon drifted down the hall, so she knew Rosy didn't sleep much either.

Together she and Rosy sleepwalked through preparation of breakfast and other morning chores. Olivia's thoughts never drifted far from that prison on the corner of Carry and 20th Street. Was Will cold, or hungry? Did he get any sleep? Was he worried about her and the children? *If I've heard nothing by early this afternoon, I'll ask Daddy to intervene, even though Will wouldn't want me to do that.*

"Mom?" James dropped his books on the table with a thud and stood beside Olivia as she dished up breakfast.

Startled, she held the spoon above the skillet of golden scrambled eggs and turned to gaze into her son's eyes. "Yes?"

"I think I should stay home today to…you know…help you until Dad comes home."

Olivia moved the skillet from the heat, "James I appreciate your offer, but I think you better get all the school you can. I'll be all right. Your father will be home soon."

"But Mom, what if…"

She didn't let him finish. "James, we don't live by *what ifs* and *if onlys* in this house. You know that. Besides, you need to go and look after Betsy."

"Betsy? No one would hurt her…would they?"

"James, I don't know what anyone will do. All this talk of war seems to drag people into an unholy frenzy. I would just feel a lot better if you were with her."

"All right," he answered with some reluctance. "But promise you'll send Samuel – or maybe Blackie – after me if you need help."

"That's an excellent idea, James. Blackie could find you. If he shows up, you'll know to bring Betsy home right away."

"I can do that," he said, glancing at Betsy who shuffled into the room looking more like a little old woman than a ten year old.

"Hey Betsy," he said. "Everything will be all right."

"But Daddy's not here. That man will make him join the *Volunteers* and we'll never see him again." Betsy brushed at the tears that trickled down her face. James rushed to put his arms around her.

"Hey, do you think Mom would send us off to school if there was *real* trouble?"

"No, but…"

"Well until we know there is trouble bad enough for us to stay home, we'll go – like normal. Blackie will come after us if Mom needs us and I'll bring you home. Okay?"

Betsey glanced at Olivia, who could only nod her approval. The lump in her throat wouldn't let her speak.

"Okay," Betsy said.

"Now, let's eat those beautiful eggs before they get cold and we have to feed them to Blackie."

Blackie slapped his wagging tail on the floor as if to urge them to let the eggs get cold. Betsy giggled and James took her hand and offered a prayer for his father and the food. Olivia turned her back and held her breath to keep her tears of pride from ruining the moment. When she turned around, Rosy's face glistened, but a smile spread across her face.

***

Olivia threw her cape over her shoulders and watched from the porch while Blackie ran alongside of James until he and Betsy turned the corner. When they were out of sight, the little dog ran back to Olivia, tail wagging.

Olivia smiled at the dog and stooped to cup his shaggy head in her hands. "Good dog, Blackie," she said. "For a street mongrel that James rescued two years ago, you are the most gentle, sweet tempered and intelligent animal that I know." She rubbed his head and scratched behind his ears. His tail wagged and his tongue hung from the side of his mouth, emphasizing his constant grin.

"Go find Samuel, now," she said. Blackie jumped off the porch and ran around the house as if a rabbit had suddenly run across the yard.

The morning dragged on. Olivia could stand the suspense no longer. *I have to do something. As soon as I nurse Lucy, I'll leave her and the twins with Rosy and have Samuel drive me to City Hall to have a talk with either Matthew, or Mayor Nelson.* Having thus set her mind on a path of action, Olivia went to nurse the baby.

She had just lifted Lucy to her shoulder, when she heard the sound of stomping feet on the front porch. A long, loud, persistent pounding at the door followed. It didn't sound like one of Will's patients. She and Rosy had already turned away several who sought medical attention and one couple who wanted to get married.

Olivia listened as Rosy shuffled from the kitchen to answer the knock. She heard a man's voice, but didn't recognize it through the closed bedroom door, nor could she hear what he was saying. She watched the door, waiting for Rosy's gentle rap. When it came, she took a deep breath and said, "Come in, Rosy."

Rosy opened the door enough to put her head around it, and said, "That Beecham man from the mayor's office is here to see you Miz Olivia." Rosy made a face as if even the feel of the words across her tongue left a bitter taste in her mouth.

"He must be here to pressure me to convince Will to join them," Olivia said. "If they were releasing him, Beecham wouldn't be here. Show him into the living room. I'll be with him when I finish with Lucy."

"Yes'em," said Rosy and closed the door behind her. Olivia made sure Lucy didn't want to nurse any more, changed the baby's diaper, held her until she fell asleep then placed her in the cradle. *Mr. Beecham needs to wait a little longer.* She took time to tidy her hair and straighten the wrinkles in her dress then sit in her rocker to meditate before leaving the bedroom. Finally, a half hour later she walked slowly to the living room and extended her hand, as if she had asked the man to morning tea.

"Mr. Beecham. How nice of you to stop by – again. I hope you have brought me news of my husband's release."

George Beecham stopped pacing and made such an abrupt turn that he had to put a steadying hand on the back of a chair. With a stiff bow, he acknowledged her greeting then plunged ahead without giving her time for further comment.

"Mrs. Brunner," he said, "surely you will have a word with your slave. You must be unaware that she has kept me waiting for almost an hour. I'm a busy man. I…"

Olivia interrupted him before he embarked on one of his famous impromptu speeches. "Mr. Beecham," she said, her eyes narrowed and her voice became level and controlled, "I do not have slaves. Rosy, my hired helper and friend, informed me at once of your arrival, but I, too, am a busy woman and I have a nursing infant to care for." She paused, gave him a smile and added, "Unless, of course, you would rather discuss your business while I nurse my baby in your presence."

Beecham's jaw dropped leaving a large round O where his closed mouth should have been. A rich scarlet color slowly crept up his neck, across his face, to the tip of his ears ending at the roots of his almost nonexistent hair. Olivia waited, almost expecting the thin gray strands across the top of his head to burst into flame. Snapping his jaw shut, he mumbled something that sounded like, "Of course not."

Olivia didn't offer him a seat so he stood awkwardly staring at her. He opened his mouth to speak, but she gave him no chance to voice his plea for her to influence Will's decision. Holding her head erect so that George Beecham, who was small and slightly shorter than her own five feet, six inches, had to look up to her. "I must say I'm not only surprised, but disappointed that our mayor has allowed *Sergeant* Parker to pull men away from their families and throw them into prison without warning. I thought he had more compassion than that."

Olivia kept her voice low with just a hint of anger. She watched Beecham pull at his collar as if it had begun to shrink. His face was still red and blotchy.

"Mrs. Brunner," His voice cracked like an adolescent entering puberty. Becoming more embarrassed and flustered, he cleared his throat and tried again. "Mrs. Brunner, the mayor sends his apologies for any discomfort you have suffered because of your husband's decision."

Olivia glared at the man. He pulled at his collar again and tried to look away from her, but Olivia's eyes held his with such force, he could hardly blink much less look away.

"Mr. Beecham," she said, "save your lies for someone who will believe them."

"Mrs. Brunner!" He raised his eyebrows in surprise.

"You heard me correctly, Mr. Beecham. My husband did not ask to stay in your prison. Because Sergeant Parker is a petulant child who cannot have his own way, he put my husband in that prison. You are here to talk me into making Will change his mind. Well, you can forget it and save your breath. Will makes his own decisions and I stand with him in whatever he does. I will intervene in any way I can to get him out of that hole, but I will not interfere with his decisions."

"But…"

"And," she continued, not giving him a chance to interrupt with his pre-planned speech, "you can tell Sergeant Parker and Mayor Nelson for me, that if my husband and his friends are not home by suppertime this evening, I will personally make a trip to Washington tomorrow to see President Buchanan. We *are* still part of the Union, are we not? The last I heard we had not yet seceded. Now, if you will excuse me, I, too, have work to do."

"Mrs. Brunner, I wish you would reconsider and talk to your husband."

"And I wish you would reconsider and leave him alone with his decision. Good day, Mr. Beecham."

Olivia turned and marched to the door, opened it and waited for Beecham to depart. He hurried out, placing his hat on his head and pulling on his coat as he stomped across the porch. She closed the door behind him and called to Rosy, who she knew was listening from the kitchen. "Prepare my best dress in case I need to go to Washington in the morning."

"Yes'em, Miz Olivia." Rosy hurried away but not before Olivia saw the grin slide across her round, shining face and light up her dark, flashing eyes.

***

The rest of the morning and the afternoon slipped by with no further word from the mayor's office – either about her ultimatum or Will's release. When Olivia heard Betsy and James stomp the snow from their feet on the back porch, she poured hot chocolate for them and the twins. The twins ran down the hall and opened the door for James and Betsy giggling and talking together as they often did.

"Mr. Beecham was here again today," said Michael as James and Betsy peeled off their outer layers of clothes. James cast a glance at his mother.

"Yeah, but Mom made him wait *hours* before she went to talk to him." Corey giggled.

"He strutted back and forth in the living room like Old Bill," said Michael. He threw out his chest, placed his thumbs in his armpits, flapped his elbows and strutted around the kitchen to demonstrate the way Beecham paced.

"Michael," said Olivia, "shame on you insulting our rooster. Old Bill might get you for that."

All four children went into peals of laughter. They all knew how many times Old Bill had flown at Michael when he went to gather eggs in the hen house.

"What did Beecham want?" James asked. "He's got Dad, what more could he want."

"He wanted Mom to make Dad join the *Volunteers*," said Corey.

"But Mom told him if Daddy isn't home for supper tonight, she's going to go see President Buchanan tomorrow," finished Michael.

"Really?" James looked at Olivia and grinned when she nodded.

"Sally's dad left yesterday for training," said Betsy, a note of sadness and fear in her voice.

"No more war talk," said Olivia. "It's bad for digestion. Drink your chocolate then do your homework."

"We don't have homework," said Corey and Michael together.

"Then go feed Blackie and help Samuel with some of the outside chores until supper is ready."

Rosy came in to help Olivia prepare supper as the boys ran out the door. Later, when Michael and Corey came in, Samuel came to the door and Rosy stepped out to the porch with him. A minute later she was back to help Betsy set the table. Olivia said, "Set a place for Will."

"Yes'em," said Rosy, her eyes wide. Betsy looked at her with eyes full of hope. Neither of them dared question Olivia.

"Did I hear Samuel go out with the wagon?" Olivia asked as she began dishing up supper.

"Yes'em," said Rosy. "The boys told him what you said to Beecham. He said he should go to the prison and wait a while – just in case."

Olivia smiled and turned back to the stove.

25 Surprise Release

Will and his friends had huddled together for warmth and slept for an hour when the guard came with breakfast – gruel and stale bread.

"Well," said Joe. "Jeannette's not much of a cook, but I'll never complain about her meals again. I hope she's all right."

"I'm sure Olivia is all right," said Will. "Samuel and Rosy will look after her and the kids, but I worry about how long they will keep us."

"They said until we come around to their way of thinking," said Joe.

"I know, but…Well, nothing we can do except pray and plan. I've been working on a map for Olivia to get her up north."

"Good idea," said Joe. "I'll remind Jeanette to go with her as soon as I can."

"Me too," said George. "If we don't get out, maybe Samuel can take messages to our wives for us."

"I'm sure he'll do what he can," said Will.

"You know," said Kenny, "the next time they cart us off like this – assuming they let us go this time – one of us should grab a Bible. It's a good thing Will knows so much from memory."

"Not much light here for reading anyway," said George.

"What do you think, Will?" said Joe. "They talk like we're going to get out of here eventually." Joe tried to laugh but it didn't sound very cheerful.

"Oh, I think they'll let us go – this time," said Will. "They only have four of us."

"Yeah," said Kenny. "They missed John and Robert this time."

"There will be other times?" asked Joe.

"Until they get what they want…" Will didn't finish. A few small pebbles fell to the floor under the window.

"What was that?" said Kenny turning toward the window.

"Sounded like…" Another ping followed by two more drew them closer to the window. "…pebbles," finished George.

"Maybe it's Samuel," said Joe.

Will moved closer to the window and picked up several pebbles from the floor.

"Will, you're taller than the rest of us," said Joe. "Maybe you can hear whoever it is."

Not wanting to cause trouble for whoever was there, Will spoke in a hoarse-like whisper. "Is someone out there?"

"Yes sir, Master Brunner. It's me, David. We heard you was in here, so Grandpa said I should come to you with news."

"Good boy, David. What is your news?"

"Some men in uniforms stopped to talk. They were laughing. Said Parker put you and Joe in jail and made you think you would be here for a long time. Then the mayor sent Beecham to your house this morning to force Miz Olivia to make you give in. She sent Beecham packing. Told him she was going to see the President tomorrow if you wasn't home for supper tonight. Grandpa thought you might like to know."

Bleak as their circumstances, the men couldn't help laughing. "Thank you David. Tell your grandfather we appreciate him sending you and we'll see him when we got out of here."

"Yes, sir, Master Brunner. Got to go. I hear a guard coming." David raised his voice and said, "I ain't doing nothing, sir. Just taking a short cut home."

"Well stay away from here," yelled the guard. "There are dangerous criminals in there."

"Yes sir," said David and started whistling.

A little while after David brought them news, they heard the key turn in the lock. The door flew open and the guard stepped in.

"Mayor says you can go – for now."

The men looked at one another, burst into laughter and left before the guard could change his mind.

***

Wind howled across the river and snow swirled around the men as they left the prison and hurried away.

"It's getting dark," said Joe. "We better start moving if you're going to be home for dinner." He slapped Will on the back and they all had another good laugh.

"Olivia sure has spunk, as Grandma Cooper would say," said George.

"That she does," answered Will, "but how long will it keep the vultures at bay?"

"Will," said Kenny, "the important thing is it worked this time.

We'll make the most of it and make sure our women know trouble is brewing and we expect them to follow Olivia's lead."

They pulled coat collars up and ducked their heads into the blinding snow. Joe almost ran into a wagon as he rounded the corner. "Where did that come from?"

"Isn't that your wagon, Will?" Joe said reaching for the side of it.

"Yes sir," answered Samuel from the seat. "The twins told me their mama told Beecham you better be home for supper. Figured I better meet you."

Not waiting for an invitation, Kenny, Joe and George all hoisted themselves to the back while Will climbed up beside Samuel.

"I'll take them home first if you don't mind, Master Will."

"Samuel we can't thank you enough. Let's go to Joe's first. Jeannette must be worried sick."

"Yes sir," said Samuel. "I stopped last night and told her you was all right and would be gone maybe a couple of days."

"Thanks Samuel."

"After they took you to the prison, I heard them say they had Master Kenny and Master George, so I stopped to tell their women folk too."

Kenny and George both sighed deeply. "We really appreciate that," said George.

"Yes, as far as they knew, we just disappeared," said Kenny.

"I know," said Samuel. "They was pretty worried."

Samuel stopped at the homes of Kenny, George and Joe then drove home. When he pulled into the backyard, Will jumped down and greeted Blackie while Samuel took the horses and wagon to the barn.

26   *Another Scare*

The children tried not to stare at their father's empty place at the table. Rosy lifted the lid from the pot of chicken and dumplings sending delicious, mouth-watering aroma across the room. Olivia opened the oven adding the flavor of baked apples to the air. They set the food on the table, Olivia seated herself and Rosy reached for her coat to take dinner to their cabin for her and Samuel.

Before she could open the door, they heard the sound of squeaky wagon wheels and clip clopping of horses and Blackie's excited yapping. Rosy grinned from ear to ear as she buttoned her red wool coat and tied her paisley print scarf around her head. Samuel was back and that was Blackie's special greeting for Will.

"It's Daddy," said the twins, jumping up from the table.

James looked at his mother and grinned. A great weight lifted from her heart. She winked at her son.

"Is he home to stay?" Betsy asked.

"Not if Sergeant Parker has anything to say about it," answered James, "but Mom can handle him."

Rosy moved to the porch, greeted Will and continued on to her home. Will stomped the snow from his feet while James held the door open. Betsy and the twins surrounded him with their arms before he could even unbutton his coat. He hugged them all, kissed Olivia's cheek then removed his coat.

"Were you expecting company?" He smiled at his wife.

"Will Brunner, you know that's your place. I knew you would be home."

"What did you tell them, 'Livia? David brought us news late this afternoon – something about you sending Beecham packing and going to see the president."

Olivia smiled. "I told him you make your own decisions and I wouldn't interfere, even if I could." She paused and tried to look serious, but a grin slipped across her face and the twins giggled. "I guess I might have said something about going to Washington to see the president."

Will laughed heartily and winked at James. "We all had a good laugh when David told us."

"She did," said Michael. He and Corey repeated their story, complete with actions, about Beecham's visit. Will laughed with them and gave his wife a look of admiration.

"Will, Samuel told us about Kenny and George. They're trying harder aren't they?"

Will nodded. Olivia knew her threat had worked this time. She doubted it would again.

They ate with quiet, companionable conversation. Olivia was dishing up the baked apple dessert when once again a knock at the front door sent a jolt of fear through them all.

"Surely, Parker's men aren't back already!"

Olivia glanced from Will's non-committal face to James and the other children whose eyes widened with fear.

James hesitated for a fraction of a second then rose. "I'll go," he said to his father who was also rising from his chair. He quickly returned with a more relaxed expression. "It's Mr. Rice. The midwife needs your help."

Will glanced at Olivia. She nodded and smiled at him. This was his work – his calling as much as him church ministry. She didn't mind waiting for his return from such absences.

"I'll keep the coffee hot for you," she said.

"I'll be back as soon as I can." He lifted his coat from the hook and went out the back door. Olivia heard him talking to Samuel who already had a horse saddled and waiting for him. Two horses galloped off.

27   The Promise Renewed

As she had done many times before, Olivia waited, in her grandmother's rocker, this time knowing Will was safe and doing the work he loved. Only the crackling of the logs in the hearth and the clacking of knitting needles broke the silence of the night until Blackie began yapping. She smiled, put another log on the fire and poured a cup of coffee. Will was home. Now they would have their delayed talk.

Will checked on the children, then picked up his coffee and pulled the other rocker close to the fire. Olivia waited, her brow furrowed in deep concentration, her knitting needles held motionless in her hands. So many questions, so many things to say, but the words were lost on that long path between thought and speech. She stared at the wool in her lap and the idle needles in her hands unable to make them work together. She waited for Will to speak first.

Will, lost in his own thoughts, held tightly to the mug of coffee with both hands as if holding to a lifeline in the dark. Finally, he took a sip of the hot liquid and spoke hesitantly. As much as she wanted to hear him say, "Everything's going to be all right," she knew that was only a dream. Life in general and their lives in particular, would become more difficult. He had to say fearful words of truth and she would listen.

As if reading her mind, Will spoke softly. "Things will get worse, 'Livia." He stared into the fire. "This was only another of Parker's warnings. He will do whatever he deems necessary to get what he wants."

He gave her no chance to question him – not that she could have found her voice to do so. "Parker is determined. He's not only trying harder, he's becoming violent. They beat Kenny when he resisted going with them. "

"On Parker's orders?"

"So they said, but whether he gave the order or not, he didn't apologize for it."

"Was Kenny hurt? Seriously, I mean."

"No, they stopped short of breaking any bones – this time."

Together they stared into the fire. What was it about the fire that fostered and stirred hopes and dreams? Stories of oracles leaping from the flames? The Spirit of Pentecost giving courage and power? Whatever it was, it did little to dispel the uneasiness, or offer a hopeful message.

"Would it help if we left Richmond? Uncle George lives up around Charleston." Olivia held her needles like crossed swords. They seemed to be tangling more threads than kitting them anyway.

Will's hands tightened on his cup until white knuckles reflected the orange flames that leaped around the logs. One of them shifted, sending a fresh rush of flames around the other logs, a few sparks across the grate and a whiff of smoke into the air.

Olivia waited.

Will heaved a heavy sigh. "It's a tempting idea, 'Livia, but I don't think we would make it as far as your father's plantation," he answered, shaking his head. "No, I think Joe and I and the others will be harassed until we either join the *Volunteers,* or die in that prison."

"Oh, Will, surely it won't come to that." Olivia had always felt strong and courageous – like a mountain lion. At that moment, she felt more like a helpless kitten. She shivered and clutched the knitting needles to keep her trembling hands from spilling the contents of her work over the floor. "Maybe the war will blow over, or Virginia will stay with the Union."

"I wish I could say that either is a possibility, but I don't think so. War is war and it won't matter which side we're on. Already seven states have seceded and I give Virginia about three months, or less, to follow. Then every man or boy who can walk and carry a gun will be expected to fight." Will paused, licked his lips, then finished, shaking his head, "No Olivia, Parker will keep putting me in jail for longer periods of time until he either leaves me there to die, or I give them what they want."

Another log shifted. Olivia started as if it had been a gunshot. Sparks like fireflies flew around the hearth. Crackling sounds of logs burning filled the room – a puff of smoke followed. Will placed another log on the fire, more for something to do than to ward off the cold. It was already warm and toasty in the kitchen. Yellow, orange and red tongues licked at the log – devouring it with insatiable hunger. Breathing in the aroma of burning wood, Will turned back to face Olivia, who still held her knitting in her lap, needles paused, waiting for a word of hope.

"What can we do?" Her voice fell to a whisper. "We can't just sit here and let them destroy our lives."

"Like all wars, a lot of lives will be destroyed before this one runs its course. But you're right. We can't act as if there is no threat and life will always be as it has been. Everything will change – whether we are in Richmond or Charleston. We have to consider our children. We have to plan for the inevitable and do what we can to protect them."

"Plan? How can we plan when Parker is in charge?" Olivia looked at her husband. She placed a hand over her pounding heart afraid it would stop and never start again. While Will was in prison, she had worried. Apparently, he had spent the time planning. Her sixth sense premonition sent a shiver through her. She knew what she had promised, but didn't dare think it might have to be fulfilled.

"Darling, you're as strong as you are beautiful. You're creative. You see possibilities when others see none. I trust you to do what's right and necessary. Parker won't let me leave, but maybe you can make it. You and the children can either go to the plantation, or move north to the Kanawha Valley. Your uncle will help you."

"Will! I can't leave without you!" Olivia tried to keep her face and voice calm, but the chill down her spine sent a tremble to her voice. The needles in her hand clacked together even though she had ceased trying to make them work.

"Olivia, if it comes to dying in prison or in battle, I will choose prison. Either way I will be unable to care for you and the children. You will have to be strong enough for both of us."

"Will, we can't go to the plantation. You know that. We would all be miserable. And a journey north without you…I can't believe it will come to that."

Olivia stared into the leaping flames for that sign, or oracle that the great patriarchs seemed to receive. *God spoke to Moses from a burning bush, can't He at least give me a whisper?* Aware of Will's eyes upon her, she continued to stare into the fire, unable to look into his eyes. She felt his nearness, breathed in the faint odor of yesterday's aftershave. The smell of prison hung in the air. She couldn't stand to see the pain in his eyes, nor let him see the fear in hers.

They sat in silence, eyes fixed unseeing on the flames leaping in and around charred logs. A sudden gust of wind howled around the chimney and rattled windows. Blackie added his mournful howl as if he understood the approaching changes in the lives of his humans.

Anger welled within her – anger at Matthew Parker, at the mayor, at men in general who craved war. She continued to stare into the flames watching them leap and dance with fury. Finally, as if she had received that coveted oracle, like Jonah of old, she didn't want to believe the message she was sure she heard. She didn't want to talk about war. She didn't want to talk about separation. She just wanted to hold Will, and be held by his strong arms – to be told everything would be all right. But, she knew better. They had to prepare, to know their options.

"Will, when the war comes to Richmond," she was surprised by the calmness of her voice and the acceptance of when, not if, "isn't it possible that, as James' teacher said, the plantation will be no safer than our home here?"

"Probably," he said. "I didn't want to worry you anymore than I already have." He paused, looking helpless and continued. "I'm sorry, darling, but it looks like you only have two other choices – to stay here and wait while I'm in prison, knowing I may never leave alive. I can't believe you would be safe here. It looks like going north is the least of all the evils."

"I don't want to leave you." Olivia hardly ever shed tears, but they stood on the brink of her eyes waiting permission to roll down her face. Furiously, she blinked them away.

"'Livia, my darling, we won't worry about it now, but we need to plan. If it comes to a choice of waiting for me to return from a life sentence or making sure the children are safe, you will do what's best. And remember, James was twelve in December. He's pretty good with a gun and old enough to be asked to bear arms – or at least be a part of the drum corp."

"Surely not James! He's only a child." Olivia's face reflected the horror she felt in the depth of her heart. It was hard enough to think of losing her husband to such horrors, but her son, too? Never!

"Olivia…," Will's pale face glistened with sweat, like a man dangling at the end of his rope, holding on to a thread for the sake of his wife, wishing with all his might that he could spare her and the children any grief. Knowing Will struggled with his emotions as much as she did, Olivia set her knitting aside and moved into his arms. Together their tears mingled for an uncertain future. With a resolve and strength from her lifetime of faith, Olivia held his face in her hands. Their eyes locked. Her voice trembled.

"Will, we'll both do what we have to do in the face of whatever comes our way. God will be with us. He always has been. He always will be. With His help, I will take the children to The Valley. I will protect them as best I can. I promised you once and I renew that promise now with a vow as firm as our marriage commitment. If you perish, we will mourn and move on. If you escape, you will find us."

As she did on her wedding day, Olivia sealed her promise with a kiss.

"Olivia, how did I ever deserve you? God is good. He will direct us in the midst of this evil that is upon us."

Olivia took his hand, hoping she would never have to keep her promise, but knowing deep within her heart that day would come – sooner than she wanted.

28   The Last Incarceration

The January thaw came and left bringing more snow, rain and mud into February. Threats of secession, war and arguments over slavery erupted like mini-volcanoes almost daily. Will's church tried to stay neutral, but it was difficult when everyone knew he and his five closest friends were in and out of prison as if going through a revolving door. How long before the door would be locked permanently and the six men would never return home?

Today has been the longest Saturday I've ever spent. The clock struck eleven as Olivia glanced at the calendar beside the door – February 9. *Already in this, the shortest month of the year, Parker has taken Will and the rest to prison five times. This time, so far, they have been gone three days. They've never kept them over Sunday before. Will this be the first?*

Olivia let her frustration and fear flow to the polishing cloth, as she cleaned and shined the family's shoes for Sunday's service. Rosy wanted to do it, but Olivia said she needed to release her tension.

She didn't want to think about the inevitable, but she could no more stop the thoughts than she could stop Matthew Parker. *How could I have promised to leave Richmond without Will? Surely, it won't come to that. O Lord, I don't want to leave without him. Help me do what's best.*

Olivia stared into the dying fire in the hearth. The shoes finished, the clothes all laid out for church the next morning, she would have to get some rest soon. Nights were always the hardest. She dreaded another night without Will beside her. Even Lucy was sleeping longer and getting her up less during the night. Tomorrow she would take the children to church, but how could she face the congregation without Will?

Lord, forgive my selfishness. I'm not alone in this. Matthew is harassing Will's friends, hoping that will break him. Jeannette is beside herself with fear. Lord, give us courage.

The faithful clock in the living room counted off twelve strokes of midnight – another hour gone. She rose, started toward the bedroom,

but stopped when she heard the sound she'd been listening for –
Samuel driving the wagon into the backyard and Blackie's greeting to
Will. Every night that Will was in prison, Samuel took the wagon and
waited near Libby until midnight in case they released the men.

Choking back tears of relief, Olivia stirred up the coals in the
stove and set the beef stew back on the hot part. *Will is home again,
but how long will it be before they take him again?*

The door opened and a blast of cold air swirled around the room
lifting the edge of the tablecloth. Will shut the door and threw *The
Enquirer* on the table as if he'd only been out for the evening paper.
She knew Samuel had bought the paper, the way he did every evening
– for Will if they released him, for her if they didn't.

Olivia couldn't wait for him to remove his coat. She flung herself
into his open arms. They clung to each other – he like a condemned
man squeezing life into his leaking spirit, she to siphon his love and
return it to him. Regaining control of their emotions, Will reluctantly
pulled away and hung up his coat, while Olivia poured him a cup of
steaming coffee.

"Thanks," he said, taking a sip. He was quiet for a minute –
staring into his cup. Finally, he bit his lip and said, "I know the
children are asleep, but…do you suppose…Could I just…look at
them…for only a minute?"

"They would be disappointed if you didn't." Olivia said. With a
sudden stab of pain, she realized that as hard as it was for her to get
through these separations, at least she had the children. Will had no
one, except Joe and the other four friends. "Why don't you check on
them while I take care of the stew?"

Will returned, eyes moist. He sat and stirred his coffee, staring at
the leaping flames in the fireplace.

"There's hot water if you want a bath." Olivia nodded at the
washtub used for baths as well as for washing clothes. It was still by
the fireplace where the children had used it earlier.

"That will feel good. Why don't you read the paper to me while I
eat and then I'll bathe?"

Olivia sat across the table from him and scanned the headlines.
Alarmed, she sucked in her breath and read, "Jefferson Davis Is
Elected President. The Confederate Provisional Congress elected
Jefferson Davis President of the Confederate States today. The new
capital will be in Montgomery, Alabama, where Davis will be
inaugurated on the seventeenth of this month. President-elect Davis
plans to lead the southern states in forging a new nation – with or

without war."

Olivia paused watching her husband eat. She was afraid to ask, but she knew they didn't feed him – or if they did, it was very minimal. Didn't they know if they starved him, he would be of no value to them, even if he gave in to their demands? She sent food by Samuel as often as she could – never knowing how long he would be at Libby – or if he really got it.

She continued to read while Will finished the stew and picked up the pans of hot water. Then she laid aside the paper and watched him pour the water into the tub being careful not to spill a drop, as if he savored even the sound of clean water running free. With the same kind of care, he removed his dirty, sweaty clothing. She was stricken to see his ribs like a piece of corduroy. She tried not to notice, but her heart lurched at the thought of what he must be going through.

Olivia waited until he was settled, then taking the cloth and soap, knelt beside the tub and gently washed his back, biting her lips until she tasted blood to keep the tears from falling. How many more times would she be able to offer this simple ministry of love to her husband? Maybe none.

***

Another five days of harassment passed. Olivia and Rosy tried to keep things as normal as possible for the children. The cinnamon aroma of cookies baking filled the house. The twins wandered into the warm kitchen and leaned with elbows on the table watching Rosy pull the cookie sheet from the oven.

"Hey they look like hearts," said Corey.

"That's 'cause it's Valentine's Day," said Michael. "That means Mom and Rosy love us."

"You mean they don't love us if they don't bake cookies?" Corey asked trying to look wide-eyed and anxious, but the mischievous giggle escaped as he covered his mouth.

"You boys know you is loved more'n anyone else in the whole city of Richmond," said Rosy, smiling broadly and handing each of them a warm cookie from the pan.

Suddenly a hard rap, followed by an insistent pounding at the front door, interrupted the cozy feeling they had momentarily enjoyed. Rosy, with flour up to her elbows, started toward the hall.

"I'll get it, Rosy. It's Beecham," Olivia said. "I know the sound."

Olivia removed her apron and took her time walking to the living room. She reached for the door as another pounding rattled the windows. George Beecham stood with his fist raised, Corporal Stevens at his side. Olivia leaned back in case he let his fist fall accidentally – or otherwise. Lucy cried out from the bedroom.

"Mr. Beecham, I hope you have a good reason for waking my baby." She didn't invite him in, but stared into his eyes, ignoring Corporal Stevens, as well as the rapid beating of her heart. She would not let them know how scared she was.

"Where's your husband?" Beecham asked not bothering to put on his polite facade.

"*Mister* Beecham, you have harassed my husband enough in the last month and a half to know where he is."

"Get him."

"I beg your pardon?" Olivia stiffened, eyes narrowed.

"You heard me. Get him." George Beecham raised his voice and made a move as if to step inside the house.

Olivia, keeping one hand on the door, placed the other on the doorframe. Beecham would have to push her aside to enter. Corey and Michael slipped into the room and stood on either side of her.

"Mr. Beecham, I am not your servant. I'm sure that's the reason you brought *him* along." She nodded to Stevens who glared at her. "If you need to see my husband," she continued, "you know where he is. Please don't frighten his patients when you arrest him this time. I'm not qualified to treat a heart attack."

Olivia didn't wait for an answer, but closed the door firmly, resisting the desire to slam it against Beecham's nose. She stood with her back against the door until she heard the men stomp across the porch. Then she released her held breath and pulled herself away from the door.

"Miz Olivia?" Rosy stood in the doorway, eyes wide, wringing her hands in her apron.

"It's all right, Rosy. They'll take him again. Let's finish the cookies. Betsy and James will be home soon."

Corey and Michael each reached for a hand. She forced a smile as she squeezed the small hands in hers. "It's all right, boys," she said. "We've been through it before. He'll be back in a couple of days." They returned to their play, glancing back at her as they tiptoed past Olivia's room where Lucy's crib was.

"Lucy must have gone back to sleep," she said as she followed Rosy to the kitchen fighting an eerie feeling that this time was different. Somehow, she knew this time it would be longer. Had she only known.

***

Will knew before the door flew open it was Beecham again. "Get your coat, Joe," he said. "Looks like they're back. Sorry Mr. Barnes."

"What's the matter with that mayor anyway? Don't he know we need doctors too?" The patient glared at Beecham and Stevens.

"Go home, old man," said Stevens. "If we can't have these doctors, no one will."

Will looked at Joe, who cringed. They both knew this would be the last time. They would not be coming home.

29   Olivia's Turn

James and Betsy shrugged into their coats. Rosy helped Betsy with boots and scarf. "You keep that tied," she said. "Where's your mittens?"

"In my pocket," said Betsy without much enthusiasm.

James pulled on his mittens, watching his mother stare out the window. "Mom, you sure you don't want us to stay home?"

Olivia turned around. Although she tried to keep her fear and concerns hidden from her children, James was too perceptive for a twelve year old. She saw concern in his eyes – far too great for a child. Did he, too, feel this time was different?

"James, we need to…"

"I know," he held up a hand to stop her and answered before she could finish. "We need to keep our normal routine. But, Mom, it's not normal with Dad locked up and…"

"And what James?"

"Nothing. Come on Betsy. We'll be late." He tugged at his sister's arm and nudged her toward the door. Betsy picked up her books and followed her brother out the door with slow dragging steps.

"They's too worried for kids," said Rosy. "Shouldn't oughta be that way. Kids 'sposed to be happy."

"I know, Rosy. I wish…" Olivia shook her head and watched James and Betsy until they turned the corner.

"Um, um, um," muttered Rosy shaking her head. They both turned to morning chores, dragging through the morning with automatic responses. Olivia missed Rosy's pleasant humming and constant smile. A soft cry from the bedroom brought a smile from both of them.

"Lucy's the only one unaffected by all this war stuff and Will's absence," said Olivia. "Even the twins are more subdued than usual."

"Yes'em," said Rosy plopping a ball of dough on the table to roll out noodles for supper.

Olivia went to care for the baby, who had stopped crying. The twins were with her. They were six now, but since Will's frequent incarcerations they acted much older. Unlike most of their friends, they began taking it upon themselves to help her and Rosy – and even Samuel. She walked into the room where Michael held Lucy and Corey knelt on the floor making his sister laugh.

"She's wet," said Michael.

"Yeah, that's why I let him hold her." Corey covered his mouth with his hand and giggled.

"Thank you, boys," Olivia smiled at them. Lucy laughed for her brothers then reached for her mother. For an instant, everything felt normal and right.

She'd no sooner put Lucy back in her cradle when the familiar banging rattled the door and windows. Her heart skipped a beat. Had something happened to Will? Why else would Beecham be back?

Rosy tapped at her door. "Miz Olivia," she said, peeking around the door, "it's that Beecham man again with that corporal. He says he won't wait this time."

"Thank you, Rosy." Olivia realized she had been holding her breath. She exhaled in a long slow breath. Slowly she walked the length of the hall to the front room where George Beecham and Corporal Stevens stood silently waiting.

"Mr. Beecham," Olivia said ignoring Stevens, "what can you possibly want today? You already have my husband."

Stevens glared at her but said nothing. Beecham spoke as if ordering one of his slaves to do a task. "Sergeant Parker wants to talk to you – now!" he said. "Get your coat."

"I beg your pardon," she said. "I don't order my paid help around like that. Suppose I refuse to go? Will you carry me out like a sack of chicken feed?" She glanced at Corporal Stevens who stood by the door slapping his hat against his hand with a nervous motion.

Corey and Michael slipped into the room. Each took a hand and stared at Beecham who smirked at Olivia. Corporal Stevens glowered at the twins.

"We're prepared to do whatever we have to do, Mrs. Brunner," said Beecham. "We were instructed to bring you in – anyway we can."

"Those were the sergeant's exact words?" Olivia raised her eyebrows in disbelief.

"Well, not exact words," said Beecham, pulling at his collar, which released the blood flow up to his neck, ears and face, "but close."

"I see," said Olivia. His discomfort gave her courage and control over her anger. She stared at Beecham until he had to blink and look at the floor. She smiled – a soft cynical smile.

"Very well," she said. "I'll go with you. I have some questions for the sergeant myself. Rosy, please take care of the children. Corey, Michael, bring my coat and hat. You boys help Rosy with Lucy. I won't be gone long."

"Don't be too sure of that," said Beecham and jumped back as Corey kicked at him.

"Corey. That will do. We don't even kick mad dogs. Remember?"

"Yeah," said Corey.

"Cause they might bite," said Michael.

Beecham's color deepened. His fists turned his knuckles white. Olivia smiled at her boys and opened the door. Moving with a brisk walk, she seated herself in their carriage before Beecham and Corporal Stevens reached it.

***

No one spoke on the ride to City Hall. When they stopped, Olivia didn't give either of the men a chance to be a gentleman. She rose to step out on her own, forcing them both to sit while she disembarked. Several passers-by noticed, clucked their tongues and glared at the men.

Olivia breezed into the large waiting room that served all the city offices. Beecham and Corporal Stevens, red faced and breathing hard, hurried after her. Olivia smiled at the secretary who looked up as she started for Parker's office.

"Sergeant Parker is busy at the moment, Mrs. Brunner," she said. "If you will have a seat, he'll be with you shortly."

Olivia continued to smile at the woman, walked past her desk and opened the door before the secretary could get out of her chair. Parker, his back to the door in deep conversation with a Confederate officer, whirled around as the door flew open. The officer, who stood a foot taller than Parker, pushed his blond hair away from his face, his brown eyes wide with surprise.

Olivia spoke in a clear, raised voice making sure every man in the waiting area could hear her. "*Sergeant* Parker. How nice of you to drag me away from my children. Did you wish to chat with me about the abominable way you are treating my husband, or do you intend to tell me when you will release him – this time?"

Parker recovered, gave her a patronizing smile, took her arm and attempted to lead her from the room. "Olivia," he said, "I'm sorry, but you'll have to wait outside. I'm busy at the moment."

"Matthew Parker," she said jerking her arm free from his grasp and still speaking loud enough for all to hear. "You had me hauled out

130

of my home like a common criminal in front of my children, so I assumed you had some urgent information about my husband. If not, then I will return to my children." Olivia started out the door.

"Wait, Olivia." He glared. "Close the door. We'll talk now."

Olivia raised her eyebrows. "My father doesn't use that tone of voice with his slaves."

A scarlet hue similar to the one Olivia had seen earlier in Beecham, now slowly crept up to the top of Parker's shiny pate. Fists clenched, he strode passed her and slammed the door with such force that, if it had contained a glass panel, maintenance would have to replace it. The door rattled, a picture on the wall tilted and the Confederate officer winced.

Olivia put on her sternest mother-about-to-bestow-a-lecture expression as if she were going to tell him the proper way to close a door. Instead, she stared at him and said nothing. He read the look and became even more flustered. Pulling a giant-sized handkerchief from his pocket to dab at his brow, he moved closer to the Confederate officer, who barely contained his laughter. Even so, he pulled at his chin to hide the twitch at the corner of his mouth. Olivia saw it but ignored him, keeping her attention on Matthew Parker.

"Olivia, this is Lieutenant Coleman from South Carolina," Matthew said, struggling to regain his composure. "He's here to obtain recruits for the Confederate Army – especially physicians."

Olivia clenched her teeth together and held her own fists close to her sides. *I will not let that mouse of a man unnerve me.* She forced a smile, but kept her hands at her side. "I'm pleased to meet you, Lieutenant. I hope you find your *volunteers.*"

She turned to face Parker. Refusing to use his title, she continued, "Matthew, if this is another attempt to force me to influence Will, you can forget it. I would have thought a man of your upbringing would have more courtesy. I suppose next you will try to abduct my children and believe me Matthew Parker, sergeant, or not, if you touch one of my children you will rue the day you were born."

"Olivia, I'm sorry you feel we brought you in against your will." Matthew cleared his throat and tried to smile.

"Then, you don't mind if I leave since we understand each other. I *do* have a nursing infant at home."

Parker narrowed his eyes and spoke between clenched teeth. "You are free to go as soon as we have your word that you will convince your husband he is needed in the service of his country."

"Which country is that, Matthew? I thought we were still a part of the United States."

"It is only a matter of time, Olivia," said Parker once again turning a deep shade of red.

Olivia stared at him then glanced at the Confederate lieutenant, who looked more and more amused. Glancing around the room, she saw an empty chair near the window and went to it. Without a word, she removed her coat, sat down, clasped her hands over her coat in her lap and stared out the window at the bushes that dripped with melting snow.

"Olivia..." Parker went into his plea once again, but four hours later Olivia still sat, wordless.

Finally, Lieutenant Coleman, not bothering to hide his amusement, said, "I think you better send her home, Sergeant. We'll get her husband another way."

The flaming color crept back to Matthew Parker's face. "You haven't heard the last of me, Olivia Brunner," he said between clenched teeth. "We'll get your husband, one way or another."

Olivia glared at Parker. She put on her coat, nodded to Lieutenant Coleman and left the office. Corporal Stevens ran across the waiting room, pulling on his coat as he ran.

"Mrs. Brunner, wait. I'll take you home."

Olivia stopped her hand on the door. She turned and with a crisp, clipped tone of controlled anger that everyone in the room heard, she said, "I would rather walk. The air is fresher."

As if she had slapped him across the face, Stevens turned on his heels and stalked back across the room, slamming a door behind him. Olivia took a deep breath, went out the door and into a misty rain. She glanced around to see if maybe Samuel was waiting for her.

"Miz Olivia." Samuel called to her as she started down the street. "Miz Olivia, I got the wagon around the corner. Rosy sent me to wait for you." He grinned. Olivia knew he would have come even if Rosy hadn't sent him.

"Thank you, Samuel. You heard?"

"Yes'em. I was outside the window."

They rode in silence. As soon as they stopped, Samuel jumped down to help her off the wagon and Olivia hurried into the house. Lucy was crying and Rosy was pacing the kitchen floor with her. Olivia was still too angry and shaken to speak. The twins took her coat and hat and she took the infant from Rosy. The boys followed her to the bedroom.

"You okay, Mom?" asked Corey

"We were scared you wasn't coming back neither," Michael added.

"I'm fine, boys." She forced herself to be soft spoken with them. "Betsy and James will be home soon. Why don't you help Rosy get a snack for them? We'll talk later."

"Okay," they answered together, but glanced back over their shoulders as they left the room. *Life is changing too quickly for small boys. Would Matthew Parker actually put me in prison? Would he take me away from my children?*

30   Waiting in Prison

In that Libby Prison room, morning dawned even darker and grayer than in most of Richmond. The one small square window close to the ceiling let cold air in, but not much in the way of light or heat from the sun. Knowing their wives would have spent another restless night, the men in the *Non-Volunteer Cell*, as they had dubbed their now familiar quarters, paced, prayed and took turns sitting on the one stone bench.

"We're not going home this time, are we?" Joe's voice caught as if a lump of hard bread had stuck in his throat.

Will hesitated. The others waited. *They all know, but they want someone to say it.* "I don't know," he said, running his fingers through his thick hair that needed cut. "But, we all knew it would come to that, and…yes, to be honest, I feel as if this is the time."

A collective sigh like a muffled sob, filled the room. "Look, friends," said Will, "you don't have to do this. It's me they want. They're using you to force me to change my mind."

"They want me, too," said Joe.

"The only way any of us will get out of here is to join the *Volunteers*," said John. "That means fighting for what I don't believe in. My boys went north to join up. Do you think I want to fight against my own flesh and blood?"

"John's right," said Robert. "We either die here together or out there in some godforsaken place where we might never be found. At least Maggie knows where I am."

"I'm with you Will. We'll live together or die together," George said.

"Count me in," said Kenny. "At least for now we have each other for encouragement."

"You're right, Kenny. I can't say how much I appreciate you fellows. Why don't we…?"

Small stones struck the floor breaking into his thoughts. Heads turned toward the window. Will was the designated communicator, so he moved closer and spoke in a stage whisper. "We're here," he said, not mentioning any names in case it wasn't David out there. He didn't want to get the boy in trouble.

"Grandpa heard some men talking," whispered David close to the window. "They says war is coming closer. Parker took Miz Olivia in today. She refused to speak for four hours. Parker was angry. She refused his ride home but Samuel was there to take her."

"Thank you David. If you can get word to Samuel, tell him to see if he can smuggle a Bible to us and maybe some blankets. But, you be careful. Don't get in trouble because of us."

"I be careful. You done helped Grandpa Noah too much for us to forget when you need help. I'll see Samuel."

They heard a light limping step on gravel and David was gone.

"Are they going to harass our women now?"

"I hope not," said Will. "I'm not surprised they tried Olivia. She can hold her own, but…"

"I think all the women can – except maybe Jeannette," said Joe.

"We'll have to pray harder for her," said John.

"If we knew for sure this is the last incarceration, I'd send word for Olivia to leave. I know she said she would, but she'll wait until I give her the word to go."

"Why don't we give it a few more days," said Kenny. The rest agreed and settled into their routine of praying, pacing and encouraging.

31   Ordinary Life in a Changing World

March winds roared like a lion, blowing away the debris of February. Olivia wished with all her heart that her troubles could join the little whirlwinds of old leaves, paper and twigs. Will, Joe and their friends were no closer to being either released, or inducted into Sergeant Parker's *Volunteers*, than they had been two weeks earlier. Would Parker really keep them in prison until the war was over?

March 4 already – the day of Mr. Lincoln's inauguration. Will that bring us closer to war? How much closer can we be without actually declaring war? Olivia's thoughts felt as scrambled as the eggs Rosy placed on the table for the children.

"Mom, why don't God answer our prayers anymore?" Corey asked.

Olivia held her cup halfway to her lips and stared. Her trembling hands made the liquid quiver in the cup. She could feel Rosy's eyes boring into her back, waiting for her answer as much as Corey and the other children. What could she say to her six year old? It was a theological question that Will should be answering. She had her faith, but even that wavered with Will in prison and Matthew Parker harassing them every day. She wanted to tell Corey she believed God would release his father, but that might not be in God's plans for them – at least not right away. How could she explain the will of God to a child? The children all watched her, knowing she was thinking, not ignoring them.

James shook his head and gave his brother a look of disgust mixed with compassion. Holding a forkful of eggs halfway to his mouth, he said, "Corey." His brother turned his expectant gaze from his mother to his brother.

James gazed into his brother's eyes and said, "God *does* answer our prayers. How do you think Mom is strong enough to take care of us and keep going just like Dad was here? Who gives her courage to keep fighting Sergeant Parker? Who gives Betsy and me courage to keep going to school when kids call us names and turn their backs on us? God don't always do things the way we want, but God does do things for us."

James finished his sermonette and stared at Corey. Olivia was stunned. Behind her Rosy chuckled and moved on to her task of cleaning up the stove. It was almost as if Will had spoken through his son.

"Oh," said Corey. He grinned at his brother. "Thanks, James. I thought so, but I miss Dad's sermons." He giggled. Michael punched him in the arm and giggled with him.

James grinned at him. "You tricked me," he said.

Olivia took a deep breath. "James is right, Corey. We need to keep praying for courage. God is with all of us – including your father and the others in prison." She smiled at her older son, masking the pain in her own heart. She hadn't known he and Betsy fought their own battles while she struggled with hers. The time was drawing closer. Soon she would have to fulfill her promise.

***

The women, hoping their men would soon be free, fell into a routine of taking turns visiting the prison with a basket of food. Olivia knew the men never received the baskets they took, but in order to keep up the charade of believing they were, she said nothing, except to encourage them to keep doing it. In the meantime, Samuel delivered another basket to the men by way of the window while the women detained the guards. The guards always promised that the men would receive the basket and each day sent back the empty one from the day before.

Samuel took news with the food and each day the men sent messages with him urging the women to begin preparing to leave. Each day the women sent messages to their husbands that clearly said they were ignoring any threat of war – all except Olivia and Tillie. They believed, but couldn't bring themselves to do anything about it – yet.

***

March continued to creep along, pushing aside winter's cold and snow to make way for spring buds to appear. Olivia was itching to plant a garden. *Would I reap the benefits of it?*

Warning signs flashed like sheet lightning in the sky day after day. She could no longer ignore them. Almost five weeks had crawled by since Will, Joe and their friends had become virtually prisoners of war. *At least they are all together in one large cell. I hope Parker never realizes that is a mistake as far as his goal to get them in the Volunteers. Together they can talk and pray to keep up their courage.*

137

To be alone, it would be more difficult.

Olivia met with the wives – sometimes one, sometimes all – trying to help them cope and see what lay ahead. But still, they couldn't understand the severity of the problem. Jeannette was sure that if Will would just join the *Volunteers* all would be well. Olivia knew that would never happen. And yet leaving Richmond without Will was unthinkable, but ignoring her promise was even more impossible.

The twins interrupted her tumbling thoughts as they stumbled into the kitchen pushing and shoving one another. "Can we go to Joey's while Samuel gets supplies today?" Corey asked.

"Yeah, can we?" Michael added his plea.

"You won't get in Mrs. Phillips' way, will you?"

"No, ma'am," said Corey.

"We help her with Joey and Sarah," said Michael.

"All right, but you listen to Samuel and Mrs. Phillips."

Olivia gave the list she had prepared for Samuel to the boys when she heard Samuel drive the wagon into the backyard. The boys ran out to meet him and she heard Corey tell Blackie to stay. The wagon rumbled down the driveway on the way to Richmond. They would be gone until lunchtime, which would give her and Rosy time to take advantage of the mild March wind and get the wash on the line.

32   Word from Libby

Samuel stopped the wagon at the back of the Phillips' house. Corey and Michael jumped down and ran toward the back porch. "Don't you boys get in no trouble," Samuel called after them.

Jeannette stepped to the door to meet the boys. "Morning Miz Phillips," said Samuel. "You want anything from town today?"

"No thank you Samuel. Joe will be home soon. He'll take care of it."

"Yes'em," Samuel said. He tipped his cap and drove away muttering to himself. "Joe ain't goin' to be home no sooner'n the rest."

When he got to Richmond, he parked the wagon with the others slaves' wagons and walked to the general store where many of his friends gathered.

"Morning Samuel," they called. "Hear anything from Master Brunner?"

"Not yet," said Samuel. He knew some of his friends would report to their masters everything that was said in these times of "just slave" talk. He couldn't take a chance of sharing any news with his friends. It might mean prison for him and death for the others.

He stepped into the store and began gathering things on his list, which he memorized. He didn't dare let some of his friends know he could read. He would be punished and so would they. Suddenly, he paused in front of a shelf and pretended to be deciding what he needed. A conversation outside the open door caught his attention. He recognized the voice.

"It can't be much longer now," said Corporal Stevens. "The governor's getting fed up. Lincoln's going to ask for our help one time too many and we'll be following South Carolina and the rest."

"How soon do you think?" Samuel didn't recognize the voice, but could see a uniform of some kind. "Man, I'm ready to fight. We'll whip them Yankees in no time. My wife won't hardly know I'm gone 'till I'll be home again."

Laughter followed then Stevens said in his puffed-up manner, "Reckon it might be anytime now. From what I hear in Parker's office, won't be no more'n two to three weeks"

The voices moved on down the street and Samuel's friend touched his arm. "Samuel, it's your turn."

"You take it, Daniel. I just remembered I gotta go check on the twins. They can get in more trouble than a pack of wild dogs."

Daniel laughed as Samuel slipped out the side door. He made his way down the back alley to the prison where he could talk to Will through the window. He dropped a couple of pebbles through the window, cupped his hands and spoke in as loud a whisper as he could, hoping the guards wouldn't hear him. "Master Will," he called.

"Samuel? I didn't expect you until later."

"I was at the store and heard Stevens and someone else talking. Had to come and let you know." He repeated the conversation.

"Two to three weeks?" Will glanced around at his friends. "Samuel, tell Olivia it's time to keep her promise – now."

"Yes sir, Master Will."

Will's voice sounded strained, but clear. "Tell Olivia what you told me. Tell her to remember her promise. She needs to fulfill it *immediately*. Tell her not to worry about me. God will take care of us."

"Tell Jeannette to go with her," said Joe.

"And Claudia…"

"And Corinne…"

"And Maggie…"

"And Tillie."

"Yes sirs. I'll tell them all," said Samuel and left.

"He'll be back with a message when they've gone," said Will.

"We won't see them again, will we," Joe choked back a sob.

"Probably not," said Will, "unless God intervenes."

33   Olivia's Response

Distracted by Lucy's cry, Olivia dropped the shirt she was about to hang on the line back into her basket and went to nurse the baby. When Lucy was satisfied, she placed the infant in her cradle that she'd brought to the kitchen. Before she could return to the clothesline, she heard the buckboard pull into the yard much faster than Samuel usually drove. He took the steps two at a time, calling to her as he ran, "Miz Olivia! Miz Olivia!"

Olivia opened the door as he reached for it. "Samuel, what it is? Have Corey and Michael gotten into trouble?"

"No, Miz Olivia, the boys are still at the Phillips'. I told them I'd be back later and for them to stay put 'til I come for them."

"Then what...? Will...?" She felt the blood drain from her face.

Rosy had dropped the shirt she was about to hang on the line and followed her husband into the house. Samuel refused to sit and Rosy stood by his side, her arm on his shoulder.

"Miz Olivia," he said, "While I was waiting my turn at the general store, I heard some talk about Virginia joining South Carolina and the other Confederate states. I told my friend I had to go check on the boys so he could have my turn. Then I went to the prison and told Master Will what I heard. He said to tell you, 'it's time for you to fulfill your promise and take the children north as quick as you can.' The others said for their wives and families to go with you."

Bless Will. He knew I wouldn't leave until he told me it was time, but can I do it? There was no more time to think about it. She had no choice. She had promised Will.

She turned back to Samuel with her eyes locked on his and a firm set to her jaw. "Sit down, Samuel, while I fix a lunch for you to take to them if you can." Rosy, anticipating her action already had the bread and knife ready for slicing.

"Yes'em," he replied and sat in the chair she pulled out for him. He swiped his sleeve across his glistening, black brow.

Olivia rattled off what he was to tell, and not tell, Will while she and Rosy prepared food. "Don't tell Will I've been harassed by Parker. No use him worrying about me." It wasn't the first time she'd given Samuel those instructions, but she knew if Will asked, Samuel would tell him everything and David had probably already told him all he'd heard.

Glancing at the dark eyes now and then to make sure Samuel was listening and would repeat whatever she told him, she said, "Take this food to them. Tell Will I'll leave as soon as I can get things together – a day or two at the most. God will go with me. I'll tell the others. He can meet us somewhere near the Kanawha River as soon as he can. Tell him not to worry about us. You take care of him as much as you can. I trust you, Samuel, as Will trusts you. You hear?"

"Yes'em."

"And Samuel, I'll take Rosy with me if she wants to go."

Rosy turned, wiped her tears with her apron and said, "No, ma'am, Miz Olivia. I won't leave my Samuel. We'll take care of the house and try to keep them from destroying it. Then when Master Will is ready to go north we'll go with him."

Olivia smiled at the determined set of her former slave's face. She was glad she had taught Rosy to think for herself and to speak her mind. She would miss her friend, but she knew Samuel needed her more. Samuel started to say something but Rosy leaned over him, hands on hips and said, "Don't you try to make me change my mind, Samuel Brunner. We been together too long for me to go running off now. Miz Olivia's gotta think about the children, and especially Master James. They'll be taking that boy and getting him killed. She gotta go. I don't."

Samuel stood, shook his head and picked up the bucket of food Olivia had prepared. He slapped his hat back on his head and started for the door. He turned and asked, "You want I should go tell the other women?"

"Not this time. I'll have them all over here tonight and explain where we are going and why."

"Yes'em," he said and seconds later, she heard the buckboard heading back to Richmond. The sound of the buckboard had hardly died away when there was a knock at the front door. Rosy went to answer it.

Beecham again? Has Parker somehow learned that I plan to leave town? Will he lock me away from my family this time? I've lost count of the times he's dragged me to his office and made me either miss, or be late for Lucy's feeding. Olivia felt frozen to the floor until Rosy

142

returned.

"Miz Olivia," said Rosy, "Master Jefferson is here to see you. I took him to the living room."

Olivia slowly exhaled the breath she was holding. Parker wanted to frighten her into convincing Will to see things his way. Her father wanted her to take the children to the plantation until it was all resolved. Olivia knew the dilemma would never be resolved until the threat of war itself was over – and that might be years away.

34 Jefferson's Visit

Jefferson Dooley waited in the living room twirling his hat in his hand, like a steamboat wheel.

"Good morning, Daddy," Olivia said as she breezed into the room. Hiding her anxiety as best she could, she gave him a hug and a kiss on the cheek.

Jefferson caught his daughter in his arms and hugged her with so much fierceness that Olivia wondered if he somehow knew her plans. "How are you, Olivia?" He released her from the hug, but kept a hand on her shoulder.

"I'm fine, Daddy. Come and sit down. I can fix us some tea…"

"Can't stay. Have you heard from Will?"

"I just sent Samuel with lunch for him and his friends." She hadn't been able to tell her father of her promise and now she couldn't tell him about Will's message to go. The thought of leaving him without saying goodbye sent a sharp pain of grief through her.

"How long has it been this time? Three weeks? Four? What are you using for money?"

"Five weeks, two days and six hours, but who's counting? I'm doing okay."

"Olivia, I heard a rumor while I was in town. If we get into a war – and it looks like we will – he'll be needed in the army. Has he thought about that?"

"Yes, Daddy, but Will's first loyalty is to God who called him to save life not take it. His second loyalty is to his family whom he loves. It will be a useless war, Daddy. Are you prepared to fight? Are you prepared to let James go and die on a battlefield somewhere? And if the war lasts longer than the few months they predict, will it take Corey and Michael too?"

"Olivia, you don't know what you're talking about. James is too young and I'm too old. The war will be over before it hardly starts."

"I hope you're right, but I don't think so. Many old and young will die before peace replaces the guns and cannons. I know you and mother want me to go to the plantation until Will is out of prison, but I can't go do that. Will and I have talked and planned. I know what I must do and I will do it."

"Olivia, I don't want to believe you, but you're probably right." He tried to smile. "You should have been a boy. You were the closest to a son I ever got."

"Don't regret what wasn't, Daddy. We had good times. You taught me how to survive." She paused and took a deep breath. Suddenly, sensing he already knew more than he was saying, she wanted him to hear the whole truth from her.

"Daddy, Will and I have talked long and hard about the situation. Months ago, I promised him I would take the children, and whoever else wants to go with me, and move north to the Kanawha Valley."

"I sort of thought something like that was brewing. Will talked with me – asked me to make sure you went when it was time. Do you have money for that kind of a trip?" The color had drained from Jefferson's face.

"No. I don't intend to travel by rail or coach. I'll put what I can in our buckboard and with God's help we'll make it."

"Olivia, you can't be serious." Jefferson's voice shook. "You're talking about months under the best of conditions. The children are too young...Lucy..." Jefferson groped for words.

"I'm very serious, Daddy. I'm well aware of how long and how hard the trip will be. We haven't much choice. I promised Will I would protect our children as best I can. Getting them out of Richmond seems to be the best solution. I'll do whatever I have to do."

"You have other choices. You can come home and if he would just..."

"No, Daddy. Neither would make any difference. When the war comes to Richmond – and it will come – no woman or child will be safe. Whether Will dies in prison or on a battlefield he will be just as dead and I will be just as alone. I really don't think the plantation will be any safer when troops begin invading Richmond. No, I'll take the children and go to Uncle George up north. It may not be any better, but it will be an attempt. You and Mother are welcome to go with us."

"You know your mother would never leave the plantation and I guess if war comes I have responsibilities here. When do you plan to leave? I know your mind's made up, but I had to try changing it."

Olivia smiled at her father's perception. "I got word from Will just minutes before you came. We'll leave as soon as I can. It should take a couple of weeks to pack, but I'm hoping for the day after tomorrow."

"But, Olivia..."

Olivia stopped him. "Daddy, I haven't even let Samuel tell Will, but I have been taken to Matthew's office so many times I've lost count and kept there for hours knowing I needed to nurse Lucy. I keep waiting for them to lock me up the way they have Will. They have approached James several times trying to either get him to convince Will, and/or join the *Volunteers* himself. When will they stop talking and take him by force? He and Betsy have been harassed at school. No one will believe we can't – and wouldn't if we could – make Will change his mind. Will is afraid for us, even without knowing all that. I have Grandma Poff's sixth sense about it. I have to go and I have to go now."

Jefferson stared, mouth open for a minute. Finally, he said, "Olivia, I know in my heart you're right. If anyone can get a train of wagons to safety, you can do it. What can I do to help?"

Olivia burst into tears and flew into her father's arms. "Just don't hate me, Daddy. Just don't hate me."

"Olivia, I would never hate you."

"Thank you, Daddy. That makes what I have to do a whole lot easier."

"Olivia, will you accept a few items to help you on your journey?"

"As long as it's nothing extravagant. I can only take what will fit in my buckboard."

"I'll send some things around first thing in the morning. Use what you can. Leave the rest. Are you taking Samuel and Rosy?"

"No, Samuel will stay to keep watch over Will. Rosy won't go without him."

Jefferson kissed his daughter's cheek, hugged her again and said, "Goodbye, Olivia. May God go with you! When this mess is all over, we'll get together again."

"I'll look forward to that, Daddy."

Olivia watched her father's determined gait as he moved toward his horse. She smiled as she thought about how much she was like him. He mounted his horse and rode away like a man with a mission. He knew what he had to do and he would do it. She had learned that lesson from him. Now she must turn to her own mission and prepare for an impossible journey.

A feeling of sadness swept over her as the sound of her father's mount faded. She wondered if she would ever see her father again in this life. Shaking her head to erase the desire to run after him, she picked up pencil and paper and began making a list of necessary cargo and another of "if room" items.

35   More Trouble

Olivia heard the wagon pull into the backyard and glanced up from her lists. Samuel was back with the twins. She smiled when she heard the giggling and Rosy's scolding. She knew the boys were chasing each other through the laundry hanging on the line. Olivia turned back to her lists. Rosy could handle them.

All of a sudden, the cries and giggles no longer sounded like Corey and Michael playing tag in the laundry. Laugher had changed to excited, almost fearful shouts. It was time for James and Betsy to be home, but Blackie's bark was not his usual joyful greeting. Something was wrong.

She got up and reached for the door, but stopped as the twins ran across the porch. Olivia stepped back as they pushed the door open and tumbled into the kitchen.

"Mom! Mom!" Corey, wide eyed, gasped for breath. "James gots a bloody nose and a black eye."

"And Betsy's crying," added Michael.

Before she could question the twins further, or admonish them to keep their voices down, James hurried into the room with his head turned so she couldn't see his face. He slammed the door and started past her.

"James William Brunner," she said, "what do you mean slamming the door that way? And why are you trying to sneak by without so much as a hello? What is Corey talking about – a black eye and…?"

James turned around. Blood trickled from his nose; a dark coloring appeared around his swollen eye. The torn collar on his coat hung to one side. "James?"

"Sorry Mom. I hoped slamming the door would distract you and I could clean up before you saw me." James dropped his gaze. Rosy bustling in with Betsy saved him from further embarrassment. As Michael said, tears streamed down her face. Her coat was askew and mud-splattered. Rosy began to gather water and cloths for the cleanup.

Olivia stared. *What is happening to my family? They have never given me a moment's worry – especially Betsy and James.* "Betsy?"

"Are you going to whup 'em, Mom?" Corey, usually the one on the receiving end of discipline, watched wide-eyed expecting to see his mother reach for the switch she kept above the kitchen cabinet.

"Hush, Corey," said Olivia then swallowed, blinked, took a deep breath and turned to her older son. "James, take your coat off and sit down. Rosy, please look after Betsy."

"Yes'em," said Rosy and set a basin of water and cloths on the table next to Olivia. She helped Betsy get her coat off and wrapped her arms around the little girl, crooning softly to her.

With gentle strokes of the wet cloth, Olivia wiped the blood away from her son's face. "What happened, James?"

"I'd rather not say," he answered. It was a simple statement, not insolent, nor belligerent.

"I see," she said, assuming that someone had said something against his father.

From the protection of Rosy's lap, Betsy brushed at the few remaining tears that trickled down her face and spoke through her hiccups. "He…he was protecting me," she said. "Some big kid…said Daddy…was a coward. I kicked him. He pushed me down and James beat him up." She gulped and gave her brother such a look of pure admiration that he blushed and Olivia had to cough to hide her smile. Rosy gave Betsy a squeeze and hurried back outside to take the clothes off the line, not bothering to hide the grin that spread across her face.

"You both know what your father and I believe about fighting," said Olivia.

"But, Mom," said James, "even the Bible says fighting is necessary sometimes. I don't think God wanted that kid to beat Betsy, so I helped Him stop it." Olivia looked deep into her son's eyes, and felt for a brief second it was Will standing before her.

"But James, you got a bloody nose and a black eye. Do you think God wanted that?"

"No ma'am, but if someone had to receive pain, I wanted it to be me, not her."

"I see," said Olivia bursting with pride. "I think you both need to go to your rooms and thank God you weren't hurt any more than you were and ask forgiveness for inflicting pain on someone else."

"Yes ma'am," they answered together.

"Is that all he's going to get?" Corey gave her a look that clearly said, "Whip him good, Mom."

"Corey, what would you have done to that boy?"

Corey grinned. "I would beat him until he couldn't get up." He and Michael started giggling and pretending to box each other.

"Outside with the rough housing," she said then turned and called to her older son, "Oh, James, when you're fully repented, I need you to run an errand for me."

James turned and gave her a curious look, then nodded and followed Betsy upstairs. He wasn't gone long when he returned to the kitchen. Olivia had emptied the basin of water and cleaned the table.

"That was quick," she said.

"I wasn't very sorry," he said.

A smile twitched at the corner of Olivia's mouth. Then she looked more solemn and said, "When your father was home, we talked about the possibility of leaving Richmond. The time has come." She handed him a list of names – Phillips, Jones, Rayburn, Cooper and Walsh. "I'm inviting these women to go with us. I want them to come here after supper tonight so we can talk about it."

She smiled and tempered her fearful news with an added comment. "Do you think you can stay out of trouble long enough to deliver this message?"

James grinned and nodded. He took the list of names, grabbed his coat and ran out the back door. "Come on, Blackie," she heard him call as the door closed behind him. A few minutes later, she heard one of the horses' pounding the dirt as he rode off to see her friends whose husbands were in prison with Will.

"Do you want me to bake and serve something for your meeting?

"Thanks Rosy, but I don't want a party atmosphere. It will be hard enough for them to comprehend what I'm asking of them. And besides that, we don't have time to bake special things. We need every minute to plan and prepare for this trip."

"Yes'em," said Rosy as she folded clothes that she normally ironed and put away. They would go in boxes for travel instead. Olivia took a deep breath and continued peeling potatoes. She knew her task that evening would be the most serious – and difficult – meeting she had ever held with friends. Rosy would be there to help in whatever way she could and that was a comfort to know.

By the time James returned from his errand, Rosy and Olivia were putting supper on the table. Olivia gave thanks. They began passing the food and Rosy dished up stew and biscuits for her and Samuel. Olivia cleared her throat and said in as calm a voice as possible around her wildly beating heart and the lump in her throat, "Even though you are still children, I'm sure you all understand the tension building in Richmond over the possibility of war. Our nation is divided and soldiers will come to Richmond soon. Your father wants you out of harm's way. I'm taking you north to Uncle George's. We'll leave day after tomorrow."

Olivia bit her lip as she looked around the table into the face of each of her children. They all stared, forks paused, mouths open. Finally, Corey asked, "Are… are we… leaving without Daddy?"

Olivia took a deep breath and nodded. "It's what he wants us to do. He'll join us as soon as they release him, or he finds some other way out."

"I don't want to go without Daddy." Tears once again ran down Betsy's face.

"I don't want to go without him either," said Olivia, "but it's what he's asked us to do. It will be easier for him if he knows we're away from Richmond."

"Will he…get out and join us?" Michael's eyes were wide, his lower lip trembled.

"That's our plan, Michael. Only God knows for sure if our plan will work."

"Is Samuel …" started Corey.

"And Rosy…" continued Michael.

"Going with us?" They finished together.

Olivia shook her head. "Samuel will stay here to do whatever he can for your father. Rosy wants to stay with him."

"Then…" Betsy sniffed back her tears, "if Samuel and Rosy are here, we'll go to make Daddy happy."

"Yeah," said Corey and Michael together. "We'll go."

James, with determination said, "of course, I'll go, but when we get settled, I'll come back and help Samuel get Dad out of that place."

"Thank you," whispered Olivia, glancing around the table at each of her children. "After supper you can each help by sorting out clothes that don't fit and special items you want to take. We won't have much room, so think ahead. What will you need a year from now."

The impossible seemed more possible when Olivia could put it in perspective of preparation. As long as they had something to do with their hands, their minds wouldn't have to dwell on the harsh reality of separation. For the children it sounded like an adventure – at least for now. They would learn the hard work and suffering they would have to endure later. Even Olivia found it difficult to think that far ahead.

The children left the table with mixed feelings of sadness and excitement, discussing what they wanted to take. *All I want is Will.*

36　The Invitation

Rosy dried the last dish and put it away as sounds of rattling wagons and clip-clopping hooves told them the women were arriving. Chatters of greetings drifted across the yard and followed the women who chose to come through the kitchen – even Jeannette, who looked as if she was afraid the roof would fall in because she had broken a rule of etiquette.

Rosy led them to the living room while Olivia checked on Lucy. They had all talked and prayed together the last five weeks. Olivia had tried to prepare them and their husbands had told them to go with Olivia, but they couldn't possibly understand. War was unimaginable. Leaving Richmond without the men was unthinkable.

Too afraid of the horses to drive her own buckboard, Jeanette had come with the Coopers. With Joey and Sarah clinging to her skirts, she followed Maggie and Grandma Cooper into the living room. The other women had left their children home, either with older siblings or neighbors.

Betsy and James started down the hall to the back room with the twins. "We'll work on your reading while Mom has her meeting," said James then turned back to Joey. "Want to come with us?" Joey shook his head and hid deeper in his mother's skirt.

Olivia glanced at her children with a look of appreciation. She wondered what the war and a journey into the unknown would do to them. That all too familiar chill slipped down her spine and sent a shiver across her shoulders. With a mother's heart and her grandmother's sense of the future things, she suddenly wanted her children to be in on every part of this journey, including the planning.

"Betsy, James." She said to the retreating children. "Maybe you and the boys should stay and listen. We're all in this together. You need to know as much as possible."

"Really? We can stay too?" Corey's eyes danced.

"You will have to be quiet and listen. If you have questions, we'll talk later. Sit on the floor over by the fireplace with James and Betsy."

"You heard Mom," said Betsy. "You can stay only if you can keep your mouth shut. I may as well pick out a book to read. You can't keep quiet five minutes, much less through a whole meeting."

"Yes, I can. I promise." Corey crossed his arms and glared at Betsy.

"I'll kick him if he talks," said Michael. "This is really important stuff, huh Mom?"

"Yes, Michael, it's very important. If Betsy believes you're making too much noise, she'll take you to the back room."

"All right," said the twins in unison.

"Is this about the big move we've been talking about for weeks, 'Livia?" Tillie was one of the few women who believed war was imminent and the mayor was lying to them about their husbands.

"You ain't going to start that 'let's move north' nonsense again are you?" Corinne rolled her eyes and laughed as she elbowed Claudia who nodded and gave Olivia a patronizing smile.

Olivia forced a smile and glanced around the room. Everyone was present – Grandma Cooper and Maggie; Jeannette with Sarah and Joey clinging to her like ivy, Corinne, Claudia and Tillie who preferred to stand by the door. James and Betsy sat by the fireplace with the twins.

Biting back an angry retort to Corrine, Olivia leaned forward and said, "We are all friends. Our husbands are in prison together, except for Grandma Cooper. We've talked before. I'm aware that Mayor Nelson has told you that your men are comfortable and he will release them as soon as Will joins the *Volunteers*. He's lying."

"How do you know…?"

Olivia didn't let Corinne finish. "Even if Will and Joe give in, Parker wants *all* our men – and boys – if he can get them."

"Why would he…?" Claudia gave her a skeptical look.

"Claudia, the war *will* come and wars are fought by men with guns."

Jeannette rammed her fist against her mouth making it difficult to understand her words. "But surely we can just…live the way…we want…Joe can't fight…"

"Jeannette, war will destroy Richmond as we know it."

Corinne became the self-appointed spokesperson for the other women. Her angry high-pitched, soprano voice filled the room. "Olivia, you're making a mountain out of a mole hill. If Will would just do his duty they could all come home."

"Would they Corinne?" Olivia stared at her friend. "Or would they be sent to training camp and then off to fight in a useless war? In, or out, of prison, we may never see our men again."

"Olivia, you can't be serious…"

"You're just trying to scare us…"

"Mayor Nelson said…"

Olivia lifted her hand to silence them and continued. "I haven't even let Samuel tell Will – and I only told my father this morning – but since this last incarceration in the middle of February, Matthew Parker has hauled me off to his office like a common criminal more times than I can remember. He detained me hours on end, knowing I had a nursing infant at home who needed me. Parker's men have approached James several times. They not only want him to influence his father, but to join the *Volunteers* himself. He and Betsy have endured unmerciful treatment at school."

"So what's your point? It's only talk. If Will would just…"

"Is it just talk, Corinne?" She glanced at James who covered his black eye with his hand. "How long will it be before it ceases to be *just* talk? It was *just* talk when they approached Will, Joe and the rest last fall. Talk didn't get the results Parker wanted, so now they're in prison – and they are *not* being treated like guests, as Mayor Nelson would have you believe. They would not even have food if I didn't send Samuel every day to take it to them."

"We take food to them every day," said Corrine.

"And the guards give us the empty basket from the day before," said Claudia.

"The guards are lying," said Olivia.

"How do you know? Who…?"

"Jeannette," said Olivia, "Samuel talks with the men almost every day."

"But what about the food…?" Maggie started then finished, "…the guards kept it?"

"That's right," said Olivia, "But Samuel was able to get food to the men while you diverted them."

"Then it wasn't all for nothing," said Maggie. "We still helped feed our men."

Olivia nodded and continued. "As I said, my children and I have been harassed. How long will it be before they lock me, or one of my children, up to force Will to change his position? They're putting pressure on you and your husbands because they know if Will joins the *Volunteers*, the rest will follow."

Olivia paused again and looked around the silent room at the horrified expressions.

Claudia blinked, shook her head. "Olivia, you can't be serious!

They wouldn't…"

"Oh yes, Claudia, I'm very serious. I don't need to give you detailed accounts, but I simply want you to know this is not a quick, reactive decision based on a one-time scare. I've given it much thought and prayer over the last few weeks. We've all talked and prayed together. I know you didn't think I was serious, but I've tried to prepare you, as I've prepared my children, for the inevitable. And the men have told us to go."

"But…I thought…I thought you were…you know…just talking…because we can't do anything else." Jeannette's pale complexion seemed almost ghost-like in the reflection of the kerosene lamps.

"And the men were just trying to make Will feel better."

"Olivia never *just* talks," said Tillie, her deep voice a contrast to the more feminine sounds. "And men in prison don't waste words."

"Talk is useless unless we're prepared to act," said Olivia, "and it's time to act. It should take several weeks to get ready, but tension is building much too rapidly. Time is running out. We don't have several weeks."

"How long…?" Jeannette swallowed hard.

Olivia looked around the room at her wide-eyed friends. *They don't understand. How can they? It's unbelievable – even for me.*

"I'm leaving day after tomorrow," she said. "You are my closest friends and in the same lonely predicament. Your husbands want you to go with me and I want you with me, but I'll understand if you decline."

"You mean leave Richmond? Leave our men in prison? We can't…Joe will…"

"I don't want to leave Will any more than you want to leave Joe, but there's nothing I can do for him except put his mind at ease by trying to get our children to safety."

Olivia bit her lip and leaned back in her chair, glancing around the room. Even Corey sat with his mouth open, hardly breathing. Her friends looked as if an arctic blast of icy wind had blown through the room and turned them to ice sculptures.

In the few seconds it took for each to absorb what she had said, Olivia scanned the room. *Jeannette is so timid and afraid of everything. Joey is more like her than his father. His eyes reflect the fear in his mother's eyes. If she decides to go, will she be able to stand the pressure and physical exertion?*

Maggie Cooper, like Tillie, was older than Olivia by ten years.

She has three children and her grandmother-in-law, Grandma Cooper, to care for. She is steady, but overworked. Maggie is strong, but this journey will take more than physical strength.

Grandma Cooper, nearing eighty was only five feet tall – or less, thin and wiry. Her pointed nose and sharp chin reminded Olivia of a small, hawk. Her thin, white hair, pulled severely up into a tiny bun on top of her head, told her age, but her eyes snapped with youthful excitement. *She will be an encouragement to the rest of us, if she can make such a long and perilous trip.*

Corinne Walsh also had three children. She was tall and while not fat, she was on the heavy side. She was a hard worker, as were all the women, but nothing ever quite satisfied her. *Can I stand her complaining for two and a half months – or more?*

Claudia Jones had four children. Claudia definitely carried more weight than she should for her height of five feet five inches. She struggled to keep her hair in place and her stockings pulled up. *She has a hard time making a decision about anything. Claudia will go along with whatever Corinne says. They've been best friends since grade school.*

Tillie also scanned the room, an amused smile crinkling her weathered face. Tillie was tall and big boned – not fat, but big. She refused to adhere to the fashion of their day, or any other day. She made her own fashion and wore her black hair in one long braid. Although Tillie never said, many thought she had some Cherokee in her. She caught Olivia's eyes and her smile broadened.

As if that icy wind had turned to a tropical breeze, the ice sculptures melted back into flesh and blood women with question after question flying at Olivia. She threw her hands over her ears. "Wait," she said holding up her hand. "Wait. I can't hear you when you all speak at once."

"How far is it to…wherever you're talking about?" Claudia asked leaning forward in the rocker.

"Approximately four hundred miles, give or take a few."

"Olivia! How long will it take?" Claudia looked horrified.

"Two and a half months if we are lucky, longer if we aren't."

"No men? We can't go on a trip that long without no men!" Jeannette's face reflected the horror on Claudia's.

"Who will protect us?" Corinne looked at Grandma Cooper.

"God has protected us all these years," said Grandma Cooper. "When Albert and I were young, we traveled from Philadelphia down to Richmond. A trip back north couldn't be any worse."

"But Grandmother Cooper," said Maggie, "you were a lot younger then."

"Not much younger than most of you folks. Besides, I don't really matter. I'm reaching the limit of my years, anyway. Y'all got kids to protect."

"Grandma Cooper's right. We can all shoot as well as any of our men," Olivia said. "Better than some." She thought of Will's aversion to firearms.

"We'll follow a trail – others have moved before us. Will and I have worked on this plan since his first incarceration. I have a map that we worked out, based on what others have told us and what we have learned from letters from my father's family in the Kanawha Valley."

"But, what about our men? What will happen to them? How will they find us? How…?"

"Claudia, your husbands all told Samuel to tell you to go. If our men trust us to make it, surely we can trust them to find us. They have three choices – fight, die in prison or escape and connect with us along the way. Will and the others want us away from Richmond before the real fighting begins here."

"How will you go?" Tillie asked.

"I'm taking my buckboard and only the bare necessities."

"Why not the rail?"

"The rail is too expensive. The connections to the Kanawha Valley aren't that good. If the war takes off, as I think it will, the rail will either be destroyed or confiscated for army use."

"Why the hurry? It's impossible to be ready in one day."

"As I said, Corinne, I've been harassed. My children have been harassed. I'm sure if Parker learns we're even thinking about leaving he'll find some way of to stop us. They want James for the service. Are those enough reasons?"

"James? But he's the same age as my George." Corinne looked terrified.

"Then, I'm sure they're looking at George too."

"What happens if a wagon breaks down? How can we manage without men?"

"Jeannette, if a wagon breaks down, we will either fix it or we won't. And how have we managed the last five weeks without our men? With God's help, we'll walk if we must. I'll die if necessary, but I promised my husband I would make every effort to get our children out of Richmond. I intend to keep that promise." Olivia gave them such a look of determination that the questions dwindled to nothing.

"I think Olivia's right." Tillie said. "John and I talked often about the same thing. He's in there with Joe and Will and the rest. The mayor and Sergeant Parker are liars. War is coming. My two older boys went north last fall to join the Federals. I, for one, am not afraid of a fight, but I owe my younger boys all the protection I can give them."

"But Tillie, how will you let John know where you'll be?"

"There are ways. He'll find me. And if he don't, well, if I have to raise my boys alone, I'd rather do it close to friends."

"What about Indians? I heard they're pretty wild up north. "

"Jeannette, you listen to too much gossip. Most Indians have moved west. They aren't even around here anymore, and if they are, they're friendly." Olivia felt frustrated.

"Look, Will asked me to take our children north. Maybe we should have started some serious planning sooner, but I guess I didn't want to believe it would come to this any more than the rest of you. But it has and I'm leaving day after tomorrow at dawn. If you want to go with me, I would appreciate your company. If you want to stay, that's your choice. I felt it only fair to ask you. That's all I have to say. Think about it, pray about it and do what you must for the sake of your own family. Good night, ladies."

Thus dismissed, the women left muttering and moaning to one another as they accepted their coats from Rosy. The tears on her cheeks told them Olivia was truly serious, more than any amount of words could do.

"You're following the James River west?" asked Tillie.

"That's right," said Olivia.

"I'll catch you at the churchyard."

"Thanks, Tillie."

Olivia listened as the rattle of wagons and clopping of hooves faded. She didn't know if any, except Tillie Rayburn, would go with her. It didn't really matter. Come Wednesday morning, she and her children would be heading north to the Kanawha Valley, with or without her friends.

36   Jefferson's Gifts

The night was too long; sleep too short. Olivia stood by her window watching for the sun's probing rays across the horizon. Not a branch moved. Swollen tips on each branch promised that new life would once again overshadow the cold death-like sleep of winter. But, where was the promise of new life in her soul?

Words from Deuteronomy came to mind ...*I have set before you life and death, blessing and curse; therefore choose life.... Life without Will?* Again from Genesis when God spoke to Abram, *Go where I will send you... Go alone? No, God will go with us and someday Will and the rest will follow.*

Father, God, I know You are with us in this journey seeking a new life for our children. I want Will by my side, but I know You will do what is best for all of us. Give us the courage and faith to persevere.

Leaving the door open a crack so she could hear Lucy, Olivia went to the kitchen where Rosy already had ingredients out to bake as much bread as she could. Other supplies would include as many canned meats and vegetables as the small wagon would hold.

"There'll be enough left to run you and Samuel until you can do up more." Olivia didn't add, assuming they would be able to grow more. "I can't possibly take all we've canned. There just isn't room in my little buckboard. I only hope we'll have enough for the long journey. There should be wildlife to hunt and fish in the rivers and streams."

"Don't you worry none about Samuel and me," said Rosy. "We'll take care of ourselves and Master Will."

Olivia gathered basic cookware – her grandmother's cast iron skillet and Dutch oven, a large stew pot and as many other items as she thought she would have room for. "James said he could rig up a cover for the buckboard sort of like the covered wagons he's read about. We'll have to walk most of the way. There won't be room in the buckboard for supplies and us, too."

Olivia talked as she worked, more to keep the fear at bay than because she had something important to say. "We'll remove the benches Will installed for the children. Maybe I can fit Lucy's cradle in a corner."

Olivia moved packed boxes to the back porch to be ready for packing in the wagon. After Rosy put the dough aside to rise, she fried bacon and mixed pancake batter. Outside the chicken coop, Old Bill strutted to his perching post. He crowed his morning wakeup call as if he alone were responsible for bringing the sun across the horizon. Chattering children hurried to the table, too excited to think about the hard work ahead of them.

"Umm, smells good in here," said James taking his place at the table.

"Yeah," said Corey and Michael together.

"Rosy makes the best..." started Corey.

"...pancakes in the world," finished Michael.

Rosy brushed at a tear and set a platter of bacon and pancakes on the table. "Don't you go trying to butter me up none. I ain't gonna do your work for you today. Got too much of my own." She turned her back and punched down the bread dough with more force than was really needed.

Olivia nodded to her children to bow their heads. She prayed for the food, the day's chores, the men and the journey. The twins were beginning to squirm when she finished. James grinned at them, took the cooler hotcakes from the top of the stack and let them have the hot ones in the middle. They giggled and dug in.

The aroma of coffee and maple syrup mingled in the air touching Olivia with nostalgia. She would miss Rosy's cooking, among other things. The children downed the pancakes as if they, too, already missed her.

Breakfast was over – all but the scraping of the last sweet leavings of syrup from the plates – when Blackie began to bark. The sounds of horses' hooves clopped across the backyard, reins jangled and wagon wheels bumped and thumped over ruts in the yard. For an instant Olivia's heart stopped. *Has Matthew Parker sent someone to stop us – or to cart me off to jail?*

James jumped up from the table to check it out. "Blackie's not growling, so whoever is out there is a friend," he said as he reached for the door. "It's Moses," he said.

The tall black man from his grandfather's plantation stood on the porch grinning at him. Blackie sat at his heels, tail wagging, thumping on the porch floor.

"Morning, Master James," said Moses. "I brung some things from

Master Jefferson for yo' mama."

Olivia rose and followed James. "Good morning, Moses," she said. "Did you have breakfast before you came?"

"No, ma'am. Master Jefferson was anxious for me to get these to you before you started packing your wagon. He said you would be up afore the dawn." He grinned again. "Looks like he was right."

Olivia smiled in return. "Why don't you show me what you brought, then let Rosy fix you some pancakes?"

"Yes ma'am," he said. Rosy moved to the stove to add more batter to the bowl. "Me and Samuel will eat with you," she said.

Crisp air sent little puffs of white spewing from their mouths with every breath. The sky was clear and the sun would soon warm the day. The smell of spring was in the air. Already the pussy willows poked their furry little buds out for a kiss of the sun. Olivia hated the thought of leaving her trees and bushes. She and Will had put a lot of work into their yard. Olivia shook herself mentally and gasped as she focused on the covered wagon standing before her. She pressed clenched fists to her mouth to keep back a cry of surprise.

"Master Jefferson said he got a good deal from a friend. He sent a wagon to each of the other five women, too – a farewell gift, he said."

Olivia stared, speechless. Moses grinned again and left her to go eat his sister-in-law's pancakes.

"Master Jefferson sent Beauty, too," he called over his shoulder. "He said you would need a horse for scouting and carrying messages among the wagons. The other horse is for me to ride back home."

Olivia continued to stare. James said, "Wow!" Together they went to examine the covered wagon drawn by two of Jefferson Dooley's best dapple-gray mules. Almost afraid it would disappear; Olivia set a tentative hand on the canvas cover – running her hand from front to back, feeling the rough texture canvas that stretched across the width of the wagon. Then she moved her hand down the rough outer wood of the sides, over the smooth wooden seat at the front and across the cold wheel hubs and spokes.

She stood before the mules, amazed that her father would send his best pair of working mules. They looked back at her and blinked their big, dark eyes. One nudged her hand. She rubbed his nose. The other one snorted and nudged her.

"Max and Jasper," said James beaming. "Corey and I know them well. They're good workers, gentle, intelligent animals."

Corey joined them and gave the mules each a bite of apple. "They're better than horses, cause they don't need as much water or food. They're stronger and work harder and longer."

Olivia looked at Corey with surprise. "How do you know that?"

"Grandpa told me," he said.

Betsy and Michael joined them. Corey and Michael climbed in the wagon to try it out. They walked from end to end. "It's two times as long as our buckboard," said Michael, "and one and a half times as wide and the sides are higher. Now you can take more things."

"Yeah, like food for the mules and books and..." Corey laughed and climbed into the driver's seat.

"Shall I unhitch the mules and take them to the barn?" James stroked the one called Jasper. "Aren't they beautiful?"

"Yes, James – to both questions. They are beautiful and they need to be taken to the barn."

"I'll take Beauty and help James get them settled," said Corey jumping from the wagon and taking Beauty's reins.

"Then we need to start packing the wagon," said Olivia. "You're right, Corey, we can take more than I planned – that special little cedar trunk your father made for me, a few toys and books, more food and supplies – maybe even one of Grandma Poff's rocking chairs."

"Mom, when did you tell Grandpa we were going away? It must have taken a while for him to get this stuff together – for everyone yet."

"I only told him yesterday. I had the feeling he already knew. He must have either known, or suspected – I think your father talked to him before the last imprisonment." Olivia stopped, breathing deeply to clear the emotion.

"He knows people who can supply things he wants when he wants them," said James.

Olivia, her emotions under control, continued. "We can leave our work horses and buckboard for Samuel to use when your father gets out of prison."

"Do you really think he will and they can catch up with us?"

"I don't know, James," she answered with more bravado than she felt, "but at least they'll have something to travel in when they do. Take care of the mules and let's get started with the packing. We have a lot to do today if we're going to leave first thing tomorrow."

38   Saying Goodbye

The spring sun began to warm a day chilled by sadness. Olivia worked stoically, refusing to give in to the pain and sadness in her heart. As fast as she and Rosy could pack boxes and barrels, Samuel and the children loaded the wagon. With Samuel to supervise, Olivia didn't have to worry about the children's inexperience. With so much to do, she took time out only to nurse Lucy. Throughout the day, she heard the familiar laughs and giggles as well as sadness over things they would leave behind.

Rosy took time away from her preparations to slice bread and ham for lunch. " I'll fix a good supper later," she said setting the platters on the table and bursting into tears.

Olivia nodded. She understood – their last supper together. "We'll be together again, Rosy. You and Samuel will bring Will and the others to be with us soon."

"Yes'em," said Rosy dabbing at her eyes as she went to the door to call the children to the table. Even though Olivia invited Rosy and Samuel to eat at the table with the family, they always refused. Rosy took their lunch out to the porch.

Everyone was soon back to work without time for resting or playing. As the sun slid over the horizon, James placed the last box on the wagon. Olivia stood back and silently gave thanks once again for her father's generous gifts.

Feet dragging, four very tired and sweaty children took their places at the supper table. Olivia offered a prayer of thanksgiving, for the food, for the gifts from her father and a special prayer for Will and the others in that *Non-Volunteer Cell* in Libby. They ate the chicken and dumplings in near silence. Talking was impossible – crying out of the question.

Suddenly, James and Olivia cocked their heads. A sound – the hum of many feet on the move – moved closer to their house. James jumped up and looked out the window. "Looks like a mob with torches coming this way," he said.

"Sounds like a funeral dirge," said Olivia looking over her son's shoulder.

The dancing lights of lanterns and torches began to fill the backyard and reflect against the widows. Soft, muted voices filtered through the closed door and windows, words unintelligible murmurs.

"Parker? Someone looking to loot our wagon?" Olivia wondered as James grabbed his shotgun standing in the corner and started for the door.

"They got torches. Maybe they're going to burn our wagon to the ground?" Corey grabbed another gun and ran after James. Olivia followed them.

"Michael, stand guard here." She indicated the door. He nodded and grabbed his gun to stand by the door.

"I'll be with Lucy," said Betsy and ran for the bedroom.

The murmuring stopped. Samuel and Rosy ran upon the porch as Olivia and the boys came out the door. Lantern lights illuminated, not Parker's men, but Will's congregation.

Are they angry with Will? With me for leaving them? Have they been paid by Parker to stop us?

Albert Johnson, the Lay Pastor, who was looking after things while Will was gone, stepped forward. "Mrs. Brunner." He cleared his throat and tried again. "Mrs. Brunner, we couldn't let you leave without a proper send off. You know how much we admire Pastor Brunner and how much he's in our prayers. We know how hard it is for you to leave with him still in that stinking prison and how difficult it is for him. We admire your courage to do what you must do even when you would rather do something else. We just want you to know you'll be in our prayers and God will go with you and we'll do all we can to help Will – provide him with food and blankets when we can and money for Rosy and Samuel to run on 'til he gets out."

Olivia found herself with her children in the center of a circle of people who prayed for their journey. There were no dry eyes as they began to sing, *Blest Be the Tie That Binds, Our hearts in Christian Love...* It would probably be the last time they would see each other on this side of heaven. Ties of friendship would stretch to the new land, but they would never again feel the clasp of those hands of old friends.

Samuel stood with his arm around Rosy's shoulder, unashamed of the tears that streamed down his face. The congregation turned away with slow, dragging steps, still singing the hymn. Olivia allowed herself the only tears she would shed for this journey, then took the children in the house and put them to bed. Morning would come before any of them were ready for it.

39 The Journey Begins

Olivia stared out her window, where she had kept her vigil throughout the night. Sleep had been out of the question. Memories tumbled and rolled until finally Old Bill strutted out to the backyard, flapped his wings a few times, then flew to the top of the fence to call to the sun into the sky.

With a death-like grip on each arm, Olivia pushed herself from her grandmother's rocker where she had sat like a statue through the night. The chair would forever stand guard over a bed that she and Will would never again share. Filling her lungs with a long slow pull of air, she held it, filling each tiny cell of her body then just as slowly she released it back into the air surrounding her. She would save her heart for Will and begin to live again when he was able to join her.

She carried Lucy in her cradle to the kitchen. Rosy shuffled in and Olivia, not ready to face the tears already streaming down Rosy's face, returned to check the room for items she might have missed. "Please dear God, take care of Will and the other prisoners," she whispered. "Bring them safely to us as soon as possible."

As if a friend responded to her prayer, a thought occurred to her. Olivia turned to their wardrobe and took out a set of clothes – underwear, socks, shirt and trousers for Will. She picked up his Sunday shoes and a jacket from the hook on the door. Carrying them with the same love and tenderness she would carry Lucy, she took them to the wagon and added them to her own treasures and mementoes. *When Will comes to us, he will need these.*

She double-checked all their possessions, making sure everything was secure and wouldn't fall on the children, or off the wagon. Still not ready to return to the house, she started toward the barn. Samuel was already there and almost finished feeding and harnessing the mules and Beauty. He had already milked Nellie and set the bucket of warm milk by the door for one of the twins to get.

"Morning, Miz Olivia." Samuel met her as he led the mules out of the barn. "Woke early and figured I'd take care of the animals for you." A somber face, as dark as the shadows, had replaced his usual happy smile.

"Thank you, Samuel," she said. "I couldn't sleep either." Together they walked back to the wagon.

"We're livin' in tryin' times, Miz Olivia. You and Master Will shouldn't ought to have to be apart like this. Soon as I can get him out of that hole, we'll follow you up north. We'll find you, Miz Olivia. Don't you worry none about that. We'll be there, the good Lord willing."

"I know you will, Samuel. I thank God every day for friends like you and Rosy. You take care of her and don't take chances that might get either of you killed."

"Yes'em," Samuel said. He swiped his sleeve across his face as he turned to hitch the mules.

"I'll help with that," called James, running toward them.

"That's a good idea, James," Olivia said. "We won't have Samuel to help us after today." Only a slight quiver in her voice betrayed her calm appearance.

Olivia stepped back to watch James and Samuel hitch the mules to the wagon. Next, they crated half a dozen squawking hens and tied the crates to the sides of the wagon. She would leave Old Bill and the rest of the hens for Rosy and Samuel. Although she would never admit it, even to herself, Olivia couldn't bear the thought of having to kill the old rooster for a meal. He'd been a part of the family too long. Nellie, their milk cow, complained loud and long when James tied her to the back of the wagon.

Olivia returned to the kitchen where the aroma of bacon, scrambled eggs, and biscuits greeted her. Corey, Michael and Betsy were already seated. James followed her in and took his place. Olivia prayed and they all tried to eat with enthusiasm, but even Corey and Michael picked at their eggs.

Finally, rising from the table, Olivia said, "If you're finished, we need to get started."

"Yes, ma'am," they all said, leaving the table with food still on their plates – something they were never allowed to do. James scraped all the food into one plate and dumped it in Blackie's dish on the porch. The excited little dog had no trouble cleaning it up.

Olivia pulled a small calendar from one of her many pockets and drew a circle around the date – March 20. March was almost gone – winter already a memory, spring emerging in the form of little shoots of green and tiny red buds.

Tears streamed down Betsy's face as she hugged Rosy and

Samuel one more time, but she made no complaint when James helped her into the wagon. The twins hugged Rosy and Samuel then ran to the wagon, climbed in and quickly brushed their cheeks with their shirtsleeves. They sat on either side of Betsy as close as they could get without being on her lap. Olivia placed Lucy's cradle beside them, took the baby from Rosy and handed her to Betsy. She forced herself to take one last look at the home she and Will had shared for over fourteen years. She sighed, blinked and turned to the wagon.

"Corey, you can ride Beauty for now. James will drive the wagon then trade with you later. You can be the messenger for now." Olivia tried to smile at Corey and wondered if there would be anyone to share messages with other than Tillie.

James, tall and gangly, dark hair hanging in his face, extended his hand to help her onto the wagon seat, then climbed to the seat beside her and took the reins. Chickens squawked, Nellie bellowed and Blackie yapped at the hooves of the mules. As the red ball of sun peeked over the horizon, the wagon wheels began to turn, carrying them into a life of travel, adventure and fear – territory unknown to any of them.

Olivia patted her pocket. The crackle of the map she and Will worked out gave her a feeling of security. She had resisted the urge to run to Rosy and Samuel, to touch them and hug them one more time. Setting her jaw in determination, she turned and waved. Rosy's face glistened. Samuel slipped his arm protectively around his wife's shoulder. Olivia bit her lip and looked straight ahead. *There will be no more tears until I can share them with Will.*

"Give them the reins, James," she said as calmly as she could.

"Okay, Jasper and Max, let's go. Get up there." James slapped the mules' rumps with the reins just enough for them to know he was in charge. The mules responded to him with a slow clip-clop.

They were on their way.

40   Samuel's News

Samuel and Rosy watched until they could neither see nor hear the wagon. "I need to let Master Will know they're on the way," said Samuel. "Then I'll follow them 'til they're out of Richmond."

"You be careful," said Rosy. "Don't you go get yourself caught down by that prison."

"I won't," said Samuel. "I'll go ask David to do it. It's early, but Noah lives behind the newsstand. He'll be there. Then I can follow Miz Olivia." He turned and ran to the barn. Minutes later, he rode out on one of the horses Olivia had left behind.

It was too early in the morning for many people to be on the streets in Richmond, but he rode slowly, his head bowed. People were used to seeing him come for supplies later in the day, but with Will in prison and the threat of war so near, he didn't dare draw attention to himself or Noah as he approached the newsstand. Sure enough, Noah was behind his counter top sorting his inventory – tobacco, pipes, candy.

"Hey Noah," Samuel called softly, sliding off his mount to talk without raising his voice. He glanced all around to make sure no one was within hearing distance. He needn't worry. No one was around at all.

"What's up Samuel? It's mighty early for you to be out. Miz Olivia got more trouble?"

"No trouble, least not yet that I know of. Is David here?"

"Be here in a little bit. You can go get him if you want."

"No time, Noah. Would you send him to Libby with a message? Tell him to tell Master Will that Miz Olivia is on the way. Master Jefferson gave all the women wagons and mules. I'll follow 'til they be out of Richmond then I'll bring news to Master Will myself."

"Glad she got away," said Noah. "You be careful, Samuel. And don't you worry none. I'll send David soon's he gets here."

"Thanks Noah," said Samuel as he looked around again. Still no one in sight, but he walked the horse slowly through the streets, then mounted and galloped until he heard the sound of Olivia's wagon near the church yard. Staying hidden in the woods, brush and whatever cover he could find, Samuel followed.

He grinned when he saw the other wagons fall in line behind her as she passed the church. *The men will be happy to know they's all together. I'll sure do my best to get them out of that prison and take them north. For now, I'll follow the women to the edge of Richmond and then take news to Libby.*

Book II

THE JOURNEY

March 1861

1   *Unexpected Passenger*

"Do we follow the James River Road?" James glanced at his mother.

Olivia nodded. "We'll follow the north side of the James River until it turns south at the Blue Ridge Mountains. We cross north of Roanoke and head west to the New River then north again until it merges with the Kanawha and Gauley Rivers."

It had all sounded so simple when she and Will prepared the map. Neither of them had ever traveled outside Richmond and surrounding areas. Only God knew if they would reach their destination and if they did what the future would hold.

Over and over, turning wheels played off-key melodies blending with the animals to sound more like a symphony of chaos than joy. Inch by inch, foot by foot, they were on their way.

Will's church, where they all worshiped, waited just around the next bend. Olivia, afraid her friends would not be there, stared straight ahead. James nodded toward the churchyard. "Looks like we got company," he said.

Olivia exhaled as if she had been holding her breath for a very long time. Five covered wagons, like hers and Tillie on her black gelding, Zeus, waited in the parking area of the church. She and Will were married in that church. She gulped back a sudden painful memory. She waved to the other women and continued moving. One by one, each of the other wagons fell in line behind her.

James grinned and Olivia relaxed, somewhat. "Knew they'd come," he said.

Olivia nodded. She hadn't wanted to go alone, but having the others along would be a greater burden. *Will they accept my leadership? Can I lead them to safety? After all, what do I know about mules and wagon trains, much less wilderness travel?*

Oh, God, with Your help, I'll do my best.

Riding in silence, they covered the distance from their home to the Dooley plantation. The rising sun painted the mansion's pillars a brilliant red with streaks of gold. Jefferson's carriage waited at the end of the lane.

"Looks like Grandmother and Grandfather are waiting for us," said James. He glanced at his mother. "Shall we stop?"

Olivia nodded. "You all need to say goodbye to your grandparents," she said knowing deep in her heart – with her Grandmother Poff's second sight – it would be the last time they would see each other.

Jefferson helped Elizabeth from the carriage. Tears streamed down her face as she approached Olivia and the children. She hugged each one then turned to her daughter.

"I don't understand why you are doing this," she said a touch of anger in her voice. "You could have come here to stay. We have plenty of room."

"It's not a matter of room, Mother," said Olivia checking her own anger. It was so easy for her and her mother to argue and she didn't want that – not now. "I promised Will. I have to protect our children."

"But you could do that here."

"No, Mother. I'm afraid for you and all Richmond when the war starts..." she stopped and took a deep breath and changed directions. "Come with us, Mother."

"And leave your father and our plantation?"

Olivia said no more.

"You will do what you will," said Elizabeth with a note of resignation. "You always did. I will pray for God's mercy and protection for you every day."

"Thank you, Mother. That's all I ask." She rushed in to her mother's arms, shedding a few tears she had declared she would not shed.

Elizabeth returned to the carriage while Jefferson bid his daughter and grandchildren goodbye.

"Thank you, Daddy, for everything," Olivia said. She knew better than to try to say more.

"I'm glad the others are going with you. Be safe and may God go with you."

Elizabeth returned from the carriage with Moses bringing baskets of sandwiches, cookies and apples. "Lunch," she said. "Henrietta insisted. We'll give each wagon one as they pass by."

Olivia smiled, accepted the offering and climbed back on the wagon. "Let's go, James," she said and gulped back the lump in her throat as the children waved and shouted, "Bye, Grandma. Bye, Grandpa." They began a slow plodding giving the others time to bid farewell to the Dooleys.

Behind her, each wagon stopped long enough to say goodbye and to take the offered lunch basket.

"Keep them steady, James." Olivia felt her nerves begin to relax and her muscles tense against the jarring movement of the wagon as the mules picked up speed. Heavy eyelids, however, won out against the anxiety and eased over tired, sleep-deprived eyes. The soft rhythmic clip-clop and swaying of the wagon sent her into that blessed twilight of floating – neither here nor there – just being.

"Whoa, there boys," James called to the mules. His words and the pressure on the reins brought them to a very slow walk and jolted Olivia back to wakefulness. *What's wrong? Did Parker learn of our leaving?*

"Whoa," James called to the mules again and pulled firmly on the reins. "Whoa there, Max. Whoa, Jasper."

Feeling disorientated for a moment, Olivia's heart pounded as she jerked awake. Sweat gathered on her palms and forehead. "What is it James?" She forced her voice to sound calm even though she felt as if every nerve in her body would explode.

He nodded toward a clump of thickets at the edge of the woods. "Up there," he said. "Looks like one of Mr. Rice's slaves. I thought she was going to run across our path. Didn't want to hit her."

Olivia saw the woman. "It *is* Mary, but why is she carrying a bundle of rags? And why is she way out here?"

"She the one Dad was called to help with a baby last fall about the same time Lucy was born?"

"Yes, her baby was breech and the midwife needed help to save her and the baby."

Olivia felt a sinking feeling in the pit of her stomach as Mary ran to the side of the wagon clutching that ragged bundle. James slowed the mules even more until they were barely moving.

"Miz Olivia, Miz Olivia," Mary called in her deep throaty voice. "Take my Charles to freedom. He be a good baby." She lifted the squirming, crying bundle for Olivia to take. Olivia shrunk back in horror. That bundle of rags was a baby!

"I can't take him, Mary. He needs his mother."

The woman trotted along crying louder, "Please, Miz Olivia. Please take care of him." With an unforeseen burst of strength, Mary tossed the bundle at Olivia like a sack of potatoes. Without looking back, she ran into the thickets and on into the woods.

James jerked the mules to a stop and Olivia's heart skipped several beats as she leaned forward and caught the squalling infant.

"Mary, wait," she called after her, "I can't take...him... with...us." But the woman was gone, leaving bushes swaying in her wake. Olivia turned to James, her brow furrowing into a question. She held the baby close to soothe him. He stopped crying.

"Good catch, Mom," said James.

Olivia frowned.

"Sorry," he said. "I know it's nothing to joke about. Do you want to send Corey after her?" He held the reins loosely in his hands and glanced up at his brother who rode up beside them.

Olivia looked at James then Corey then Tillie, who rode up to see what was happening. She sighed. "You won't find her and it would only waste precious time. We'll just have to make the best of it. I can't blame her for wanting him to have a better life, but..." Olivia didn't have to finish her thoughts.

She pulled the tattered blanket aside and dark, round eyes with tears still hanging on his eyelashes stared back at her. The baby smiled then gurgled as Olivia caressed the smooth, soft brown cheeks with her fingertips. Tired as she was, she couldn't keep from smiling at the infant.

Charles opened his mouth and made sucking noises in search of food. Olivia sighed again and opened her bodice to feed him. Tillie laughed and said, "I'm glad she gave him to you, not me. At least you can nurse him."

"Just what I wanted – more twins to raise," said Olivia trying to sound irritated.

"What's wrong with twins?" Corey asked then broke into his familiar giggle.

"Yeah, what's wrong with twins?" Michael stuck his head over the back of the wagon seat to see Charles.

"Come on, Corey," said Tillie. "Let's ride back and tell the rest you just got a new brother." She laughed and galloped off, Corey right behind her.

"Let's go, James," said Olivia, "before word gets around and we have more slaves running after us. I nursed twins before. I guess I can do it again, but I don't want any more than two."

James grinned and gave the mules the reins to go ahead. "You might have some explaining to do when Dad catches up with us."

"Your father will understand. I'm not sure about the other women and Uncle George. I've never even met him, so I don't know his views of slavery. But I have no choice. I can't leave a baby at the side of the road like a stray dog."

"Not hardly," said James.

Charles suckled her breast then fell asleep as if he belonged with this family. Olivia smiled and handed him to Michael. "Betsy, hand me Lucy and see if you can fix a soft place for Charles back there. When we stop for the night, I'll find something more permanent. Can you manage with both babies?"

"I'll help her, Mom," said Michael.

The rocking of the wagon soon had both babies asleep. Olivia felt as if she were sitting on the back of a giant snail. *If only we could run the mules faster. If only we could outrun the feeling of impending doom that clutches and squeezes at my heart.*

As if he'd read her mind, James said, "The animals would never last the journey if they spent all their strength at the outset."

Olivia gave her son a look of admiration. "You must be a mind reader," she said. "I know you're right, but I want to put as much distance between us and Richmond as we can – as quickly as we can."

James nodded and grinned.

Olivia was glad her father had taught her children about animals. James, young as he was, understood the mules and would pace them well. With a jab of longing, Olivia was once again thankful for all her father had done to help them.

Richmond soon faded from view and rolling hills reflected golden sunlight against the new crop of grass and winter wheat. Trees, losing their nakedness of winter, offered promises of spring with tiny spots of green and pink. A robin's song drifted across the road as they passed a copse of trees. The river burbled and splashed against an occasional boulder and lapped the shores on the other side of the road. Olivia glanced at the clear, blue sky.

"I'm glad the spring rains haven't yet descended upon us. We don't need swollen rivers and mud pits in the roads."

"We'll probably have some of that before we reach the Kanawha Valley," said James.

"I know. But at least we're starting out with good weather and good roads."

Another half hour slipped by. The babies slept. Olivia once again felt herself drifting into the softness of slumber. Before she reached that solid state of non-awareness, once again James called to the mules and jarred her back to wakefulness.

"Whoa there, Max; whoa, Jasper. Slow down there. Whoa now."
What now? More babies?

2   Parker's Volunteers

"What is it now, James?" Olivia asked, shaking herself awake. "No more babies, I hope. I don't think I can handle another one."

"No ma'am," he said, "but we got company and they don't look none too friendly. Three horsemen are blocking the road ahead."

James pulled the reins and reached for the hand brake to slow the wagon to a stop. Corey galloped up to see what was happening. "Tell the women to stop and stay put, but keep their guns ready until we see what they want," said Olivia nodding at three men. Corey rode from wagon to wagon with the order.

Tillie drew Zeus to a halt beside Olivia. Tillie didn't mind wearing men's trousers so she could sit astride her horse like a man. She held her shotgun across her lap ready for use at Olivia's signal.

"Looks like soldiers of some kind," said Olivia. "We can't get around them. Just sit here for a minute and see what they want. Let them come to us."

The horsemen, holding shotguns, walked their horses toward the wagon. Two stopped in front of the mules, the third rode to the side of the wagon facing Olivia. Tillie backed away giving him room to talk. Blackie sat beside Max watching the men. Suddenly he turned his head toward the woods and started to get up.

"Stay, Blackie," said Olivia. He sat back and kept his eyes on the men in front of them.

Keeping a facade of calm, Olivia faced the men before her. She knew who they were and why they were there, but she would play innocent and ignorant. The broad shouldered, bearded man in a *Volunteer* uniform nudged his horse closer to the wagon.

"Morning, Olivia," he said, tipping his hat like a gentleman. One side of his mouth turned up in an attempt at a smile. The bulge of tobacco in his jaw made a full smile impossible.

"Morning, Elias," Olivia answered. "You're out early. Been coon hunting?"

He laughed, not a very pleasant sound, choked on his tobacco juice and coughed. He spat across the road to the field behind him.

"No ma'am," he finally said. "Been commissioned by Sergeant Matthew Parker to bring in all the horses and mules we can find. We got us a war starting and our new government's going to need all the help it can get."

"That so?" Glad the sun was to her back, Olivia kept her gaze steady. Elias Harper shifted in his saddle as if he knew he was between a rock and a hard place. "I don't remember hearing about a new government," said Olivia. "Did President Lincoln issue an order for our mules?"

"I ain't talking about Lincoln. I'm talking about President Davis," Elias drawled.

Anger flared, but Olivia forced her voice to stay low and even. "Unless the status of our state changed overnight, Elias, we're still members of the United States of America and Abraham Lincoln is our President. Was there a change I don't know about?"

Elias pulled at his collar and shifted in his saddle again. "Not yet, but it's only a matter of time. And when it comes we gotta be ready."

"When that time comes, Elias, you come and ask for my animals and I'll let you have them. Until then, they're mine and you'll only take them over my dead body."

Elias shifted again. His horse pawed at the ground and bobbed his head issuing a questioning neigh. Elias patted the animal's neck and looked back at Olivia, who had not shifted her gaze.

"Can't let you take those animals out of Virginia, Olivia. That's the law," he said.

"Whose law is that, Elias? *Sergeant* Parker's?" The look on the man's face told her she was right. She sat wordless for what seemed an eternity. When she spoke again, it was in a different direction. "I never heard of a law that says a woman can't take her family and friends to visit relatives while their husbands are in prison. We aren't even going out of the state."

"We live in a new day, Olivia. We got a new government, or soon will have. They want your animals and it's my job to take 'em. I got no quarrel with you, with Will in jail and all."

"Elias Harper you've known me since we were kids together. Did I ever lie to you?"

"No ma'am, Olivia. Can't say as I ever knowd you to lie to anyone. Everyone could trust Olivia Dooley." Elias turned his head, spat tobacco juice again then swung back around, swiping his mouth on his sleeve. A strong tobacco odor hung in the air. He gave her his crooked, half smile again. Olivia didn't return it.

"Then you listen to me, Elias Harper," she said. "You tell your sergeant, the mayor and any of your other Confederate friends that they can have my horses and mules, even my milk cow if they want her, as well as all the rest of the animals in this wagon train, just as soon as they get us to my uncle's place in the Kanawha Valley. You can go with us and bring them back, or I'll send you a letter when we arrive at our destination to let you know where we are. You can come and get them. Otherwise, you'll have to kill every woman and child on this train in order to take them." Olivia didn't raise her voice or lower her eyes. *He knows we won't give up without a fight and Parker will be lucky if any of his men survive to tell the story, but he needs to save face somehow.*

Three guns clicked ready for firing in and around the wagon – probably more in the other wagons that she didn't hear. She waited.

Sweat popped out on Elias's brow. His raised eyebrows told Olivia he, too, heard the children cocking their guns. She knew he wasn't too keen on killing women and children for a few animals. The other two men watched their leader, waiting for his order. He stared for a minute longer then as if he suddenly realized her graceful offer of a way out of the dilemma, the corner of his mouth turned up into his half smile. He motioned the two men behind him to lower their guns.

"Olivia Brunner," he said relaxing in his saddle, "I'll tell the sergeant he has your word on that. You send me word when you get settled and I will inform him. He can decide then if he wants to go after them. Good day, ma'am. God speed on your journey." He tipped his hat, turned his horse and the three of them rode across the meadow.

Olivia didn't turn around but, took a deep breath and said in a shaky voice. "Thank you, children. Now put the guns away, please."

"Yes ma'am," said Michael and Betsy.

"We just dare them to take our animals," declared Corey from beside the wagon, sliding his gun back into the saddle holster. Olivia smiled as she heard Betsy and Michael put the safety on the guns and set them aside.

"Olivia, do you think that was a smart way of handling them? Will Parker accept your offer?" Tillie had heard the exchange.

"He might, but I doubt it. He'll hound us as long as he can. We need to stop talking and get out of here before he sends others who won't be as easy to talk out of it as Elias Harper was. Once we're in The Valley, I doubt Parker will send for our animals."

Olivia faced forward and said, "Give them the reins, James. Let's move out of here before someone else tries to stop us." Tillie and

Corey returned down the row of wagons giving the rest the news. Blackie gave one last longing look at the forest and ran to catch up with Max and Jasper.

"Wonder what he saw back there in the woods?" James asked when Blackie ran ahead of them.

"I noticed. He wanted to go investigate. Probably a rabbit or squirrel."

"Maybe."

"You don't sound too convinced. Did you see something while I was talking to Elias Harper?"

"Not exactly – just a feeling. I think Samuel is following us – at least until we get out of the area so he can tell Dad we're on the way."

Olivia stared at her son. Then she smiled. "I hope you're right. Blackie did seem to know whoever or whatever was hiding there. Your father will rest a little easier knowing we have matters under control."

"Yeah," he said and slapped the reins to tell Max and Jasper to move along.

Hills and valleys slipped away, merging into the background they once knew as home. The clip-clop of the mules, yapping of Blackie as he ran from wagon to wagon and bellowing of Nellie added to the creaking of wagons once again sent that symphony of travel that would soon be embedded in their mind so that even in sleep they would wonder if they were still moving. Olivia searched for more signs of ambush– more soldiers, more slaves with babies or disgruntled Virginians. Sleep would have to wait now for nightfall. Who knew what they might encounter next.

"Olivia, I thought I saw movement behind us," said Tillie riding up beside the lead wagon. "Should I go check it out?"

"James noticed it too," said Olivia, "while I was talking to Elias. Off to the right in the woods. He thinks it was Samuel. Blackie wanted to go to him. If it was, he'll let the men know we're safely on our way."

Tillie nodded. "I'll let the rest know so they won't worry so much," she said and turned Zeus toward the other wagons.

Like a disjointed caterpillar, the wagon train crawled up one small hill and down another. Around them birds chirped, wind whispered through the trees, wagons creaked and groaned, mules clip-clopped along and Nellie bawled. Finally, James broke into Olivia's reverie.

"Mom, do you really think Dad will find us?"

"Of course, he will child. He said he would, didn't he?" Olivia looked straight ahead, unwilling to look into his wide, trusting eyes."

"Mom, I'm not a child any longer. I'm twelve. Some kids my age are enlisting."

Olivia jerked around and gave her son a sharp look. James stared back with Will's hazel eyes. Even his voice was becoming deeper and richer in timbre. When had he grown up? He was no longer a little boy, but not quite a young man.

"James, you're right, son." She sighed. "I've been so caught up in this war and what I had to do to keep you children safe, that you grew up without me knowing it. I suppose I'm lucky they didn't try to pressure you into the army." Startled by her son's expression, Olivia's face lost its color. "I know you said they approached you, but…"

"Yes, ma'am," he said without dropping his gaze. "They tried. I told them I would have to talk it over with Dad when he got home."

"James…" She stopped, speechless. What could she say? With a sudden rush of gratitude, she realized she didn't face the journey alone after all. They were all in it together. "James, you're right," she said. "You and George Walsh are the only *men* we have in this wagon train. You need to know all that I know – which isn't much. If something happens to me along the way, you can take charge and get the rest to safety."

"Mom, ain't nothing going to happen to you. We won't let it."

"Yeah, Mom, we'll protect you." Corey rode alongside the wagon listening.

James sounded so emphatic and so much like his father that Olivia almost laughed, but checked herself in time. This boy/man needed assurance, not ridicule. And Corey? Was he only six?

"Thank you, boys, I'm sure you'll do your best, but all the same, things do happen." She pulled out the map that she and Will had spent hours and weeks putting together. "Now this is where we are and this is where we're heading. We need to move at least eight to ten miles a day. There are clearings along the way where we can circle the wagons for protection. Some have been marked. If we start early each day and push hard we can get to our destination, hopefully in time to plant gardens."

James reached for the map to examine it then handed it to Corey who gave it to Betsy and Michael.

"Uncle George, Grandpa Dooley's brother, lives in the Kanawha Valley area, called The Valley." She pointed to the area on the map as Michael handed it back to her. "You can see it's still in Virginia, but the last I heard from Aunt Molly, they're more Union than Confederate and she thinks they'll secede from Virginia."

James turned his head and coughed to smother a laugh.

"Is something funny?" Olivia scowled at him. *Am I expecting too much from him. After all, he is only twelve.*

"Sorry," he said. "It just struck me as funny for Virginia to secede from the Union then western Virginia to secede from the seceding."

Olivia gave him a blank look then burst into laughter. In her concern over the serious change in their lives, she had forgotten her son's sense of humor. "War does strange things to states and people," she said. "Now back to the Dooleys in The Valley. If anything happens to me, you find them. They'll help you get the little ones settled. You take care of them until your father shows up. You got that?"

"I got it Mom. But…will Dad show up?"

"James, I certainly hope so, but I know how difficult it will be for him. All we can do is pray and trust the good Lord. That's what your father would tell us to do. In the meantime, we'll do our best and trust God to do the rest."

"We'll make it, Mom," said Corey.

"Yeah, and so will Dad," said Michael from behind her.

Yes, she thought, *with faith like that, how can we fail?*

The sun moved higher in the sky, making the day unseasonably warm for the end of March. Tillie rode up beside the wagon once more. "We stopping for lunch, 'Livia? The women are getting weary and the kids are getting hungry and restless."

"We aren't on a Sunday afternoon picnic, Tillie. We can't stop except for emergencies until we stop for the night."

"Mom," said James, reaching over to lay a hand on her arm, "the mules have to have a rest. We don't need to pull off the road and set up camp, but we should give them rest and water. They can nibble on the grass at the side of the road."

Olivia frowned and wanted desperately to lash out at James and Tillie for slowing them down, but she knew they were right. None of them was used to the kind of work they had cut out for themselves. She looked up at Tillie who waited for her answer.

"We'll give the mules some water and let them graze on whatever is there. Tell the women we'll take about a half hour then we're moving on. There's no time for cooking, but we have the lunch baskets Mother gave us as we left. We'll cook when we stop for the night. We can't waste two to three hours every day to cook lunch. It would take six months to reach The Valley."

3   *Libby*

As the morning grayness valiantly tried to send a little light to the dark dungeon of the room in Libby Prison, the men rose from their blanket-bed on the cold, hard floor and looked toward the window square near the top of the outside wall as if seeking a message from God. It would be several hours before the guard brought food – if he even bothered.

"Do you think the women will make it out of town before Parker stops them?" Joe asked the question that they all were thinking. Sleep had been out of the question, so the men had spent most of the night praying for their women and children, who would be leaving for an impossible journey later in the morning, the Lord willing.

"They'll make it, Joe," answered Will. "We have to believe they'll make it."

"If the rest go with Olivia, they'll all make it," said Kenny

"That's if…" The sound of small pebbles hitting the floor caught their attention.

"Samuel?" whispered Robert

"Is there trouble with the women?" asked George.

"Never sure if it was friend or foe passing through the alley by the window, Will moved closer to the window and said softly, "Someone out there?"

"It's me, Master Will," whispered the small voice outside the window.

"David? Is something wrong?"

"No sir, Master Will. Samuel sent me to tell you Miz Olivia is on her way. He said he will follow her until she's out of town then he'll come let you know."

"What about the others?"

"He didn't say nothing about the others – just Miz Olivia."

"Thank you, David. You better leave before someone sees you."

"Yes sir."

The other men looked at Will, fear and anxiety etched on already strained faces.

"Surely they went with her," said Joe, close to tears.

"I know Tillie went," said John. "My guess is they were meeting her somewhere – probably the church lot. Samuel sent David to let us know Olivia is on her way and he would follow her, but she hadn't reached the church yet. That's probably where the rest will meet her."

"I think you're right, John," said Will. "He went to Noah and asked David to come to us as soon as Olivia left our place. He'll let us know more later. Jefferson gave them all wagons and mules. There's no reason they wouldn't go."

"Oh yes there is," said Joe. "Jeannette is scared of her own shadow. I can't imagine her driving a team of mules 400 miles or so."

"The others will help her," said Robert. "I'm sure Grandma Cooper will take her under her wing. But, I think we better pray some more. I don't have any fingernails left to chew on."

Will smiled in spite of his anxiety for Olivia and the children and slapped his friend on the back. "I think you are right. I'm sure Grandma Cooper will be on that wagon train even if Maggie and the kids don't want to go."

Robert laughed. "You're right. As old as she is, she would never pass up an adventure like that and Maggie won't let her go alone."

"How old is Grandma Cooper?" asked George.

Robert laughed again. "I don't think even she remembers, but probably somewhere near eighty."

"Can she take that kind of journey?" asked Kenny.

"She'll go or die trying," said Robert.

"I never thought about the possibility of…" Kenny couldn't finish his thought.

"I'm sure they will all have a lot of hardships, sickness and maybe even death," said Will. "They are all – except Jeannette – well seasoned with life's experiences. They'll do their best."

"Please pray hard for Jeannette," said Joe. "I'm not sure she can…" he voice broke. The rest gathered around him and they settled down to pray until they heard the guard coming with food – such as it was.

The guard – this one was named Bert – ran his ring of keys along the wall of bars. "Wake up! Wake up!" he called then laughed as if he had told a funny joke. "Here's your fine breakfast of ham and eggs with biscuits dripping with melted butter and lots of hot coffee."

Bert set the tray on the floor inside the door and backed out laughing again.

"Ha, ha," said Robert sarcastically to the closed door. He picked up the tray of gruel, dried bread and water. He carried it to the center of the room where he set it on the floor.

"We won't have Olivia sending food anymore, so we have to learn to get along with what they give us," said Kenny.

"Maybe Rosy will send something when Samuel gets back," said Will.

The men sat around the food, joined hands to form a circle and waited for Will to ask God's blessing on it.

"Bless the food and the hands that provided it," prayed Will. "May it nourish us and may we be thankful for it."

"Amen," answered the six in unison.

***

Bert returned later to collect the tray. "Looks like a beautiful day," he said. "Good day to be thinking about gardens and spring clean-up." He laughed heartily and slammed the door then turned the key in the lock.

"Someday…" Kenny didn't finish his thought, but rammed his clenched fist into the waiting palm of the other hand.

"Don't let him get to you, Kenny," said John. "The world is full of jerks like him."

"At least the women have good weather to start their journey," said Robert. "It's still March and they could have had anything from rain to snow."

"Guess I didn't' think of that," said Kenny. "Thanks for getting me back on track."

***

The morning dragged by until sometime midafternoon when once again, small pebbles hit the floor. Will moved to the window and lifted his face toward the little sun that streamed in. "Yes? Who's there?"

"It's me, Master Will – Samuel."

"Are they all right," Will asked.

"Yes sir. The rest met her at the church. They stopped at Master Jefferson's. He was waiting at the end of the lane for them with baskets – food I suppose. About an hour later, one of Mr. Rice's slaves stopped them and gave Miz Olivia something. I couldn't see what it was. Then they was almost out of town when three of Parker's men stopped them. They wanted the mules and horses. I think they intended to take them. Miz Olivia stared them down. All the women and some kids had guns ready. Finally, the three rode off. I don't know what kind of deal Miz Olivia made, but they looked happy and the wagons moved on. Soon's they was out of town and stopped to rest the mules and eat some lunch, I left. They be on their way."

"All of them went with her – even Jeannette?" Joe whispered.

"Yes sir, Master Joe. They all had wagons and mules. Miz Jeannette looked mighty scared, but she was with them."

"Thank God," said Joe and swiped at his eyes.

"Rosy sent some ham sandwiches for you. I'll bring food when I can. And I will get you out of this hole and up north with those women and children. I promise you that sirs. I promised Miz Olivia and I intend to keep that promise."

The men all exhaled together as if they had been afraid they would miss a single word if they breathed. Samuel had whispered, but they all heard.

"Thank you, Samuel. You be careful."

"I will, Master Will. I got you and my Rosy to think about."

Samuel was gone. The men fell to their knees in thanksgiving. They ate half the sandwiches slowly. The other half they hid in their blankets for a later time when there would be nothing.

**

The rest of the day, they took turns pacing for exercise then settled in to wait for the unknown. Night fell and the square in the wall revealed twinkling stars in a midnight blue sky.

"Do you suppose they are sleeping under the same stars?" asked Joe, then gave a choked laugh – half sob. "Somehow, I can't picture Jeannette sleeping under the stars – or even in the covered wagon, for that matter."

"She'll get used to it," said Will. "They all will."

Somewhere a dog howled and further away another answered.

"Will?"

"Um?"

"Is it too fanciful to think that they can hear our thoughts calling across the miles like those strays calling to each other?"

"Olivia would say that makes perfect sense."

4   Lost Wagon

The brief lunch over, the wagons moved on with loud grumbling added to the cacophony of wagon noises. After squinting into the sun all afternoon, it was a relief to see it begin to drop toward the horizon. Tillie pulled Zeus to a slow trot alongside Olivia. "We stopping soon?"

Olivia glanced down at the map in her lap. "According to my map, there should be a clearing not too far down the road."

"Want me to ride ahead and check it out?"

Olivia thought for a minute. It was going to take some getting used to being in charge of a wagon train and giving orders. "Why don't you take George Walsh with you? James and Corey can ride back to tell the others and check for any potential problems."

Tillie, never one for long conversations, nodded and turned Zeus to the wagon behind Olivia. Seconds later, she thundered by with George holding on to her.

Olivia took the reins. "James, you go with Corey and tell the others we'll soon be stopping. Tillie will have a fire started – I hope."

James jumped from the wagon seat to Beauty's back behind his brother and they rode down the line with the information. Michael climbed over the seat and sat beside Olivia. The clearing she had been watching for was around the next curve. Flames of fire were leaping skyward in the center of the site. Olivia turned her wagon and began forming a circle around it, leaving tracks for the others to follow.

"Where's Corey and James?" Michael asked, looking around when they stopped.

"They'll be here," said Olivia frowning as she watched the others move into the circle

"Maybe they're lost." Michael's eyes were round with fear.

"Don't be silly, Michael," said Betsy climbing down from the back. "How can they get lost when they're with the wagons?"

"Betsy's right," said Olivia. "They're probably making sure all the wagons know where to turn."

However, Olivia couldn't stop the feeling of impending doom as she and Michael unhitched the mules and tethered them to a bush so they could graze. She would have James and George Walsh make some kind of temporary corral for all the animals.

She glanced up as the last wagon stopped in the circle. *There are only five. There should be six. Who's missing? As if I need to ask?*

"Betsy, keep an eye on Charles and Lucy. I'll see if Tillie knows anything about the missing wagon."

"Okay, Mom."

Olivia started toward the fire. "Tillie, do you know…?" The sound of Beauty galloping toward them stopped her words. Corey's familiar prelude to trouble interrupted her and set her heart racing.

"Mom! Mom!"

Corey galloped in, stopped so abruptly that Beauty reared and he slid off her back. Olivia reached for the reins to settle Beauty. "Whoa there, Beauty. Corey, where's James and…?"

Corey picked himself up, brushed at the seat of his pants and said, "Mrs. Phillips' wagon was lost when we went to tell them."

"Wagon lost? How could a wagon get lost?"

"We rode back along the trail until we found her. She was back quite a ways – probably close to a mile. Sarah was crying and Joey looked like he was ready to cry. Mrs. Phillips' face was all red and streaked and she was trying to make Sarah quit crying. James stayed to drive her wagon in. He said to tell you they would be here soon."

Olivia scowled, but said as evenly as she could, "Thank you, Corey. Help the Rayburn boys and George with the animals. Michael, take the other children along the edge of the forest and gather more sticks for the fire. Don't go into the forest, just the edge. Watch for snakes and poison ivy. It's a little early in the year for either of them, but as warm as it's been today we need to be on watch for unseasonable dangers."

"Yes ma'am," said the twins in unison. Michael took off, gathering children as he ran. Corey ran to help George make a rope corral for the horses and mules.

"We got twigs and some small logs for the fire," said Michael as he and the others brushed debris of their scavenging from their clothes and hands.

Lucy and Charles made sure that everyone within the range of hearing knew they were hungry. "There's a stream over there," Olivia nodded behind her. "See if you can get some clear, clean water to boil."

"Okay," said Michael. "Come on guys," he called to the others as he grabbed buckets and headed for the stream.

Olivia went to feed the babies. Tillie had the meal preparations under control. Soon the aroma of stew wafted over the camp. Olivia finished feeding the babies, left them with Betsy and started over to help Tillie. Coffee burbled in the pot and the stew smelled wonderful. Pots of water bubbled around the outer edge of the circle sending streams of rising steam. Hearing the sound of Jeannette's wagon approaching, she changed directions. Jeannette's face was still red and blotchy and tears hung on her eyelashes. Olivia waited for her to get down from her wagon.

"What's the problem, Jeannette?" Olivia tried to be compassionate and understanding, but it was difficult to push aside her irritation.

"Oh, Olivia, I'm not cut out for this. The children are afraid. I'm scared of the horses. I don't know how to survive this kind of life."

"Jeannette, they're mules, not horses and we're all scared. None of us know how to survive. We're going to learn together. We have to. Why did you come with us if you feel this way?" She knew, but had to ask.

"Because Joe said I should. He told me to do what you said. But, I just want to go home and be with Joe," she wailed. More tears gushed down her face.

Olivia grabbed her by the shoulders and shook her – not hard, but she was far from gentle. "Jeannette, stop that crying this instant."

Surprised by Olivia's sudden attack on her, Jeannette stopped crying, eyes wide, mouth open. Olivia continued, "We all want to be home with our husbands, but it's not going to happen any time soon. Crying won't change anything. Now, go with James. He'll show you how to take care of your mules. Joey, you go help the boys find more firewood before it's too dark. Sarah, you come with me. You can help Betsy with the babies."

Olivia sounded abrupt and uncaring even to herself, but she couldn't spend the entire journey crying with Jeannette. Tears were a luxury they couldn't afford. Hard work and lots of it was the only way to keep them sane – at least keep herself sane.

The aroma of wood burning and savory stew simmering had groans of anticipation coming from all around the camp. Children chased each other around the circle getting rid of pent-up energy.

Olivia and Maggie sat on stones holding the babies near the fire ring. Tillie stirred the stew once more then turned to Olivia.

"The stew is done. How shall we call the others to the *table*?" Tillie laughed as she looked around the circle, bare except for a few stones and logs the boys had pulled up for a place to sit.

"I have Nellie's bell," said Olivia. "I took it off her after our lunch break. I'll go get it."

"That would work," said Tillie. "I'll hold Lucy while you get it, unless you want me to go."

"I know where it is. I could get it in the time it took me to tell you how to find it." She handed Lucy to Tillie and ran to the wagon, returning in a minute or so with the bell. "Here, you ring it, since you prepared dinner."

Tillie gave Lucy back to Olivia, took the bell and gave it a few hardy shakes. Everyone came running, assuming there was either an emergency or dinner was ready.

"If everyone will get their eating utensils, the stew is done," said Tillie. "The bell will be the signal for mealtimes, so when you hear it, bring your table service." Again, she chuckled because they had no table.

"Yea," cried the children as they ran to help their mothers get the dishes.

As if by signal, once they were all around the fire, they stopped talking and waited for someone to pray.

"Olivia, would you pray for us on this our first night out? We can take turns after that," said Tillie.

Olivia was startled. She hadn't expected to become their spiritual leader as well as their wagon master. Even the children looked at her with expectation. She nodded and cleared her throat.

"Lord, You've been good to us this first day of our travel. You know we don't want to do what we're doing, but it seems to be the only way to protect our children. Bless our travels. Bless the food we have prepared. Bless our men that their hunger and other needs will be met. May our night's rest be complete that we may have strength for tomorrow. In the name of our Lord Jesus, we pray. Amen."

No one needed a special invitation to begin filling plates. Children laughed and giggled, women scolded and talked. Olivia stood back and watched with wonder – *our first meal together. Our first day is ending. We are one day away from Richmond – one day closer to our destination.*

Oil lanterns hung by each wagon, either on poles or on the end of the wagon, giving an eerie light around the outer edge of the circle. The campfire in the center gave light as well as warmth as the night air became cooler. Olivia gazed at the twinkling stars. *There will be frost on the ground by morning.*

Children, who were supposed to be down for the night, giggled and laughed, whined and complained. Mothers, still sitting around the campfire, too tired and weary to discipline, yelled at children too tired and keyed up to listen. Older children sat around the fire with the adults, listening to plans for the coming days, weeks and months.

"Olivia, we can't push like this," said Corinne. "We have to stop for a rest more often and take longer lunch breaks – long enough to fix a decent meal. Poor Jeannette is beat. She doesn't have an older child to help like most of us do."

"Corinne, this trip is going to take two and a half months minimum. You want to make it six months, or longer?" Olivia glared at her friend.

"Well, no, but…"

"No buts about it. We have to keep pushing. It's the only way. We don't know what kind of weather we'll run into. Today was nice, but we can still get rain, or even snow that will slow us down."

"But, it's so hard," wailed Jeannette.

"I know it's hard, but we'll just have to ignore our pain and sorrow and push on. Until we are safe in The Valley, we can't take time for a pity party. If we do, we may as well invite the soldiers to come and take our animals and supplies."

"Well, I don't think we can hold up with the kind of schedule you've set for us. We didn't know how hard this would be." Claudia waved her chubby arms to include the entire group, looking for support from them. She got nods from Corinne and Jeannette.

"I didn't know how hard it would be, either," said Olivia, "but I have a feeling today was easy compared to what we'll endure before we reach The Valley. I can't even guarantee that some, or all, of us won't die before we get there. Life is uncertain in the best of times. A journey into the unknown increases our chances of danger, but I promised Will. You don't have to stay. We're only a day's journey from Richmond. If you want to return in the morning, I won't be offended."

"Olivia's right, Corinne, we have to keep moving. We'll make it." Maggie pushed loose strands of hair from her face and rubbed her tired eyes. She spoke with a note of weariness in her voice.

"She certainly is right," said Grandma Cooper. "I'm an old woman and I might not make it at all, but with God's help I'll go as far and as long, as I can. If Maggie can handle it with the kids and me, and Olivia can manage with two infants, the rest of you can do it."

Olivia, surprised, smiled at the older woman. Grandma Cooper winked at her and added, "I just hope Olivia knows how to give a decent burial if I don't make it."

"Grandma Cooper!" Olivia said. "You wouldn't do that to me – would you?" Although she tried to laugh, that all too familiar foreboding sent a chill down her back.

Grandma Cooper laughed a soft clucking sound. "I hope not, but we never know, do we? Now, if nobody minds, I'm going to find a place to lay my weary bones. I've got a big day ahead of me tomorrow."

"I think that's an excellent idea. We leave at daybreak. We need to appoint guards." Olivia, sure she couldn't stay awake another night, offered for the first watch anyway – just to get them started.

However, James said, "No, I'll take the first watch."

"And me," said Tillie.

The rest volunteered, or were appointed, setting a schedule for the next several days, then began moving toward their wagons – their homes for the next few months. Olivia checked the children, glanced to the southeast where home used to be and breathed another prayer. *O Lord, will we get out of here before the war catches up with us? Protect us and our men, Lord. Give us courage for this journey.*

Having put her life in the hands of God, Olivia crawled under the wagon beside the twins. James would join them after his watch. Betsy was in the wagon with the babies. Olivia had learned to sleep without Will beside her during the harassment and incarceration. Now, she would have to learn to sleep without the comfort of either Will or a warm bed. She would sleep on the cold, hard ground, knowing Will would have nothing better.

Tired as she was, sleep would not come immediately. On her back, she watched the stars and, like the patriarchs of old, tried to count them.

"Mom," whispered Michael, "I didn't know nighttime was so dark."

"Or so noisy," added Corey. "What are all those sounds?"

"Crickets and frogs mostly," said Olivia. "Maybe some raccoons, possums or night birds. You'll get used to them and know what they all are by the time we get to The Valley."

"Are there any bears and wildcats?"

"Maybe, but they won't come near our campfire. They don't usually attack people."

"You sure it's not ghosts out there?"

Olivia smiled in spite of her weariness. "I'm positive it's not ghosts, or bears or wildcats," she said.

"Okay," said the twins and were soon lightly snoring.

Although the ground was hard and it poked and jabbed her body, weariness finally overtook her. Olivia slept until the first streaks of dawn spread across the sky waking her with a start. *Where am I? Have I been dreaming?*

5   Routines Set

Signs of life rustled and twittered as nature's morning symphony spread across the forest. Fingers of red and gold massaged the gray, predawn sky. Olivia lay motionless, listening. She rolled over and tired achy muscles reminded her she hadn't been dreaming. Pain attacked every nerve fiber and muscle in her body as she crawled from under the wagon. Clenched teeth held back the groans. At least she managed to keep from waking the boys – probably because they, too, were exhausted.

Holding a lantern in front of her to light the pathway, Olivia stumbled across the frosty ground a short distance into the woods where James and George had dug small trenches the night before for their toilet – one for boys and one for girls separated by a small cluster of trees. She went from there to the bubbling stream, gasping as she splashed the icy water on her face. Filling a bucket, she carried it back to the camp to begin breakfast.

She was almost back to the camp, when she met James and George. "Did I wake you? I thought you would need more sleep since you had guard duty last night."

"I got plenty of sleep," said James. "Corey and Michael are up, too. We tried not to wake Betsy and the babies. George and I added fuel to the fire for cooking. We'll feed and water the animals so they'll be ready to go."

Michael joined them with another bucket in hand. "Thought I'd milk Nellie so we can have milk for breakfast."

"Good idea," said James. "Come on, we're headed that way."

Olivia took the water to the circle of fire where Maggie was gathering cooking utensils and already had fresh coffee on. Corey managed to gather a few eggs from the crates before the chickens stepped on them. Blackie ran from wagon to wagon barking as if it was his job to waken everyone. Throughout the camp groans and cries of pain accompanied little puffs of white with every breath in the cold, frosty air. The aroma of coffee and burning wood drew the rest to the circle where a large pot of oatmeal bubbled away.

While the rest finished eating and lingered over coffee, Olivia and Betsy fed Charles and Lucy. Betsy fed Charles some oatmeal while Olivia nursed Lucy. Then they switched and Lucy got oatmeal while Olivia nursed Charles. Even though Olivia concentrated on the babies, she could hear sounds of discontent across the camp.

"Why are they angry?" asked Betsy.

"I don't know for sure," said Olivia, "but they're probably tired and scared."

She looked up as the other women approached – all except Jeannette, who took Sarah and Joey back to her wagon. As Betsy had said, Claudia and Corinne looked and sounded angry. Maggie, Grandma Cooper, and Tillie were simply curious.

"Olivia, we need to talk, again," said Corrine.

"All right," said Olivia. "I'm listening."

"We think you're being too hard on Jeannette," said Corrine.

"We heard her crying off and on all night. She's not going to make it if she keeps that up," added Claudia.

"What do you suggest we do?" Olivia handed Charles to Betsy to put in the crib she had made from one of her wooden boxes.

"Maybe we should send her back to Richmond," said Claudia. "She'd be better off and so would we."

"Can't do that," said Olivia. "Joe gave her orders to go. She would no more disobey his orders than she would her daddy's when she was growing up. Besides that, we can't send her back alone. Who wants to go with her?"

"Too bad someone didn't teach her to be a little more independent," said Corrine.

Tillie turned her gaze from Claudia to Corinne to Olivia. She and Olivia both had a flash of insight and smiled at each other. The smile softened Tillie's hard, homely features and Olivia remembered that smile was one of the qualities that had drawn her to the woman years earlier.

"Well," said Tillie, "if no one taught her, then it looks like it's up to us to help her learn. Might be a good idea to put her wagon in the middle of the train – so she don't get lost again."

Olivia smiled up at her friend. "I think that's an excellent idea, Tillie."

"Why don't I ride with her today," said Grandma Cooper. "She's younger than most of you and probably feels the loneliness more."

"Grandmother Cooper, are you sure you're up to that?" Maggie frowned.

Olivia looked from Maggie to Grandma Cooper and back to Maggie. She knew Maggie had not been fully convinced it was a good idea to bring an elderly person on such a perilous trip in the first place. However, when Grandma Cooper decided something, no one was going to stop her. She would have come with them with, or without, Maggie.

"Of course I'm up to it. I have to ride somewhere. These old legs won't let me walk as much as the rest of you youngins." Grandma Cooper squinted at Maggie and pounded her cane on the ground to emphasize her point.

Maggie threw her hands up in a gesture of giving up. "You send Corey or Tillie after me if you…"

"If I what? Get tired? Feel sleepy? That'll be a part of the journey for as long as it takes to get where we're going. I'll be fine. I'll send for you if I need you." Grandma Cooper gave them a toothless grin.

"Thank you, Grandma Cooper," said Olivia. She understood Maggie's worry – her husband in prison, his grandmother in her care. *What if something happens to her? There is nothing either of us can do except be as watchful as we can. Grandma Cooper makes her own choices, but I still feel responsible for the safety of my women and children and I will protect them all as best I can.*

She smiled and winked at the frail-looking old woman and added, "Just don't die in Jeannette's wagon. That would completely unbalance her."

Grandma Cooper laughed her soft cackle. "That's for the good Lord to decide, Preacher Lady."

"Preacher Lady?" Olivia gave her a startled look.

"I know, your husband's the preacher, but that makes you as close as we get to one on this journey." Grandma Cooper laughed again at Olivia's expression. Still chuckling to herself, she started for Jeannette's wagon, planting her cane firmly on the ground with each step.

"Preacher Lady?" Olivia said again and shook her head.

Olivia knew Grandma Cooper was right. She wasn't a preacher, never would be, but she would have to give what spiritual encouragement she could. *What else do you have in store for me, Lord? All I ask is for help to keep these women and children safe on this journey.* That nagging sixth sense told her she should have begged for mercy, rather than simply asking for help.

Finally, they were almost ready to move out. Olivia looked around for James. He was usually close by. He had already hitched Max and

Jasper to their wagon. It wasn't like him to disappear without saying something to her. Irrational fear rushed over her. Had Parker's men…?

"Where's your brother?" she asked Betsy. "The wagon is ready to roll."

"Here he comes," answered Betsy.

Olivia felt the fear and tension ease as James loped up, ready to climb aboard. She didn't ask where he'd been. He would tell her if it was important.

"I'll walk awhile this morning," she said. "Then, I'll drive this afternoon while you walk. We all need to keep up some exercise."

"All right," he said climbing aboard. "I helped Mrs. Phillips hitch her mules to the wagon. She's scared of them, but she'll get over it. They're good mules. She'll be third in line, so she shouldn't get lost." James grinned at his mother.

"Hopefully," Olivia couldn't keep a twinge of sarcasm from her voice. James laughed, sounding so much like his father that Olivia caught her breath. "At least if she starts dragging, Tillie will crack the whip – figuratively, of course. Thank you, James for helping her, but help her learn. Don't do everything for her."

"Yes ma'am."

"I'll send Michael back later to drive her team so she can get some exercise."

James flicked the reins, called to Max and Jasper. Once again, the disjointed caterpillar was on the move. Blackie ran along beside them, barking at the mules. Nellie complained loudly. She'd been used to wandering free in their pastureland. The chickens squawked in their crates. Wagons creaked and groaned. Another day stretched before them, teasing with adventure, warning of possible danger.

The sun climbed higher into the sky. Children cried and complained. At noon, when they rested, Corey called to Michael. "Let's get some water from the creek for Max and Jasper."

"Okay," said Michael jumping from the wagon where he had been helping Betsy with the babies.

"Better check on Jeannette," said Olivia as she took Lucy to nurse. "She might need help. Make sure her mules get food and water."

"Yes, ma'am," called the twins.

The boys fed and watered the mules and horses while Olivia finished feeding Lucy and Charles. Betsy got out sandwiches and cookies for lunch. Olivia felt no desire for food, but forced herself to eat. She knew she had to keep up her strength as well as supply milk for the babies.

Long before the rest were ready to move on, Olivia took the reins. Watching for possible trouble, she started moving to a barrage of complaints from behind her. Tillie rode up beside her.

"Everyone is finally in their wagons and moving," she said. "Claudia and Corinne were trying to have a picnic. Jeannette thought she would have time to make Sarah and Joey take a nap before we moved."

Olivia frowned.

Tillie grinned. "They'll catch on soon enough."

"Yeah," said James walking beside the wagon. "They haven't quite got the idea that we're not on a pleasure trip." He laughed and ran ahead playing tag with Blackie.

Betsy sat beside Olivia with pencil and tablet in hand.

"What you doing?" Michael asked poking his head through the opening in the canvas.

"I'm drawing pictures and writing about things we see so we can show Daddy when he comes."

"That's great," said Michael. "Be sure and draw one of Mrs. Walsh and Mrs. Jones trying to have a picnic." Michael giggled and Betsy scowled at him.

"That's a very good idea, Betsy," said Olivia around the lump in her throat, "Making a book for your father that is." She wondered if Will would ever see the pictures and read the account of their journey, but Betsy's faith and the children's energy and resilience sparked her own courage.

Spring bugs hummed and buzzed – even a butterfly floated by now and then. Children slept, played or talked in low voices to one another. The afternoon seemed so quiet and peaceful that war, prison and Matthew Parker almost seemed to belong to another world. *Maybe this won't be such a bad trip after all. Even Nellie has stopped bawling.*

Suddenly Blackie's excited yapping broke the peaceful lull. He ran up beside Beauty, as Corey galloped up shouting, "Mom! Mom! One of the Jones kids fell off their wagon. Looks like his arm is broke."

6 Doctor Olivia

Olivia felt the blood drain from her face. She pulled harder on the reins, more to steady her own shaking hands than to stop the mules. They seemed glad for any opportunity to rest awhile. "Whoa Max. Whoa there Jasper. Whoa, now."

She sat for a minute hoping she hadn't heard what she thought Corey has said. *Maybe it was my imagination – a mirage like the ones they talked about in western stories.*

"Mom?"

"I heard you, Corey." She sighed and ran down a mental list of what she needed to do. "James, you take Beauty and ride ahead and find us a decent place to stop. Corey, come up here and take the reins."

Corey jumped from Beauty's back to the wagon seat. James took his place with such speed and smoothness the horse hardly had time to know there was a change in riders.

"Keep the mules calm so they don't run away with the wagon. Michael, hand me your father's medical bag. You and Betsy stay with the babies. Blackie, come with me." He had started after James.

Her racing thoughts kept pace with her feet as she ran back to Claudia's wagon at the end of the line. The little black dog trotted along beside her. *I helped Will before he and Joe went into partnership. He taught me some basics. I even helped him set a few bones. But can I do it alone? What if it requires surgery? How can I take a child's life in my hands?*

Olivia heard Claudia's voice rising in loud complaints even before she reached their wagon. "Of all the stupid things to do," yelled Claudia. "You haven't got a grain of sense. If I told you once I told you a hundred times not to play around on the wagon while it's…"

Olivia came around the wagon and interrupted her. "Claudia, Corey said you had an accident back here."

"*I* didn't have an accident. That stupid son of mine fell off the wagon trying to see how far he could lean over. It's a good thing we're the last wagon. He could have been run over."

Bobby sat in the middle of the road surrounded by children. He rested his forearm in his lap and supported the elbow with the other hand. Tears streamed down his face.

"Move aside," said Claudia. "Let Olivia in there so she can take care of him." The children opened a passageway for her then squeezed back to watch. Blackie moved in beside Bobby and licked his face, then sat beside him while Olivia examined the arm.

"Did you find out how far you could lean over, Bobby?" Olivia asked as she stooped beside the boy. He squeezed his eyes and sniffed then gulped a big swallow of air to shut off the tears. It didn't help. They continued to flow.

"Yes ma'am." He hiccupped. "I reached...all the way...to the ground."

The others children giggled and Bobby scowled at them. Olivia examined the arm. The wrist joint was out of place. There was no tear to the skin and no blood. She heard Beauty and looked up as James rode back to her.

"There's a good place about a mile up the road – a clear stream running from the mountain and lots of fire wood. If we push we can be there in twenty minutes or so."

"Thank you James. Take Michael and start gathering firewood."

"I'll take George Walsh and go with them," said Tillie mounting Zeus. "Tommy, take care of the wagon."

"Yes, ma'am," said Tom as he ran for the wagon ahead of Claudia's.

"We'll have a fire going by the time you get there," called Tillie over her shoulder as she thundered off after James and Michael, stopping only long enough to give George a hand and hoist him up behind her.

"Bobby do you think you can hold on until we reach the camping spot? Then we'll be able to do the job right."

"Yes, ma'am," His lower lip quivered. "You won't..." He gulped again. "You won't have to cut it off...will you?"

Olivia turned away from him to close the medical bag, but also to get herself under control. She fought the smile that played at the corners of her mouth, but she fought harder to control the urge to slap Claudia. She was sure that's where Bobby got the idea she would have to amputate his arm. She turned back to Bobby as she stood.

"No, Bobby, it's only a simple break. By the time we get to The Valley it'll be all better."

Claudia rolled her eyes and yelled at the other children. "All right. Everyone get back to your wagons so we can get started.

"Come on, Bobby," said Olivia. "Why don't you ride with me? I'll give you something for pain until we get there."

Bobby glanced at his mother to see if it was all right. "Go on," said Claudia. "You aren't any good to me anyway until she gets you fixed up. I should have known this would happen. You are always…"

Olivia and Bobby didn't hear the rest of her tirade, as they walked back to Olivia's wagon. She helped Bobby up then climbed up beside him.

"Corey, don't dally, but watch the bumps. James will be there to help you begin the circle."

"Does it hurt a lot?" Corey looked at Bobby with wide eyes.

"Yeah, but your mom will fix it for me." The painkiller was working and tears no longer streamed down his face. "You sure are lucky."

"I know. Mom can do anything," Corey bragged.

"Boys!" Olivia felt her cheeks flush and didn't know whether to laugh or cry.

"Well, you can," said Corey.

"Watch where you are going or we'll all be swimming in the river." Olivia tried to divert the attention from herself.

"No we won't," said Corey and giggled the way he usually did. "Jasper and Max are too smart to do that."

"There's James. Let's get these wagons circled."

As promised, Tillie and the boys had a blazing fire that sent sparks skyward. It didn't take long to gather and fill pots with water that was soon steaming. Olivia sent Michael for Claudia. She had waited long enough. The pain medication was wearing off and pain returning to Bobby's arm.

"I'll need help setting his arm," she said when Claudia hesitantly approached her.

"Well, I don't know what you expect me to do," said Claudia, shrinking away. "I can't stand the sight of blood."

"Claudia, there is no blood. It's a simple fracture – a bone out of joint."

"I can't do it. He's my kid."

"What does that have to do with it? Never mind." Olivia glanced around for one of the other women to help her. Corrine and Jeannette weren't even there. Maggie, Grandma Cooper and Tillie moved closer.

"I never did anything like this before," said Tillie, "but tell me what to do and I'll help any way I can."

"I'll help," said Maggie.

"Me too," said the frail voice of Grandma Cooper.

"James went to find something to use for splints. I've given Bobby another pain killer, but it is still going to hurt." She glanced at Claudia who stood off to the side looking as if she were going to be sick.

Forcing the sarcasm from her tone, Olivia called to her, "Claudia, someone needs to keep the rest of the children away from here. I'm sure Bobby doesn't want them watching."

A look of relief spread over Claudia's face. "I can do that," she said gathering the children and moving them to the opposite end of the camp just as James arrived with the pieces of wood he had found.

Olivia looked at the flat pieces and then at James. He shrugged and she smiled. He had torn apart a wooden crate. Of course, there wouldn't be any flat, clean branches and twigs from the woods. She was glad he had thought of it.

"Let's clean them as thoroughly as we can," she said. "While James and I clean the splints, you three tear that sheet into strips."

A little later, Grandma Cooper folded a piece of the sheet and placed it in Bobby's mouth so he would have something to bite down on when the pain hit. Grandma Cooper put her arms around his shoulders and held him while Olivia and Tillie pulled the arm, snapping the joint back in place. Maggie held the splints in place while Olivia wrapped strips of the sheet around and around the arm to hold the splints in place.

Grandma Cooper removed the cloth from Bobby's mouth and wiped the tears that were running down his face. "You did real fine there, boy. Why once I helped set the arm of a grown man who passed out when I just reached toward his arm. You're a brave little man."

"I am?" Bobby gulped back his tears.

"You certainly are," said Tillie, "but, let's make this a one time event. It's no fun for us either."

"Okay," he said. "Can I eat?"

"Are you left handed?" Olivia winked at Grandma Cooper and Tillie.

"No ma'am," he answered looking confused.

"Then you should have no trouble eating since it's your left arm that's broken. The medicine I gave you won't interfere, unless it puts you to sleep. Just be careful with the arm for a few days. Keep the splint on the arm for about six weeks and keep it in a sling for a while."

Bobby went to see the other children and brag about his splint.

Olivia stared after him, feeling weak in the knees.

"Drink this," said Maggie wrapping Olivia's hands around a cup of hot coffee. "James put it on before tending to the mules."

"Maybe you better sit," said Tillie leading her to a log.

"You did mighty good," said Grandma Cooper. "That's only our first emergency. The next one won't be such a shock."

"When I promised Will I'd take the children north, I didn't know that included becoming a doctor," said Olivia. "I wonder what else the Lord has in store for me?"

"Maybe you don't really want to know," said Tillie.

"Probably not, but I'm sure glad I have a good medical team for back-up."

They all laughed and Tillie, Maggie and Grandma Cooper left to give Olivia a few minutes alone to recoup her strength.

***

Later, as the traumatic day faded into twilight, Olivia took her turn as guard with Jeremiah Cooper. Slowly she walked around the outer perimeter of the wagons listening for any unusual sounds and watching for any movement beyond the wagons. Everything seemed secure. She returned to the circle where Jeremiah poked at the fire in an effort to stay awake. He was only ten, but was determined to do his share. Olivia sat on a log beside him.

"The moon looks like a tiny sliver of fingernail," Jeremiah said, leaning his head back to look into the sky.

"It's waning," said Olivia. "Soon there will be no moon for a few nights, then we'll start getting a sliver turned the other direction."

Jeremiah thought for a minute. "I never saw the stars twinkle like that before. I feel like I could reach up and touch them, maybe even pick a few like I pick blackberries."

"It does look different out here away from the city." Olivia smiled.

"What's that chirping noise? Sounds like it's over by the stream."

"Some folks call them spring peepers. They're frogs calling to their mates, getting ready to make a home for themselves and all the little tadpoles that will become new frogs."

"Can you see them?"

"If you're careful and walk as quietly as possible you might. But your lantern would probably scare them into silence."

"Are they big?"

"No, just little frogs – maybe the size of your thumb." Jeremiah frowned and she added, "And they don't bite."

He laughed, poked the fire again and added more twigs.

202

Somewhere in the woods, an owl hooted its question, "Hoo-Hoo?"

"What's that?"

"That's an owl, probably calling her mate. Listen, maybe he'll answer."

They sat in silence for a minute or two. In the distance, an answer came with another, "Hoo-Hoo?"

"Mrs. Brunner, if we keep calling in our hearts, like that owl, maybe our dads will answer us, too? Is that possible?"

Olivia bit her lip, tousled Jeremiah's hair, and said, "Jeremiah, with God all things are possible."

"That's what Grandma Cooper says too."

Olivia went to check on the animals then walked from wagon to wagon once again. When she returned, Claudia and George were there to replace her and Jeremiah. She said goodnight and crawled under her wagon thinking about all the children with them – Jeremiah, barely ten, George and James only twelve, Bobby, seven and all the others. Would they all survive the long journey? Could she cope with losing one of the children? Or even one of the adults?

"O God, give me courage," she whispered, "and keep my charges safe."

7   Richmond

"How far do you suppose they've gone?" Kenny stared up at the square of light as if expecting a message to drop from the mouth of a pigeon flying by.

"It's only been a little over a week," said George. "They can't have gotten very far yet."

"If they've had as much nice weather as we've had in Richmond," said Robert, "They've covered at least 70 or 80 miles."

Will pulled two folded pieces of paper from his pocket. The rest gathered around him as the opened the first – a calendar.

"It's been about ten days since they left," he said. "They left on the March 20 and today is March 29. If they travel eight miles a day, you're right. That's about eighty miles."

"Olivia will push them," said Kenny.

"But the mules will need to rest somewhere along the way," said John. "If not, they'll give out on her."

"Jefferson has taught the children much about animals and their care," said Will. "Olivia grew up on the plantation. She'll learn to pace them."

"How far are they going?

"About four hundred miles."

"Then they're almost a quarter of the way," said Robert with a note of cheer.

"Do you suppose Parker will be harassing us today? I'm getting a little tired of his daily questioning and pushing us to join the *Volunteers*." Kenny rammed his hands in his pockets and paced around the small room.

"Yeah," said John, "always the same ploy: 'Don't you want out of there? Wouldn't you rather be outside in the sunshine? All you have to do is sign up with the *Volunteers* and convince your pal Brunner to join.'"

"And always we say, 'Thanks, but no thanks.'"

"I doubt they'll be around today," said Will. "They seem to take the weekends off."

Lost in thought, the friends fell into silence – silence except for the outside intrusion of men yelling, hums from boats on the river and horses clopping down distant streets.

Quietly Joe lifted his head and asked, "Is there any chance we will ever see them again – in this life, I mean?"

They all looked to Will for an answer – hungry for a taste of hope.

Will closed his eyes, brushed his hands across them, wishing with all his heart he could tell them what they wanted to know. They waited. Finally, he sighed deeply and held out his hands as if inviting them to the communion table. "I wish I could say, 'yes we'll soon be out of here,' but the reality is that I just don't know. All of life's obstacles are stacked against us. If I were a faithless man, I would say we have no chance. But, I believe, that God can and does still work miracles.

"But will He?"

"I'm not God. I don't know. It just might be we are needed here more than there as far as God's plans go."

"Then, it sounds like all we can do is pray to be where God wants us to be and ask for courage to live or die for Him."

"That's about it George," said Will.

"And pray for our women who must be as concerned as we are. I can't imagine them crossing the wilderness."

Joe suddenly laughed. "I can barely imagine Jeannette crossing a Richmond Street alone."

"Their job is to get the children to safety," said John. "Ours is to uphold them in prayer."

"Then I suggest we get to our work," said Will.

8　*Sabbath's Rest*

Unseasonably warm and dry days of early spring crept along much like the slow-moving disjointed caterpillar-like wagon train. With each turn of the wagon wheels and clopping of the mules' steady hooves, miles accumulated slowly but not nearly as quickly as Olivia would have preferred. Only ten days – eighty miles – less than one quarter of the way.

Wearily Olivia rolled her head to loosen her neck muscles. Michael and Betsy dragged themselves along beside the wagon listening for Lucy or Charles. Even the babies seemed too tired to cry. Behind them, Olivia heard Sarah screeching and other children whining, crying and complaining. Mothers, too tired to yell, ignored them.

"Mom," James glanced at Olivia. She didn't answer, but turned toward him, so he continued. "You look more tired than you should," he said as if reading her mind. "The others are getting weary, too – especially Grandma Cooper."

"It's a long trip, James. You didn't expect it to be any different, did you? Rain will come soon enough making travel more difficult."

"I know, but it's been a week and a half since we left Richmond. If we're going to make it to The Valley, we're going to have to rest once in a while – I mean *really* rest. Even God rested after six days."

"James William Brunner, are you preaching to me?" Olivia tried to sound stern, but she knew he was right. Routines had become so predictable that it seemed even the babies cried on schedule and complaints were heard so often that the complainer had only to speak the first words and the rest joined with the ending. A smile slipped across her lips in spite of her weariness.

"Yes ma'am. I guess I am." He grinned.

"You're probably right, James. Even the mules look tired. The weather's been so perfect I hate to take time off our travel. Who knows when the rains will come?"

"That's all the more reason to rest," said James. "We're bound to run into more emergencies and hard times. If we don't renew our strength, how can we fly like eagles?"

"James, I think you are confusing your Scriptures, but you're right." Olivia paused, lost in thought for a few minutes. She checked her map and said, "There should be a nice mountain stream at our next stop. Tomorrow is Saturday – a good day to take a break – do some laundry and maybe bake some bread."

"How do you expect to bake bread?" James cocked his head and gave her a curious glance.

Suddenly the world looked brighter – as if the sun had pulled a depressing fog away. Feeling a rush of excitement, she said, "You and George are a good team. You'll figure out how to put together some kind of an oven for us."

James threw back his head and laughed. The gloomy sky lost its haze. Hope pushed fear aside once more. Olivia's heart lurched at the sound. She hadn't heard that joyful sound from her son – or any of the children – for many days. *They are still children – not adults. They need time, if only a few hours, to just be children.*

Max and Jasper plodded along and as they rounded a curve in the road, Olivia caught her breath at the beauty of the clearing. She couldn't have anticipated such a field of emerald surrounded on three sides by trees popping out with green leaves and pink and white blossoms.

"It's beautiful," she whispered. James nodded.

A fragrance of spring filled the air – pine trees, blossoms on wild cherry and apple trees. Along one side of the field, a spring-fed stream snaked its way in and out of the woods and on to wherever it cared to meander. The distant mountains looked like tiny, lacy scallops against the sky. The James River bubbled along on the other side of the road, carrying their whispered hopes and dreams back to Richmond – back to loved ones left behind. *This will be a perfect place to rest and be refreshed.*

When the evening stew was ready to serve, the women shuffled to the fire outside the cook tent. Lack of enthusiasm, drooped shoulders, heads so low chins rested almost on chests gave the air of a funeral procession stopping for a brief rest before proceeding to the final resting place. Too tired to even grumble and complain, each one waited for word from the cook that supper was ready. Even the savory stew smelled bland and unappetizing.

Olivia lifted her hands to get the attention of lethargic and grim adults and docile children who looked much too old for children. All sat closed-mouth, chins in cupped hands waiting because there was nothing else to do – and no energy to do it if there was. Suddenly, Olivia felt a tingle of fear. If Parker's men – or anyone else – attacked them in this state of apathy, would they even be able to defend themselves? James was right. Pushing on was important, but so was rest.

"Before offering our prayer of thanksgiving," she said, "I have been given a suggestion that needs the vote of the entire group."

Tired, weary eyes popped open, wide with wariness. Backs stiffened and a collective sigh rippled around the campfire. "Now what torture do you have in mind for us?" Jeannette spoke, but Claudia and Corinne nodded in approval.

Olivia smiled. "Actually it was James' suggestion. He thinks we need a Sabbath's rest."

"Rest?" Claudia tested the word as if it were a foreign language.

"Yes. Our bodies need renewed. The animals need a day to…"

"A day? You mean…stay in one place? For a whole day?" Corinne, afraid she hadn't heard correctly, tried to hide her excitement.

"Yes," said Olivia, "if we all agree, we'll rest tomorrow and leave after we worship Sunday morning."

A few seconds passed as the intent of her words sank into dull, travel-numbed minds. A tentative clap from one of the children brought more claps until the entire circle erupted into applause. Olivia quieted them then prayed for the food and for the rest they all needed.

As if struck by an electric current, life sparked the weary travelers. Excited chatter accompanied the stew, which all of a sudden smelled spicy and mouth-watering good. Claudia and Corinne's habitual complaints carried above the chatter, "'Bout time we stopped…thinks we're pack animals… only women…"

The meal finished, Olivia smiled as she sat outside her wagon. Everything was back to normal. The babies were asleep. Betsy was with her friend, Martha. The boys sat around the campfire exchanging stories and jokes. The women sang, laughed, chattered – and complained.

Olivia sighed deeply, enjoying her solitude and the sound of laughter. *Who would've thought two weeks ago that I would be sitting at the edge of a camp of wagons? When I promised Will I would take our children to The Valley, I had no concept of the hard work, loneliness and complaining we all would endure.*

Suddenly, she heard something behind her and turned to see what it was. Before she could focus on the dark shadow, something hit her head. She felt herself slipping into a soundless darkness.

9   Kidnappers Return

The sound of many marching drums brought Olivia out of the darkness. Drums? Indians? She shook her head to clear her thinking and immediately remembered there were no Indians. The pounding, pulsating pain was in her head. *Where am I? How long have I been unconscious?*

Slowly she opened her eyes, but was unable to move her arms and legs. Ropes cut into her wrists behind her back and into her ankles. Olivia struggled against the rising panic and concentrated on her surroundings. She listened for something that would give her an indication of people, activities or location. A gentle up and down movement accompanied the sound of water slapping against the sides of whatever she was in – presumably a boat of some kind. *Am I dreaming or are we moving?*

Her eyes became accustomed to the darkness. *Looks like a square room. I'm on a narrow bed or cot. At least my mouth is free and I can breathe. No point in calling for help. They – whoever they are – would have used a gag if there was any chance of anyone hearing me call out. Footsteps above – two different sounds. So, I must be in the Captain's cabin, but why?*

The cabin door flew open and slammed against the wall. Footsteps, accompanied by a bouncing light of a lantern, descended the stairs. Olivia closed her eyes and lay motionless, forcing her breathing to be slow and even. Body odor, so strong she could hardly breathe, filled the stale, muggy air around her. Even with her eyes closed, she knew the man had moved closer and held a lantern over her. It took all her will power to keep her eyes closed.

The man laughed, sounding more like a growl than cheerful laughter. He called to the other person on topside. "She ain't awake yet, but she ain't goin' no place. Won't do her no good to yell. No one will hear her out here. We should be a mile downriver by now."

"You shouldn't a hit her so hard. Sergeant won't like it if you killed her." The second voice grew louder and stronger. The second man apparently joined the first one in the small room.

"She ain't dead. She was breathing when I put her…" The growling voice suddenly stopped yelling. "Hey, who's running this boat?"

"Don't be stupid," said the second man. "We can't run at night. Hard to tell what we'd run into. We took a chance going this far. Come morning we'll head on back to Richmond."

"Oh. How much we gettin' for this one?"

"Plenty."

"Why do they want a woman anyway?"

"I don't ask questions. I just do as I'm told and collect my fee. Sergeant wasn't too happy we let the kids slip away from us. We gotta make sure she don't run."

"She ain't goin' no place." The obnoxious-smelling man laughed again.

Olivia's heart beat so fast she was sure they would hear it if the smelly one ever quit laughing and yelling. Her mind raced in step with her heart. *There are only two. No more footsteps above. These must be the men who tried to take Corey and James last October? But why? Who wanted them – or me – except…? Sergeant? Surely, Matthew wouldn't… Yes, he would.*

O Lord help me. I can't leave my children out here in the wilderness alone.

Olivia opened her eyes a thin slit to see what was happening. The little man, who joined the first one, took the lantern and hung it on a hook over a small square table. Pulling a deck of cards from his pocket, he sat at the table and started shuffling them. The big man sat opposite him, his back to Olivia. While they played, from the darkness of her corner, Olivia took note of her surroundings. *I'm on a lower bunk in what I assume is the captain's quarters. I've never been on a boat before, so I'm not sure what things are called.*

Something jabbed her hip every time she moved even a tiny bit, so she tried to ease away from it while not seeming to move. A sharp prick on her hand sent a pain up her arm. In a moment of panic, she pictured a cottonmouth with its fangs in her hand.

She held back the scream that rose in her throat and forced her breath to stay slow and even. *I can't let fear take over now. Snakes aren't hard and I would've felt its movement. It's too early for them to be out – especially at night. My fingers feel wet. Blood? A knife! Maybe I can cut the ropes.*

"Hey, you cheated!" The big hairy man yelled and threw the cards on the table.

"What you gonna to do about it?" The little man with the scarred face laughed a wicked, evil laugh.

"I'll kill you," yelled the big hairy man, "that's what I'll do about it." He jumped up and slapped his hip as if reaching for a weapon. "Hey, where's my knife? You stole it!"

The little man laughed again. "You probably lost it when you grabbed the woman. You had it with you, didn't you?"

"Yeah, I guess." He didn't sound sure. He dropped back onto the chair, picked up his cards and said, "Play cards and don't cheat again."

Olivia slowly exhaled the breath she had been holding while they argued. *Could that be his knife under me?* The men resumed their game. With slow easy movement, she managed to get in a position for the knife blade to rest on the ropes. She bit her lip and winced each time the sharp blade made contact with her fingers and hand. Finally, the rope gave way at the same instant she heard a thump on the deck above her. The men looked upward.

"What was that?"

"Probably a raccoon. We had one the other night. Remember? You were so scared you wet your pants." The little man cackled and the hairy man pounded his fist on the table, scattering the cards and coins.

"Don't you make fun of me," he roared. "I'll throw you overboard and take the woman back myself and collect all the money."

"Sure you will. Who you goin' to take her to?"

"I'll take her to that sergeant fellow. If he ain't the one what wants her, he knows who does. I seen you talkin' to him."

"You think you're so smart. Well, I'll tell you…"

Before he could tell him what he thought, the door to the cabin flew open again. Both men jumped up knocking over their chairs and table.

"Somebody's up there."

"Oh, it's just the wind."

"Ain't no wind blowin'."

While they argued about what to do, Olivia quickly cut the ropes around her ankles; not at all sure, she could take on two men – especially when one was as big and strong as a bear.

The little man started up the steps with his knife drawn. He fell backward onto the hairy one, who grabbed the knife, kicked his unconscious friend aside and took two steps up. He, too, fell backward with James on top of him. Corey followed. Both boys tried to hold him down, but he roared and flung Corey off as if he were a yapping pup.

James tried to hold on but the man slammed him against the wall and raised his knife.

Olivia jumped from the bed, holding the bloody knife. She rammed it into the man's hairy hand. He bellowed and let go of James and the knife. He lunged at Olivia with his bare hands open ready to close around her neck.

Tillie flew through the door, landed on him, knocking him to the floor. Corey hit him over the head with a chair. He tried to get up and James hit him with the other chair. Finally, he slithered unconscious on top of his colleague.

Corey ran into Olivia's open arms while James reached out a hand to Tillie. "Mom, you're bleeding." James reached for her hands.

"Just a few minor cuts getting the rope cut behind my back. The big guy thought he lost his knife on shore, but it was on the bed under me."

"What'll we do with these two?" Tillie stood straddling the unconscious bodies, dripping water on them.

"They'll recover," said Olivia. "Leave them there, pull up the anchor and let them drift down river until they either wake up or hit an obstacle."

"You sure you want to let them go?" Tillie asked.

"This is their second failed attempt to get what Matthew Parker wants. I don't think they'll be too anxious to go back to Richmond."

"Parker?"

"They didn't name him, but said a sergeant in Richmond. How many sergeants in Richmond do we know who would go to this much trouble to get what he wants? Let's get out of here and back to camp. We can fill each other in on the way."

James and Tillie hauled in the anchor then they all jumped overboard and headed for shore where they turned and watched the boat drift downstream, carried by the current.

When they arrived back at camp, Olivia told her side of the story while Maggie took care of her cuts. Then James, Corey and Tillie told how Blackie took off barking and growling. They saw the man carrying Olivia to the boat. Blackie tried to stop him, but the man kicked the little dog out of the way and continued to run. They saw him jump onto the boat. It was already moving downstream when they got to the river's edge. They ran along the road until the kidnappers dropped anchor then the three of them swam to the boat.

"How did you know they would drop anchor? What if they'd just kept going?" Corrine asked.

"Because those are the same two men who tried to kidnap Corey last fall," said James. "They told him they were anchored because they couldn't travel at night."

"Well, I don't know about the rest of you, but I've had quite enough excitement for one day," said Tillie. "I'm glad we're resting tomorrow."

"I agree," said Olivia, "and thanks for the rescue. I don't think I could have handled those two alone."

"Sure you could, Mom," said James, "but we wanted in on the fun."

"Yeah," said Corey. "Besides, we told you we wouldn't let nothing happen to you."

"Yes, you did, didn't you? Well, as I said before, we're all in this together. We need each other. Now, I'm with Tillie. I'm ready for some rest."

But, tired as she was, the sky was turning its soft morning gray before Olivia could finally close her eyes.

Will we ever be safe? Will must be alive yet or Parker wouldn't be still trying to get me back to make him change his mind.

10 The Storm

Weeks earlier, the Blue Ridge Mountains had appeared as tiny scallops against the clear blue sky. Now they loomed like green-haired giants filling the space beyond the valley. Each day pushed Richmond deeper into memory and pulled The Valley nearer to reality. Another week and a half slipped by since their Sabbath rest. Still the warm, dry weather held, giving the women a false sense of security. Today, however, was unseasonably hot and sticky, pressing everyone into tense, edginess.

Pushing hair from her sweaty face as she drove the mules, Olivia listened for any sound of trouble. Skinned knees, stubbed toes, snakebites, bee stings – anything could happen. With constant vigil, she watched the river. Parker had tried once he would not hesitate to try again. But Olivia was not only concerned about intruders, but also the water level. They'd had no rain since they left Richmond three weeks earlier, but with the unpredictability of southern spring, heavy rains in the mountains that they never saw could send floodwaters to the river.

As if thinking about rain magically induced it, the sky began to turn from a few white clouds to dark, rolling storm clouds. It was so gradual that the women hardly realized the change. A breeze caressed her face and Olivia glanced skyward. With a sigh of resignation, she noticed that the clear, sunny morning had become a cloudy, muggy afternoon.

A storm is brewing. Maybe we can get a couple more hours before it hits. As if giant fingers upended an inkbottle, clouds suddenly loomed black. Moving air massaged her sweaty, sunburned face with cool fingers momentarily then suddenly pulled away to nothing. *The calm before the storm? Is that thunder in the distance? Hard to tell above the rattle of the wagons and squawking of the wheels. Better start looking for a place to stop.*

***

James trotting alongside the wagons on Beauty, stopped to chat with Jeannette. The cool breeze whipped her hair out of her face. "That felt good," she said. "Even the movement of the wagon hasn't given much breeze today. I feel like my clothes are glued to me."

"Good weather for a storm," said James. "I hope the rain holds off until we can stop for the night."

"Rain?" Jeannette's fearful attitude had become almost a joke among the rest. Everything terrified her.

"Yeah, you know, rain – those tiny little drops of water that fall from the sky." James grinned and she laughed – something she seldom did.

"I know what rain is, James," she said. "I was just surprised. We haven't had any since we left Richmond. I thought your mother ordered dry weather for the whole trip."

James, surprised at Jeannette's attempt at humor, laughed with her then stopped to wait for the next wagon to catch up to him. The calm suddenly abandoned them. Wind became wild and gusty and had a chill to it. Lightning shot back and forth among the clouds in the eastern sky behind them as if giving orders to an army of lumbering black soldiers. A distant rumble answered. *Better check with Mom.* James turned and galloped back to Olivia.

***

"Mom, it looks awfully black behind us." Lightning flashed across the sky. Thunder rumbled over the mountains from the east. "Want me to ride ahead to find a place to stop?"

Olivia's brow creased. *If we stop for the rain, it might be several days, or even a week, before we can move again.* She sighed and nodded to James. "We have no choice," she said.

Zeus reared as Tillie stopped beside them. "Why don't I go with him? We can begin to clear a path if necessary and gather fire wood before it gets wet."

"Thanks, Tillie. That's a good idea."

Olivia waved a green flag to the wagons behind her – a signal to pick up the speed. Children who were not already in a wagon jumped in whatever one was closest. They all could see and feel the approaching storm. She heard Michael and Betsy scramble into the back of their wagon.

"I'll wait and help Mrs. Phillips," yelled Corey.

The marching clouds picked up speed and surrounded the wagons. As if someone had pulled a giant shade over the sun, a gray, twilight-like haze covered the land. Clouds churned and tumbled. Thunder rumbled across the sky, bumped into mountaintops and fell grumbling into the distant valleys. Lightning poked and prodded the clouds as a

216

captain pushes his troops to battle. Dropping temperature raised goose bumps on hot, clammy skin.

"Betsy, cover the babies, so they don't get cold," Olivia shouted.

"I did, Mom," Betsy answered. "Michael helped me."

Assuming the children were in a wagon, Olivia snapped the reins sending the mules into a gallop adding more dust to the swirling wind. *I hope James and Tillie find a place out of the range of a flash flood.*

Clouds tramped over and around the dark skies. Screams from wagons behind her blended with howling wind through the wagons. Speed and uneven roads rocked the wagons from side to side like her grandmother's rocker.

O Lord, please keep the wagons from turning over into the river, Olivia prayed as she snapped the reins again and called to the mules, "Come on Max and Jasper. Move it. Get this wagon rolling before that storm hits full force and puts us in the river."

Fat drops of rain began to dot the road, splattering the dust like an egg dropped in a bowl of flour for noodles. Nothing so good would come of this splattering. Smell of rain filled the air.

As if the mules understood and wanted to please Olivia, Max and Jasper, ears back, eyes wide, pulled and galloped with all their strength, slowing only for a curve in the road. Behind the wagon, Nellie bellowed, competing with the thunder and shrieks of children.

At last, she saw him. James waited in the middle of the road and pointed to the clearing. She pulled on the reins. "Whoa there boys. Slow it down, now. Looks like we found a place for the night."

Tillie had a small fire burning in the center of the clearing, but had to fight to keep it burning. Flames leaped and licked at nearby trees as if they were hungry animals locked in a cage of stones. Wind pulled the flames this way and that as if trying to free them, but Tillie fought back, keeping the angry flames within their prison.

Olivia chanced a glance at the river across the road drifting along several feet below the bank before she turned into the clearing. *Unless we're stuck here with several days of hard rain, there should be no danger of flood. Trees and shrubs will give us some protection from wind and driving rain. We'll be safe enough while the storm passes.*

As if released like a herd of frightened cattle, the dark clouds rushed at them, retreated and rushed again – a warning of what was to come. After three dry weeks of relatively good traveling, would they lose their wagons and animals to a storm now? *No time to worry, not that it would do any good.*

"Tie down anything that's loose," shouted Olivia above the

roaring wind. "Get the cook tent over the fire or we won't cook anything tonight"

***

"Come on Corey," called James. "We'll help the women with the tent then tend to the animals."

"Okay."

"Michael, you and the others gather some more wood before it gets soaked."

"Okay," called Michacl.

When the tent was secure, James called to Olivia, "We'll corral the animals now and stay with them until the worst of the storm is over."

"All right. Watch for falling limbs." Olivia called to the retreating boys.

James, George, Tom and Corey unhitched the mules from all the wagons and led them to a copse of trees. Blackie yapped at their heels as if urging them to hurry. Wrapping ropes from tree to tree, the boys formed a corral keeping the mules close together.

Corey pulled a bellowing Nellie. He was almost to the corral, when a loud crash of thunder frightened the cow. She bolted pulling the rope from Corey's hands. He grabbed for it.

"It's all right, Nellie. I've got you. We'll go with the mules…"

Eyes wide with fright, Nellie balked. Another crash of thunder caused her to kick at Corey and jerk the rope from his hands again. Then she ran.

"Nellie, come back! Nellie. Nellie." Cory's cries were lost in the booming thunder. James came to his side to help. "She broke loose and ran away," cried Corey.

"It'll be all right, Corey. We'll look for her when the storm lets up some. She can't have gone far."

"Yeah, we need to keep the mules safe. We can't travel without them."

James put an arm around Cory's shoulder and pulled him into the corral where the four boys tried to keep the mules calm.

11   Duel Disasters

Thunder rolled and roared – sounding like a troop of frightened soldiers running across the wagon tops in search of the enemy. Lightning flashed. Eerie shadows shot in and through the wagons and surrounding woods. Wind rocked the wagons and tossed leaves and twigs around as if it were autumn, not spring.

Olivia glanced at the cook tent, puffing out like a giant balloon. *Tillie and Maggie will fight hard to keep the fire contained within its boundaries. For now, I'll have to find refuge in the wagon with Betsy and the babies. The other women will have to do the same.*

Olivia, Betsy and the babies sat crushed together in the small cleared space at the back of their wagon. While Olivia nursed the babies, wind whistled around them and rain pelted the wagons. Air quickly became stuffy and humid. The smell of body odor, wet clothes and fear permeated the air.

"I don't like this," said Betsy, holding Charles close to her while her mother nursed Lucy. "What if the wagon turns over?"

"I don't like it either, Betsy," said Olivia. "I don't think the wagon will tip over. We have a lot of weight in it."

"Olivia…" The frightened voice came from outside.

"Is that Mrs. Phillips? Maybe her wagon…"

"Hold Lucy and Charles. I'll see what's wrong."

Olivia unfastened the end flap and opened the canvas cover. Jeannette held a screeching, screaming Sarah. Tears ran down their faces mingling with the rain. Joey clung to his mother's wet skirt.

"Scoot back as far as you can so they can get in out of the rain – not that it will do much good. We're all soaked anyway." Olivia moved a couple of items and made room.

Jeannette handed Sarah and Joey up to Olivia, then climbed in herself. Sarah screamed with every exhaled breath setting both babies to crying.

"Jeannette, what's wrong? Is someone hurt?"

Tears still trickled down Jeannette's face, but she finally managed to shake her head at Olivia's question. Olivia wanted to slap her to get her attention and stop Sarah's screaming. She gritted her teeth and waited, while she and Betsy tried to calm the babies.

Jeannette held Sarah close and the screaming ceased. Olivia spoke above the steady stream of rain that pelted the wagon. Thunder roared overhead as if releasing the fury of all the weeks of storms held at bay. "Now, tell me what's wrong. Is someone hurt?"

Although she asked, Olivia had the feeling it was only another of Jeannette's fears. No one was hurt. No one was in danger. She was simply afraid of the storm.

"I'm scared," whimpered Jeannette. "I hate storms."

Olivia spoke through clenched teeth. "Jeannette, this is certainly a bad storm. I understand you are afraid, but you are simply going to have to learn to control your fears. I can't have the entire camp in a panic every time we get a little storm."

"If you don't want me here, I'll leave," sniffed Jeannette. "I'll go back to my wagon."

Before she could move, however, lightning flashed so brightly that for a brief second Olivia could see the fear etched on Jeannette's face. Almost simultaneously thunder boomed as if applauding the lightning for making a direct hit. Jeannette screamed. Sarah screamed. The babies cried. Olivia gave in to her desire to slap the woman. The screaming stopped. The crying stopped.

"Now," said Olivia, clenching her stinging hand into a fist at her side, "you will conduct yourself like a woman – a mother of two children. You are not ten years old. You are almost thirty. This storm is nasty, but it might not be the worst we'll encounter. If you are to arrive in The Valley and wait for Joe, you'll have to grow up. Now, sit there while I finish nursing my babies. By then, maybe the worst of the storm will be over."

Olivia put Lucy back to her breast. Jeannette tried to shield Sarah and Joey so they wouldn't see. Olivia smiled to herself knowing that Jeannette also felt uncomfortable watching her. She kept her eyes averted as much as possible – looking anywhere except at Olivia.

Then Olivia took Charles. Jeannette's eyes widened, as if it were the first time she saw Olivia nursing the baby – and it probably was. She had made a point of not being near Olivia while she nursed them.

"Olivia, how can you let that…that…Negro…?"

"Jeannette, I have been nursing him for three weeks. What would you suggest that I do? Let him starve? He's only a week older than Lucy and needs nourishment. It really is none of your business." The women glared at one another. "I think the worst of the storm is over,"

Olivia said. "You can take the children to the tent and wait for supper if you don't want to go back to your wagon."

Silently, Jeannette climbed out of the wagon. Taking Sarah and Joey with her, she splashed across the circle to her wagon. She had hardly left when she was back.

"Olivia."

"Now what?" Olivia didn't bother to hide her irritation.

"That loud clap of thunder," Jeannette said. "The lightning hit a tree. It's on my wagon."

Unable to find her voice, Olivia stared back. Rain drummed steadily on canvas wagon tops. Wooden wagon tongues extended thirstily soaking up the falling water. Jeannette stood like a street waif from a Dickens novel and waited for Olivia to make everything all right. Rain dripped from her chin. A child clung to either side of her soaking skirt. Wind pulled at her hair, whipping it across her face.

Olivia shook her head and forced herself to respond. "There's not much we can do about it tonight. We'll have to wait for daylight to see what we're doing."

"But…"

"You and the children can sleep in the cook tent tonight. The worst of the storm has passed, but I'm sure there'll be more rain before morning."

"You won't leave us here when it's time to go, will you?" Jeannette's lips trembled.

"Jeannette, we're in this together. We'll get to The Valley together. No one will be left behind, unless we bury them."

Suddenly, Olivia thought of Grandma Cooper. How was she handling the storm? Surely, Maggie would've called her if there was trouble. She would check on her later.

Olivia watched Jeannette pull Sarah and Joey with her and splash her way to the tent. The flap opened, sending firelight leaping into the dark, outer edge, then it closed, swallowing the three soaked pilgrims and the brief spark of light. Olivia stared after her feeling an almost overwhelming desire to sit down and cry. Shaking herself free of such frivolous thoughts, she called to Michael, who answered her from Tillie's wagon.

"Jeannette has a tree on her wagon. Check the other wagons for trouble while we have a lull in the storm," she said.

Michael and Tillie's son, Tom, splattered around the circle and Olivia sat on the back of her wagon pondering her next move – see about Jeannette's wagon, check on supper, or get Nellie milked.

"Mom?" Olivia blinked. James and Corey stood before her, soaked and looking apprehensive. "We have a problem with the animals," said James. "Is everything all right here?"

Olivia's heart faltered then began to race. *If we lose any of the mules...*"How bad?"

"Only Nellie. She bolted and ran before we could get her in the corral. We tried to stop her, but thought we needed to stay with the mules until the storm was over. Corey and I will go look for her."

"You're right. We can't afford to lose the mules. We have a problem here, too, but we'll have to wait until morning to know how bad it is and what we can do about it. A tree fell on Jeannette's wagon."

"Anyone hurt?"

"No," Olivia couldn't keep back a sarcastic smile. "She and the children were in our wagon. They were afraid of the storm. I sent Michael to check for other problems. See if you can find Nellie. Stay together and don't go too far.

The boys each took a lantern and started toward the woods. James checked his gun and made sure it was loaded before he left.

Michael met Olivia and Betsy as they took the babies to the cook's tent. "No other problems that we can see," he said. A boom from the woods startled them.

"Was that a gunshot, or thunder?" asked Tom.

"Probably, thunder," said Olivia. *I hope.*

Minutes later Corey returned, tears streaming down his face.

"We...we need...help to butcher Ne...the cow," he sobbed. "She was in a ditch, both front legs broke."

Olivia wanted to hold him. He was only six. But he was trying to so hard to be brave. They all were.

"I'll go with you," said Tillie.

"And me," said Maggie grabbing another lantern.

Olivia sighed deeply. They would eat meat for a few days, but there would be no more milk for the children. The chickens were also gone. No more eggs.

Her eerie sixth sense prickled the back of her neck. Somehow, she knew their troubles up to now had been small in comparison to what lay ahead. Her thoughts wandered to that hole on Libby Street in Richmond. *Do they feel the storm, too?*

12   War Begins

Thunder crashed outside the prison bringing the men upright on their floor beds. Still dark, they couldn't see anything, but each knew the rest were awake.

"Was that a cannon?" Kenny whispered.

"Are we finally at war?" Joe added.

A brilliant light flashed for a few seconds, followed by another boom. A collective release of held breath spread across the room.

"Lightning and thunder," said John. "Could be just as disastrous for our women."

"If they've had the same weather we've had," said Robert, "they've been able to make the best time they could. This might slow them down, but it won't stop them."

"Jeannette is scared to death of storms." Joe didn't really expect an answer. He was just thinking aloud.

"I expect she'll get over a lot of her fears before they reach The Valley," said John. "Tillie and Olivia won't coddle her."

"They can't," said Joe. "I understand that. There's just too much at stake for one person to want – and get – all the attention. She won't like it, but you're right Tillie and Olivia will help her get over her fears."

"I expect the storm will make up for lost time. It's been unseasonably warm and dry and like you said they've been able to make good time. I just hope they don't hole up somewhere and wait for the sun to shine." Will paced as the spoke, so accustomed to the dark that he could avoid stepping on anyone.

"Olivia won't let them do that," said Robert. "And Grandma Cooper will stand with her."

***

After breakfast, they heard the guard – this one named Homer – descending the stairs. The last several days, Parker had been harassing them again. Who would he take today?

The key rattled in the keyhole, the door slowly opened enough for a man to walk through. "Brunner," called Homer. "Let's go. Parker wants to talk to you."

"Anything new?" asked Will as he started out the door.

"Don't know. None of my business. I just do as I'm told and I can go home nights. You could too if you would…"

Will interrupted. "If I would become a puppet for Parker. No thanks."

They walked up the steps with Homer holding a gun to Will's back. "I hear your women folks ran off and left you."

Will remained silent.

"Another man, I would bet."

Still Will said nothing. They were outside Libby and walking toward the courthouse. Rain fell fast and furious; thunder boomed; lightening flashed.

"Move along," said Homer. "You might not care about getting wet, but I do."

"He who follows Parker's orders, gets wet," said Will with a smile playing at the corner of his mouth. Homer pressed the gun harder against his back. "Shut up and move it," he said.

They reached the courthouse, but instead of going in the front door, Homer stopped him. "This way," he said, nodding toward the right alley. "We'll go in the back. Decent folks don't like to see prisoners."

"Parker is afraid one of us might tell them what's going on," said Will and was rewarded with another poke in the back by the barrel of Homer's gun.

They proceeded down the alley then turned left to the back door which opened into a short hallway. "In there," said Homer.

Will turned the knob of the door and walked into a bare room with a table and a straight-backed chair. The room was small and square with another door opposite the one they entered.

"Sit," barked Homer as if he were commanding his dog. Will ignored his tone of voice and sat down. Such as the old, wobbly chair was, Will felt a small sense of gratitude. He had not sat on a chair of any kind in weeks.

They heard heavy footsteps outside the other door. It flew open and Parker stood as tall as possible, trying to fill the doorway with a terrifying form. As far as Will was concerned, he was still a short, bald, loser. He said nothing, waiting for Parker to say the first word.

"Well, Brunner. You look a little wet. I wonder if the women are feeling the storm?"

"I'm surprised you care," said Will.

"They'll turn back, but it won't matter if they don't. I sent a new recruit to bring back their mules. They can't travel without them."

Will clenched his teeth and held his fists in his lap. He would not rise to the bait. He knew Olivia would never turn back – with or without the mules. She would walk the rest of the way if the recruit succeeded – which he seriously doubted he would.

"All you have to do to protect them is join our *Volunteers*. The war is getting closer each day. Do you think our soldiers will let them pass unharmed, and if they do, will the Federals let them go?"

Will sat staring at his hands, refusing to speak. Parker stepped closer and backhanded him.

"Look at me when I'm talking to you. I asked you a question, I expect an answer."

"I'm not one of your minions," said Will between clenched teeth. "I owe you nothing. But, I think you have seriously underestimated the courage and resourcefulness of those women. They will survive and get to where they are going with or without the animals and in spite of soldiers on the march."

Parker stared, the crimson red of hatred and anger creeping up his neck to his ears until his entire head looked like the sun rising on a cloudy day. "Get him out of here," he yelled at Homer. Then he turned back to Will. "This is the last time I will ask to speak to you or any of your pals. You can rot in that prison for all I care. If you change your mind, tell Private Mills. Maybe I'll grant you an audience, maybe not."

Before Will could stand, Parker turned and stalked through the door, slamming it behind him.

"You really ticked him off today," said Homer taking Will back to the prison.

"Because he knows I'm right," he said.

When he returned to the prison, Will told the others what Parker had said.

"Will he really take their mules?" asked Kenny.

"He sent a recruit," said Will.

"Just one?" said John. "Tillie could handle him all by herself." He laughed and the others joined him.

"I doubt Blackie will even let him get close to the mules and if he does, the women will take care of him. They are all intelligent enough to take on a trip like this. They won't let their guard down."

"What about the rain?"

"They'll get wet. Jefferson had those wagons made with the very best canvas he could find. Won't keep out all the water, but it'll help.

They won't let a little rain turn them back."

"Looks like we need to increase our prayers," said Joe.

***

Two days later the rain was still falling off and on. Pebbles alerted the men that someone was at the window.

"Yes?" Will stood close to the window and spoke softly.

David spoke from outside. "Master Will, Grandpa Noah sent me with the news in today's paper. Fort Sumter has been fired on. All across the south, they are saying this means war. Richmond is waiting to see what Lincoln will say or do."

"Thanks, David. If there is more news maybe you can get it to Samuel. He tries to come shortly after dark."

"Yes sir, Master Will."

David left and the men sat quietly in a circle on the prison floor.

"Fort Sumter. That's in South Carolina isn't it?" said Kenny.

"Yes, but it's the property of the federal government. When Lincoln became president he avoided threats of force, but promised to protect "the property and places" in the south that belonged to the federal government." John had studied history and kept up with events since the hanging of John Brown.

"Then it will depend on how Lincoln reacts to Charleston's attack as to what the nation will do," said Robert.

"That and the reaction of the south – and more importantly Virginia. We'll have to wait and see what Samuel tells us tonight."

Samuel didn't have much to add when he came later that night, except that there was revelry – which the men could hear – in the streets of Richmond. There was no doubt as to which direction their intentions lay.

13   Horse Thief

Two long, wet days crept by. Using saws, axes and any other tool available, the women and children cleared the tree from Jeannette's wagon. Olivia fretted. *When will we be able to move on? We don't dare wait for the rain to stop. Sometimes these spring rains last for weeks.*

A third day ended – another day of intermittent drizzle and downpours. It was impossible to stay dry. Olivia put the babies down for the night and looked forward to crawling under the wagon – wet or not – and disappearing in the blessed, darkness of sleep. It was still early, but weariness was taking its toll.

"Mrs. Brunner," Jeremiah called to her as he splashed across the puddles. "Grandma Cooper wants to see you if you have a minute."

"Is she ill, Jeremiah?" Olivia reached for Will's medical bag that she had learned to keep near at hand. The older woman hadn't exactly been joking earlier about Olivia doing a funeral. With all the rain and dampness it was hard to tell what was wrong with her.

"No ma'am." He gave her a toothless grin and added, "She said you was younger'n her and could come to her easier'n she could come to you."

Olivia laughed with relief. "All right Jeremiah. Corey, you and Michael stay with Betsy and the babies."

"Okay, Mom."

Olivia lifted up her skirt and followed Jeremiah. She stepped over scattered branches and around larger puddles then squished through the wet grass and weeds. The Cooper wagon was beyond Jeannette's. Grandma Cooper sat on a chair under a canopy Maggie and the boys set up for her. A lantern from the back of the wagon spread its light on the open Bible on her lap.

"You wanted to see me, Grandma Cooper?" Olivia squatted beside the chair and nodded to the Bible. "Can you read that in this light?"

Grandma Cooper laughed her soft cackle. "No, can't see it all that well in daylight, but it gives me comfort just laying here in my lap."

Olivia nodded. She understood.

"I just want to speak my mind on the running of this show," said Grandma Cooper.

Olivia smiled at her. "Oh?" She waited.

"We got spoiled with all those weeks of sunshine. I figured the rain might cause some to think we should sit here until the sun shines again. I think, come morning we ought to move on, rain or no rain. We got Jeannette all fixed up. No reason to sit when we could be moving."

"I couldn't agree more," said Olivia. "Are you well enough? Maggie was concerned about your cough earlier."

"Wet weather makes my bones hurt and probably the dampness makes me cough, but I can keep going until the good Lord sees fit to take me home."

"Thank you, Grandma Cooper," said Olivia as she gave the older woman a quick hug.

"For what?" She gave Olivia a curious look.

"Oh, just for being here and for helping me to make a decision."

Olivia returned to her wagon and sent Michael and Corey around to tell everyone they would be moving on come morning – rain or no rain. Then she waited for the aftermath. Sure enough, it wasn't long before Claudia splashed across the clearing toward her.

"Olivia, we can't move in the rain," she said.

"Why not?" Olivia turned to face her.

"We'll get wet. Some of the kids are coughing already."

"We are already wet and if the kids have a cold, staying here won't make them any better no more than moving on will make them any worse."

"What about Grandma Cooper? She can't travel in this kind of weather."

"I just talked to her. She's anxious to get moving. We move at daybreak, Claudia. No more discussion."

Olivia turned to check on the babies and felt Claudia's knife-like stare jabbing her back. She ignored it and soon heard Claudia stomping back to her wagon, splattering mud and complaining to everyone she met. A duet of complaints from Corinne and Jeannette joined her. Olivia ignored them all and prepared for travel come morning.

***

At last, everyone seemed settled. Corinne and Jeremiah were on first watch so Olivia crawled under the wagon and even on the hard, damp ground, was soon asleep. Heart pounding, she was suddenly jarred awake. Something was wrong. She glanced toward the tent where Claudia and George were on second watch. *They don't seem concerned. Maybe I was dreaming.*

She waited, eyes open, ears straining. Blackie, on his stomach, pulled himself between her and James and whined. He licked their faces. *Blackie! That's what woke me.*

"What is it, boy?" Olivia and James whispered together so softly she wondered if Blackie even heard. He licked her face again and started backing out from under the wagon. James, on his elbows, pulled himself out. Olivia touched her fingers to his lips to signal him not to make a sound. She clutched her shotgun and crawled out beside him.

Blackie started toward the corral, stopped and turned to look at James and Olivia.

"The corral," whispered James.

Olivia nodded and reached for Blackie's collar. Holding it tightly so she wouldn't lose him, they crept along the outer ring of the circle toward the corral. A low growl came from Blackie's throat when they were in sight of the roped-off area. A man had his hand on the corral rope.

Olivia let go of Blackie, stood and shouted, "What do you think you're doing?" Her voice sped through the forest, back to the campfire, sending forth a cry of alarm from Claudia.

Just as Olivia shouted, the clouds parted, allowing the moon to shed some light on the man who raised his arm and threw what looked like a long, silver dagger. The moonlight gave it an evil sparkle as it whizzed through the air.

"Down!" Olivia shouted. She hit the ground and felt James fall beside her. The knife whistled over their heads, landing in the tree behind them with a twang. Blackie lunged for the man's throat, knocking him to the ground. He held him motionless with bared teeth inches above the soft, white flesh of his neck.

James jumped to his feet and stood over the man with his gun. George and Claudia arrived with a lantern. "What's going on?"

"Let the man up, Blackie," Olivia said. "You make one false move mister and I'll let him have you for a midnight snack. We have four guns aimed at you. If you get away from the dog, we'll fill you full of holes. Now, get up slowly and keep your hands where we can see them. Move back to our fire where we can talk."

"Looks like we got us a would-be horse thief," James said to the other two.

"How did he get here? We didn't hear a thing." Claudia

229

stammered.

"Yeah, except for the crickets there wasn't any noise at all. Even they stopped chirping and everything was quiet."

James shook his head and gave them the look of a schoolteacher explaining to a dull student. "George, when crickets stop chirping that's a sure sign someone, or something, is close by."

"Really?"

"Really. Come on let's find out who this man is and why he's trying to steal our animals."

The man stumbled, pulled himself up and stumbled again, all the while keeping his eye on the little black dog that nipped at his ankles. When they reached the ring of stones that surrounded the campfire, Olivia nodded for him to sit on a stone near the fire.

"James, maybe you and George better take a lantern and check the ropes in case he managed to cut through any of them. Keep an eye out for any of his pals. Wake Tillie and tell her we need another gun out here."

"I'm here," said Tillie from behind her. "Who can sleep with all the commotion? What's going on?"

"Grab a lantern, George," said James. "Let's go."

"We caught him trying to steal our mules and horses," Olivia said to Tillie. She turned to the man before them. "Now, who are you and why were you trying to take our animals? Talk fast before I reward Blackie for his vigilance. It's been a while since he wrestled with a man."

"Don't let him hurt me," the man whimpered. "Name's Robert White...I...just joined the *Volunteers*...need..."

"*Volunteers*? Where?" Olivia asked, but was sure she knew the answer before the spoke again.

"Richmond, ma'am. With a war on our heels, we need mounts."

"Why ours – so far from Richmond? How did you even know we were here and had what you wanted?"

"Sergeant Parker told me. He said you were only women and it would be easy. He said he'd make me a corporal...if'n I brung back all your horses and mules."

"How many are with you ?"

"None. Sergeant Parker thought I could ride faster alone. I'm a really fast rider. That's why he wanted me in the *Volunteers*."

"We've been on the road more than three weeks. You been following us all that time?" Olivia stared at the man.

"No, ma'am. Not all that time. The sergeant sent me out about a week ago. He knew you was following the river. I just caught up to you 'bout an hour ago. Saw your campfire and thought I could get the animals and be gone afore you woke to stop me."

"You saw the campfire. Didn't you know we'd have guards?"

"Just thought you didn't know that much...Parker said..."

"Yeah, we know," said Claudia. "We're *only* women."

"You're stupid, you know that," said Tillie. "Anyone knows better than to leave a fire, or animals, unattended."

"But you *are* just women. How was I to know...?"

"That we were smart enough to take proper precautions to keep us safe?"

The man hung his head too scared to even look embarrassed. Olivia shook her head in disgust.

"What are we going to do with him?" Claudia asked.

"Out west they string up horse thieves," said Tillie without a hint of a smile.

The man whimpered and cringed. Blackie yapped as if agreeing with her.

"We can't have murder on our hands," said Olivia, "but it's tempting. Tie him up for now. We'll have a meeting before breakfast and decide."

James returned alone to report the damage. "George stayed with the mules. He'd – he nodded toward the thief – just started to cut through the rope. George and I will keep watch at the corral the rest of the night. It's almost dawn anyway."

"Good idea," answered Olivia. "He says he's alone, but he might be lying. I'll keep Claudia company."

"I'll put on some fresh coffee and haul water for breakfast," said Tillie. "It's my turn to cook anyway."

Morning dawned with more gray clouds hanging low. A misty drizzle surrounded the camp but at least there was no wind. One by one, the others arrived at the campfire and were startled at the sight of a stranger sitting there – a man yet!

"Who's that and why's he all tied up like that?"

"Wait until everyone is here," said Olivia, "then we'll explain."

When all were around the fire, Olivia offered the morning prayer. While Tillie dished up the oatmeal, Olivia told the others about finding the man trying to steal their mules and horses.

"Give him some breakfast while we decide what we should do with him," said Olivia.

"I say we shoot him," said Claudia.

"We could tie him to a tree and leave him," said Corinne.

"We can't take him with us and I won't condone killing him. We'll have to send him back to Richmond." Olivia frowned.

"What if he goes to Parker?"

"Oh, he'll have to go back to him," said Olivia. "He's in the *Volunteers*. If he doesn't go back, he'll be AWOL. But, he'll go empty handed and my guess is he'll wish we'd let Blackie have him by the time Parker finishes with him. Get his horse, James."

James found the man's horse where he left it a half mile back. "Tie his hands in front of him loose enough he can eventually get free," said Olivia. "Put him on his horse and give him the reins. He has a long ride ahead of him and we don't want him to die in the saddle. Put his gun in its holster."

"What if Parker sends more soldiers?"

"I've given it some thought," said Olivia. "It took this one about a week of hard riding to reach us. It'll take him longer to get back to Richmond, especially if he gets smart and takes his time, or heads north away from Parker. So even if he goes back, and Parker sends more men, we should have another three weeks to get more distance between Richmond and us. We're already close to half way. Maybe by then we'll be too far for it to be profitable for them."

"I hope you're right, Olivia," said Tillie. "We haven't much control over whatever Parker decides to do. We'll just have to be more diligent and move on."

James grinned as he led Private White to the road. "Tell the sergeant, better luck next time. But, if there is a next time, the thief won't get off so easy." He slapped the horse's rump and watched it gallop down the road with White holding on for dear life.

14   Lost River

Patiently Max and Jasper waited in front of the wagon, hitched and ready to move out on another wet, rainy day. James rubbed the nose of each mule, speaking softly to them, telling them what good mules they were.

Olivia smiled as she heard his words of encouragement. *Even the mules work better if they are appreciated.*

James turned. Echoing her thoughts, he said, "They like to have a little praise now and then."

Olivia nodded and patted the soft velvet noses.

"Do you want to drive first?" asked James.

"I'll walk. I've been thinking about it. The road is getting softer and muddier in places. We need to lighten the wagons as much as possible. Right now, all we can do is remove people. If we really get stuck, we might have to leave some things behind."

Corey, Michael and Betsy joined them. "What about Lucy and Charles?" asked Betsy. "Do you want Michael and me to carry them?"

"We might need you to help push. We'll leave them in the wagon and you can stay close by in case they try to get up."

"Okay."

"It looks like the rain is making up for lost time," said Corey.

"Yeah," said Michael. "I guess Mr. Rain Cloud wants as much time as Mr. Sun had."

The twins punched each other and giggled at Michael's joke.

"Well, I sure hope not," said Olivia, "but you might be right, so we better get moving. We won't get far in the mud. Corey, you and Michael go tell the rest we want everyone walking."

"They won't like that," said James.

"It can't be helped," said Olivia. "Let's move."

A new sound was added to the already creaking and groaning of the wagons and the grumbling of the women and children – squish plop as they stepped in mud and lifted their feet for the next step.

Michael and Corey began to sing. "Squish, plop; squish, plop; wagons keep moving; please don't stop."

The rest of the children giggled then picked up the tune and rhythm. Olivia and James smiled.

"Someone's going to yell at them to stop," he said.

"Then we'll sing with them," said Olivia and started singing the silly little tune with the children, who laughed and sang louder. No one dared tell Olivia to stop.

The road curved inland, becoming rougher and less muddy – at least for a while. This made it possible to move a little more easily, but now they had to watch for large stones that could cripple a mule or break a wagon axle. But the greatest problem was that the river no longer bubbled along in view.

"Looks like more mud up ahead," said James.

"Get ready to push and pull," said Olivia to the children behind her."

Tillie rode up and saw the problem. "I'll tell the others to leave their wagons and come help you over this bad area."

"Corey and Michael, you pull Max and Jasper. We'll push from the back."

The rest of the women and children helped push until Olivia's wagon was out of the immediate danger of sinking into the boggy mire in the road. When her wagon was on dry land with room for the other wagons behind it, they all went back and repeated the process with the second, then third until all wagons were clear. By the time they had finished, the sun was already dropping behind the distant mountains.

Tillie swiped her hands across her face leaving as much mud on her face as she had wiped off. "Are we near our stopping place?" she asked. "Or do you want me to find one?"

"I think we're only about halfway to our next stop. Better find something. Take James with you."

***

The cook tent meant to hold only a few persons, somehow expanded so they could all gather around the struggling fire. The rain had stopped for the time being but everything was wet and soggy.

Michael, Tom, Corey and Jeremiah stumbled into the tent loaded with fairly dry sticks and small branches.

"Where did you find that?" Maggie grabbed for it and eased some under the cooking pot.

"There was a cave…," said Michael.

"And a cliff that stuck out over it," finished Corey.

"We thought we might sleep there tonight," said Jeremiah.

"It's not far," said Tom.

"We'll see after supper," said Olivia.

The meal was eaten with a minimum of grumbling. At least the dry branches the boys found created enough heat to thoroughly cook the stew. The boys sat together giggling and talking about the cave. The girls laughed and played with Charles and Lucy.

Claudia, Corinne and Jeannette sat to one side grumbling among themselves. Olivia glanced at the three malcontents and braced herself knowing she was in for another onslaught from the irrate trio.

"Olivia, are you sure we're on the right track?" Claudia asked.

"We can't see the river anymore," said Corrine.

"I thought we would follow the river the whole way," said Jeannette.

Olivia sighed and reached into her pocket for the map. She spread it on her lap and showed the women where they were, where the river was and where they were going.

"I don't understand." Jeanette whined.

"It's quite simple," said Tillie. "We follow the road. If the road runs beside the river, we see the river. If the road moves away from the river, we don't see it."

"Well, I feel better when we see the river," said Claudia. "I just hope we aren't lost."

Olivia, tired of the grumbling and complaining, picked up the babies, said goodnight, told Betsy she could stay a while longer then left the tent. The temptation to strike back – verbally, if not physically – was becoming too great.

"Let me carry Charles," said James following her out.

Back at the wagon, James sat beside his mother on a damp log while she fed the babies in preparation for bedtime. He'd seemed lost in his thoughts. Suddenly he chuckled.

"Want to share your joke, James?" Olivia tried to keep the bitterness from her voice. *It's not his fault we are all so weary. Every muscle in my body aches from pushing and pulling wagons through mud and up hills. My clothes cling to my sticky, sweaty body and I know the others are just as miserable. What can James possibly see as funny about the situation? I certainly don't see anything to laugh about.*

The look on her son's face was far too mature for his age and his words weren't those of a child. "Things are hard right now," he said. "Supplies are low and everyone's tired, but it'll get better."

"James, don't get philosophical on me."

He smiled, ignoring her bitter sarcasm. "I just remembered a comment Mrs. Phillips made the day of the big storm – something like she thought you had ordered dry weather for the entire trip."

"Does she think I'm God – or His prophet? Does she think I can control the weather?"

"Actually," he said, in all seriousness, "I think they all do – think you're close to God, that is. Everyone has to have someone to look up to and respect – especially when life is so hard. You're our leader, so you're the one they look to."

Olivia stared at her son, overwhelmed by his wisdom. "James, are…are you sure you're only twelve?" Suddenly, the corners of her mouth twitched. He grinned and she broke into laughter. The bitterness and discouragement began to evaporate.

"You're probably right," she said. "They expect me to be more spiritual and knowledgeable and when they see that I'm human just like they are, they become frightened. They'll get over it."

"Yeah," he answered. "That's what I thought."

"Corey and Michael ran from the cook tent. "Can we sleep in the cave?"

"Yeah, can we?"

"I don't know. How deep is it? What if it's a bear's den?"

"It's not really a cave," said Michael.

"It a huge rock…"

"Big as a house…"

"With an overhang…"

"We can build a fire…"

"And stay warm and dry."

"What will you do when the fire goes out?"

"We'll take turns staying awake."

"Why don't I go check it out?" said James rising from the log.

"Thanks James," said Michael.

"Yeah," said Corey. "Say, maybe you can stay with us."

"And chase away the bears."

"And keep our fire going."

Olivia smiled as the boys left. It was good to hear their childish chatter and giggles in the midst of all the grumbling.

James returned and got his gun. "George and I will stay with them," he said. "Tom and Jeremiah are going too. We can see the corral and the camp from there. Should be all right."

"Thanks, James. They need a little diversion."

"I know," he said and grinned. "We all do."

15   Muddling Through the Mud

Day after day rain splattered on and around the weary travelers. A hostile atmosphere almost as thick as the morning fog crept through the camp each evening. What little sense of adventure the women and children had when they began the journey had long since deserted them. Mothers yelled at children and children yelled at each other, or the mules and Blackie.

Even with all the rain, clean water was at a premium. No streams were near only mud-laden puddles lay along the road. Each night children gathered wet soggy branches that made smoky fires with barely enough heat to boil coffee. The boys tried in vain to find another cliff overhang with dry wood. Meals were becoming not only tasteless and bland, but were often semi-done. Saturated ground made even poorer beds for sleeping.

"We should have stayed in Richmond," said Claudia not bothering to lower her voice.

"At least we would have cooked meals and dry beds," said Corrine.

"I think she's lost and is leading us to our death. Then she'll take our wagons and mules and sell them for her and her kids and that…that…black baby." Jeannette's voice rose to a shrill shriek that broke into a sob.

Olivia turned to respond, but Tillie laid a hand on her arm.

"Let me," said Maggie. She walked over to face Jeannette. "Jeannette, I know you are scared and lonely. We all are. But we chose to come with Olivia. Someone has to lead a group like this. We chose her to lead. We are following the only road available. As long as we have a road to follow, we're not lost. Please, for your sake, and the sake of your children, try to overcome your fears."

"You just say that because you're *her* friend." Jeannette nodded toward Olivia.

"Jeannette, we are *all* her friends – and each other's friend."

"Well, I didn't want…"

"After you eat, why don't you take Sarah and Joey and go to bed.

You're tired. We all are."

Claudia, Corinne and Jeannette barely spoke to Olivia, when they took their dish of warm stew. Tillie, Maggie and Grandma Cooper shook their heads.

"They act like children," Grandma Cooper said. "They need a good horse whipping."

"Now Grandma Cooper," said Olivia. "It's not that drastic – yet."

"You mark my word. Those three will cause you more trouble than you can shake a stick at before this trip is over."

"You're probably right, but we'll deal with it – one problem at a time. It's all I can manage. If they don't want to go with me, they can go it alone or turn back. I'm doing all I can to get us to safety. No one told me when I married Will I would have to become doctor, preacher and wilderness guide."

Grandma Cooper laughed her soft cackle. "Bet Moses didn't have it any easier."

"No, but at least he had a burning bush, then the cloud by day and a pillar of fire by night to guide him. What do I have?"

"Well," said Maggie, sipping her lukewarm coffee, "it seems you have good kids, good mules, a good map to follow and good friends to listen to you and advise you."

"That's right," said Tillie. "Moses didn't have none of those and he had a lot more grumbling to listen to than you do. You only have three grumblers. He had more'n you could count. Remember how the Israelites grumbled at Moses because they didn't have food. They said they'd been better off in Egypt." Tillie laughed at her comparison.

Olivia had to laugh with her friends. "You're right of course. God is good and God is with us. I couldn't ask for more except…" She bit her lip and concentrated on her coffee.

"You want Will," said Grandma Cooper, patting Olivia's hand. "You'll have that, too, in God's own good time,"

"I hope you're right, Grandma Cooper. I hope you're right," Olivia said and placed her other hand over the older woman's hands that felt like tiny skeletons wrapped with fine silk under her own, callused fingers.

"Not meaning to change the subject," said Tillie smiling because she knew that was exactly what she meant to do, "how are we fixed for supplies?"

"We need to take inventory," said Olivia, thankful for the distraction from painful memories. "I know we're getting low. We've been as conservative as possible, but children have to eat."

"Why don't I take a couple of the kids around and get a list of what everyone has," said Tillie. "Then we can make menus for as long as our supplies last. We can start looking for wild vegetation that's edible and let the boys hunt and fish more. We aren't near the river right now, but we will be."

"Thanks, Tillie," said Olivia. "Take Jeremiah and Michael with you. They're both good with numbers."

"I'll do that, as soon as supper is cleared away."

***

Supper finished, Olivia took the babies to her wagon to put them to bed. Betsy, who had been talking with her friend Martha Cooper, started to get up.

"You stay awhile," said James. "I'll help Mom."

Betsy glanced at Olivia for approval. Olivia nodded. "Thanks James," said Betsy.

"Michael, you and Jeremiah, come with me," said Tillie. "We need to do some inventory."

"You aren't going poking around in *our* wagons, are you?" Claudia glared. Corrine and Jeannette stood with their hands on their hips.

"That depends," said Tillie.

"On what?" asked Corrine.

"On whether you will come and show me what you have or if you stay here crabbing about things you can't do nothing about."

"You can't make us," said Jeannette, sticking her lower lip out into a childish pout.

"Don't need to," said Tillie. "That's what I've got Michael and Jeremiah for." Tillie turned and started to Jeannette's wagon.

"That's mine," screeched Jeannette sounding more like Sarah than an adult.

Tillie said nothing but kept walking, Michael and Jeremiah beside her. She nodded for the boys to climb into the Phillips' wagon, but Jeannette whipped around them and climbed into it.

"What do you have in the way of provisions for meals?" asked Tillie.

"What I have is mine," said Jeannette.

"Jeannette, have you been cooking your own meals? Or have you been eating with the rest of us?"

"Well, I might want to go back. I'll need..."

"Jeannette, no one is going back. As hard as it is for us, it would be even harder for one lone wagon to retrace our trail. Now, stop wasting time and tell me what you have and how much."

Jeannette stared then opened a wooden box. "It's all in there. Take what you want."

"We don't want to *take* anything right now. We only want to know what we have among us so we can plan meals until we get somewhere to buy more supplies."

Finally, Tillie and the boys left with their list started. Corrine and Claudia had watched the interaction with Jeannette, so were ready when Tillie arrived at their wagons. Maggie and Grandma Cooper met them with a list in hand.

"We figured we'd save some time," said Grandma Cooper. "This is what we got. We got a few dollars between us in case we come to a store to buy more."

"Thanks folks," said Tillie. "Come on boys. Let's check my supplies now."

When they returned to Olivia, she handed them her list. "This is what I have left," she said. "My supplies are low, so I'm sure the rest are too. Unless we find somewhere to buy some basics soon – and how can we find something when we can't even move – we'll be in trouble long before we reach The Valley. Maybe we should have taken a different route through Lynchburg."

"I don't think so," said Tillie. "We needed to avoid larger towns as much as possible – especially if the war has started."

Tillie and the boys added up the supplies and confirmed their suspicions. Everyone else was as low on supplies as she was – except Jeannette. At least she still had some of the basics they would need.

Olivia looked into the eyes of her friend. "Have I led them away from the war only to let them starve on the journey?"

"Olivia, remember Moses," said Tillie. "The people grumbled about food and water, but God provided quail and manna. God might not give us manna and quail, but God will provide."

"Thanks Tillie. I needed to be reminded of that."

16   *Virginia Secedes*

Another week crept by. Each day the men paced, worried and prayed. Would their women and children make it to safety? David brought news that war had been declared. More states seceded. Later that night, Samuel came and told them more.

"It be bad news," said Samuel through the window. They could hear riotous yelling, singing and chaos from the streets. "I think I was followed, so I just brought you the newspaper. I wrapped some food in it for you. There be someone at the end of the alley. Gotta go."

Samuel disappeared. They heard footsteps stomping down the alley. Then all was quiet except for the street noise.

"Read it Will. We still have a little light from the candle," said Joe.

Will held the paper with shaking hands then handed it to John. "You read it. My eyes are bothering me tonight. Things seem blurred."

"Will?" Joe sounded distressed. The rest looked at him.

"Read it before Homer comes," said Will, wanting to draw the attention away from himself.

John took the paper and read, "President Lincoln called on loyal states to furnish 75,000 soldiers and President Davis asked for 100,000 volunteers. Virginia, North Carolina, Tennessee, and Arkansas have joined the South. Maryland, Delaware, Kentucky and Missouri stayed with the North. Some of western Virginia will go with the North."

"Then we are now Prisoners of War and considered traitors," said Joe.

"Looks that way," said Will. "Parker said he would not send for us again, but if you want to change your mind and fight with Virginia…"

"Will, don't be ridiculous," said Joe. "We have been in here together almost two months now. We all knew this was coming. That's why we sent our women and children away. And what is wrong with your eyes? How long…?"

"I'm fine, Joe. I don't know what's wrong. Things just get blurry then they clear up."

"You need to see an eye doctor."

Mary Lu Warstler

"Like I'm going to see one in here?"

Joe slammed his fist against the wall then shook his hand against the pain. "I hate this hole. I hate having our women out in the wilderness. I hate war. I…"

Robert laughed. "Did you run out of hate?"

Joe glared at his friend, even though it was too dark now for Robert to see him.

"It's all right, Joe," said Robert. "We all feel the same way. I don't think there is a man alive in his right mind who relishes war and killing and all that goes with it."

"Then why are they so hell-bent on having a war?" Joe's last word was lost in a smothered sob.

"Because they are infatuated with the distorted image of war," said Will. "The honor, the prestige, the glamour. They don't realize their women and children will die and their homes will be burned to the ground. When the war is over, if they are still alive, they will have nothing left worth saving. Then the horror of war will come too late."

"You're right Will. We need to double our prayers for our women, but we need to uphold all those who are going blindly after the glory that is not there," said Kenny.

"Let us pray for courage for our women and ourselves. The war has begun."

17   The Rainbow

Another morning dawned with clouds caressing the mountaintops, creating a mist and pulling tentacles of fog from the valleys. Humidity hung in the air, giving a sheen to already warm bodies plodding through mud, pushing wagons and coaxing weary mules to move.

"I'm sick of mud," wailed Jeannette. "I'll never get Sarah's dresses clean. Joey don't even try to stay clean."

"Where's the river?" We ain't seen it for days." From the side of the wagon where she was walking, Corinne jerked the leather straps of the mules. Both turned their heads and gave her a hard stare.

"We're lost, ain't we Olivia?" Claudia yelled at Olivia, who pretended not to hear.

The road will eventually veer back to the river. I've told them often enough and even showed them the map, but Claudia, Corinne and Jeannette just can't comprehend. To them the map is only a scrap of paper with meaningless lines scribbled here and there.

Olivia brushed the sweat from her face leaving brown streaks across her forehead. *Will we really have three weeks of rain now? It's been over a week since we sent that horse thief back to Parker, but we've only gone the equivalent of one day's travel. If more of Parker's men come after us now, we could never outrun them in this mud. Our only hope would be to meet them in a clearing where we can protect one another better.*

***

Three more days of pushing and pulling. Olivia, like all the rest, was mud caked and bone weary. *How much more of this can we tolerate?* Her foot slipped. Falling to her knees behind her wagon, she was too weary to pull herself up. Leaning her head against the back of the wagon, she prayed, *Lord, we're doing the best we can. Give us strength for this task and patience for our journey.*

"Are you all right, Mom?" James and Corey sloshed through the mud to help her up. Michael kept Max and Jasper straining so the wagon wouldn't roll back on her.

"I'm all right," she said reaching for their hands, slathering them with more mud. "Just taking a prayer break." She smiled at her boys as they helped her to her feet.

James grinned then said, "I hope you asked for some dry weather."

"No, just help to endure with what we have."

"A sign would be nice," said Corey. "You know, like a dry road, or…"

"A rainbow!" Betsy called excitedly. Arcs of vivid, brilliant color connected the river to the road. Heads down, shoulders against the wagons, no one had noticed the river was once again beside them. Suddenly, the fishy smell of the river was stronger than the clay smell of mud.

"It is," called Bobby. "It's a rainbow and it's not even raining. Just like when God gave a rainbow to Noah."

"It's the moisture in the air," said James.

"When did the river come back?" asked Jeannette, bringing Joey and Sarah to the front of the line.

"It never went away," said Grandma Cooper. "Olivia told you we would be beside it again."

"Can we sit a minute?" Claudia looked to Olivia.

"I don't think the wagons are going anywhere," she answered.

As if someone had said, "Rest," women and children moved to the grassy banks of the river. Blackie ran and rolled over and over in the wet grass.

"Hey," said Corey. "Blackie's taking a bath. Let's join him." The boys ran to the grass, dropped down and rolled around, laughing and giggling while they removed some of the mud.

The women and girls knelt or sat in the wet grass to watch the rainbow, as if they had never seen one before. An awed silence fell like Sunday morning prayer time. Grandma Cooper, unable to sit on the ground, leaned on her cane. Tears streamed down her face. Her voice trembled as she sang, "O God our help in ages past…"

The rest joined in, "Our hope for years to come; Our shelter from the stormy blast, and our eternal home!"

18   Search for the Bridge

Mud was finally a vivid memory. Women and children alike were bone weary, but least they were able once again to ride in the wagon part of the time. James was driving while Olivia took in the scenery, while watching and listening for trouble of any kind.

"Mom?" said James.

Turning to face him, she waited to hear what was on his mind. He cast a sideways glance at her.

"We should be getting close to the bridge. Do you think someone should ride ahead and check it out?"

Olivia smiled. "I suppose you intend to be that *someone.*"

James grinned and nodded.

"Probably would help to know what's coming. In the morning, why don't you take Beauty and scout it out? Once we cross to the other side of the James River, we should be only a few days from New River and then not far to the Kanawha Valley." Olivia felt a tingle of excitement. "We have a long way to go yet, but we're over halfway."

***

Olivia woke to the chatter and singing of wildlife. The sky was beginning to take on a golden glow. It would be a good day for travel – hopefully no rain. Crawling from under her wagon, she started to the cook tent. Water was already boiling for breakfast oatmeal.

"Coffee's done," said James as she approached the fire. He was poking it and adding twigs to the leaping flames, sending them up to lick the coffee pot. "Mrs. Rayburn and I thought we might as well begin breakfast since our watch was ending. I packed a lunch and fed the mules and horses already."

"You've been busy."

"Yes, ma'am." He grinned. His face shone with excitement. He mounted Beauty and turned toward the road.

"You be careful and don't take any chances. If you don't find the bridge by midafternoon, come back and try again in a day or two."

"I'll be careful," he said. "I'll try to be back by dinner time. I'm sure I can find the camp."

Olivia pulled the map from her pocket. "If we don't run into rain, we should be here by nightfall." She pointed out the spot for James. He nodded and headed down the road.

Tillie came to stand beside Olivia and watch James ride off. "Should he be going alone?"

Olivia startled, turned to Tillie. She stared for a moment, a sinking feeling in the pit of her stomach. "I…I…didn't think…oh, Tillie I really made a big mistake, didn't I? Maybe I should go after him. What was I thinking?"

Tillie laid her hand on Olivia's shoulder. "You were thinking like a wagon master. All our children have matured beyond their years. You did what any wagon master would do. You sent a scout ahead. James will be all right."

"But, he's only a boy. I guess I forgot that."

"He's no longer a boy, Olivia – not quite a man – but no longer a boy."

"You're right, Tillie, but…"

"I hear the others stirring. Let's fix breakfast."

***

Breakfast eaten and the camp cleared, the women began to hitch the wagons and mules. Corey looked around and finally asked, "Mom, where's James. He always…"

"He left early to scout for the bridge. He should be back by the time we stop for the night, or shortly after. Can you and Michael hitch the wagon?"

"Sure, come on Michael."

With a minimum of grumbling and complaining, they were soon on the road – their disjointed caterpillar creeping along to the next destination. Watching for ruts, they didn't move as fast as Olivia would have preferred, but no need taking a chance of breaking axels or wagon wheels. By late afternoon, Olivia began looking for James, straining to see someone approaching. When they pulled into their camping site that evening, James still hadn't returned.

"Does James know where we're camping?" Corey asked as he unhitched Max and Jasper that evening. "Want me to help George with the corral?"

"Thank you, Corey. Yes, James knows where we are and he can see the campfire from the road. He'll be along shortly." Olivia was worried, but didn't want to worry Corey.

"Do you think he's lost?" Corey wasn't so easily fooled.

"He can't be lost, Corey. He's following the same road we're traveling."

"Maybe a bear got him." Olivia almost laughed, but Corey looked so serious that she bit her lip to keep it back. Suddenly she remembered, *Corey is only six, not sixteen. Tillie was right. They are all maturing too quickly.* She smiled at her son and tousled his hair the way Will used to do.

"He has his gun and Beauty. They could escape from a bear if he meets one on the road," she said.

"Did he take lunch with him?"

"Yes, now, go help George and don't worry about your brother. He can take care of himself."

Olivia had convinced Corey, but it wasn't so easy to convince herself. Supper time came and went and still James had not returned. No matter what she told Corey, Olivia was too worried to sleep. *I shouldn't have let him go alone.* She joined Maggie and George, who were on guard duty.

"I can't sleep," she said, trying to sound casual.

"James not back?" It was more a statement than a question. Everyone knew James wasn't there.

Olivia shook her head.

"He'll be back soon," said George. "He's probably scouting out the camping area and the hunting prospects."

"He's right," said Maggie. "James won't take any unnecessary chances. He has enough moonlight to see the road."

"I know," said Olivia. She smiled at their cheering words, but deep in her heart, she still worried. Anything could have happened – Parker, wild animals, accident.

Close to midnight, they heard Beauty's galloping hooves and all three breathed a sigh of relief. Olivia realized Maggie and George were almost as worried as she was. She went into the tent for the stew she had saved for him. "He'll want to take care of Beauty before he eats," she said and set the stew on the fire.

"I'll help him," said George and started toward Olivia's wagon to meet James.

The boys returned and sat around the fire. "You want us to leave?" Maggie asked as James began to eat.

"No," said Olivia, "stay, but…"

"I understand," said Maggie. "Some folks can't handle too much information at once – especially if it's bad news." She glanced at George.

He nodded. "Yeah," he said. "Later is soon enough."

Olivia smiled and between bites, James gave them his report. "There's a nice clearing across from the river about two days from here, if the weather is good. But…the bridge is impassable."

Olivia sucked in a sharp breath. Maggie groaned. He glanced from one woman to the other and continued. "It was deliberately disabled…probably soldiers…burned out in the middle."

"Soldiers? Surely not…" Maggie started.

"Will said it would probably come to that. We'll have to double our vigilance."

"Which side?" George turned to James.

James hunched his shoulders and continued. "Hard to tell, but parts of the bridge are hanging on each side. There's no middle. I tried crossing the river with Beauty, but the water is almost up to her head. We'll have to wait for the water to go down, find another crossing or repair the bridge."

Olivia sighed deeply, a habit she abhorred and realized she was quickly falling into. Maggie said nothing, but shook her head in dismay.

"Thank you James," said Olivia. "We better get some sleep. I have a feeling it's going to be a long two days. We'll give it some thought and maybe come up with something by the time we get there."

Following a short night of fitful sleep, Olivia woke before dawn to the sound of a rumble much too close. *Have the soldiers caught up with us?* She gripped her gun and crawled from under the wagon to listen closer. A flash across the sky followed by another rumble confirmed her fear. Not soldiers – more rain!

19 Samuel's News

Samuel knew better than to ride one of the horses, or take the wagon to town for supplies. He didn't need much – was running low on money anyway. Walking with a slow, limping gate, he made it to the general store without notice. He mingled with what few friends were left. Many had been forced to join the *Volunteers*. Others had run away – or simply disappeared.

Slowly making his way around the store, pretending to look for supplies, he listened for conversations that would help Will and his friends.

"How you doing, Samuel," asked his old friend, Daniel. "Must be pretty lonely out there without the missus and the children."

"It sure is Daniel. Rosy and I miss them something fierce. This war's got everything topsy-turvy. How you doing Daniel?"

"I'm too old to fight, so they don't want me, but they took my son and grandson."

"We keeps praying, Daniel. That's what keeps us going."

"You got that right," said Daniel. "See you around. I gotta pick up my daughter-in-law at the Percy place. She been cleaning for them."

"You take care," said Samuel and turned back to looking. Finally, he found what he was looking for. Old Zeke offered his back room to some of the soldiers to come in out of the rain and warm themselves. Samuel loitered near the door that was slightly ajar. He couldn't see who was there, but he knew the voices – Stevens and a new man. That was good. Corporal Stevens liked to let the new men know how important he was.

Watching from the corner of his eye for Zeke, he leaned closer to hear.

"You really that close with Sergeant Parker?" The young recruit sounded awed.

"Of course I am. He hardly makes a move without consulting me."

"I hear there was some recruit rode in here late last night and wanted to see Parker. Something happening out there?"

"Naw, That was Private Robert White." Stevens laughed.

"Sergeant sent him out to catch up with those women and bring back their mules. He was gone over two weeks and came in empty handed."

"He couldn't get the mules? From a bunch of women?"

Stevens laughed again. "He said they all had guns and a vicious dog that tried to tear his throat out. He said they tied him up and left him to starve, but he managed to get loose and ride back to Richmond."

"Did Sergeant Parker believe him?"

"He knew the women had guns and a little black dog. But he figures they put White on his horse and sent him home. Anyway, White will never be a corporal. He's still a private. Sergeant put him in charge of prisoners."

"What happened to Homer."

"Got promoted."

"Some of the men were talking about a bridge that they blew up because Parker didn't want those women to cross it. What was that all about?"

Stevens laughed again. "There's a bridge – or was – that crossed the James out west of here. The road then leads north toward the New River. Parker figured those traitors' wives would be heading that way. He sent some men out to blow up the middle of the bridge so they can't cross. The river will be too high to cross with all the rain. They'll be stuck."

"That the same women with the mules?"

"That's them."

"What's Parker going to do? Let them die there? Go after them again?"

"He plans to wait about another week when they'll be starving then he'll send another soldier after their mules."

"Won't the mules be half dead too?"

"Maybe, but Parker don't care. He just don't want the women to make it to Charleston."

"We going to be *really* fighting soon?"

"I hear the Confederate Government will be moving their headquarters to Richmond sometime next month. I'm sure we'll see some real fighting then."

"We still need horses and mules?"

"We always need them."

"How about those traitors in Libby? They have horses."

"You know, Private Moore, I think that's an idea we need to take to Sergeant Parker."

"Do you think he'll give me a promotion?"

"Let's go see," said Stevens. "He should be back from lunch by now."

Hearing chairs scrape on the floor, Samuel quickly turned away from the door. With his back to the men as they passed him, Samuel reached toward a sack of flour. The men ignored him and hurried out. Samuel left the flour and hurried home. *I can't let them come and take Master Will's horses. How will I get him to Miz Olivia?*

***

Samuel ran into his cabin. Rosy was cleaning something – she was always cleaning something.

"Samuel Brunner, what in the world…nothing happed to Master Will did it?"

"No, but I heard Stevens and another recruit talking at the store. They plan to take all the horses of the men in prison. If they take Master Will's horses, how we going to get him out of Richmond?"

"What can we do? Maybe hide them in the woods?"

"They would look there."

"Maybe we can pretend they's sick – or hurt. We could wrap their legs and…"

"That might work…no, they would insist on a horse doctor looking at them."

"Maybe take them to Master Jefferson's."

"Not much time. But it might work if I take them through the woods. If they find me, I'll say they ran away and I was just gathering them up."

"You do that Samuel, but hurry. That Parker don't waste no time when he gets something in his head. You go. I'll stall them."

"You come with me. I don't want them…"

"Don't worry about me, Samuel. We gotta think about Master Will. Now hurry."

Samuel nodded and ran to the barn. He brought the two horses out, rode one and led the other through the woods.

***

The stars began to dot the sky as Samuel took news to Will and his friends. Dropping the pebbles in the window, he waited for Will's response.

"Yes?"

"Master Will, things is getting worse out here. I knows they ain't good in there neither. I'm working as hard as I can to think of safe way to get you out."

251

"I know you are, Samuel. We appreciate it, but don't get yourself and Rosy hurt or killed in the process. Do you have news?"

"Yes, sir," Samuel chuckled as he told him about the horse thief who came back empty-handed. Then he told them about the plan to take the horses.

"Rosy and me worked out a plan. I took your horses to Master Jefferson. He said he would keep them for you."

"But what did they say when the horses weren't in our barn?"

"Rosy told me she was all in a stew when they came. She was crying and carrying on. Told them the horses broke out of the barn and ran off into the woods right after I left for town earlier. She tried to find them, but couldn't."

"They believed her."

"Not at first. But when I got home, they asked me about it. I told them I was in town. I had a sack of flour to prove it. Zeke saw me talking to Daniel."

"Thank you Samuel, but if danger starts building too much, you get you and Rosy out of here. Maybe take David with you."

"I ain't going no place without you and your friends, Master Will. You can count on that."

20   Mutiny

Two wet, soggy days later and the weary travelers were back to pushing and pulling their wagons inch by muddy inch on the water soaked roads. Olivia hoped James was wrong and they would soon be able to cross the river, but she knew her son too well. He would not say the bridge was impassible if there were any way at all to cross it.

Grumbles and complaints rose and fell while women took a brief rest from their backbreaking task. "Maybe the bridge is only slightly damaged on one end," said Claudia.

"Yeah, what does a kid know about bridges anyway?" answered Corinne.

"What does Olivia know about any of it? She just wants to be..." Jeannette saw Olivia looking at her and turned her head as if to check on Joey.

"Don't pay them no mind," said Grandma Cooper. "We're all getting weary, but we'll get there – bridge or no bridge."

"She's right," said Tillie. "Don't let them get you down. Got enough mud to do that." Tillie grinned and Olivia had to smile at her friend's attempt at humor.

Two and a half more days passed before they finally crept into a circle in the clearing across from the bridge. One look at the muddy brown water and the mangled bridge and they all knew James had not been wrong. It would be a long time before they could cross the river there – if ever.

James and Tillie walked to the bridge with Olivia while the other women began preparations for supper. "I was hoping you were mistaken about the severity of the damage," said Olivia.

"I'm sorry I wasn't."

"Whoever destroyed it didn't intend for anyone to cross the river here," said Tillie. "Like James said, looks like the middle is burned out."

"And the water is too deep and running too swiftly to try to cross on horseback, much less with wagons," said James.

"How long you figure it'll take for the river to go down?" Tillie squinted across to the other side.

"Longer than we have provisions for," said Olivia.

"Maybe we can make some kind of raft and…" James stopped and hunched his shoulders. "Don't worry about it Mom. God will show us a way."

"He's right, you know, Olivia," said Tillie. "In the meantime, I think I'll help the kids catch some fish for supper. I don't know what Maggie is planning, but I'm sure a little extra meat in our diet won't hurt."

"Good idea," said Olivia. "And Maggie will appreciate your help."

"And the rest wouldn't?" Tillie gave her a look of mock surprise then laughed. "Come on James. Get your brothers and the other boys. Shouldn't take us long to haul in enough fish for tonight. We'll work on tomorrow when it gets here. Olivia, you go feed your babies and then rest your weary bones for a change."

"Sure I will."

***

After she fed the babies, Olivia put them on a quilt where they sat cooing at each other. She sat on a log outside her wagon trying to think through their dilemma. *What can we do, Lord? How will we ever get across the river? You parted the waters for Moses, but I'm not Moses. Our supplies are getting so low. I promised Will I would take care of our children. You said You would supply all our needs. I do trust You, Lord, but right now, I need courage.*

A gunshot, followed immediately by another, jerked Olivia from her meditation. *That came from the woods. I thought the boys were still fishing. Has Parker's men caught up with us?*

Olivia saw Tillie grab her gun and start for the woods. The boys must have come back with her. Betsy and her friend, Martha ran for the wagon to watch the babies and Olivia grabbed her gun and caught up with the other women.

Branches crackled and a pair of crows scolded, as someone ran through the woods toward the camp.

"Mom! Mom!" Corey's usual prelude to trouble added to the fear and gave Olivia another spurt of energy. She met him as he darted from the woods, stumbled over a root and righted himself.

"Corey?"

Before she could ask him who was hurt, he yelled again. "Mom, James and George got a deer!"

Olivia stopped, stunned. Holding her chest, she tried to force her heart rate back to normal. James and George struggled under the weight of a young buck they dragged behind them as they emerged from the woods. She felt a rush of anger, tempered with pride. She wanted to give Corey a good shaking for scaring her half to death, but she wasn't sure she even had enough strength left to stand, much less scold.

"Corey, I told you not to run yelling like that," James gave his brother an angry glare. "You scared Mom and the other women. They probably thought someone got shot."

"But…" Corey suddenly looked at his mother's pale face. "Sorry, Mom. I didn't mean to scare you."

"We thought sure one of you got your head blowed off," said Tillie. "Don't you boys know better'n to go off with guns without telling someone where you're going? You should have told me when we finished fishing."

"Tillie's right, boys. Certainly we're excited and proud of you for your fine hunting ability, but please let someone know the next time you decide to go hunting."

"Sorry, Mom, I guess we goofed," said James. "We didn't mean to scare anyone. We just didn't want to get anyone's hopes up in case we came back empty handed."

"Well," said Olivia getting her breath and her wits back, "now that you have it, what are you going to do with it? Do either of you know how to dress a deer?"

"No," said James with a grin, "but I think we're about to learn."

***

Cloudy, rainy weather continued for three more days – sometimes a drizzle, sometimes a downpour. Occasionally parting clouds reminded them the sun was still in the sky. Finally, more blue sky than clouds filled the day. Still they waited for a miracle, or at least some insight on how to cross the river.

Standing on the riverbank, Olivia stared at the muddy flow. On either side of her, the boys hauled fish for supper.

How long before we can cross the river? Olivia prayed in the silence of her heart. *It continues to swell from the rains. Is there anything we can do about the bridge? Our provisions are running dangerously low. We're doing the best we can, Lord. I know You will help us. Give me the patience and courage to wait.*

She sighed. *Not only do we know nothing about building a bridge, we don't have any materials if we did know. Maybe I should send James and George to look for another way?*

Feeling the answer must be yes, Olivia gathered the fish the boys had caught and went back to begin supper.

Later that evening, while Olivia got the babies down for another night, the other women milled around the fire. Angry voices rose and fell. Even the evening song of nature and the wonderful aroma of wild flowers could not abate their fear and anger.

Betsy looked up at her, eyes wide with fear. "Why are they so angry, Mom?"

"Because they're all tired and afraid," Olivia said.

"Aren't you tired and afraid, too?"

Surprised, Olivia turned to face her daughter. "Yes, Betsy, I guess I am, but someone has to stay calm."

"Oh."

"Don't worry about it, Betsy," said James coming around the wagon. "Mom can handle them anytime. Right, Mom?" He winked at her. "I'm going to check on the animals then turn in early since I have guard duty with Mrs. Rayburn the second watch." He started toward the corral area, but suddenly stopped to listen, as the angry voices grew louder. The women were moving closer to their wagon.

Olivia's sixth sense tingled. It didn't take her grandmother's second sight to hear trouble in those voices. She saw James step behind the wagon.

Softly she said, "Betsy, get in the wagon with the babies. Lie down on the floor and don't move unless I tell you to."

Betsy climbed into the wagon and did as she was told, except she too, clutched her gun and held it ready.

"We'll drown if we try to cross that river," shouted Claudia. "We can't make it."

Jeannette whimpered, "We should have stayed in Richmond. We're all going to die in this wilderness and our men-folk won't even know where to come looking for us."

"Who does Olivia think she is, God Almighty?" Corinne grumbled.

Swinging lanterns sent menacing, shadowy fingers toward Olivia as the women marched like a determined posse toward her wagon. Younger children were down for the night, but older ones joined the parade looking for excitement. Jeannette, however, afraid to let Sarah and Joey out of her sight, even at bedtime, dragged them along. Joey stumbled. She jerked him up and kept moving.

Olivia prayed. *Lord, help me stay calm. They're travel-weary and frightened. I trusted You in Richmond and I trust You now.* With this affirmation, she reached for her shotgun. Stepping out in front of the approaching women, she fired one shot into the air, leveled the gun and prepared it to fire again.

"What in the name of thunder are you doing?" bellowed Claudia clutching at her heart. "Do you want to bring every soldier in the neighborhood down on us?"

"And your shouting and waving torches and lanterns won't? That's assuming soldiers *are* out there in the first place," answered Olivia.

"Well, someone destroyed that bridge," said Corinne. "We can't get across that river. The children are all tired. We're tired. We're nearly out of provisions. We're only women for heaven's sake! We can't do this. You're leading us to our death." They pressed forward another step.

Olivia raised her gun. They stopped. Breathing in heavy gasps, eyes wide, Claudia and Corinne stared. Jeannette hung back, clinging tightly to Joey and Sarah. The others watched with amusement.

"She can't kill all of us," shouted Corinne and started forward.

"Stop where you are!" Olivia raised her voice for the first time since they left Richmond. She heard two more guns click ready for firing. "I don't intend to kill anyone. We are all friends, after all. I don't intend to turn back either. One step closer and you'll be digging buckshot out of your hides for weeks to come."

"She's bluffing," said Claudia.

"'Livia don't bluff," said Tillie leaning against a tree, letting a smile play at the corners of her mouth.

"Now, all of you listen to me and you listen real good because I'm not going to repeat myself." Olivia's eyes narrowed, teeth clenched, she spoke through tight lips. "You all know I left Richmond because I made Will a promise."

Olivia lowered her voice. She now had their attention. There was no need to shout. Neither did she take her eyes from Claudia's face. "You will either go with me, or you won't. I'm taking my children north. God Almighty parted the waters once. If He has to do it again, He will. If not, He'll show us another way. Now, if you want to go with me – fine. If not, go on back the way we came and may God go with you."

The angry women and Olivia stared at one another. Jeannette turned and stomped back to her wagon. Children who had come looking for a good fight sighed with disappointment and followed their mothers back to their wagons.

Tillie laid a hand on Olivia's shoulder. "I'm with you all the way, Olivia. We'll find a way." Olivia nodded. She didn't trust herself to speak. She knew her voice would be as shaky as her knees.

"Tillie's right," said Maggie, "and Grandmother Cooper said to tell you she'll swim across the river if need be, or she'll wait until it shrinks however long it takes."

Olivia felt a rush of gratitude. "Tell her I appreciate her confidence," she said.

Maggie and Tillie left and Olivia spoke to her children. "Thanks for your help and support, James and Betsy."

They didn't answer. They didn't need to. She heard them set the safety catch on their guns. Then James left to check the animals and Betsy settled down to sleep with the babies. Olivia dropped to her knees. *Thank You, Lord, for what You are about to do. We'll make it to The Valley and with Your help Will and the others can find us.*

21   Captain Barnabas

In spite of the encounter with the angry women, sleep came almost immediately for Olivia. She vaguely remembered James getting up for the second watch. Startled out of a deep sleep by a hand on her shoulder, she threw her other hand over her mouth to keep from crying out. Glancing at the sky, she saw streaks of red against the gray horizon. Close to dawn.

"Mom," James whispered.

"James, is something wrong?"

"There's someone here you need to meet."

"More trouble? Parker's soldiers?"

"Nothing like that. An answer to our prayers, possibly."

Cautiously Olivia followed James to the campfire. A short, plump man with a bushy, white beard and mustache squatted drinking coffee and talking with Tillie. His captain's cap almost covered white, bushy eyebrows. An unlit pipe bounced up and down in his mouth as he spoke.

How could I have slept through the arrival of horses and/or wagons? How did he creep up on us? Blackie would ...

"Mom," said James, "this is Captain Andrew Barnabas. Captain Barnabas, my mother, Olivia Brunner. Mom, Mrs. Rayburn and I think Captain Barnabas might be able to help us." James glanced at Tillie for confirmation. She nodded. James threw another piece of wood on the fire and handed his mother a cup of the strong, black coffee.

"I'm glad to meet you, ma'am," said the captain, extending a chubby hand. "You have a fine boy here – smart and observant. I thought I was quite good at hiding until I felt a gun in my ribs." Captain Barnabas chuckled and took a sip of coffee.

Olivia wrapped her hands around her cup, sipped the contents and stared at the man. Hot liquid slid down her throat. She waited for it to speed through her body. The captain watched her as if they were playing chess and it was her turn to make the next move. Tillie and James stood back, giving her time to think.

Finally, she took a deep breath, one more sip of coffee and said,

"Pardon me if I sound skeptical, Captain, but who are you, why are you here and how did you get here?"

Tillie sipped her coffee and leaned forward to catch the warmth of the fire. "James and I been talking to Captain Barnabas for the last half hour or so," she said. "I think you need to hear what he has to say."

"All right," said Olivia taking another gulp of coffee and sitting on a stone beside Tillie, close enough to share the warmth of the fire. "Let's hear it."

The man laughed – a jolly sound – and said, "I apologize for sneaking in on your camp, but I saw the campfire and smelled the coffee. I can never resist a good cup of coffee."

"But where is your horse? And, surely you aren't alone out here in the wilderness." Olivia stared, trying not to sound either gullible, or cynical.

The man laughed again, sending a ripple across his belly. He took a draw on his unlit pipe, removed it from his mouth, looked it over and tapped it against a stone. Then he began refilling it from the tobacco pouch he pulled from his pocket. He explained while he worked with his pipe.

"No, ma'am, I'm not alone," he said, "but, I'm not with any army either. I don't ride a horse; I ride the river."

Olivia lifted her eyebrows. He hurried on as if anticipating her questions. "I run a barge service. I have a crew of a dozen men on my steamboat, *The Adventurer,* over there on the river. I figured with a war coming, I should invest in special made barges to haul everything from people to cannons."

Olivia felt uncomfortable with so many men nearby, but said nothing while Captain Barnabas continued. "I was supposed to meet a company of Confederate soldiers here about ten days ago, but got held up and didn't make it on time. I guess they didn't want anyone to cross the river. Looks like they used a torch on the bridge."

"Confederate soldiers?"

"Yes ma'am."

"Then we are at war?"

"You didn't know?"

"We've not seen a newspaper or talked to anyone outside our own group since we left Richmond on March 20."

"I saw your fire," said Captain Barnabas, "and thought maybe the soldiers were waiting for me. When I saw the wagons, I knew you wasn't soldiers, but I was curious. I tried to check it out very quietly. Didn't want to get my head blowed off, but I thought someone might need help in crossing the river. Intended to go back to the boat and wait 'til morning to approach you." He chuckled again and winked at James.

"That is all very interesting, Captain, but I don't understand what all that has to do with us or how you think you can help us."

"I have three barges tied together over there on the river. I was supposed to take the soldiers and all their equipment back to Richmond…"

Olivia interrupted. "Richmond?"

"That's what the orders said."

"Olivia, do you suppose Parker…?" Tillie spoke over the edge of her cup from which she had started to drink.

"Wouldn't put it past him," said James. "Guess they figured they would wait until we were weak or dead then come back and the take our mules."

"That would be Sergeant Matthew Parker from Richmond?" Captain Barnabas looked surprised.

"Yes," said Olivia. "Do you know him?"

"Not personally. He's the one who hired me to pick up his men."

"He wants our husbands in the *Volunteers* – or army, I guess it is now. They all went to prison rather than join. We left with the children to go to relatives up north. Parker has tried several times to stop us."

"I see," said Captain Barnabas. He grinned. "But doesn't look like he's any match for you folks. Your son told me your wagon train needs to get across the river. What do you say we beat him again? Be glad to take you across the river and move you up river a little closer to your destination. There's an easy access back to the main road about eight or ten miles upriver."

Olivia stared at him. Finally, she said, "Which side of the war are you on?"

Captain Barnabas laughed again. "Me? I'm trying to stay in the neutral zone."

"I see," said Olivia giving him a shrewd look. "In other words, you'll take whichever side is willing to pay your price."

Captain Barnabas threw back his head and laughed a hearty laugh. He looked at James and said, "I see where you get your courage and smarts, son." He turned back to Olivia and said, "That just about sums it up, ma'am."

"Well, Captain Barnabas, since we aren't soldiers, how much do you expect to charge us to take so many that far?"

"My dear lady, it will be my pleasure to help you. I just had the best coffee I've had in years and a piece of venison that melted in my mouth. If you could come up with five dollars a barge it would be well worth my while."

Olivia saw James wince. She knew he hadn't thought about a charge. "One other crucial question, Captain, do your men know how to behave like gentlemen around ladies? I would hate to send you on your way with them full of holes because they tried to take advantage of my women – or children."

Captain Barnabas looked surprised. "I never thought about that possibility ma'am, but I will personally guarantee their behavior. If any of them get out of line in the least, I'll save you the trouble and shoot 'em myself."

"We're low on supplies, but if your men want breakfast we'll share what we have."

"That's very generous of you Mrs. Brunner, but we have a cook on board the boat. He'll take care of our men and provide sandwiches for all of you at noon while we're on the river."

Olivia smiled and extended her hand to shake his. "Captain Barnabas, we have a deal." She turned to her son and said, "James, why don't you go wake the other women and tell them to come to the circle. We need to work out the details with the captain."

"Mom, I didn't…"

"It's all right, James," she said as they walked toward her wagon. "Your grandfather gave me a few five dollar gold coins for emergencies and supplies. Now hurry along. We want to get started as soon as possible." James continued to the other wagons to wake the women while Olivia dug into her hidden stash of coins from her father.

A sudden pang of tenderness and longing washed over her as she saw her father standing in her living room, hat in hand, almost begging her to let him help. Once again, she was thankful for his gifts. Not even James knew about the gold coins Jefferson had given her – "in case there is a war and our current money is useless," he'd said. She was saving them to buy supplies and help get settled, but there would be enough.

With the help of Captain Barnabas, we can make up at least part of the two weeks we were delayed by weather.

22   *Wagons on the River*

James and Tillie handed each of the women a cup of hot coffee as they stumbled, bleary-eyed to the campfire. Olivia returned from her wagon with three five-dollar gold pieces. She gave one to the captain and showed him the other two.

"When we have everything unloaded safely on the other side of the river, I'll give you the other two coins," she said. The captain laughed his hearty, jolly laugh and pocketed the coin.

"What's the big idea?" Claudia complained. "I was getting used to sleeping late. It's not like we're going anyplace." The confrontation of the previous night apparently forgotten, Claudia was winding up for her long tirade of complaints when she noticed Captain Barnabas. "Who's that? And why's he here?"

"If you would shut your mouth long enough, we could tell you," said Tillie. Claudia glared, but said nothing more. Maggie smiled and Grandma Cooper's eyes sparkled as she sat in her straight-backed chair the women kept for her with the cooking tent. She leaned forward, resting her hands on her cane.

Olivia raised her hands for quiet. "This is…"

Before she could finish her introduction of Captain Barnabas, Jeannette shuffled into the circle. Joey held tightly to one hand, his other thumb stuck in his mouth like a cork. Sarah on the other side, drug her feet and whined.

Olivia shook her head. *I should have known Jeannette wouldn't leave the kids asleep in the wagon – not even for a short meeting in the safety of the camp circle.* She waited until James took Joey and Jeannette sat on a stone with Sarah on her lap. Tillie handed her a cup of coffee.

Once again, Olivia raised her hand for quiet so she could introduce the captain. Blackie jumped to his feet, snarling and growling. He plunged toward some shrubs between the road and their campsite. James set Joey down beside Jeannette, picked up his gun and followed Tillie. The other women clutched their ever-present shotguns and waited.

Captain Barnabas grinned then called out, "If that's you Scottie, you better show yourself with your hands in the air." He laughed his jolly laugh and a tall, broad shouldered man stood and lifted his hands in the air. James motioned with his gun for the man to join the captain.

"This one of your men?" he asked.

"My right hand man," said the captain, "First Mate Scottie McDonald."

"Sorry about the reception," said James, lowering his gun, "but you're lucky you don't have teeth marks on your neck."

"You can put your hands down," said Olivia. "James, get him some coffee. I was just going to explain to my women who your captain is."

"You're all right, then sir?" The young man asked in a thick Scottish brogue. "We were concerned when you didn't return."

"I'm fine, lad, just drumming up some business since we missed the soldiers. This is Olivia Brunner and these women are in her wagon train." He nodded at the women around the fire.

The young man took off his dark colored knit cap, exposing a head of bushy red hair. He nodded to Olivia and the others then accepted the steaming cup from James.

Olivia turned back to the women. "As I started to say, this is Captain Andrew Barnabas. He runs a barge service on the river."

"Another riverboat? Who'd they try to kidnap this time?" Corinne glared at the men.

"They didn't try to kidnap anyone," said Tillie. "They want to help us."

"Help us? How?"

"Well, why don't we just let Captain Barnabas tell us?" Sarcasm was lost on Corinne.

Captain Barnabas gave Olivia a curious look. "Kidnap?"

"A couple of men on a riverboat tried to kidnap my mom a few weeks back," said James, "but we stopped them and sent them drifting back toward Richmond in the middle of the night."

"Must be the boat we saw awhile back hung up against the rocky shore. It won't be going anywhere for some time to come."

"Well, Captain Barnabas isn't like those two," said James. "He's offered to, not only take us across the river, but will deposit us several miles upriver. That will save us a couple days of travel over land."

Olivia's glance took in the women's expressions. She knew them so well by now that she could predict their responses. Jeannette would be afraid; Corinne would question; Claudia would be skeptical;

Maggie and Tillie would be willing to try it; Grandma Cooper would revel in a new experience.

Finally, Jeannette swallowed as if something had stuck in her throat. "You mean he'll take us – wagon and all – on the river? We'll sink and drown."

"Yes, Jeannette. He'll take the wagons, mules and us on the river and no, we won't sink. He carries entire companies of soldiers with all their equipment – including cannons – on his barges and they don't sink."

"Olivia, are you sure this man knows what he's doing?"

"It's his life, Corinne," said Olivia. "He's been running barges for a good long time. Both armies trust him to carry their equipment."

Olivia smiled at Captain Barnabas, who chuckled. He punched his First Mate's arm and said, "She's a smart one, Scottie."

"What if we get to the middle of the river and sink?" Jeannette shivered. "I don't like water. I don't believe all that weight won't sink the barge."

"Jeannette's right," said Claudia. "What do we know about barges and rivers and…"

Even though Olivia expected opposition, she was still irritated and tired of all the complaining. She interrupted. "We don't really know much about a lot of things, do we Claudia? What did we know about horses, mules and wagon trains before we started this journey? I told you before, any of you are welcome to turn around and go back anytime. If we stay here, we can't cross the river until it recedes enough to drive the wagons over, or until we can rebuild the bridge. That might be weeks, or months – or never! Captain Barnabas has offered us an alternative way to cross it and move us further on our journey at the same time. The rains have put us behind by at least two weeks. You are all welcome to do what you will. My wagon is going on that barge. If we sink, we sink. If we don't, we move on."

"I'm with Olivia." The frail crackly voice of Grandma Cooper surprised them. Heads turned to her and she narrowed her eyes. "I ain't never been on a barge afore. Matter of fact, I ain't never been on a boat. Ought to be exciting."

Maggie gave Grandma Cooper a look of awe and admiration. She laughed then teased the older woman. "Grandmother Cooper, what if it sinks and we all drown?"

"Then I'll die happy and Olivia won't have to bury me." She cackled and started back to her wagon. The mirthful laughter of Captain Barnabas, Scottie and Olivia followed her halting, cane-jabbing walk.

"If we're leaving today, we'd better get moving," said Tillie. "Whose turn is it to cook?"

"Mine," said Corinne.

"What are we having?" Claudia asked as she and her friend turned toward the cook tent.

"Oatmeal."

"Again?"

"You got a better idea?"

Their voices faded, Captain Barnabas and Scottie returned to *The Adventurer* to let the other crew members know what was happening.

Olivia turned to her morning routine of taking care of the babies and packing the wagon. James, too excited to eat, took care of the horses and mules and was ready to help when the men met the wagons at the edge of the river. A fearful hush fell over the circle of women and children.

"It'll never work," said Claudia.

"We'll all drown," wailed Jeannette.

They all stared. A steamboat with the name *The Adventurer* painted across its sides throbbed and putted behind the barges. Like a long black river snake, the barges stretched ahead of the steamboat. None of them had ever seen anything like those long floating, almost flat boats. No oars or motor, only the power of the steamboat would give them life and send them moving up the river. Even the adults stared with open mouths.

Finally finding her voice, Claudia spoke for the rest. "How will we get the wagons on those things?"

Olivia eyed the barges with the rest. She glanced at the mules and wagons then back to the barges. "I don't know any more about it than you do, Claudia, but the captain and his crew know what they are doing." *At least, I hope so.*

"You're right, ma'am," said Scottie, doffing his cap. "Captain Barnabas knows his barges and he knows the river like the back of his hand. He could move an entire city if he had to and not lose a single article. He'll take good care of you folks. Don't you worry none about that."

"That's right," said Bert, a tall black man with bulging arm muscles. "I been with the captain ever since I was freed. He knows what's what all right."

"How do they move?" James asked. "Does the steamboat push or pull?"

"The steamboat stays behind the barges," said Scottie. "It pushes, rather than pulling them. We'll have you lassies and lads loaded and moving up the river by noon."

"How fast will we travel?"

Scottie grinned at James. "You ask a lot of questions, laddie."

"Since I'm not in school, I got to learn when I can." James returned the grin.

"That makes a lot of sense," said Scottie turning his cap in his hands. "Well, it used to take fifty men to push a boat with barges like these up the river. They used long poles and pushed against the current. Would've taken all day to go a couple of miles."

"Like us pushing our wagons through the mud," said James.

Scottie raised his eyebrows in surprise, glanced at the assortment of women and children and shook his head, then continued, "With our steamboat we can move eight to ten miles in an hour."

"An hour?" James' eyes widened. "It takes us all day to go that far on land on a good day."

"I don't understand how you even got this far." Scottie shook his head again.

Bert smiled exposing more gums than teeth. "The good Lord done helped 'em, man. That's how they does it. The good Lord be with 'em."

Olivia smiled. "You're right, Bert." She noticed him watching Charles and Lucy sitting on the ground at her feet gurgling at each other. "This is Charles and Lucy," she said. Then she gave him a shortened version of how Charles came to be with them.

The man's eyes widened and he said, "No wonder the Lord is good to you. You is good to others."

Olivia thought about all the hard times since they left Richmond and the reason for leaving in the first place. She smiled at the man again and said, "Thank you, Bert, for reminding me that God is with us, even when the going is rough."

Captain Barnabas called to Scottie and Bert, who tipped their hats and went to join him. By noon, with the help of the older boys, the crew had the barges loaded. Corey, Michael, Jeremiah, James and George stayed with the horses and mules that were all on the first barge with higher sides. The wagons were divided between the other two barges. The women and the rest of the children climbed aboard the steamboat.

Grandma Cooper, as excited as the children, stood with Captain Barnabas at the helm, watching the children, the river and taking in as much as she could. Turning to Olivia, who had walked with her to the helm, her excitement bubbled over.

"I don't often want something other than what I have, but this is one time when I wish I was younger and my bones weren't so achy."

"Are you in pain, Grandma Cooper? I can give you something…"

Grandma Cooper waved her hand as if chasing away a pesky fly. "No pain…no more'n usual anyway. I just want to dance and run like the little ones."

Olivia laughed. "Well, I'm sure your heart is with them."

Grandma Cooper chuckled. "That it is. And I'm just glad the good Lord let me live long enough to ride the river."

Captain Barnabas laughed with them. He reached into a small cabinet-like structure and pulled out another cap like the one he wore. Placing it on Ethel's head, he said, "Grandma Cooper, I appoint you Assistant Captain of *The Adventurer* for the duration of this trip up river to your next camping place."

Wearing the cap like a queen, she held the wheel and grinned widely as the boat began to move. With the captain's help, she guided the barges to the center of the river shouting "Yahoo."

They were on their way.

***

Darkness settled around them and stars twinkled in the sky as Blackie swallowed the last bite of fish. Captain Barnabas and his crew had joined them and contributed to the meal. James refreshed his coffee and sat beside Olivia and the captain.

"How far did we travel today?"

Captain Barnabas answered, "We're about fifteen miles north of the destroyed bridge. If the Confederate soldiers come back looking for bones to pick, they're going to be mighty surprised."

James laughed. "I know a certain sergeant who will be even more surprised – and angry."

"Well, we're certainly thankful to you for your help, Captain," said Olivia.

"Like Bert said, 'The good Lord helped you.' We were just His tool. And we've had more enjoyment and good food than we've had in a long time. Best fish fry I ever attended."

"The vegetables you brought added some variety," said Tillie. "Thanks for reminding me of a different way to cook them. I learned that as a child when if visited my grandparents, but haven't used since."

Cook nodded. "Learned to cover them around the edges of the fire like that as a boy. Saw the Indians do it." Then he stared at his captain. "You saying my cookin's no good?"

"Cookie, you're the best man I have for *The Adventure*, but you have to admit sometimes food just needs a woman's touch. But now, we better get back to *The Adventurer*. Maybe if you show me your map, Mrs. Brunner, I can help you adjust it from here."

Olivia got the map and she and Captain Barnabas moved to the end of her wagon under the lantern. He went over it and marked a new trail to New River.

"About another two, maybe three, day's journey and you'll reach a small town here." He marked an X on the map. "A little further on – maybe several days travel – will be a town called Riverton. About a day's time from there is New River Crossing. I haven't had any dealings with either of them – mostly saw them in passing, but you should be able to get enough supplies to see you over the mountains. If the weather holds, you could be in the Kanawha Valley by early June."

Olivia thanked the captain again and he left for other adventures with his steamboat and barges. She fed the babies, put them to bed and settled under the wagon for the night. Under a cloudless sky, frogs, crickets and other night noises sang their night song. The odor of fish hung in the air, competing with river smells and spring flowers from the mountain. Somewhere in the trees above her, an owl sent its familiar question, "Hoo-Hoo?"

She waited, hardly daring to breathe. There was no answer. Had that lonely owl lost its mate? She held her breath, waiting, hoping for its answer. Then she heard it – faint and far away. Above her, the owl once again asked its question. The answer came closer. Olivia released the breath she had been holding.

Her mate is coming to her. Surely, mine will come too, won't he?

23　New Territory

Glad to be across the river, the women rose early. Excited to be ready to move again, they even laughed and joked about the ever-present oatmeal. James smiled at his mother, who had just finished feeding Lucy. "How long do you suppose that will last?" he said.

"Until we make camp tonight," she said.

James laughed. "You're probably right. Don't we move inland away from the river again?"

"Yes, by noon we won't see the river for several days. This time, maybe they'll be more willing to trust our map."

By the time they made camp, the three grumblers were sitting with heads locked together re-hashing old complaints: "...expects too much...", "...not work horses, after all...", "...never see our men again..."

James shook his head, smiled at his mother and started toward the corral.

***

Two days passed without incident, or major accident. Supplies continued to dwindle. With Blackie's help, the boys brought in enough rabbits to flavor the stew and add meat to their diet.

Shortly after noon on the third day, they veered inland and came upon the Y in the road that Captain Barnabas had marked on the map. Three painted wooden arms had fingers pointing in the three directions of the Y: Richmond 250 Miles – behind them; Gauley Bridge 75 Miles – to the left; and King's Corner 1 Mile – to the right.

Tillie, riding along beside Olivia's wagon, took a closer look at the signs. Raising up in her saddle and shading her eyes, Tillie peered toward King's Corner.

"Doubt we can take all six wagons into that small town," she said. "Why don't James and I see what kind of supplies we can find in King's Corner? You can keep moving and we'll catch up with you. Can't be too far from a place to stop for the night." Tillie waited on Olivia's answer.

"They'll only have a small general store. Probably can't get everything we need, but…maybe some basics until we reach Riverton." Olivia reached into her pocket and threw a couple of gold coins to Tillie. "Get what you can with these."

Tillie's eyes widened at the two five dollar coins. "You got many more of these?"

"Enough to supply us with basics once more and hopefully get us set up with garden seeds and supplies when we get to The Valley."

"Your father?"

Olivia smiled and nodded.

"He's a generous man, 'Livia, and he raised a generous and thoughtful daughter. I don't know if anyone ever told you, but he made it possible for all of us to have wagons and mules for this journey. We owe him much."

"Thanks, Tillie. You're right. We couldn't have made it this far without his help. Now get those supplies so we can cook some supper tonight."

Olivia smiled and slapped the reins at Max and Jasper as Tillie and James thundered off to King's Corner. Olivia followed the road toward Gauley Bridge. The wagons curled into their circle and Maggie and Claudia had the campfire blazing, coffee boiling and the stewpot on when Tillie and James rode into camp on Zeus, leading Beauty like a loaded pack mule.

The meal finished, Maggie and Grandma Cooper started cleaning up. Claudia, Corinne and Jeannette sat sipping coffee looking like thunderheads ready to burst.

Hoping to abort another confrontation, Olivia took a sip of coffee. "Is there a problem?"

"It would have been nice if you had told us Tillie was going to shop," said Corinne.

"Maybe we wanted something, too," added Claudia.

Jeannette stared at the fire, but spoke under her breath. "She's the *boss.* She's the only one who decides what we need."

"What was that Jeannette?" Olivia heard her but knew Jeannette hadn't intended for her to hear.

"Nothing."

"I'm sorry if you all feel left out," said Olivia, "but King's Corner is a very small town."

"So?" Claudia gave her a hateful look.

"Not big enough for six wagons," said Tillie.

"Well, one of us could have gone," said Corinne.

"We'll keep that in mind next time," said Tillie. "Let me know

271

who wants to ride Zeus and Beauty then double up on Zeus on the way back, leading Beauty."

Olivia took a sip of coffee to keep the smile from her lips. Not many of them would even go near Zeus, much less ride him.

"Well, you folks can sit and grumble all night if you want to," said Grandma Cooper, hanging the dishtowel across a line strung from the tent to a tree. "These old bones are ready to quit for the night."

"Good night Grandma Cooper," said Olivia. "Betsy, we need to get the babies down."

***

Another night faded to morning. The rising sun sent bright rays through the forest as if combing hair with fingertips. Leaving all nature awakening, the rays dropped down on the waking campers, tickling them with a sense of excitement. New terrain awaited. Mountains of western Virginia loomed ahead, while behind them, the James River flowed back to Richmond.

Mourning routines had become so usual that the train was moving before the women and children hardly knew they were finished with breakfast. The new road was more narrow and the river often flowed at the bottom of deep gullies and ravines – something else to strike fear into the hearts of some.

The sparkling river water flowed below the road. "Did you know that New River is the oldest river in North America?" said James.

"I didn't know that," said Olivia. "Who told you?"

"I read that in a book I got at Worthington's."

"The water looks a lot rougher than the James River," said Olivia.

"It is – partly because of the boulders and falls. And did you know the river flows south to north instead of southward?"

"Is that right? That's unusual."

"There will be deep canyons and a lot of rapids over boulders."

"According to the map the river won't be as close to the road as the James was. The mountains are steeper. It's going to be tougher going up and down them."

"But we're getting closer to our new home," said James with a look of excitement.

24   *Confederate Soldiers*

Grumbles continued like a stewpot set to simmer – not quite boiling over, but constantly bubbling. Olivia, aware of the tension, watched the women while watching for trouble along the way.

It had been almost a week since they left Captain Barnabas. Olivia's familiar premonition of possible danger gripped her heart. *The women? Grandma Cooper is too old for this kind of trip. Parker? He has tried several times. Some new danger? Plenty of new animals and dangers to face. Could be almost anything, but it feels like someone following us. It's unnerving, but it is only a feeling. I can't frighten the others on the basis of a feeling.*

She listened more intently and watched the wooded areas. *James also seems to be watching more cautiously than usual.*

Olivia felt the hairs on her neck begin to prickle as if an electrical storm was approaching. The sky was clear. Unease increased.

"As soon as we can find a clearing," she said to James, "Maybe we should stop early.

James nodded. "Good idea. I think we're being followed."

Olivia felt a heavy weight lift from her shoulders. "You feel it too?"

He nodded.

"Do you hear or see anything?"

"No, just a feeling mostly," he said. "A certain way the road curves, sound echoes differently. I'm sure I hear a number of horses back there – not running fast, just trotting along, as if trying to equal our speed."

"You have a good ear, son. I've suspected it, but I don't hear anything. And, you're right, we'll have a better chance of protecting ourselves if we can reach the next clearing and form our circle. Why don't we speed up a little?"

"You think it might be Parker's men waiting to catch us after dark?"

Olivia shivered at the thought. "Possibly, but it could be almost anyone – thieves, soldiers or maybe no one."

Tillie rode alongside the wagon. "Olivia, I think a number of riders are following us. When I was at the end of the train, I saw a dust cloud a couple of miles back. Want me to ride ahead and find us a clearing?" Corey rode up to the other side.

"Good idea, Tillie," said Olivia. "James, you go with her. Corey, you come drive the team. I'll keep watch."

"Yes, ma'am," James answered grabbing his shotgun. He handed the reins to his mother and jumped to Beauty's back as Corey jumped off and took the reins from Olivia. Tillie and James thundered off in search of a camping place. Olivia waved a green flag.

"Keep them moving steady until we get all the walkers in the wagons, then speed up until we catch up with Tillie and James. We don't want to cause panic, but don't want to dally either. There should be something in the next valley."

"We're on back here, Mom," called Betsy from the back. "Joey ran back to be with his mom."

"Let the mules trot when you can, but watch the curves, Corey."

"Okay. You heard her Max and Jasper. Let's get down the mountain. Get up there now. Move it!"

At the foot of the mountain, James guided the wagons into a clearing. As each wagon pulled into the circle, Tillie barked orders.

"Get your guns. Stay behind the wagons. Betsy, Martha, take the little ones to the woods. Corey, Michael, Jeremiah, Tom, under the wagons. Come on now, everyone move it."

Olivia, glad Tillie got the women started, grabbed her gun and started for the entrance of their circle while the women took their assigned "battle stations," guns in hand.

"Come on Joey and Sarah," called Betsy. "Martha, get Lucy. I'll take Charles."

"Where we going?" Joey grabbed his sister's hand and ran with Betsy and Martha.

"Over there," said Betsy. "We can hide in those trees." Betsy carried Charles in one arm and her gun in the other. They ran for the group of trees where they would be out of the line of fire should there be shooting.

The twins took their guns and slid under their wagon. Jeremiah and Tom went under Tillie's wagon. Olivia stood where she could see the road. James moved in behind her – Blackie at his side. They waited – nerves taut, palms sweaty. The sound of horses drew nearer. Dust swirled in the air. The breeze carried the odor of sweat – man and beast. Parker? Soldiers?

Finally, the riders came into view. "Confederate soldiers," Olivia muttered, not sure if that was good or bad. *We're still in Virginia, but what's the status of our state? Parker has already tried several times to take our animals. Will these soldiers do the same?*

"Tell the others it's a dozen or so Confederate soldiers and for them to hold their fire unless the soldiers make a move to harm us." She spoke to James without turning.

"Michael, Corey," he called to his brothers, "you go tell them. I'll keep Mom covered."

She heard the twins crawl from under the wagon and move to the women with her message. The soldiers stopped on the road outside the clearing. Olivia took a step forward where the officer in charge could see her. Holding her shotgun as if she meant to use it, she waited for him to speak.

"We ain't looking for trouble ma'am," the man called. "I'm General Robert Martin, Confederate Army. I just want to talk to the wagon master." The general had moved his horse a step or two ahead of the other men.

"Keep talking." Olivia held her gun steady and kept her unblinking eyes on the man's face.

One of the men reached for a gun. Olivia heard the click of a shotgun behind her. The general motioned to the soldier, who moved his hand away from the pistol. General Martin took a good look at Olivia and said, "Where's all your men folk?" He raised himself in the saddle and tried to peer over the wagon into the circle.

"All back in Richmond, either fighting, or in jail 'cause they won't," she said.

"You're all women and children? And you came all the way from Richmond?"

"That's right. We left there the end of March, been traveling most of the time since, except for some time held up by the weather."

"With no help from your men? Impossible."

Olivia narrowed her eyes and glared at him. "Mister, nothing's impossible if a person's determined enough and follows God's command."

The officer, who looked to be her father's age, chuckled then replied, "I can see that, ma'am. Where you heading?"

"We have friends and relatives in the Kanawha Valley." Olivia glared again and shifted her eyes to include the company of men behind him, who were looking around the wagon at the women and children. "If any of you boys got ideas about finding pleasure here, forget it or you won't have any brains left to have any more ideas. We might be women, but we'll protect our young ones and ourselves, or die trying. We've come too far to be stopped now by a bunch of juveniles in uniform."

The general threw back his head and laughed. It was a sound of merriment, not ridicule. Then he said, "I think you would do just that, ma'am. Like I said we don't want trouble. We're on our way to Richmond. Saw your wagon train and thought we'd check it out for runaway slaves and AWOL soldiers."

"AWOL soldiers?" Olivia felt confused and then alarmed. "We heard we were at war."

"Yes ma'am. We are. The Yankees fired on Fort Sumter the twelfth of last month. Mister Lincoln asked for more troops and Virginia rebelled. They seceded on the seventeenth. You're still in Virginia and if you don't go any further than western Virginia, you should be safe from the Union soldiers. Have you seen any men in these parts at all?"

"Only Captain Barnabas and his crew, who gave us a ride upriver on his barges. He missed the army troops and needed the work." She grinned at the general whose eyebrows shot up almost to his hairline. Before he could respond she continued, "If you want to search our camp, you can come alone and do it. I'll not have all those men in here with my women and children." Olivia stared over the barrel of her gun that she had not lowered during their conversation.

The general dismounted and said, "Stay put men." He stepped closer to Olivia, towering over her. She pointed the gun toward the circle and followed him, keeping the gun in her hands, but pointed it toward the ground.

"Sorry ma'am," he said removing his hat to expose a shock of white hair, "but I have to do this."

She nodded, turned to James and with a quick nod toward the remaining soldiers, signaled him to stay and make sure no one moved. He nodded in return. Corey and Michael moved to his sides. Blackie sat at his feet.

Olivia followed the general around the circle, where he glanced at all the women and children with guns of various kinds. Slowly he stepped from one wagon to another, looking inside. He glanced behind the wagons and saw all the children huddled near a tree. Charles chose that moment to cry. Betsy looked alarmed and tried to quiet him. The general went closer with Olivia right behind him.

"Where's the darkie's mother? She's a slave who'll have to go back with us."

Olivia didn't lower her eyes. "She's not with us – never was. She threw the baby at me as we left Richmond. He'll be ready to work in about ten years if you want to take care of him that long."

The general shook his head. "I get your point ma'am. You got some paper and a pencil?"

Olivia nodded toward Betsy. She gave Charles to Joey, who sat on the ground, leaning against a tree holding Sarah's hand. Charles started crying again and a look of panic spread across Joey's face, but he didn't say a word. Betsy climbed into the wagon and emerged with paper and pencil. The general lifted his foot to a wagon wheel to make a writing surface on his knee, scribbled a note, signed his name and handed it to Olivia. "This should protect you from any of our Confederate soldiers. Can't speak for the Feds. Good luck to you on the rest of your journey."

"Thank you, General." Olivia took the note, glanced at it and slid it into a pocket. She bit her tongue to stop the flow of words that might cause more trouble. She wanted to ask about Richmond, the prisoners, her father's plantation, her own home. As much as she wanted to know about these things, she was more anxious for the soldiers to leave – to put distance between them and her women and children.

General Martin mounted his horse, saluted her and turned south. The sound of the hooves died away leaving dust to settle back to the road and the weeds along the side. A soft breeze whispered through the trees and the smell of spring blossoms erased the smell of days' old sweat and masked even the irritating dust. The men were gone, but Olivia continued to stare at where they had been. One by one, the women and children gathered behind her.

"What was that all about, 'Livia?" Tillie asked.

"Why didn't you ask about our men?"

"Claudia, sometimes you have to leave well enough alone," said Tillie. "Suppose our men folk have escaped and we ask about them. What do you suppose the soldiers would think?"

"They'd think we're hiding them that's what," said Grandma Cooper. "Personally, I think Olivia did a marvelous job and so did the rest of you. No one panicked. No one got trigger-happy. I think we met that crisis like professional soldiers." She jabbed her cane on the ground to emphasize her point.

Nerves stretched to the limit, released emotions like pebbles from a slingshot, sending giggles, laughter and a few sobs around the group. Olivia's nervous laughter died away and she said, "Thank you

Grandma Cooper. We needed that little speech. I think we were all scared out of our wits, but you're right, we rose above our fear."

"Now, that we're done patting ourselves on our backs," said Maggie with a twinkle in her eye, "what did he write on that paper?"

Olivia pulled the paper from her pocket, held it in front of her and read, "This is a wagon train of women and children. They have my permission to travel to the Kanawha Valley to be with relatives while their men are away." It was signed, "General Robert Martin, Confederate Army."

Olivia slowly folded the paper and put it in a pocket of her skirt. They were safe – for now. Another four to five weeks and they would be at their new home – she hoped.

25　The Curse

The sound of the Confederate Soldiers' horses faded, but the women were still keyed up and baffled. Looking from one to another, Claudia asked what they were all thinking, "What do we do now? I was all ready for battle."

"Feels sort of like a bowl of raised dough that suddenly goes flat," said Maggie.

"Well, it's too late to start moving again," said Olivia. "We could maybe get another hour or hour and a half of travel time in, but…"

"It's hardly worth the effort of getting everyone back in place," said Tillie. "We may as well take the extra hours and catch our breath."

"You're probably right," said Olivia. "I think I'll clean and straighten my wagon – prepare for an early start in the morning."

"Today is Sunday," said Jeannette. "We aren't supposed to work on Sunday."

"That's right," said Claudia.

"We could just have a quiet prayer time," said Corinne.

"Should we skip our evening meal?" asked Tillie. Her sarcasm was lost on the three *grumblers.*

"Of course not," said Claudia.

"Then how are we going to fix it without working? And how did we manage to get this far today without working?"

Claudia, Corinne and Jeannette glared at Tillie then turned and stomped back to their wagons.

"We're going hunting," said the boys giggling and laughing as they headed toward the woods. .

"All right," said Olivia.

Although she heard the boys, the sound of gunshots startled her. She moved toward the sound of voices – just in case they needed her. Corey waved and called to her as the boys popped over a ridge. This time he knew better than to scare her with his shouting.

"Mom, look what we got."

"You all did a good job, boys," said Olivia eyeing the six rabbits.

"Get them cleaned and we'll have rabbit stew for supper. I'll see if I can scare up a few vegetables. We'll have us a feast tonight."

James laughed as he led the boys to the camp. He knew a feast would simply be the same old stew with a little meat rather than vegetables only.

Soon the savory smell of rabbit stew wafted around the camp bringing even the most skeptical to sit around the fire in anticipation, enjoying the mouth-watering aroma. Even the complainers should have been able to admit that it had been a good day. They'd met the Confederate soldiers who gave them permission to travel rather than taking them back to Richmond with the mules. They had a couple extra hours of leisure. And now...rabbit stew!

"That sure smells good," said Grandma Cooper as Jeremiah helped her to her chair. "Reminds me of the time my Albert went hunting in a blizzard." She leaned on her cane and stared off into the distance as if seeing her beloved husband standing near the woods. "We didn't have a thing in the house to eat..." Grandma Cooper smiled at the children's eager, upturned faces and launched into one of her famous stories that kept both the children and adults enthralled.

"He brought in the biggest rabbit I ever saw," she said. "It must have been as long as my trusty cane! Made the best rabbit soup you could ever imagine. It made so much that three days later, as we were finishing the last of it, we suddenly began hopping all over the house. Albert hopped out the door, through the snow drifts and the next day he returned with..."

The children, eyes wide and mouths open, waited breathlessly for the ending. Jeremiah giggled and asked, "More rabbits?" The children all laughed and giggled.

Grandma Cooper laughed her soft cackling sound with them then said, "No, not more rabbits. He came in soaking wet, icicles hanging from his fingers and nose. He carried a four-foot fish frozen like a plank from the woodshed. We had fish until..."

The children giggled and laughed some more and one said, "You swam around the house."

Grandma Cooper laughed again with the children. "You're too smart for me tonight."

While the children laughed and begged for more stories, Claudia, Corinne and Jeannette glared, arms crossed on their chests. Sounding like a teacher reprimanding an unruly child, Claudia said, "Really, Grandma Cooper, do you think it's proper to lie to the children like that?"

The children all stopped laughing, tears forming in their eyes as if Claudia had punished them instead of rebuking Grandma Cooper, whose face clouded. But she said nothing.

Michael jumped to his feet, faced Claudia with his hands on his hips and said, "You leave Grandma Cooper alone. She don't lie. She tells us stories to help us forget Richmond." He turned his back on Claudia, faced the older woman and said, "Tell us another story, Grandma Cooper. Please."

Claudia, her red-face clashing with her plum-colored dress, reached toward Michael and opened her mouth to give him a good scolding. Olivia raised her eyebrows and glared. She didn't say a word, but her warning look was clear. Claudia snapped her mouth shut, turned around and stomped away muttering about women who lie and children who have no respect for their elders.

Olivia was surprised at Michael, who had never been aggressive or rude to an adult before. She would talk to him later, but she knew, as Michael must have sensed that Grandma Cooper needed the encouragement now. She nodded to Grandma Cooper, who jumped into more stories about how Albert and she had survived in the early days of their marriage.

By the time Olivia announced, "The stew is done," Grandma Cooper had told several more stories.

"Let's gather around the fire for our blessing," said Maggie, "then we'll dish it up."

After everyone gathered, Olivia began, "Lord, You are our rock and our salvation. You give us food and the love of stories. Show us the way and we will follow You. Bless this food. Bless us. Bless our men and send them to us. Bless our journey. Amen."

"What kind of a prayer was that?" Claudia grumbled. "Doesn't even use proper words."

"Just because her husband's a preacher, she thinks she knows more than the rest of us," said Corinne. "I can't wait to get to a *real* church service with a *real* preacher."

Tillie, who stood beside Olivia, laid a hand on her friend's shoulder. "Don't pay them no mind, 'Livia. They never went to church that much when they had a chance."

Olivia smiled at her friend. "Thanks, Tillie. I guess I was letting them get to me."

Lips smacked and spoons scraped across the empty plates. The crackling fire and chatter of birds in the trees added to sounds of the contentment. Hearty laughter and childish giggles rose in waves.

Between General Martin's note and the rabbit stew, a feeling of wellbeing and hope settled over fatigued, travel-weary women and children. Evening fog began to fall around them like a soft woolen shawl. Tomorrow they would be back to business as usual with the hard work of moving a wagon train across the mountains. But, tonight would be a night of celebration. They had met danger and rebuffed it. They were safe – at least for now.

"Hey, let's have some music," said Michael. He pulled out his harmonica and blew a few notes on it.

"What's that?" asked George.

"It's a harmonica. Grandpa bought them off a ship heading back to Germany. The man said he couldn't sell them in America."

"When did you get that?" Corey eyed his brother suspiciously.

"Grandpa gave me six of them."

"When? How come he didn't give me one?"

"Cause you was off getting yourself kidnapped. Then we got home and Lucy was born. I put them away and forgot until today. I found them in my stuff."

"Oh. Do you still have some more?"

"Sure, Grandpa showed me how to play it. I'll show you." Michael ran to the wagon and returned with five more of the instruments. George, James, Corey, Jeremiah and Bobby each took one. After lots of laughter, they managed a simple tune.

"Hand me a couple of spoons," said Grandma Cooper, clapping her hands and stomping her feet.

"Spoons? You want more stew?" Jeremiah gave his great-grandmother a dubious look.

"Shucks, no, lad. I'm going to play music with you boys."

"Music? With spoons?"

Grandma Cooper laughed and placed the spoon handles between her fingers of her right hand, backs together and began clacking them together – one against another, using the left hand to alter the sounds and rhythm. The children laughed and others tried it.

"Let's have a band." Corey began to gather other *instruments*. Lids became cymbals and pans became drums. Someone took the dinner bell. Soon everyone was dancing, singing or playing an instrument of some kind – almost everyone. Claudia, Corinne and Jeannette scowled.

"Come on," Tillie called. "We may as well enjoy ourselves tonight. It might be a long time before we can relax like this again."

"It's disgraceful," said Claudia.

"Today is the Sabbath in case you've forgotten." Corinne glared at Olivia as if she should know better.

"I'm aware of what day it is, Corinne," said Olivia. "I'm also aware of the need for releasing tension. We've been on the road for over a month and a half, with at least four or five more weeks to go. Like Tillie said, it might be our last chance to relax for a while." She shivered as if her words were a prophecy.

"Just you wait," wailed Jeannette." God will punish you for acting like heathens on His day."

"Jeannette, even King David danced for joy. God doesn't punish good. He punishes evil."

"You'll see," cried Jeannette. "You'll all see. Something bad is going to happen. I just know it is."

"Jeannette," said Olivia with more exasperation than she intended, "we have several more weeks of travel through the wilderness, with the possibility of running into Union soldiers, wild animals, unpleasant weather and who knows what else. Of course, we're going to run into trouble. That's life."

"You just wait, Olivia Brunner. You'll be sorry."

Jeannette grabbed Joey and Sarah and dragged them back to her wagon. Claudia and Corinne left also with their younger children. The older ones refused to go. Olivia muttered to herself, "Yes, Jeannette, I'm sure I will be *sorry*."

Tillie heard her and laughed. She said, "I think we'll all be sorry before we arrive, but we'll be much happier once we are there."

"I hope you're right, Tillie. I hope you're right." Jeannette's words had left an uncomfortable, uneasy feeling in the pit of her stomach. How sorry would she be?

26   *Jefferson Seeks Information*

Jefferson Dooley, lost in thought, left the Richmond Post Office. He had hoped to hear from Olivia. *She's been gone eight weeks now. She must be getting close to Cabin Creek. It can't be easy to lead a group like that on a short trip, much less all the way to the Kanawha Valley. And with the war now a reality, both northern and southern soldiers will be patrolling the area.*

"Hey, Jefferson. You look like you're miles away."

"Yes, I guess I was, Andrew." He shook his friend's hand. They moved away from the doors.

"Still haven't heard from your daughter?"

"No."

"Don't worry, Jefferson. Olivia can take care of herself."

"I know she can take care of herself. It's taking care of the others that I worry about. Women can sometimes balk at another woman being boss."

Andrew, Jefferson's longtime friend laughed. "I think Olivia can handle them. She's too much like her father." He laughed again and slapped Jefferson on the back.

"I guess you're right. Her hands are too full to write."

"Probably no place along the way to mail anything anyway. She'll let you know when she reaches her destination."

"Thanks Andrew. I knew all that but I needed someone to tell me."

"Say did you hear the latest war news?"

"What's that?"

"I heard that Corporal Stevens talking earlier this morning."

"I think Matthew is sorry he ever took that blabbermouth on," said Jefferson and chuckled.

Andrew laughed with him. "You're probably right, but he said the Confederacy is moving their capitol to Richmond."

"Did he say when?"

"Just within the next week or so."

"Andrew, that will be *big* trouble for all of us."

"I know. The men in Libby…"

"The big-shots will have a circus and those boys will be the entertainment." Jefferson cringed.

"Maybe Matthew can do something. You've done a lot for him over the years."

"All I've done pales in comparison to the one thing I didn't do."

"Olivia?"

Jefferson nodded. "But I might just give it a try. Good talking to you, Andrew. Say hello to Lucinda."

"And to Elizabeth." Andrew tipped his hat and continued into the post office while Jefferson moved toward Prince.

He mounted the horse and found himself moving toward Will's house. Maybe Samuel or Rosy will know something.

***

He rode around to their cabin. Rosy was raking the garden area getting it ready to plant early vegetables. She stopped, leaned on the rake and waited for him to dismount.

"Morning, Rosy," he said. "Is Samuel here?"

"Morning, Master Jefferson. No, sir, Samuel's not here right now. You want me to send him out to your place?"

"No, I was just wondering if you folks had heard anything from Olivia."

"No sir. We ain't heard a word. Course she wouldn't send us no letter. I doubt the post office would give it to us if she did. We ain't supposed to know how to read."

"You're probably right." Jefferson smiled at his former slave. He was glad Olivia had freed her and Samuel. "I know you folks have other means of communication," he said.

"Ain't heard nothing there either. Samuel and me prays for them all the time just like the Bible says."

"I'm sure she feels it Rosy. How about Will and the others? Do you hear from them?"

"Master Jefferson, we could be in *big* trouble if word got out that we took food and news to them."

"I know that Rosy. Whatever you say is between us. I can't say how much I appreciate what you and Samuel do."

"Is there any chance they will let him out?"

"I don't see any right now, Rosy. And from what I hear, things are getting worse. Maybe I'll talk to Matthew Parker and see if he will let me visit. I'll tell him that maybe I can make Will change his mind."

"If you do, will you let us know how he is. Samuel can only

whisper to him from that little window when he takes food to them. He heard them saying something about Master Will losing his eyesight."

Jefferson groaned then mounted Prince. 'I'll see what I can do. I'll let you know."

"Thank you sir. God give you help."

***

Jefferson rode back to Richmond and stopped in front of the City Hall. He stepped into the spacious waiting room and walked to the secretary's desk.

"Good morning, Miss Campbell," he said. "Could I see either Sergeant Parker or Mayor Nelson?"

"Good morning, Mr. Dooley. The mayor stayed home this morning – a touch of the flu, he thought. I'll see if Sergeant Parker can see you?"

"Thank you."

Miss Campbell walked to Parker's door and knocked, then opened it enough to speak to him. She turned around and motioned for Jefferson to go in.

"Good morning, Matthew," Jefferson said as he reached to shake hands.

"Mr. Dooley! It's been a while. What can I do for you?"

"Just wondering if you can arrange for me to see my son-in-law. It's been a couple of months since he's been in there. Thought maybe I could get him to change his mind now that Olivia is out of danger."

"You've heard from her?"

"No, but I'm sure she's doing all right."

"You think you can convince Brunner now that the Confederates will soon have their headquarters in Richmond. When that happens, he won't have another chance. They'll try him and his friends for treason. I told him a while back I would not approach him again. It's up to him now."

"Then let me try. He is my son-in-law after all. I would hate to see him hanged, or shot and know that I didn't even try to help him."

Parker pulled at his chin for a couple of minutes, then said, "All right." He reached for a piece of his stationery and a pen, scribbled something on it and handed it to Jefferson Dooley. "Here's a note to the guard. He'll let you in. If Brunner or any of the others tries to escape you'll find yourself in there with them."

"I understand," said Jefferson. "Thank you. I know we have our differences, but I knew I could rely on you to be a gentleman." He left the room with the note and walked to Libby. There he presented it to the guard on the main floor, who opened the door to the stairs and pointed to them. "Down there," he said. "Kyle will let you in."

He reached the bottom of the stairs, which even at noon seemed stuck in permanent grayness. The guard held a lantern closer to the note then unlocked the door. "Just rattle the bars when you're ready to leave," he said.

As Jefferson walked into the cell, six sets of eyes watched him. Cautiously they approached him.

"Mister Dooley?" Joe spoke softly as if he were used to keeping what was said between them.

"Yes," he said holding his hat in his hand feeling awkward. What do you say to men who have been in prison for several months?

Will approached him with Robert's help. "Why are you here, sir? Surely they didn't…"

"No, Will. I'm not a prisoner – yet. But I had to see how you are faring. Your eyes? They're bad?"

"Yes sir, but I can see some things – especially if I'm in the sunlight."

"Not much of that here."

"No sir."

"I told Matthew that I would try to convince you to join the Confederate Army. That was the only way he would let me in to see you. I know your answer, so we won't waste time on that. He said the Confederacy is moving their capitol to Richmond within the next week or so. That will mean sure death for all of you."

Will gave a sardonic chuckle. "I don't think he will really want me now. But the rest of you could get out of here and…"

"You stay, we stay," said Joe. The rest nodded.

"Are you being fed well?"

The men laughed. "If you call a bowl of gruel once a day being fed well."

"But at least every other day – sometimes more often – food mysteriously falls through the window."

"I understand," said Jefferson. "Let me think on this. I'll figure out something to get you out of here."

"Don't get yourself in trouble," said Will.

"And don't tell Parker that Will's sight is bad."

"I won't. I'll just say you're thinking about it. Maybe that will give me one more chance to get in here and see what I can do."

"Thank you for coming," said Will. The rest nodded and Jefferson went to the bars and asked to be let out.

27 Hooked a Big One

Dense cream soup-like fog settled in the valley during the night. By morning, it was impossible to see a foot in any direction. Olivia and the boys emerged from under the wagon.

"Where's the campfire?" Corey rubbed his eyes and glanced toward a small red glow where the fire should be burning.

"It's there," said James, who took his lantern and with his extraordinary sense of direction helped his mother and Betsy get the babies to the tent where it would be easier for her to feed them. George was already there, helping Maggie with the fire.

"Hard to see out there," he said.

"Yeah," said Corey.

"Feels like walking through a dream," said Michael.

"Or a nightmare," said Corey. Then he giggled.

"Dream or nightmare, we need to feed the mules," said James.

"What if we get mixed up and feed one twice..."started Corey.

"And leave one out?" finished Michael

James pushed his brothers out of the tent. "Then you will have to give them your breakfast," he said."

The boys' giggles faded and Olivia's smile went with them as Claudia arrived.

"Olivia, we ain't moving the wagons in this fog, are we?" She shoved her children into a corner of the tent and glared at Olivia who didn't bother to answer.

Once the rest were there for breakfast, a myriad of grumbling accompanied the morning oatmeal – both from inside and outside the tent since they couldn't all fit inside. "The fog's too thick to see your hand before your face..."

"...not even sure where my mouth is..."

"...dampness sinking right into my bones..."

"...children take pneumonia..."

"...should have room for everyone inside the tent."

Breakfast over, Olivia ignored the complaints and prepared for the day's journey. While the rest finished breakfast and were still near enough to hear, she announced, "It will probably take us longer to get hitched and ready to roll this morning, but keep at it. Take your time. I don't want to have to set arms or legs before we move out. As soon as I can see the road from my wagon, we move."

"Olivia, we can't..."

"Yes we can, Claudia."

"But, we'll..."

"Take your time, Jeannette."

"Olivia, you can be so stubborn. Why can't we just wait for the fog to lift before...?"

"Corinne, if we wait, we'll only get a couple of hours of travel time. We need to move, even if we go slower."

"But..."

Olivia took Lucy from Betsy and started to her wagon letting their complaints blend into the fog. James took Charles and walked close to his mother. Betsy followed behind, holding to her mother's skirt to keep her sense of direction.

With the babies settled in their beds, she turned to James and said, "Help them get the right mules to the right wagons. We don't want any broken legs – on the mules, that is."

James laughed and his soft chuckle faded as he moved toward the corral.

By feel and by memory more than sight, Olivia took care of her preparation. By mid-morning, a narrow section of road like a crinkled brown ribbon became visible along the edge of the river. Olivia waited another hour until she could see a wider ribbon of road.

"Let's move," she said. "Corey, lead Beauty and walk in front of Max and Jasper. Take it slow and stay close. Michael, tell the rest to stay as close as possible to the wagon ahead of them. Someone from each wagon should walk with their mules."

"Yes ma'am," answered both boys together.

"I'll stay and help Mrs. Phillips with her mules," said Michael.

Corey walked the horse to the road. Michael reported to the others then went to walk with Jeannette's mules. James signaled Max and Jasper to move. They stayed on the heels of Beauty and Corey.

Unlike the road along the James River, this mountainous path carried the travelers high above the river. A sheer drop to the bottom of a ravine awaited them if they missed a curve in the road. Each wagon followed on the heels of the one ahead of it. One of the women or boys led the mules, watching the edge of the road. The fog held the sun at bay until late afternoon and then allowed thin fingers of light to sift through it. Hot humid air replaced the foggy wetness.

When they finally stopped for the night, once again the grumblers took up their chorus. "How far did we go today? A half mile? We may as well have stayed where we were," said Claudia.

"Even a snail could move faster than we did," said Corinne.

"No ma'am," said Corey dropping a load of wood beside the fire. "I saw a couple of snails along the road. We passed them and left them in the fog."

"Don't be a smart mouth," said Claudia and Corey ran off giggling with the other boys.

"However much it was, we moved," said Maggie, "we are that much closer to our destination."

"That's right," said Tillie. "Things are going to be tougher so you better get used to it."

***

Seven more days crept by with the mules struggling up slopes, straining against the loaded wagons. Everyone had to walk including the drivers. Even Grandma Cooper walked to remove as much weight as possible. Olivia and Betsy carried Lucy and Charles tied on their backs papoose style. As they had done earlier when the roads were thick with mud, they pushed and pulled to take some of the strain off the animals. Each time a hill was crested, they rested ten minutes, as much for themselves as for the mules.

Supplies were once again very low. Strength waned. Afraid for the children, Olivia cut the adult rations of food in half. She pushed aside her own bowl of oatmeal. *How can I eat it when the rest are so hungry and tired?*

"You eat that Olivia Brunner." Maggie stood over her, hands on hips, reminding her more of her mother than her friend.

"I can't, Maggie, not when…"

"Olivia, you are eating for three. If your milk supply goes we'll have to feed two more – and we don't have the kind of food we can give infants."

"But…"

"No buts. We'll make it. The rest of us adults are on half ration until we can get more supplies. The boys will hunt and fish. The children won't starve."

"But, I can't…"

"You can and you will," said Tillie who joined them. "We'll force it down you if we have to."

Olivia looked up at Tillie who was twice her size knowing she could – and would – do it.

"Yeah, Mom." She hadn't heard James come up behind them. "George and I are *halfers*, too."

"No…" Olivia started to protest. She saw the glint of determination in his eye. He stood with his arms crossed, legs apart, looking so much like his grandfather that she felt a sweep of homesickness. She sighed, reached for the bowl and forced every bite into her mouth, willing it to stay down.

That afternoon they approached another valley. A sparkling waterfall cascaded from a mountain stream that tumbled down the slope then slowly meandered across the back of the field and into the forest. She stopped to study it.

"Is there a problem?" Tillie's horse pawed at the ground.

"No," said Olivia, "no problem. I was just struck by the beauty of that clearing. Want to check it out?"

"Sure," said Tillie and nudged Zeus to the meadow. She returned with a grin. "It's perfect for a break," she said. "Ought to be some good fishing in that stream."

Olivia turned Max and Jasper into the clearing. Under the waterfall was a small pool. *A bath and clean clothes will boost morale.*

"Looks good," said James after he checked the pool. "The creek bed there is a part of that cliff. Should be safe enough for even Lucy and Charles."

"Thank you, James," said Maggie. "It will feel good to soak these hot, weary feet."

"Come on guys," James called to the boys. "We'll go fishing upstream a ways."

"But we…" began Corey.

"Want to swim," finished Michael.

"We will…later. The women need us *men* out of the way." He grinned as Betsy's cheeks turned a deep shade of pink.

"Just keep an eye on the *boys*," Olivia responded as James and the boys followed the stream into the woods.

The women enjoyed their bath – even in cold water – then sat around a blazing fire to dry their hair. They jabbed the fire with sticks and added large pieces of fallen trees to give greater warmth. Every available bush, tree and open piece of land held wet clothing.

"It feels so good to be clean," said Maggie.

"Yes, it does," said Olivia. She took a sip of her coffee, enjoying the mixed aroma of coffee and wood burning. "The boys should be back soon with a mess of fish. They'll want to bathe and swim before supper."

Shouts from the returning fishermen sifted through the trees.

"Sounds like you might be right. We'll have fish for supper if we have nothing else," said Maggie.

Olivia's smile suddenly turned solemn as she heard the familiar, "Mom! Mom!"

"That's Corey's trouble call," she said, as she picked up her skirts and ran. The others followed and met the boys as they ran toward the camp.

"Mom," cried Corey gasping for breath, "Michael's got a fish hook in his head. It's all bloody and…and…everything!"

Olivia sighed. Would she ever get used to the emergencies that seemed to pop up at the most unexpected moments?

James led Michael by one hand and carried a stringer full of fish in the other. Each boy – even Michael – carried a stringer filled with mostly trout. Olivia gave Michael's fish to James and turned him around. Sure enough, there was a hook caught in the back of his head. She would have to cut the hair around it, remove the tangle of line and pull the opposite end of the hook through. Not serious, just painful and frightening for a small boy.

Jeannette began backing away from the group, eyes wide, fists crammed against her cheeks. "I told you there would be trouble. I told you. Just you wait, Olivia Brunner. There'll be more, you'll see." Her voice rose in pitch and volume with each word.

"Will someone take her to her wagon," said Olivia through clenched teeth, "so I can tend to Michael?"

"Nurse Cooper reporting for duty, Doctor Olivia," said Grandma Cooper. "We're all set up."

Olivia, always surprised by Grandma Cooper's wit and humor, forgot Jeannette's outburst and laughed. "Come on Michael. This is going to hurt me more than it will hurt you."

"Sure it will," giggled Corey. Michael glared at him then trudged ahead of his mother into the cook tent, where Maggie and Grandma Cooper had set up a *medical station* in one corner.

With a minimum of blood and tears, Michael lost a small patch of hair and a tiny piece of skin. The other boys, looking serious and sympathetic, waited for him outside, expecting a lecture from Olivia when she walked out with him.

"I don't know which one of you hooked my son," she said as seriously as she possibly could, "but he doesn't look like a fish to me and I refuse to clean him for supper. Next time, get your fish from the water, not the shore."

The boys stared. James laughed and Corey giggled. The others, relieved they wouldn't be punished, laughed too. They gathered around Michael and treated him like a hero. As they hurried to the creek for their turn in the water, he gave them a blow-by-blow account of the removing of the hook. Olivia smiled. Michael's vivid imagination would embellish the truth.

Olivia felt a prickling sensation – someone watching her. She glanced around the wagons. Jeannette stood beside her wagon glaring at Olivia, mouth moving as if talking to someone who wasn't there. Olivia shivered. Somehow, she didn't think Jeannette was praying.

Olivia shook her head and retuned to help Maggie clean their nurse's station. There wasn't much to do except empty the washbasin and put away the surgical instruments. Once again, Olivia was glad she had brought Will's medical bag with her. She'd almost left it in Richmond, thinking she wouldn't know what to do with it if she did have a need.

In spite of the earlier commotion, they all enjoyed the fish and a time of relaxation. The boys played music and Grandma Cooper told stories – one about the time that Albert came home with a fish hook in his hand and she had to help him remove it. "The hook, not the hand," she said and they all laughed. Michael listened with elbows on his knees and chin in his hands, his eyes wide with understanding of Albert's plight.

28   Discrimination at Riverton

Another six days dragged by. Even the knowledge that they drew nearer to their destination each day did little to lift the anxiety level. Nerves stretched tight as if waiting for some disaster. Children bickered and complained, tempers flared and tension among the women became so sharp Olivia often felt the prickle of someone staring at her. She worried about Jeannette, but what could she do? She wasn't God.

According to the map, they should be close to a couple of small towns. Knowing they needed to rest as well as replenish their supplies, Olivia sent Corey and Michael on Beauty ahead to scout out a stopping place. She was beginning to question her wisdom in sending the twins when Tillie rode up beside her wagon

"The boys been gone a long time," she said. "Want me to go look for them?"

"Maybe you should…never mind. I see them coming."

A cloud of dust on the horizon grew and scattered debris around them as Beauty galloped to the other side of the wagon and stopped.

"We found a neat place," said Corey

"Nice stream," Michael added.

"Not far…"

"…only a couple of miles…"

"…sign said…"

"…Riverton one mile…"

"…population eight hundred…"

"…went to see their store…"

". . . grumpy old man . . ."

"…told us to get out…"

"Corey, Michael. I didn't tell you to…"

"I tried to tell him, Mom," said Michael, "but he was doing the steering." Michael covered his mouth and giggled while Corey glared.

"All right, but next time…"

"We worry when you boys are gone too long," said Tillie.

"Sorry," they said together.

"No harm done – this time," said Olivia. "How far to that clearing?"

"Probably a couple of hours. Doubt you can reach town before the store closes."

"We're due another rest anyway," said Olivia. "Let's get to that clearing then see what we can do. Today is Saturday and we won't be able to shop until Monday. Maybe we can rest and go to a *real* church service tomorrow. Was there a church in the town, boys?"

"Yeah," said Corey.

"Up on a hill," said Michael.

***

The sun slipped over the horizon, sending its morning rays on an excited group of women and children. They splashed water from the mountain stream on their faces and shivered, as much from anticipation as from the cold water. Then they searched through their meager belongings for something suitable for church.

"George and I will stay to guard the camp," said James, while Olivia and Betsy dressed the babies.

"I'll stay with the boys," said Grandma Cooper. "I would only slow everyone down."

"We can walk with you," said Corey and Michael.

"Thank you boys, but I'm afraid my old legs won't take me that far. I'll stay here and pray."

Amid excited giggles and lots of chatter, the rest began the trek into Riverton to worship.

"You taking the babies?" Claudia asked.

"You could leave them with the boys and Grandma Cooper," said Corrine.

"I could," said Olivia," but I never left them with Rosy when I went to church in Richmond. They'll be fine and Grandma Cooper and the boys will enjoy their solitude."

"Grandma Cooper will probably give the boys a service complete with song, Scripture and sermon," said Maggie. They all laughed at the thought.

"There'll be trouble," muttered Jeannette as if she hadn't heard all the conversation.

***

Arriving in town, the women and children started down the only street toward the church at the other end.

"We look like a bunch of rag-tag beggars," said Claudia. "My clothes droop on my shoulders like they belong to someone else."

She'd begun the journey carrying far too many pounds, now she was almost as slim as Olivia. "I'll be surprised if we don't get a lot of stares."

"Won't make no difference to God," said Corinne marching along like a soldier to battle. "We can worship as good as the next one."

Holding tightly to Joey and Sarah, Jeannette whispered, "I don't like people staring at me." She hung close to Claudia and Corrine.

People on the street did indeed stare at the six women and odd assortment of children who marched through the town like a small army off to battle. The only church in town, as the boys had said, was a white frame building on top of a hill overlooking the community. Its steeple stretched heavenward, fresh white paint gleamed in the sun. The bell echoed across the valley calling worshipers to church.

Olivia tried to reassure them. "Don't worry about people looking at us. They probably don't get many visitors, especially a whole string of women and children with no men."

Olivia slipping into her pastor's wife role, smiled and said "Good morning" to anyone she met.

Like a holiday parade, they marched down the street, up the path to the church and climbed steps to the building. Olivia led the way, carrying Charles and Betsy walked beside her with Lucy. Two men stood talking at the door. Olivia decided the one in the black suit and white shirt was probably the pastor.

Shifting Charles to her left arm, she extended her right hand. "Good Morning. I'm Olivia Brunner. We're passing through and stopped to worship with you this morning."

"Mornin'." The man seemed neither interested in introducing himself, nor inviting them into the sanctuary. He stared for what seemed several minutes, then finally, ignoring her outstretched hand, said, "I'm Reverend Martin Bragg."

Olivia stiffened her back, shifted Charles back to the right arm and stared back at the man. He was probably in his early fifties and looked as if he had enjoyed more than his share of chicken dinners and church potlucks. He squinted at Olivia and then at Charles, but offered no other information.

Undaunted by his rudeness and lack of hospitality Olivia started to go past him into the building. He put out his hand to stop her. Olivia raised her eyebrows and he pulled back the hand that had touched her arm.

"I'm sorry ma'am, but you can't go in there with him." The pastor nodded at the baby in her arms.

"I beg your pardon," said Olivia giving him an even more surprised look. *Maybe I misunderstood him.*

The man shook his head and repeated, "You can't take him in there."

"That's odd. This is a church isn't it? The house of God? A place of worship?"

"Of course it's a church and we're about to begin worship." The pastor's face began to turn a mottled shade of red. He pulled at his collar that suddenly seemed to become too tight.

Olivia stared at him and said in her clear, no-nonsense voice that carried to the rest of the women, as well as to the congregation already gathered. "I distinctly remember the words of Jesus when he said, 'Suffer the children to come unto to me and forbid them not.' I've never heard of a church that outright refused to admit a child."

"It's not the child, ma'am," the pastor said. "It's the color of his skin. There's a colored church over the mountain."

"But we aren't over the mountain, are we? We are here. We hoped to buy supplies before we move on."

"I'm sorry ma'am, but the stores are all closed today, it being Sunday and all. They open tomorrow morning at nine."

"Pastor Bragg, I'm not a heathen. I know stores are closed on Sunday. I didn't mean I wanted to buy supplies today. We'll do that tomorrow."

"We don't sell to colored folks here," said the man talking to the pastor. Olivia had almost forgotten he was there.

"And you are...?"

"Morgan. Tyler Morgan. I own the only general store in town." He pushed out his chest as if he had just told her he had been elected United States President. "We don't sell to no coloreds," he repeated. "You'll have to go over the mountain."

Olivia stared at them with her mouth open. The other women began to squirm with uneasiness. Finally, voice sharp and biting, cheeks flaming, Olivia replied, "So, you are saying that because I am fulfilling my Christian duty and caring for someone else's child, I can't worship or buy supplies?"

"Sorry ma'am, that's the rules of our town fathers."

Betsy held Lucy up for her mother. "Here Mom, you take Lucy. I'll take Charles back to the wagons."

Olivia continued to stare at Pastor Bragg until he had to turn away. He looked like he would have run away if there had been an out for him. With her eyes still boring into the man, Olivia spoke to her daughter, "No, Betsy. As long as Charles is a part of our family, if he's not welcome, then neither are we." Olivia continued to stare. Pastor Bragg and Mr. Morgan dropped their gaze. Olivia retreated down the wooden steps.

"I told you there would be more trouble," said Jeannette as Olivia stepped off the last step to the dirt road.

Olivia glared at her. "If you want to stay and worship with a church full of hypocrites we'll wait for you. Otherwise, we're leaving as soon as the mules are hitched to the wagons."

"But, what about our supplies?"

"You heard the man, Corinne. They won't sell to us."

"They won't sell to you. The rest of us can buy."

"Don't be naive, Jeannette. We're in this together. As long as Charles is in the wagon train, they won't sell to any of us."

"She's right, ma'am," said the pastor who had followed them down the steps. "I'm sorry, but I don't make the rules. Where are your men folks?"

Olivia turned and gave the pastor a searing stare that made him squirm. "Would it have made any difference in the unchristian attitude of this town if our men were with us?"

Pastor Bragg clenched his fists, his face a deep shade of red, lips stretched like gauze over his buckteeth. Olivia thought that if she'd been a man, he would have hit her.

"I didn't think so." She turned and walked away with such brisk steps that even Betsy had to trot to keep up with her.

***

The wagons rattled through Riverton as the worshipers were leaving church. Olivia stared straight ahead. Children gawked and town-folks tried to turn away and ignore them.

"Are they afraid they'll see Charles?" Betsy leaned on the back of the seat.

Olivia, too angry to answer, pretended not to hear. James winked at his sister. "Yeah," he said. "They're afraid he'll cry and they might actually believe he's a baby."

"Oh." Betsy frowned, not always understanding her brother's humor. Olivia turned to reprimand him and found herself fighting a smile. Finally, she laughed.

"Your brother is right, Betsy. Some folks are afraid of the truth, but there are others who are more compassionate. We'll find them."

The afternoon passed without further incident. The wagon train rolled through another small town called New River Crossing as the sun began to set. Twilight gave them enough light to get settled for the night.

***

The evening meal over, Olivia began preparing the babies for bed. Jeannette, Claudia and Corinne tromped over to her wagon. Olivia sat on a log nursing Charles while Betsy put Lucy to bed.

"You're going to leave him here while we go for supplies in the morning, aren't you?" The three women, glared at her.

"I won't be a hypocrite about it, Claudia," she answered without looking up. "If they can't sell to us because we have a Negro baby, then we'll continue on as we have. There's plenty of fish and game. The boys are getting to be experts. We'll survive with the Lord's help."

"Olivia, you can be the most stubborn mule I have ever met. We tried to tell you that baby would be trouble for us." Claudia's angry words fell flat. Olivia wasn't listening.

"We say you leave him here." Corinne tried her luck. Olivia ignored her, letting them stew in silence for a while. Then she raised her head and focused on Jeannette. "Will you leave Sarah and Joey here?"

They all knew Jeannette would hardly go to the toilet area without her children.

"Of course not," answered Jeannette.

"Then why should I leave my children?" Olivia was, as Claudia said, being stubborn, but she would make her point now, even if she changed her mind later. She did not intend to shop with the distraction of children and babies at all. Neither did she intend to take the other women with her.

"Olivia, that's different. They're my children." Jeannette looked horrified.

"And Lucy and Charles aren't mine?" Her eyebrows lifted in mock surprise.

Jeannette turned red and raised her hand to slap Olivia, who narrowed her eyes and spoke through clenched teeth. "I wouldn't do that if I were you," she said. "We've been friends too long to end it this way. If you prefer to take over this wagon train and move us across the mountain wilderness, I'll step aside anytime the rest agree."

Jeannette turned around and stomped back to her wagon like a three-year-old having a temper tantrum. Claudia and Corinne glared at Olivia, then turned and followed Jeannette.

299

29 New River Crossing

Olivia watched red and orange probing fingers stretch across the eastern horizon while she nursed the babies. Tillie and Betsy would feed them oatmeal later in the morning. She heard James quietly harnessing Max and Jasper. He would lead them to the road and wait for her there.

Olivia put the babies back to bed and woke Betsy. "I'm leaving now," she whispered. "Should be back by midmorning. See Tillie if you have any problems."

"Yes ma'am," answered Betsy.

Blackie followed Olivia to the road, tail wagging. James helped her mount Max then settled himself on Jasper's back.

"Stay with Betsy, Blackie," he whispered. The little dog gave him one last longing look then ran back to the wagon. As the sun slipped fully over the horizon, Olivia and James were well away from the camp. She smiled at the thought of the women's reaction when they came to breakfast and found her gone.

As if reading her mind, James said, "There'll be some angry folks at the camp shortly."

"I know," she answered, "but it's best this way." He nodded and they rode the rest of the way in silence.

Too early for the store to be open, the town stretched before them with only a light here and there to indicate life inside buildings. Like most towns, the streets were dirt, but sidewalks of wooden planks paralleled the street. Sturdy brick or log buildings stood side-by-side, narrow alleys between them and identifying signs above the doors. The Federal Bank nestled close to the protection of the New River Crossing Police Station. Several saloons and a hotel dotted both sides of the street.

Halfway through town was The General Store, a large building of split logs. A covered porch extended the entire width of the building, one step up and parallel to the wooden sidewalk. Several rocking chairs, upside down barrels with checkerboards and a sign on the wall invited folks to "sit a spell." Olivia and James sat in the rocking chairs to wait for the store to open. Rocking back and forth brought nostalgic memories of more pleasant days with her grandmother's many rockers.

"Care for a game while we wait?" James reached for a checkerboard barrel.

Olivia smiled, understanding her son's intent to relieve her painful reverie. "Are you sure you want to get beat so early in the morning?" She reached for the black checkers and began putting them on the squares.

James set the red ones in place and said, "This is the only way I'll ever beat my mom."

They both laughed and launched into the game of wit with surprising enthusiasm until they saw a man approaching the store. He nodded to Olivia and James, who stood as he reached for the door.

"You're out mighty early," said the man as he propped a brick against the door to hold it open. Somewhere inside a bell jangled when he pushed the swinging screen doors. "You're strangers here. Must be with that wagon train that went through here last evening."

"Yes sir," Olivia answered, abandoning the game. She grinned at James, who was close to winning. "Name's Brunner," she said. "We're traveling to Kanawha Valley and ran low on supplies. They wouldn't sell to us across the mountain because I have a Negro baby with us. If that's a problem for you, say so now, and we'll move on."

Olivia stared up at the tall heavyset man. His broad shoulders squared and he lowered his head exposing the silver white hair combed to one side. He had rolled his plaid shirtsleeves halfway up his forearms. Suspenders hung across his shoulders like long fingers reaching to hold on to his pants – front and back. He gave her a quizzical look then said, "Hank Miller, here. My wife and I run this store for almost thirty years afore she died last fall. Not that it matters – just curious, really– but, how come you got a colored baby and not his mama?"

"She threw him at me as we rode out of Richmond then ran away."

The man nodded in understanding then changed the subject. "Them your mules?"

"Yes, we rode them in hoping to lead them back with the supplies."

"Mighty purty animals. Look like good workers."

"They are," answered James with a note of pride. "This is Max and that's Jasper." He gave them each a pat on the nose as he spoke.

"Come on in. Why don't you take a couple of apples over there to

Max and Jasper, while I see what we can fix you up with?"

"Thank you, sir. They'll like that." James took the apples to the mules while Olivia handed Hank Miller her list.

"I have a buckboard around back," he said. "Might be easier to carry your goods. We can hitch one of your mules to it. The boy can bring it back 'fore you leave."

"Thank you Mr. Miller. That's mighty generous of you."

"Most folks call me Hank," he said as he began gathering her items. "Your men folks tied up with the war?" It was more a statement than a question, but Olivia nodded in answer. She didn't want to get into a long discussion or explanation. She just wanted to get her supplies and move on. Maybe they could be on the road again by noon. Dark clouds formed off to the southwest. It would be rough going with more rain and mud.

"Too bad you ain't settlin' around here," said Hank. "Could use a good boy to help out." He nodded toward James who carried the supplies to the wagon. "The good Lord never blessed us with kids. Don't have sons or grandsons."

"Maybe you'll find someone in town to help out," Olivia said.

"Maybe," he answered and gave her the total for the supplies.

"Can I send a letter from here? I need to let my relatives know approximately when we'll arrive."

"Sure can. Mail runs Monday and Thursday. Go out this afternoon. If you have it there, I can stamp it and drop it in the out-bag."

Olivia pulled the letter from her pocket and handed it to Hank. Then she dug into her bag of coins and pulled out enough to pay for the letter and the supplies.

"Gold coins. Ain't seen any of these for a long time. Hope you ain't carryin' too many of them with you. Could be dangerous."

Olivia smiled. "Thank you for your concern, Hank. My daddy gave me a handful. Should have enough left to get settled up north."

"I don't want to take all your money, ma'am." He started to hand back some of it.

"Thank you, but we have relatives who'll help us out. These supplies should get us to The Valley. You have to make a living too."

"I have Jasper hitched to the wagon, Mom," said James. "I'll ride Max. You can drive the wagon then I'll bring it back while you get the wagon train ready to go."

Hank Miller called after them as they started back to the camp. "God bless your journey. If'n you decide not to tackle the mountains,

302

be mighty glad for you to settle here."

"Thank you, Hank," Olivia called, waving to him. "God bless you for your help."

***

Hands on hips, scowls across angry faces, Claudia, Corinne and Jeannette met Olivia as she pulled the wagon into the clearing, "You *knew* we wanted to go," screeched Jeannette.

"It's been months since we were inside a store," said Corinne.

"I've lost so much weight I need some new clothes," said Claudia. "I'd hoped to buy some calico and muslin."

"And when did you plan on making new dresses?" Olivia threw the question over her shoulder as she and James began unloading the wagon. "There'll be time enough for calico when we get to The Valley," Olivia continued. "We still got mountains to climb. We don't need to load the wagons with any more weight than is necessary. Now let's get these supplies divided among the wagons and get ready to move."

"I have room for this," said Tillie hoisting a sack of flour to her shoulder.

"I'll take the potatoes and other vegetables," said Maggie.

They soon had the wagon unloaded. "Start hitching your mules," said Olivia. "James will take the buckboard back to town. We'll be leaving as soon as he gets back. The day started out with a clear sky, but it looks like more rain ahead of us."

James returned Hank Miller's buckboard. With grumbling and complaints from the three disappointed women, Tillie directed the distribution of the rest of the supplies among the wagons. Olivia felt that familiar prickle between her shoulder blades and turned to see Jeannette, who gave her such a hard, evil stare that she couldn't stop the shiver that ran up her spine. *Something is happening to that girl's mind, Lord. But what can I do? This journey is so impossible .Only You can help me bring them all to safety?*

"You know, Olivia," said Grandma Cooper, who had witnessed the silent exchange, "You ain't God. Only He can understand her. She needs help, but not from you. With God's help, we'll make it. Remember Jesus said, 'With God nothing is impossible,' or something like that."

"Grandma Cooper," said Olivia giving her an appreciative glance. "Are you a mind reader?"

"No," answered the older woman, "but it don't take no mind reader to read the face of a friend – or one who is on the edge of

303

insanity." She nodded toward Jeannette.

Olivia tried to ignore the chill that persisted. She could almost hear Jeannette's words, "You'll be sorry, Olivia Brunner. You'll be sorry." How much more sorry could she be?

"All right," she called to the others. "I hear James coming. Let's get ready to roll."

30   *Union Soldiers*

Once they had replenished their supplies, spirits rose and reaching The Valley seemed more possible. A mixed sense of excitement and tension prevailed. The May weather was unseasonably warm – more like late June.

It had been two days since they stopped at New River Crossing. While Claudia and Corinne had forgotten their anger over not going shopping, Jeannette held onto hers. It seemed to Olivia that she stacked one angry event onto another.

She can't keep all that hostility inside without blowing up. But, what can I do? Should I confront her? Or simply wait it out? We're all tired and our nerves are on edge. Lord, we need Your calming touch.

Olivia lay under her wagon, slapping at mosquitoes knowing she needed more sleep, but unable to turn off racing thoughts. *Soon the sun will push over the horizon and we will push on to another camping site. How many more? Ten? Fifteen?*

Finally, the smell of fresh coffee and crackling campfire were more appealing than the hard ground and bugs. *I may as well go sit with James and Tillie.*

Before she could move, however, she felt vibrations on the ground that jarred her nerves and rattled the lantern still hanging on the back of her wagon. *Surely, that wasn't an earthquake.* She listened closer. *Not an earthquake, but pounding of horses' hooves. Someone is headed this direction on horseback.*

Olivia called to Corey and Michael as she pushed herself from under the wagon. "Wake the women. We've got visitors." Tillie, James and Blackie were already at her side. Corey and Michael grabbed their guns and ran from wagon to wagon.

"Sounds like only two, maybe three horses," said Tillie as the riders drew nearer. She was right. Two riders turned into the clearing.

"Stop where you are unless you want to be shot full of holes," Olivia called to them.

The men stopped so suddenly they had difficulty controlling the horses.

"We need help, real quick," yelled one of the riders getting his horse settled. "We saw your campfire and thought maybe you have a doctor in your group."

"No doctors here," said Olivia. "What's the trouble?"

"Accident about a half mile up the road. We were sleeping and heard this loud crack. Next thing we knowed a huge tree limb fell on our captain afore he could move. He's pinned. Couple of strong men could help us lift it off and get him out."

"We don't have any men," said Olivia.

"But…"

"We can help, though," said James. "I'll get Max and Jasper."

"Yeah, we can do it." George had joined them.

"How bad is he hurt?" Olivia asked.

"Don't know. He's unconscious."

"Maybe I better go with you. Tillie if we're not back in an hour, take charge."

"I'll get some water on to boil and gather some bandages. If he can be moved, be easier to help him here," Tillie said over her shoulder as she moved toward the cook tent.

"Corey, grab a couple of lanterns. You and Michael take Jasper. James and George take Max. I'll take Beauty."

"It's not far – maybe half mile," said the soldier.

What have we gotten ourselves into? Olivia wondered as they rode after the soldiers. This could be a trap. She glanced at James. *He, too, looks wary, but alert. Even if it is a trap, we can't let a man die because we're too afraid to help. Lord, it's in Your hands.* Olivia prayed as they galloped back to the soldier's camp.

The smell of smoke from the campfire drifted out to meet them before the soldier said, "Right around that bend there." He led them into a small clearing. The campfire sent shadows darting around a fallen tree limb almost a large as an entire tree. Olivia slid off Beauty and ran to the man trapped under it.

"Bring the lanterns over here," Olivia called to the boys. A sigh of relief whispered through her lips as she examined the man by lantern light. The sudden light of the lantern made him squeeze his eyes shut. He was conscious, not crushed, but firmly pinned underneath. But where was his right arm?

"Who are you and where did you come from? Private…" The captain tried to sit up but could only lift his head a few inches. He gasped in pain and let it fall back to the ground.

"I'm Olivia Brunner from a wagon train down the road. Your men came seeking help. Can you feel the fingers in your right hand?" Olivia didn't want to waste time on nonessential questions at the moment.

The captain spoke between clenched teeth, "Yes, ma'am. And if you will pardon my language, it hurts like..."

"I get the picture, Captain," Olivia interrupted him. "It is Captain, isn't it?"

"Captain Robert Martin, the Third. Private Hall, why is this tree on me and why...?"

"It would take more than two or three men to lift that tree branch and you're hurt." Olivia answered before the private could say a word. "I'm not a doctor, but I'll do what I can after my boys get the limb off you."

"Boys? If my men can't..."

"Captain, we're all you have. Trust us."

While Olivia talked to the captain, the men helped the boys tie strong ropes around the tree limb. They started to fasten the other end of the ropes to the mules, but James yelled, "No, not that way. You'll crush him."

"Boy, who do you think you're talking to? I'm a U. S. soldier and that's my captain."

"Yeah," said James, "well he's going to be your dead captain if you try pulling that tree limb over him to get it off."

"You got a better idea?" The man retorted.

"You gotta lift it up – not drag it," answered James. "Corey, Michael, tie these ropes around your waists and climb that tree next to him. Get to that strong limb up there and drop the ropes over it."

"Okay," The twins answered together. They scrambled up a tree as if they were created to climb. When they got to the limb, Corey dropped one rope and Michael the other. James and George caught them and tied them to Jasper and Max.

"All right now, when we lift the tree limb, pull him away from it as quick as you can in case these ropes let go."

Two soldiers got ready to grab the captain under the arms and the third stood ready to go under the limb to lift his feet. Olivia stood back, holding her breath, both proud of her boys and scared to death of what they were doing.

"Okay, on three," called James. He turned to the mules. He grasped Max's halter; George grasped Jasper's "All right fellas. Come on now Jasper and Max. Let's pull that limb up. You can do it. Here we go." As he counted, he and George gently pulled the mules forward. "One – pull fellas pull. Two – you got it. Pull a little harder. Dig in those hooves. Three – give it all you got," he shouted.

James and George pulled and Max and Jasper dug their hooves into the earth and pulled with all the strength they had in them as if pleasing James was their main intent in life. The limb went upward. The men grabbed the injured captain and ran with him away from danger. When James knew the man was safe, he said to the mules as he and George rubbed their noses, "Good job, boys, Let it down now. Nice and easy. Back up a little. Good job."

"Hey James, keep the ropes tight. We're coming down," Corey called from the tree limb.

Olivia saw what they were about to do and put her hand over her mouth to keep from screaming. It would have been too late. Corey and Michael twisted their bandanas from the corners, threw them over the taut ropes and holding them close slid down the ropes. Corey landed on Max's back with a thump and Michael landed on Jasper's. The mules turned their heads and gave the boys a surprised look.

The soldiers stared at Olivia and the boys while their captain lay on the ground where they dropped him. His expression said he would have used very strong language had he not been in the presence of women and children. Olivia regained her breath and knelt beside him. He had to be in pain, but she wasn't sure of the source. Swift fingers probed his neck and back. Everything seemed intact. He winced when she checked his ribs and the arm that was obviously broken. His legs seemed to be all right. Satisfied the injuries weren't too serious, Olivia leaned back on her knees and looked at his boyish face – *far too young to be a soldier, much less a captain.*

"Do you think I'll live, Doc?" He tried to grin around the pain.

"That all depends on what you get into after I patch you up," she answered.

He tried to laugh, but it sent a spasm of pain across his face.

"Do you think you can ride your horse to our camp about a half mile south of here? Or do we need to fix a litter to carry you?"

"I think I can handle a half mile. Private Hall, bring me my horse."

***

Tillie had water boiling when they returned to the camp, but Olivia was glad she had nothing worse than a broken arm and a few scratches to fix. While she gathered what she needed, Bobby Jones ventured over to the captain, who sat on the ground near the fire,

308

leaning against a log.

"I broke my arm," said Bobby.

"Did a tree limb fall on you, too?" Captain Martin smiled at the boy.

"No, I was trying to see how far I could lean over the wagon without falling and I leaned too far."

"Did it hurt much?" asked the man.

"Yeah, but Mrs. Brunner set it. It's all better."

"Mrs. Brunner is a pretty good doctor, huh?"

"She's not really a doctor. Her husband is, but they put him in jail cause he wouldn't join the army. My dad's there too. She's taking all of us to The Valley so we'll be safe."

Olivia, embarrassed by Bobby's unauthorized praise of her abilities, said, "Bobby, do you have chores?"

"Yes ma'am," he answered. He grinned and added, "I'm just telling him what a good doctor you are so he won't be scared."

"Thank you, Bobby. Now go do your chores so we can take care of Captain Martin's arm. You didn't want anyone watching when I set your arm. Captain Martin doesn't either."

"All right." Bobby ran behind the wagon, but Olivia and the captain both knew he was watching. She started to tell him again to leave, but the captain shook his head.

"It's all right," he said. "He needs to know even a grown man hurts and will probably yell when you set the bone."

"Bite this," she said placing the thick cloth in his mouth. Tillie helped her set the arm. She wiped the beads of perspiration from his brow. James handed him a cup of strong coffee.

Olivia left her patient to recover from the trauma of having his arm set. The babies were awake and wanted breakfast. She saw Bobby sit down beside the captain, who seemed to like children. With a jolt of apprehension, she looked around for his men. They were busy helping the children with the chores – hauling water, feeding the animals, getting them hitched to the wagons, filling water barrels and whatever else they could do. The other women kept their eyes on them.

After feeding the babies and changing diapers, Olivia went to check her patient. He leaned against the log finishing his second – or third – cup of coffee. He looked pale, but otherwise none-the-worse for his accident.

"Are you feeling better, Captain?" she asked.

"Except for maybe a plaster cast, my own doctor couldn't have done a better job. And you have some smart kids here. Don't suppose I could recruit a couple of them."

Olivia smiled while she studied his face for a minute. Then she said, "Captain, James and George are the oldest children in our camp. They are just barely twelve. Corey and Michael who went up – and down – the tree are only six. They all seem older because they have to be."

Captain Martin's brow lifted. He shook his head and sipped at his coffee. "People who start wars don't think about things like that," he said with a faraway look in his eyes. "You got far to go?"

"About another week to a week and a half. We go north to Gauley Bridge where we'll cross over. Only a few days from there." She smiled at the man.

"Better go on to Carnifex Ferry. There's supposed to be fighting at the bridge sometime in the next couple of weeks – not sure when, but better if you miss it. Got a map?"

Olivia showed him her revised map that Captain Barnabas had made for her. He showed her another route to the ferry, only a little out of the way. "Don't let Old Jake McCoy overcharge you to get across."

"Thank you," said Olivia.

"Don't suppose you've seen any Confederates about? We were sent to scout the area."

"A couple of weeks ago. They told us Virginia had seceded."

"That's right," he said. "I don't suppose you've heard the Confederates have moved their headquarters to Richmond."

Olivia paled. "That's not good," she said in almost a whisper.

"No, I'm sorry to give you bad news. If I ever run across your men, I'll do all I can to help them on their way. But they'll have a hard time of it."

"General Robert Martin wrote a note giving us permission to travel through Confederate territory and granted us safety from Confederate troops to the Kanawha Valley."

"Could I see the note?"

Olivia reached into her pocket and pulled out the folded note. The captain looked at it and smiled.

She gave him a curious look. The names were the same. "Relative?"

"Grandfather," he said. "We don't agree on a lot of things, but he's a good man. You got a pencil?"

"Betsy, bring Captain Martin a pencil please."

He followed Betsy to the wagon and grinned as he took the pencil in his left hand. He lifted his foot to the wagon wheel the way General

Martin had done and using his knee as a writing board, wrote something across the back of the Confederate General's note. "Good thing I'm left handed," he said, winking at Bobby, who followed him like an adoring puppy.

Bobby giggled. "I broke my left arm," he said, "so I could still do things with my right hand."

He handed the note back to Olivia then tousled Bobby's hair. "Carry on, soldier," he said.

"Yes sir," answered Bobby and saluted the captain who then mounted his horse. His men followed him.

"Thanks for your help and your hospitality, ma'am. I hope the rest of your journey is uneventful and your men folk can soon join you."

"Thank you, Captain. Take care of that arm. Keep it in the splint and in the sling for at least six weeks."

Captain Martin grinned and saluted her with his left hand. They turned and galloped south. The women gathered around her to hear the note. "Union soldiers are gentlemen too. We agree with General Martin. It's signed, Captain Robert Martin, III."

31 Richmond Becomes Capitol

Samuel had gotten in the habit of checking with Noah before taking food to the prisoners in case there was any news they should hear. Soldiers patrolled the streets most of the day. As he made his way to the newsstand, keeping in the shadows, he thought, something's going on today. Noah was behind his drop-down counter waiting for the papers.

"Something is going on Noah," Samuel said as he leaned against the wall, trying to be inconspicuous.

"I know, Samuel," said Noah. "I don't know what, but I can feel the tension in the air. David's late. The paper's late. I got a bad feeling about this."

"I'm with you Noah."

"I hear the wagon. Maybe the paper will tell us something."

"Here comes David. Looks like he's seen a ghost."

"Come here boy," called Noah. "What's going on? Are you hurt?"

"No, sir," said David. "Just scared. "Some soldiers stopped me. Tried to make me join them, but they got distracted and I ran. But I'm scared they'll come and get me – even with my bad leg."

"You get going," said Samuel. "Keep to the shadow and go to Rosy. She'll hide you till I get home. Hurry now."

"Grandpa…?"

"Go, boy. Samuel's right. Something is happening and you need to get yourself away from here. Samuel and Rosy will help you."

David gave his grandfather a hug and ran into an alley. He was gone by the time the wagon arrived and dropped the bundle of papers on the platform. Samuel set the papers on Noah's counter top, cut the ties then picked up the top paper.

"Hey there nigger, what you doing. You can't read."

"I knows that," said Samuel to the young soldier who yelled at him. "I just moved the torn copy so's you folks can get a good copy to read. I can use this to start a fire in the cook stove."

The men laughed and pushed him aside and began taking the papers. Some gave Noah his money, some didn't. When the soldiers were all gone, Samuel looked around to make sure no one was near. He lifted the paper and read to Noah, "Confederate Government Moves to Richmond. Today, May 21, the Confederate government will set up their offices in Richmond, Virginia where they will be closer to the action and to the Federal Government in Washington. We are expecting great things from our new government."

"This be bad," said Noah. "I can hear singing and shouting already. They be celebrating like they did when that Brown fella got hanged."

"I need to let Master Will and Master Jefferson know. Don't you worry about David. We'll get him on his way to the Underground Railroad. Maybe you better come too, Noah."

"I's too old to run, Samuel. They already took my eyes. They may as well take the rest of me. Just get that boy to safety."

Samuel slipped through the alley and worked his way to the back of Libby where he intended to talk to Will. Soldiers were guarding the prison, all around. He paused to listen as two stopped to talk.

"These prisoners been in there for months. Why does Parker think they might try to escape now?"

"Because things are changing. We're no longer in charge. The Confederate government is. They'll try the men and hang them for treason. If they get wind of that, they might panic and try to escape."

"Not likely to happen."

"At least we're not in there polishing Parker's boots." They both laughed and continued on their rounds.

Samuel staying in the shadows made his way out of town. Somehow, he would have to get to Master Jefferson. He had already taken all the horses to him. Maybe he could go through the woods. He stopped to listen before crossing the road. Hearing horse's hooves approaching he waited behind a tree. Jefferson Dooley passed him on the way to Richmond. Samuel gave a sigh of relief. *If Master Jefferson is going to town, he will hear the news, so I need to get home and help Rosy get David out of here.*

***

Jefferson Dooley heard the revelry before he even entered Richmond. *What is going on?* He rode down Main Street toward the Court House and Parker's office. He didn't need to ask. All the military brass going in and out of the government office building told him the Confederate Army had arrived. Richmond was now the Capital of the Confederate States.

He could see that the drunken revelry was getting out of hand and it was still early evening. He dismounted and made his way through the jostling crowd to the mayor's office. Inside the once spacious waiting room, desks, chairs, men and artillery took up more space than any men who waited to see the mayor had ever done. Someone had pushed Miss Campbell's desk to the far corner. She was stuck between the wall and her desk. She didn't look very happy.

"Good morning, Miss Campbell," he said as he approached her desk. "Is the mayor in?"

"I'm not sure, Mr. Dooley. As you can see, things are rather chaotic in here. If I could get his desk away from me, I would get out of here as fast as I could."

"Why can' you…" he stopped. "Oh, someone set a small cannon in front of your desk. Here, let me move it." Laying his hat on the desk, he moved the heavy article and pulled the desk away from her. "Is that better?"

"Thank you so much, Mr. Dooley. If you see the mayor, please tell him I quit. I won't work in this kind of environment."

"I'll tell him. Say hello to you father."

Miss Campbell didn't take time to answer. She almost ran for the door. One of the young men reached to grab her. Jefferson grasped his arm. "I wouldn't bother that lady, if I were you," he said.

The man started to reply, but Jefferson squeezed his arm tighter. He jerked away and went back to doing whatever he had been doing. Jefferson made his way to the mayor's office. He wasn't there. He went to Parker's office. Matthew was seated behind his desk looking like he had just lost a most valuable object. Maybe he had. He raised his head and looked up as Jefferson closed the door.

"Evening, Matthew. It seems a little hectic out there."

"It's not a good day, Mr. Dooley. They're taking over."

"Did you think they wouldn't?"

"Mayor Nelson and I thought we would at least be in on their talks."

"And you're not?"

"We're no better than the freed slaves in town. They order us around like we were dirt."

Jefferson bit his tongue to keep from saying, "I told you so."

"It's looking bad for the men in Libby. They want to bring them out and parade them down the streets then tell them they are free and shoot them in the back when they run."

Jefferson felt the blood drain from his face. "And the mayor will allow that?"

"He has no say. *They* are in charge. *They* are going to round up all the slaves and freed slaves to make them either work for them or join the ranks of the army. Mr. Dooley this isn't at all what I envisioned for Richmond when the war came."

"It isn't what any of us envisioned, Matthew. I have to try to save my daughter's husband."

"You will end up in there with them."

"I have to try something."

"Maybe things will settle down in a day or two, but if I find out they are going to move faster than that, I'll let you know. I don't like cold-blooded killing. At least on the battlefield, the enemy is armed and hopefully trained to protect himself."

"But they still die – both sides. I'll stop back tomorrow."

Matthew dropped his head on his desk and Jefferson walked away. He hurried to Prince and rode home.

32   Tragedy at New River

Hot, sunny days had replaced the long days of spring rains. Occasional storm clouds and brief showers kept the travelers alert for flash floods and muddy roads. Up and down hills, around sharp curves, like a slow moving caterpillar, the wagons picked their way along narrow mountain roads barely wide enough for them. Nerves taut, hearts heavy with anxiety, women and children alike watched warily for any hint of trouble.

Bone weary, eyes heavy for want of rest, Olivia pulled her well-worn map out for what seemed the dozenth time that day. James smiled. She ignored him.

"We can't be too much farther from that crossing," she said.

James, who had memorized the map, said, "Probably about another day – or two at the most."

"I want to time it to arrive in the morning, so we can all cross in the same day. I don't want half of us on one side of the river and the rest on the other side when night falls."

"Not a good idea," said James. "We'd have some women in a worse panic than they usually are." He glanced around him. "We seem to be in a fairly clear valley. Might be a good idea to stop early and do some last minute inventory and planning."

"That sounds like a good idea," said Olivia. With more enthusiasm, she began to look for a place to camp. As they rounded a curve in the road, Olivia caught her breath. "Over there," she said, pointing across from the river. "Why don't you check it out. I'll hold Jasper and Max in check."

James jumped down and ran across to the clearing. Michael followed. "I'll go with him," he called back to Olivia as he ran. The clearing turned out to be a beautiful green field. A clear, bubbling stream ran along the back edge and meandered back into the forest.

"As much as I want to reach our destination, I don't think anyone will mind stopping early," she said.

James grinned and nodded. "It's been a little more than a week since New River Crossing and we are near the crossover point."

Wagons slowly crept into their circle. Weary boys began unhitching mules to corral them for the night. Throughout the camp groans and moans rose above the burble of the water – river on one side and creek on the other. Olivia ran her hand across Max's back as James unhitched the mules.

"They're getting tired, too," said James.

Olivia nodded. "I know." She paused then said, "We'll give the mules a rest. First thing in the morning, you and Corey can ride ahead to check out Carnifex Ferry – at least see how close we are to it. Should only take a few hours by horse."

"How long should it take once we get to the ferry?"

"Once we're across, we ought to hear from Uncle George almost anytime – maybe two or three days."

"We'll leave before breakfast tomorrow and should be back by late afternoon," he said and turned to lead the mules to their resting spot.

Olivia wanted to relax and just enjoy the beauty around her, but she dared not let her guard down. Anything could happen yet. She kept a close eye on the babies. During one of their Sabbath rests, James had made a collapsible, portable, fence-like structure for them. Lucy and Charles sat on a blanket inside their fence and gurgled to each other. James found his mother grumbling to herself when he returned from caring for the animals.

"Is something wrong?" he asked

Olivia whirled around, startled. "I didn't hear you coming," she said then laughed. "No, nothing's wrong. The *girls* are complaining because we stopped too early. They think we should've kept going so we can get to The Valley sooner."

James laughed with her. "The girls – meaning the three complainers?"

Olivia smiled and nodded.

"If we'd kept going," said James, "they would've complained because we didn't stop sooner. You can't win with those three."

"You're probably right. Maybe we should've moved on. We have another three or four hours of daylight, but we can't be far from Carnifex Ferry."

"I think you're right, Mom." Then he changed the subject. "Since it is still early, why don't George and I take the kids and see what kind of fish we can catch for supper? We'll watch the hooks and stay away from the river's edge. The water looks rough out there. Sounds like a waterfall not too far downriver."

"That's an excellent idea, James. Fresh fish again for supper might spark a little enthusiasm."

The boys, laughing and joking about getting a hook caught in their head, started across the road to the river. Olivia began to relax until angry words from Jeannette's wagon reminded her of potential trouble and Jeannette's unstable condition.

From the beginning of the journey, they had determined that each woman would look out for all the children – reprimanding, correcting and praising. But discipline and punishment would be strictly each mother's responsibility. Olivia didn't always agree with the other women's method of discipline, but she wouldn't interfere. Each respected the others' privacy as much as possible, but living in such close proximity to one another made it impossible not to know what was happening around the circle.

Jeannette, never one to cope with even small problems, seemed to be losing control of her temper more often than the other women – or even the children. Her raised, shrill voice made everyone wary. They watched her with concern – even Corinne and Claudia. Not wanting to hear, her latest tirade at Joey, the women tried to ignore her. Joey seemed to receive the brunt of Jeannette's anger and fear more than Sarah. Even the other children shivered in fear at her scathing words.

"Why can't you ever do anything right? Why can't you be more like Sarah?" Jeannette's voice rose in volume. Although his words were not distinguishable, Olivia knew Joey had responded. A loud crack followed his voice. Olivia flinched. Had Jeannette slapped the child that hard?

"Don't you talk back to me. You watch your sister. And don't you…"

Olivia tried to ignore Jeannette's screams as much as possible, but saw Joey jump from the wagon and run her way. Had there been a door on the back of the wagon, Olivia was sure he would've slammed it. Looking like a storm cloud pushed by gale force winds, he ran across the center of the circle and almost into her.

"Whoa there, Joey. What's the problem?"

"Sorry, Mrs. Brunner." The frail little boy rammed his hands in his pockets. "Nothing," he said, then hung his head. "I just need to control my temper."

Olivia had to bite her lip to keep from laughing. That was Jeannette talking. With as much seriousness as she could manage, she said, "I think we all need to watch our tempers, Joey. It's been a long trip and we're all getting on each other's nerves. We'll soon be in The

Valley and can go our separate ways. Then we'll be good friends again." She smiled and laid a hand on the red print on his face then tousled his unruly brown hair, which like all the boys, needed trimmed.

He attempted a smile, but his eyes were far too sad for such a small boy. "I know," he said. Olivia wanted to hold him the way she did Charles and Lucy, and would have if Sarah hadn't chosen that moment to run toward them shrieking. "I wants to go, too. I wants to see the water."

Joey yelled back at her. "You can't go. Mom said for you to stay here." He turned and ran toward the river. Olivia knew Jeannette didn't allow him to fish – or even go near the river for any reason. She suspected he was being disobedient this time, but she also knew James and the other boys would watch him. Sarah was a different story. Sarah wouldn't listen to them.

"Sarah, why don't you come play with the babies? We can…"

Sarah turned with hands on hips, stamped her foot and screamed, "No! Leave me alone. I hate you. You a mean old woman. I go with Joey." She ran screeching after her brother, leaving Olivia stunned.

Jeannette stepped from her wagon and yelled after them. "Joey, you come back here and watch your sister. Don't you go near that river! You let her get hurt and I'll whale the daylights out of you."

Olivia glanced at Jeannette who sent such a scathing look at her that she felt her skin prickle and looked to see if blisters had formed on her hands and arms. *Is Jeannette losing her mind completely? Surely, I haven't been that hard on her. Whatever, her problem, Jeannette needs to know the children went to the river.*

"Jeannette, they went to the river," Olivia called.

"Mind your own business, Olivia Brunner. I told them not to go. They won't disobey me."

"Jeannette, they…" A blood-curdling scream from the river stopped her.

Betsy and Martha ran to the babies as Olivia lifted her skirts and ran toward the river. She met James coming toward the camp. "Sarah fell in…Corey jumped in to help…both carried away…get Beauty…rope…catch them."

33   *Carried Away*

Neither James, nor Olivia stopped. James kept running for rope and Beauty. Olivia continued across the road and down the sharp embankment to the river. At the edge of the river, Joey screamed and fought Michael, who struggled to hold him back. Blackie bounced around them, nudging them away from the river's edge. Olivia grabbed each boy by an arm and yanked, jerking him from the brink of the river. Beauty galloped down the road above them and Blackie after her.

"We don't need any more of you in the water." Olivia's voice was sharp.

"It's my fault," cried Joey. "I want to die too."

"What do you mean your fault," Jeannette screamed from behind them.

"Keep your comments for later," Olivia ordered. "We need to get the children."

"I told you this would happen," yelled Jeannette. "I told you this would happen."

"Jeannette, if you can't keep your mouth shut and help us then go back to your wagon and bury your head or something. Michael, come with me. We'll go along the river bank."

"We'll go the road," yelled Tillie. "Call us if you need help down there."

They all ran, leaving Jeannette still shaking Joey as if she could shake time back to the past and prevent the tragedy.

"There they are." Michael pointed to the middle of the river. "Corey has Sarah, but she's still fighting him. He can't swim in the rapids with her squirming like that."

"You're right," said Olivia picking up her skirts to run. "It's all he can do to hang on to her and keep their heads above the water.

Oh dear Lord, help us to get to them in time. Olivia prayed as she ran.

They rounded a bend and James was there with a rope tied around his waist. "Stay, Blackie," he yelled as he jumped into the water. The current immediately pulled him downstream toward the falls. The little dog sat twitching, ready to jump in and follow his master. He waited. Olivia saw the rope pull taut and stop her son's downstream movement. He had tied the other end around a tree about three feet from the edge. James started swimming toward the center.

He intends to grab Corey and Sarah as the rapids sweep them downstream.

"If he misses them, the children will go over the falls," Olivia said, hearing Tillie come up behind her. She pulled at her dress, scattering buttons. "The rope won't be long enough," she said and slipped out of her dress and shoes. Tillie untied the rope from the tree and she and Michael held the rope taut while Olivia took the end from the tree and tied it around her waist.

"Take my hand," Tillie yelled as Olivia slid into the water. Tillie fell to her stomach, leaning over the edge. "Grab my feet," she called back to Michael. Joined by the other women, he grabbed her feet and legs and held on, feeling the pull of the water as Tillie held to Olivia.

Olivia went as far as she could while keeping hold of Tillie. It wasn't much, but added four or five feet to the length of the rope for James. Her arms ached from the pull, but she didn't dare let go or they would all go over the falls. Screams from the road told her Jeannette had caught up with them. She blocked out the sound. The water, up to her chin, splashed over her face, blurred her vision. She wanted desperately to go out farther – to swim with James and catch the children. Only the clutch of Tillie's hand around her wrist gave her courage to keep her common sense.

Finally, Tillie began pulling her back. James either had the children, or he'd missed them and they were gone. Slipping and tripping over stones and roots, Olivia backed toward the bank, where the water only reached her waist. Once she was out of the current and could stand without being sloshed about, she swiped the water from her face. Her heart pounded in her chest. Breath came in short gasps.

Brushing the water away from her eyes with the back of her hand, Olivia saw them – James holding desperately to Corey and Sarah. While the women pulled the rope, she grabbed it and began to help. James could barely keep his own head above the water while holding the children's heads up. They both looked unconscious – or dead.

James hit the bank beside Olivia. Maggie snatched Sarah from him. Corinne grabbed Corey. Claudia gave James a hand and pulled him out of the water. Tillie helped Olivia. Blackie whined and wiggled, but stayed out of the way.

321

"Somewhere I read of midwives in the Bible who blew air into the mouths of newborns when they wouldn't breathe on their own," said Olivia taking Sarah in her arms.

"We gotta try something," said Tillie reaching for Corey.

Jeannette screamed and clawed at Olivia's arm trying to take Sarah from her. Maggie, Claudia and Corinne pulled the distraught mother away from her. They struggled. Jeannette's ear-splitting screams stopped as Maggie slapped her so hard the sound echoed across the river above the sound of the rolling rapids.

Olivia continued to breathe for Sarah until the little girl coughed. Sarah started heaving and Olivia turned her over on her stomach, pressing her back until the child began throwing up river water. Gently Olivia pressed more water from her lungs until Sarah cried and struggled.

Beside her, Corey, pale and coughing, raised his head and looked to his mother. "She all right?"

"You both are," Olivia said and sat down with a thump as Jeannette snatched Sarah from her. Olivia felt as if her knees had turned to jelly. "Get them back to the camp and into some dry, warm clothes," she said. "I'll be along in a minute."

Olivia sat on the bank of the river trembling, her face buried in her hands. Sounds of concerned voices and crunching stones faded as the rest moved toward the camp. Jeannette's screams faded. "It's all her fault. My baby's going to die. She caused it because she…"

Olivia sat until only the river filled the silence around her. She waited for her heart to stop pounding in her ears and her hands to stop shaking. Startled by a sound behind her, she turned to see Maggie standing with her dress over her arm.

"Would you like some help getting back into this?" Maggie, holding Olivia's dress, extended a hand and grinned at her friend's startled look.

"I thought everyone had gone," she said reaching for Maggie's hand.

"I figured you might need help once the shock wore off."

Olivia didn't need to explain for Maggie's sake – only for her own. "The wet dress and shoes would've pulled me under."

Maggie nodded in understanding. Between the two of them, they got the wet rope off her waist and her dress on. Maggie even found most of the buttons Olivia had ripped off in her haste. She would sew them back on later.

"Olivia," Maggie paused as she helped with the buttons that

remained. She took a deep breath then hurried on, "Thank you for caring enough to stand up to us even when we aren't very nice." Maggie gave her friend a quick hug then ran. Olivia was embarrassed. She wasn't used to receiving praise for her work as wagon master.

Olivia struggled up the embankment, slipped and grabbed a sapling to keep from falling. A hand wrapped around her wrist and pulled her the last foot or so to the road.

"Thank you, James," she said as her son threw back his head to remove the wet hair from his face. "You were terrific, you know."

James blushed then said, "You weren't so bad yourself."

She put her arm around his shoulders and smiled at her son.

"You want to ride Beauty?" James asked, grasping the reins.

"It's not that far, but my knees do feel a little weak." James helped her onto the horse then swung up behind her. Blackie trotted along beside them, tongue hanging out the side of his mouth.

34   *Fire and Prison*

Samuel woke early, having hardly slept. He smelled smoke as if all Richmond was burning. *All those drunken fools probably set a few barns on fire.*

He stepped out to the porch. The acrid smell was stronger. He started toward Will's house. Rosy followed him out to the porch.

"Where you going? Is Will's house…?"

"Don't know," said Samuel, "but I got a real bad feeling 'bout this. Get David and move him to the woods. You know the place. If I ain't there by nightfall or if soldiers come looking, move on to the Railroad. Don't wait for me."

"Samuel Brunner, I won't…"

"Don't argue with me, woman. You get that boy safe. I got to make sure Master Will is going to be all right. Don't like what I been hearing in town."

Rosy brushed at her tears, ran down the steps and kissed Samuel on the cheek. "You be careful and take care of yourself. Me and David will be all right."

Samuel waited to watch Rosy and David running toward the woods then he turned toward town. He stopped and ran behind the house, when a galloping horse raced into the Brunner's yard. The rider dismounted and ran, not to Will's, but to Samuel's cabin.

"Samuel, Samuel."

It's Master Jefferson. "Yes, sir," he called as he stepped from behind the pile of wood.

"Samuel, they…they…"

"Here, Master Jefferson. Come sit on the step. What…"

Jefferson swiped his tears and gulped back a sob and sat on the step with a thud. Samuel sat beside him ready to help him if he should pass out. *Something mighty bad happened to put him in this state.*

"The soldiers… the drunken so-and-so's…they burned the plantation."

Samuel sucked in his breath. "Miz Elizabeth? Mattie? Henrietta?"

"Elizabeth, Henrietta and all the other slaves are dead. I found

Moses with Mattie in the barn. He said he was taking her to the woods. He knew a place."

"Yes sir. I just sent Rosy and David there. Told her if I don't show up by nightfall for her to get the boy and herself to the Railroad. Moses will meet them at our special place."

"They'll be here, Samuel. You have to go to."

"No sir, I ain't goin' no place without Master Will."

Jefferson dabbed at his eyes. "Samuel you are a true friend. I'm going to see the mayor and what I have to say will probably get me thrown in prison too. I'm hoping I can recruit Parker's help. I know he has done all he could to get Will in the *Volunteers*, but he's not at all happy with the way things are going. When I tell him Elizabeth was murdered by those cutthroat renegades, I think he'll help me. Don't get yourself caught and stay near the prison if you can. We'll need you."

"Yes sir, Master Jefferson. I'll gather some supplies and hide them where we can get them later. God go with you, sir."

***

Jefferson ran back to Prince and headed toward town before he had hardly mounted. He raced down Main Street and stopped before City Hall. It was too early for anyone to be there on a normal day, but today was not normal. Soldiers milled around the streets as if they had been there all night.

Jefferson dismounted and ran inside and without speaking to anyone. He barged into Parker's office. Matthew looked up at him bleary-eyed. He either hadn't slept or had been crying, or both. Jefferson ignored his looks and with a voice of authority said, "Come with me to the mayor's office." He turned before Parker could say anything and walked out of the room.

Jefferson pushed the mayor's door open and found Mayor Nelson in conversation with a Confederate General.

"What's the meaning of this outburst? Parker get that man out of here."

"Yes sir," said Matthew. He laid a hand on Jefferson's arm. "Come with…"

Jefferson jerked his arm away and stomped to the mayor's desk. He leaned on it so he was face to face with Nelson. "You, sir are a murderer. And so are they." He turned and pointed his finger at the General."

"Mister Dooley! What are you talking about?"

"Your renegade soldiers came to my plantation while I was in town trying to talk some sense into some people. They burned my buildings to the ground, slaughtered all my cattle and sheep, killed all my slaves and … and…" A sob escaped, but he continued. "And murdered my beautiful wife, Elizabeth. You are as much a murderer as the men who did the deed."

Behind him, Jefferson heard Parker suck in his breath. He turned and glanced at him. He had turned white; his fists balled at his side.

The mayor, red-faced stood. "Parker, arrest that man. No one comes in here and accuses *me* of murder. I don't care who he is."

"Is this true?" Parker asked the General.

"Possibly. I gave the order to burn the traitor's homes and kill all their slaves. They might have gotten a little out of control and included some of their families. Tomorrow we will parade the traitors down Main Street and then shoot them. And that, sir, includes you as of now! Sergeant take him to Libby with the others."

With a trembling hand, Parker took Jefferson's arm and led him from the room. "Come with me to my office while I get my jacket and keys," he said, his voice quivering.

Inside the room, he whispered to Jefferson Dooley. "Sir, I…"

"You didn't know," said Jefferson. "But you can help me now."

"How?"

"Just lay the master key to Libby on your desk. I'll steal it. You know nothing about it."

"And when you escape? Where will you go?"

"I don't know and I wouldn't tell you if I did. This isn't your problem."

"Yes it is. Had I known this would be the result, I would never have pushed…"

"Parker, get that man to the prison."

"Yes, sir. I had to get my jacket."

As they walked to the prison, Matthew held tightly to Jefferson's arm, the key already in Jefferson's possession.

"Mr. Dooley, you get them out of the prison and I'll see that you get out of town – alive or we'll all die together."

Jefferson nodded. "Talk to Samuel."

He led the man down the stairs to the cell. Six men looked up. "Unlock the cell," Parker said to the guard. "In you go, Dooley. You shouldn't have called the mayor a murderer."

Matthew Parker turned and walked away. Jefferson Dooley turned to explain to his son-in-law and friends.

35   Waiting

"Sorry we didn't get any fish," said James later as he warmed himself by the fire. "We were sort of interrupted."

"That's all right. We still have some dried beef. We'll have soup. I think everyone will need the broth as well as whatever vegetables we have."

Olivia set a pot of water on the fire and added the dried beef and some onions. For several hours, the tantalizing aroma invited the hungry travelers to gather around the fire to talk and wait. Fear was reluctant to release its grip. Death had come too close – and still lurked, waiting for one – or more – of their number. Only Jeannette refused to bring her children. She would care for them in her own way.

Although everyone, except Jeannette, already waited beside the fire for supper, Olivia rang the supper bell. Jeannette brought bowls for her and Sarah. "Sarah needs to stay in the wagon until she is well," she said, answering the unasked question.

"Jeannette, bring her out here," said Claudia glancing at Corey who sat huddled with his friends close to the fire– wrapped in a blanket like a caterpillar in its cocoon. "Don't make an invalid of her. She needs to be where it's warmer – to move about to keep pneumonia from settling in her lungs." Olivia was glad Claudia said it.

Jeannette ignored her and turned to go back to her wagon without answering. Olivia called to her. "Jeannette, how is Sarah? Does she have a fever? Can I…?"

"No! You stay away from her. She's not all right," Jeannette said. Had she been a dog, a snarl would have followed her words. "She almost drowned and will probably take pneumonia. And it's your fault." Jeannette whirled around to leave.

"Jeannette." Olivia laid a hand on her arm to stop her. Jeannette jerked away and splashed hot soup on both of them. "Jeannette, you're behaving like a child. What about Joey? You only have enough for two."

"It's his fault. He pushed her into the river. He's being punished. He won't have another bite of anything to eat until she gets better."

Jeannette's voice had risen to a high-pitched scream. The other women, even Claudia and Corinne looked at her as if a monster had suddenly appeared where Jeannette stood.

"Jeannette, you're overcome with fear and grief," said Olivia. "You can't punish a small boy by refusing him food. I've never interfered with any of you in your discipline, but you will send Joey out here to eat, or I will take it to him. You won't starve him for being a child."

"Keep out of it Olivia Brunner. It's all your fault anyway."

In an effort to keep her temper, Olivia clenched her teeth, squeezed her hands tightly into fists, which hung at her side. It didn't work. She the lost the battle, but kept her voice low and even. "Jeannette, make up your mind. If it's my fault, then punish me. If it's Joey's fault, then punish him correctly."

"Both of you are at fault," she screamed.

"Then hit me and get it out of your system." Olivia extended her chin. Jeannette gave her a scathing look, turned and stomped away.

Olivia waited long enough for Jeannette to return to her wagon and for Joey to come to the fire. When he didn't come, she took a bowl of soup and went to Jeannette's wagon, not sure how she would be received.

"Jeannette," she called. "I brought supper for Joey. Please send him out here."

"Go away. He's asleep."

Olivia heard the child sobbing and hiccupping inside the wagon. "Jeannette, either you send him out, or I will come in and get him."

Jeannette came to the back of the wagon with her shotgun aimed at Olivia. "You take one step into my wagon, Olivia Brunner and I'll blast you to kingdom come."

"And there won't be enough of you left to bury throughout the whole state of Virginia, Jeannette," said Tillie from behind Olivia, who had been so lost in her thoughts and concern that she hadn't heard the rest following her.

"That's right, Jeannette," said Claudia. "You're not thinking clearly, child. It's not Olivia's fault and it's not Joey's fault. It was an accident. Accidents happen on trips like these."

"Well, I didn't want to come and she made me," said Jeannette.

"That's not true," said Corinne. "Your husband told you come with us. He trusted Olivia to get us safely out of Richmond, just like our men did. You're too afraid of your own shadow to trust anyone. Now put that gun down and send the boy out here. If you want to take care of Sarah by yourself, then do it, but you can't starve the boy in the process."

Jeannette stared, wild-eyed. She gave Olivia a look of pure hatred, but lowered her shotgun. "Get out of here," she said and pushed Joey from the wagon. His scream echoed through the camp as he hit the ground. James ran to him.

For a brief second the women all stared with wide, horrified eyes. Olivia had never seen James so angry. Had Joey not needed calm, compassionate care and had Jeannette been a man, she was sure he would have gone after her with fists doubled. He couldn't, but she could. Teeth clenched, fists doubled, she made a move toward Jeannette. Tillie's firm hand gripped her shoulder.

"Won't help matters, 'Livia," she said.

Olivia stood rigidly staring at Jeannette, who stared back with a blank, faraway look in her eyes. She knew Tillie was right, but she wanted to vent her anger in the worst way. Both of Joey's eyes were swollen almost shut and turning very dark colors. His right arm hung limp beside his body and Olivia knew without looking that there were bruises over his entire body.

James lifted the boy and carried him with long, determined strides to their wagon. Olivia shook her head and followed. As she left, she heard the other women talking to Jeannette. She didn't know, or care, what they said. At that moment, Jeannette ceased to be her friend.

Once again, Maggie, Grandma Cooper and Tillie assisted her in her role as *Doctor*. They set Joey's arm and put cold cloths over his bruised face. Grandma Cooper fed him some soup while Olivia took care of her babies. Betsy made room for Joey on the wagon floor beside her.

Once the children were asleep, Olivia fell quietly to her knees. *O Lord, I don't understand. She's in Your hands, as we all are. This is such an impossible journey. It is only by Your grace and mercy that we have come this far. Take away my anger and give me compassion, if not understanding.*

Olivia rose, knowing sleep would not come anytime soon, so she joined James and Tillie who had early guard duty. They all stared into the fire, hoping for an oracle or some insight. Finally, James broke the silence.

"How could she do that to him? He tried to take Sarah back to camp. She was just being a little brat like she usually is. She pulled away from him and got too close to the edge. Corey jumped in to get her. She fought him until they were caught in the current."

Olivia took a deep breath. Pity had replaced her anger. "James, I don't understand. I only know we all deal with fear differently. Jeannette wasn't cut out for this kind of life. None of us were. Most of us have learned to live with life as it is, whether we like it or not. Jeannette never learned that. I'm not sure even Joe could help her through it any better."

"You're probably right, 'Livia," said Tillie. "It's unfortunate that she took her fears and anger out on the boy, but to be honest, right now I'm more concerned about Sarah."

"Surely, you don't think she would…"

"Not deliberately, but it's almost like she expects Sarah to die. If she goes into pneumonia, she just might. I wonder if Jeannette is capable of caring for her."

"Do you think I should take Sarah, too?"

"I don't know, 'Livia. Maybe her love for the child will get through to her."

Olivia continued to stare into the leaping flames. As warm as it was, a cold chill wrapped its icy fingers around her.

36   Another Cell Mate

"Mister Dooley, why…?" Robert moved closer to him. "You aren't here to visit this time."

"No," said Jefferson, a sob escaping his throat.

"Come and sit with us," said Will. "Sorry we can't offer more than the floor."

Jefferson eased himself down on the folded blankets with the other men and told them what was happening outside the prison.

"Elizabeth dead?" Robert's whisper held a note of sadness and perplexity. "Why?"

"Because the Confederate government wants to establish who is boss and they will not tolerate anything that even looks like treason. They knew I was related to Will, so I was included in their destruction."

"But surely the mayor knew…"

"The mayor's hands are tied. He has created a monster and can't control it."

"Parker…?"

"Surprisingly, he's our only hope. He has finally realized what is happening and doesn't have the stomach for the kind of brutality the General is bringing to Richmond."

"Do you think he can do anything if the mayor can't?"

"He already has." Jefferson reached into his pocket and pulled out the key to the cell. "I got this in Parker's office while he turned his back to put on his coat."

"Does he know?"

"Yes."

"Will he be waiting with a firing squad if we try to escape?" John stood with his back to the guard so he couldn't see what the men were doing. He could only hear muffled whispers.

"I don't know," said Jefferson. "I only know this is our only chance and we have to give it a try. If we don't leave tonight, we'll all be shot tomorrow – after they parade us up and down Main Street."

"I will only slow you down," said Will. "You will leave me

and…"

"No!" said Robert. The guard turned toward them. He lowered his voice. "We will not leave you. We have been in this together from the beginning. We'll not scatter like scared chickens now."

"Robert is right," said Kenny. "Either we will all make it, or we'll all perish together."

"But…"

"No, buts about," said Jefferson. "I didn't get myself thrown in prison to get you out just to have you say, 'no thank you.'"

"But how…?"

"Will, what has happened to your faith and courage during these months of imprisonment? Olivia is risking her life everyday getting those other women and children to The Valley. I'm sure she has moments of despair, but she will keep going because she promised you she would. She'll either make it or die trying. Are you willing to sit here and do less?"

Will's temper flared. "You know as well as I do I would have done anything to keep her from taking that perilous trip. I'm not God. I'm just a …"

"Servant of God who is ready to give up when you are finally given a miracle?"

Tears ran down Will's face. "I can barely see in the daylight. I'll slow you down and get you killed."

"Maybe your eyesight is going, but if what I've heard and read is true," said Joe, "your other senses are heightened. You'll be able to hear and sense danger before the rest of us will. We'll help you and you'll help us. It's the way it's always been and it's the only chance we have of being with our wives and children again."

Will sighed. "I know you're right, but…"

"No buts about it," said Jefferson. "We only have one shot at this and we have to work it out carefully and trust God for the rest. Matthew went to see Samuel. I'm not sure what they will do. Our job is to get out. I have the key but there is still the guard here and others in and around the prison."

"Kyle – our guard – always leaves around dusk for dinner. No one guards us for almost an hour."

"No one?"

"We asked him once if he wasn't afraid we would leave. He laughed and said we couldn't open the door and if we did manage, we'd still have to go out the front door where anyone would see us."

"Ah," said Jefferson, "what about the side door on the basement level?"

"Didn't know there was a side door."

"Matthew told me about it on our way over here. This master key fits all the doors in the building. I asked him to talk to Samuel. Hopefully, he'll be waiting for us – if he believes Matthew."

"They'll start looking for us as soon as Kyle returns," said Robert.

"The river runs near here," said Kenny. "Maybe we can get to it."

"We'll have to swim up river, or we'll go over the falls," said John.

"Will we have strength enough to do that – swim up river, that is?" Joe glanced at Will.

"But that's exactly what they will expect us to do," said Jefferson. "To go downstream would be suicide."

"So we go downriver," said George.

"Seems the only way. We can stay along the bank and hopefully Samuel can pick up us with the wagon and get us out of town."

"We can't just leave in a wagon," said Will. "Not out in the open."

"You're right," said Jefferson. "There wasn't enough time to think and plan. Our first step will be to get out of here. We'll just have to trust Samuel and Matthew to come up with something after that."

"Sounds like we better do a lot of praying in between times," said John. "Our women did it, we will to."

"We don't know that they made it," said Joe.

"We don't know that they didn't," said John. "I'll always believe they did – even if we don't meet up with them somewhere."

"You're right, John. We'll…," The chair scraped the floor outside the cell as Kyle stood and stretched.

"He's going early tonight," said Kenny. He raised his voice, "Hey, Kyle, you hungry tonight?"

"Yeah, your wife fixing a special dinner? Bring us some leftovers," said Robert.

Kyle laughed. "Yeah, sure I will. Be a long time afore I taste my wife's cooking again."

"Oh, is she ill?" asked John. "We got a couple of doctors here if you need them."

"She ain't sick, but since the big fellows came to Richmond, all soldiers have to live in barracks or tents and eat at the mess hall – pig slop if you ask me."

"Sorry about that. Let us out of here and we'll go find a nice fat pig to roast."

Kyle laughed again. "Wish I could take you up on that. They

ought to at least give you one last meal. But…"

"Oh, well, just a thought. Enjoy your pig slop. It's probably a step above what we get."

Kyle laughed again and started up the stairs.

"We need to hurry," said Jefferson. Before he could move to the door, a couple of pebbles landed on the floor.

Will moved toward the window. "Yes," he said waiting for whoever was out there to speak.

"Sergeant Parker says go to the river, upstream to the bridge, cross to the other side in the shadow. We'll be there with a wagon. Hurry and be careful."

"Suppose it's a trap?" asked Joe.

"Don't know," said Will, "But like Jefferson said, it's the only chance we have. Let's go for it."

Jefferson opened the cell door. The men followed him out and down a long dark hallway that had very little use. The door at the end opened to a dark side alley. The river ran so close the falls sounded like thunder.

"This way," said John who took Will by the hand and ran down the alley, keeping close to the side of the building. Two guards were at the far end of the back of the building. They turned and went down the opposite side street. The men ran for the river.

Easing down into the cold, water they clung to the grasses along the bank to keep the current from carrying them down river.. The bridge was about a quarter of a mile up river.

"Can we swim it?"

"Why don't we hold on to the bank's greenery as long as possible and pull ourselves along. When there ain't no roots or trees to hold onto, then we can swim," said John. "I'll lead. Jefferson you bring up the rear. The rest of you guys keep an eye on Will and stay together."

Oh God, Will prayed as silently as they moved in the water. *We trusted You with our women and children. Now we are trusting You to get us to them. And if we don't make it, keep them safe.*

They were almost to the bridge when the siren began wailing indicating prisoners had escaped. Will felt his heart sink. *Will we make it to Samuel before getting caught? Will the soldiers catch Samuel before we get to him?*

37   The Wait is Over

Morning dawned and with it the need for familiar chores. Corey crawled out from under the wagon with the others and moved toward the animals to help with their care and feeding.

"Corey, you need to rest more." Olivia placed the back of her hand against his forehead. "No fever, but we don't want to take any chances."

Corey coughed. "I'm okay," he said. "I can help James with the animals."

"Stop and rest if…" Corey left her talking to herself as he ran to catch up to James.

Jeanette didn't come for breakfast. Claudia and Corinne took bowls of oatmeal to her wagon. Olivia walked with them. Jeanette reached her hand out to take the bowls and grunted her thanks as she withdrew into the wagon.

"How is Sarah doing this morning?" Olivia called to Jeanette's retreating back.

"She's asleep."

"Do you want me to check her?"

"No."

"Does she have any fever?"

"No."

"Call me if you need anything."

Jeanette didn't bother to answer. Olivia turned to Corinne and Claudia. "Let me know if she needs help." They nodded and she returned to her chores and waited.

***

Two more days passed and the wagon train, rolled into a ball like a frightened caterpillar, waited for the danger to pass. Children played and talked in hushed whispers. The silence that replaced Jeanette's screams and Sarah's screeches filled hearts with more fear and tension.

Olivia remembered Tillie's earlier concern. *Each time I try to check on Sarah, Jeanette insists she's all right – just sleeping. Why don't we hear something from the wagon – crying or coughing? And why don't they come to the circle with the rest of us for meals? Today, as soon as I get the babies down for an afternoon nap, I'll insist on seeing Sarah.*

Joey, arm in sling, bruises still visible, watched her and Betsy with wide eyes. "Can I help?" he asked.

"Sure," Olivia said. "See if you can get a couple of clean diapers for me from that stack in the corner of the wagon."

Joey struggled into the wagon, found the diapers and almost fell as he tried to climb back out. Betsy reached to help him down.

"I'm sorry," he said.

"It's okay, Joey," said Betsy. "You're still sore and weak, but you're getting better." She smiled at the boy, who smiled back at her. Olivia's heart swelled with pride at the thoughtfulness of her daughter.

The babies asleep, Olivia turned her attention to Joey. Fear and sadness ran down his face in great drops of tears. "Mrs. Brunner, why don't Mommy love me like you love your kids?"

Olivia's heart skipped a beat. She put her arms around him and pulled him close to her. "Joey," she said, "your mommy is sick and Sarah is sick, so she can't think clearly. She does love you and she would show it if she could. Right now, she just doesn't know how to love anybody, but it's not your fault, Joey. You didn't do anything to cause her sickness."

"When do I have to go back to our wagon?"

"Not until she's better." Olivia hoped that would be soon. She didn't understand illnesses of the mind, but she wondered if Jeannette could ever be trusted with this child again.

"Thank you," he said and climbed slowly into the wagon to nap with the babies.

Olivia felt James and Betsy watching her. How could she explain? James smiled and gave her a quick half-hug.

"I'm going to check on the animals," he said. He ran toward the corral before she could say anything, but Betsy looked at her with a frown far too mature for a child of ten.

"Mom?"

"Yes, Betsy?" Olivia made room on the log for Betsy and slipped an arm around her daughter.

"Is the kind of sickness Mrs. Phillips has catching? I mean…"

"Will I, or the other women, get it?"

Betsy nodded.

"No, Betsy. It's not contagious like measles. Mrs. Phillips' mind has never had to live with so much trouble. The rest of us have had more practice."

"Will she get better when Sarah gets better and we get to our new home?"

"I hope so, Betsy, but if she doesn't, we'll all have to pitch in and help her until Joe comes."

"Okay," she paused then added, "I hope she gets better, but I'm sure glad you won't get whatever she's got." She threw her arms around her mother's waist and Olivia hugged her close.

O Lord, give me strength to endure and be strong for the children You keep putting in my care. Olivia prayed as she began slowly walking toward Jeannette's wagon. *Even if Jeannette is still angry, surely she would ask for help for her sick child. Wouldn't she? Corey is getting better. Sarah should be too, shouldn't she?*

Claudia and Corinne met her as she approached Jeannette's wagon. "Olivia, we've got to do something," said Corinne. "Jeannette is starving herself as well as that child. The plate we took her for lunch hasn't been touched. Neither was breakfast or last night's supper."

"I was just on my way to see her. Surely she would have called me if Sarah was feverish or needs medical help."

"I don't know, Olivia. She hasn't been outside the wagon for two days – not even to go to the toilet area. The wagon smells like a tub of dirty diapers," said Corinne.

With a more determined gait, Olivia crossed the inner circle to Jeannette's wagon. *Will I have to take Sarah from her, too?* She felt like a reluctant hangman on the way to the gallows, but she couldn't let Jeannette starve Sarah. Corinne was usually negative about everything. Surely, she was over-reacting.

"Jeannette," she called, "I need to know how Sarah is doing."

"She's asleep and it's none of your business." The sound was muffled – hidden inside the wagon.

"I'm sorry, Jeannette, but it is my business. We're holding up the train, waiting for her to recover. Corey is up and about. She should at least be able to come and sit by the fire for her meals. I want to see her."

"Go away. You can't come in here. She's fine."

"Jeannette, I'm coming in. I have to see for myself."

Jeannette stuck her head out the back. Olivia was shocked at her disheveled appearance. Her hair hung in oily strings, over her face and down her back. Red, watery eyes stared over the barrel of her gun, which shook in her hands. "Go away. This is my home. You can't come in."

Olivia, aware the other women had joined her, knew they were eager to help and anxious about Sarah. She felt relieved they were there. "Jeannette, I *will* come in and *you* will put that gun down this instant." Jeannette's eyes widened, but the gun continued to shake in her hands.

"Drop the gun, Jeannette," said Claudia, who stood closer to the wagon. "Olivia's the wagon master, as well as our only medical person. She has a right to know about all her charges. Now give me that gun before you hurt someone and let her in there to see to Sarah."

Jeannette glared then dropped the gun. Claudia passed it to Corinne and stepped up on the wagon step. She held Jeannette aside so Olivia could climb into the wagon.

Olivia caught her breath, not only at the awful smell, but also at the unkempt appearance of the child, who lay still as death on a blanket on the narrow aisle of the floor. Still in the dress she had on when she fell in the river, her face was pale and pasty looking. Kneeling beside Sarah, Olivia placed the back of her hand against the child's forehead and jerked her head around to give Jeannette a questioning look.

"How long has she had this fever and what are you giving her for it?"

"What fever?"

"Jeannette, she's burning up! How can you not know she has a fever? All you have to do is touch her and…"

"No," Jeannette screamed. "I can't touch her. She'll die and I'll be contaminated."

"Jeannette!" Olivia thought she was beyond shock, but gasped as if Jeannette had thrown a bucket of ice water in her face. "How…how do you feed and clean her…?" One look told her Jeannette didn't touch the child for any reason, which explained the awful smell and uncombed hair, the sunken cheeks and sallow skin.

Olivia clenched her teeth, shook her head and picked Sarah up.

"No! Don't touch her," screamed Jeannette, grabbing Olivia's arm. Olivia jerked away to keep from dropping Sarah.

"Claudia…" Olivia didn't need to say more. Claudia wrapped her arms around Jeannette and held her while Olivia handed Sarah down to Tillie. "Take her to my wagon," she said.

"You have your hands full," said Tillie. "We'll take her to mine." She turned her gaze back to Jeannette. "And you better get down on your knees and pray that she pulls through this."

"She's going to die," yelled the distraught woman as Tillie walked away carrying the limp little body like a newborn. "I know she will because Olivia allowed dancing on the Lord's Day." Her screams fell on deaf ears.

"There's a blanket in that box in the corner," said Tillie when they got to her wagon.

"Here's a bucket of warm water." Maggie set the bucket beside the wagon. "Let's get her clean first then wrap the blanket around her."

"Throw those filthy clothes in the fire," said Claudia. "I'll see if I can get something clean from Jeannette."

"I'll go with you," said Corinne. The other women helped Tillie wash and wrap Sarah in the blanket. Sarah neither woke, nor cried out while they worked over her feverish body.

"Let me give her something for the fever," said Olivia and tried to give her the liquid. Most of it ran out of the corner of her mouth.

"Try some soup," said Grandma Cooper, holding a bowl of lukewarm broth. That, too, dribbled down her chin. Sarah couldn't swallow, any more than she could cry out. She didn't even whimper.

They all tried, but about midnight the inevitable happened. Sarah stopped breathing. Olivia tried everything she knew, or had even heard about. She pressed on the heart, breathed into her open mouth, rubbed her cooling limbs. Nothing helped. Cold, dry skin replaced the burning fever.

Sarah was dead.

38   A Grave on the Hill

Head bowed, steps dragging, Olivia moved toward Jeannette's wagon. When she promised Will to take the children north, never in her wildest imaginations could she have pictured this setting. *How do you tell a mother her child is dead? Jeannette is on the edge of insanity. Will this push her over that edge?*

Even so, it was her responsibility to tell Jeannette. Claudia and Corinne walked with her, for which she was thankful. As they approached the wagon, they heard Jeannette inside muttering unintelligible words.

"Jeannette," called Olivia. "Jeannette, we need to talk to you."

"Go away. I don't want to talk to anyone. I want to go home. I hate this place. I hate this trip." Jeannette opened the back of the canvas and put her head out.

"Jeannette, there is no home in Richmond anymore," Corinne's voice was soft and soothing. "Joe will come to us as soon as he can and your home will be up here with him."

"Joe won't come. He hates me."

"Jeannette, whatever gave you that idea? Joe loves you." Claudia couldn't hide her shock.

"No he doesn't. He only has eyes for *her.*" Jeannette glared at Olivia.

Olivia was speechless. Her mouth opened, her jaw dropped. She stared at Jeannette, blinked and snapped her jaws shut. How much more shock would she endure from this woman? Surely, she had misunderstood Jeannette, but Claudia, too, stood with her mouth agape.

Claudia found her voice first. "Jeannette, that's ridiculous. Joe has never looked at another woman since he married you. He would have to be insane to think he could..." Claudia again was at a loss for words.

"You're wrong. All he ever talked about was her. Olivia this and Olivia that. Olivia knows how to cook. Olivia takes care of her children. Olivia can read and understand. Olivia..." Jeannette choked and dropped to the floor with her fists in her lap.

"Jeannette, that doesn't mean he wanted Olivia instead of you. It only meant he admired her and Will and the way they worked together." Corinne tried to hide her astonishment.

Olivia, remembering their reason for being there, shook her head. "Jeannette, we'll talk about that at another time," she said. "Right now, we have more important matters to discuss."

"Sarah?" Jeannette's eyes widened. She raised herself to her knees, hair hanging in strings down her pale and hollow face.

"Yes," said Olivia. "She died a few minutes ago." There was no easy way to say it.

Jeannette did the predictable. She screamed like a banshee and jumped from the wagon with her hands ready to go around Olivia's neck. Corinne and Claudia grabbed her but she still screamed and clawed at the air. "You did it. You killed my baby. You'll be sorry, Olivia Brunner. You'll be sorry. Just wait until one of your precious kids dies. You'll be sorry."

Olivia, believing this would happen, was prepared. Corinne and Claudia held Jeannette while Olivia poured a sleeping potion down her throat. She choked and continued to scream, "You killed my baby and now you're trying to kill me. God will punish you Olivia Brunner. God…will…pun…ish…"

"Let's put her in my wagon until morning," said Claudia. "We can clean hers while she sleeps."

Although Jeannette was not a big woman, it took the three of them to carry her to Claudia's wagon and get her settled. Knowing she would sleep several hours, Claudia and Maggie took buckets of water and rags to clean the smelly floor of Jeannette's wagon.

"I'll stay with her," said Corinne, "just in case she wakes."

"Thank you," said Olivia. "Grandma Cooper, would you help Tillie? I think…"

"I'll help her prepare the body. Where will we bury her?"

"I'll have the boys dig a grave in the morning."

"We need a coffin of some kind. We can't just stick her in the ground," said Claudia.

"I'll find something," said Olivia.

She slowly turned to her wagon while the other women took care of Jeannette. She wanted to cry with her friend, but Jeannette was no longer a friend. Now she understood why. *All this time she has been jealous. If only she had talked about it, we could've worked it out.*

The women all walked like half-dead souls, shocked and numb.

Sarah's death had been a blow to them all, but Jeannette's accusations were just as shocking. Tears would come in time, but for now, details would keep them moving. Death had entered their circle of protection and stolen one of their children. Would the death angel leave without more?

James waited near the fire. Olivia didn't need to explain. He'd heard Jeannette's cry. Everyone within a mile of the camp would have heard.

"I made fresh coffee," he said and handed her a cup.

"Thank you, James. When it gets daylight, will you and the boys dig a grave? Find a place that won't get washed away and we can cover it with stones large enough to keep animals from digging it up."

"Yes, ma'am."

"We can put her in the wooden chest your father made for me." Olivia's voice was flat and toneless.

"Mom, you can't give her…"

Olivia held up her hand and shook her head. "Don't say it, James. It's all we have."

"It won't make any difference to her," he said. "She'll still hate you."

"But, I won't hate myself." Olivia looked into her son's eyes and for an instant was looking into the eyes of Will. She blinked and he was gone, but he had smiled at her. She now climbed onto the wagon seat where she opened the canvas and found her cherished gift from Will. She placed the box on the seat beside her. One by one she removed its treasures – pictures of her family, keepsakes from the children and Will, a piece of hair from the tail of her favorite pony when she was young, the faded, dried rose Will had given her the first time he came to call. These memories might be all she would have left of the past. She sighed deeply. She would find another place for her treasures.

A small pillow that she'd made for James when he was born fit in the chest. Jeannette would have a blanket to wrap Sarah in – or should have.

She carried the chest to Tillie's wagon and set it down without a word. Tillie glanced at her, knowing what it was and how much it meant to her.

"She won't appreciate it."

"I know." Olivia said. She turned and walked away, her heart heavy with unshed tears. She couldn't break down now. They were too near *home*.

***

No one slept after Jeannette's screams – no one except Jeannette and the younger children. Before the sun even rose, Maggie and Grandma Cooper had a pot of oatmeal cooking. The aroma of coffee, wood burning and that special smell of the river rose toward heaven. Olivia wondered if it was, as the Psalmist said, *a sweet offering to the Lord.*

After breakfast, James gathered Michael, George, Jeremiah and Tom and started toward the small hill across the stream.

"Can I go too, Mom?" Corey pleaded. He had risked his own life – all six years of it – in an effort to save Sarah. How could she say no? And yet…

She bit her lip. "Corey, I don't you want to…"

"I'm all right. I won't get too tired. I'll just watch. Maybe I'll pick some flowers for her grave."

Olivia caught her breath. How did her children become such caring adults at such a young age? She nodded then called after him. "Stop and rest if you get tired." No matter how much she tried to erase Jeannette's words, they continued to haunt her – "just wait until you lose one of your precious kids," she'd said.

Anger flared at the thought. *I might lose one of my children to this trip yet, but I will do everything in my power to prevent it. I won't let them starve in the process.*

By early afternoon, the boys returned and Olivia gave them some lunch. "We found a spot up on that hill overlooking the river." James swiped at the sweat running down his face with his shirtsleeve as he took the sandwich his mother handed him.

"Jeannette should be waking soon. We'll give her time to get up and make some decisions. We'll have to move on tomorrow. I sent a letter to Uncle George from New River Crossings. They'll be looking for us."

"Speaking of Jeannette…" James didn't need to finish his thought. Screams assaulted their ears. Olivia sighed and walked toward Claudia's wagon, where Claudia and Corinne stood with Jeannette. Jeannette was incoherent, screaming to the top of her lungs – one scream after another.

Olivia stepped up to her and slapped her across the face. Stunned, Jeannette held her hand to her face and stared at Olivia, who clenched her fists at her sides – more to stop the stinging of her hand, than from anger. Jeannette opened her mouth to scream again and Olivia raised her hand.

"Keep screaming and you'll look like your son," said Olivia. "You're not a child. You've suffered a tragic loss, but you're an adult, so act like one. I'm sorry about all of this, but there's nothing I can do to change it. You have chosen to suffer rather than survive. I can't change that either. Now what do you want done about burying your daughter. The boys dug a grave. We have a casket for her. What do you want us to do?"

Olivia stared at Jeannette, waiting for an answer. The words had been hard, maybe even cruel, but Jeannette wouldn't understand any other language at the moment. She'd beaten her son and let her daughter die from lack of care. She would have to live with that, even if she chose to blame someone else.

"We'll take her with us," said Jeannette. "I won't leave her alone in this wilderness."

"Jeannette, that's not an option. We cannot take her with us. We will bury her. What do you want done about a service. I have Will's Book of Ritual and can…"

"No! I don't want you near her. I can take care of everything myself. I'll stay here with her. I won't leave her."

"Jeannette, you aren't making sense," said Corinne. "You can't stay here. We have to move on in the morning. You can't stay by yourself."

"I can if I want to." Jeannette stuck out her lip in a childish pout.

Claudia shook her head and gave Jeannette a disgusted look. "You're acting like a three year old. Even Sarah wasn't as childish as you are. You can't stay here and that's that. Who would bury you when you starve to death or, worse yet, are killed by some animal?"

"You're just trying to scare me. I won't leave her."

"Jeannette, the boys have dug a grave on the hill over there." Olivia nodded toward the hill beside them. "They'll fill it in after they lower the casket into it then pile rocks on top to keep animals out. You can stay beside the grave as long as you wish today. Tomorrow you will go with us if we have to tie you in one of our wagons."

Olivia turned to Claudia and Corinne. "The casket is ready whenever Jeannette is. I'll stay here with the babies while the rest of you go to the grave. James will bring Joey." She turned back to Jeannette and said, "If you even so much as give him a dirty look, I'll beat you to within an inch of your life. He has a right to say goodbye to his sister."

Jeannette glared daggers at Olivia who turned her back and walked with resolute steps to her wagon.

"Do you want me to stay with you?" James watched the others walk toward the hill.

"No, take Joey. Keep him at your side. Don't let him near Jeannette, or the grave. We don't want another accident. Grandma Cooper can bring him back while the rest of you fill in the grave and pile stones on top of it."

"Come on Joey." James took the little boy's hand and led him up the hill.

Olivia sat on her log and prayed while Charles and Lucy played in their makeshift play area. *O Lord, if I have done wrong forgive me. Jeannette needs help, but I don't know what to do. Comfort her; I can't. Take little Sarah into Your arms.*

Laughter in the play area caught her attention. Charles, his rich, dark colored skin and Lucy as fair as a Lily of the Valley, rocked together on their knees. Then they helped each other to stand. She watched in awe, as they stood together, giggled and fell back to the ground, clapping their hands and laughing. If only all of life could be so beautiful.

39   Left Behind

With a heavy heart, Olivia turned over on her back, hands behind her head. From under the wagon, she listened as the night sounds gave way to those of a new day. She watched the gray sky turn pink and yellow with the rising sun. The forest was alive with singing, chirping and cawing. Aware of the hard, lumpy ground beneath her, she felt as if she'd wrestled with the Lord throughout the night like Jacob of old had done. She'd tried to keep all her charges safe, but they would leave behind, not a pillar of stones, but a grave piled high with them.

Since the beginning of the journey, a nagging, internal voice told her they would bury at least one along the way. She never expected it to be one of the children. Would there be others before they reached The Valley? Grandma Cooper? One of her boys?

Olivia shivered and dragged herself from under the wagon. All night, even in her half sleep, she'd heard a rhythmic clink, clink, clink – metal against stone. James sat by the fire, hunched over something, pounding, deep in concentration.

"You didn't sleep much," she said reaching for the coffee pot.

"No ma'am. I had something to do." He continued chipping at a large stone between his legs. "I'm almost done. If you have to leave before I finish, I'll catch up."

Blackie, stretching on the ground beside James, lifted his head, following their conversation with his eyes.

"If it's important to you, James, we'll wait." She was curious, but he would say more when, and if, he was ready. She put a fresh pot of coffee on to boil and made other preparations for breakfast.

"You want some fresh coffee?" Olivia asked when it was ready. She held the coffee pot over the cup watching the black liquid flow into it, breathing in the rich aroma.

"Yes, thank you," James answered and continued to pound the chisel against the stone.

Finally, he straightened his back, rolled his head from side to side raised one shoulder then the other. He held the stone up for Olivia to see as she brought his coffee to him. "I'll take this up to the grave then

I'll be ready to help you get started."

Olivia looked at the stone and caught her breath, bit her lip and turned away murmuring, "That's beautiful, James."

On the stone, he had carved an angel and the words:

Sarah Marie Phillips
May 1, 1857 – May 29, 1861
Forever a child

"Did Jeannette stay at the grave last night?" Olivia asked as he stood, stretched again then lifted the heavy stone.

He nodded. "Mrs. Jones and Mrs. Walsh stayed with her. I'll tell them breakfast is almost ready."

"Let me know if they need help getting her back down here."

James nodded and started toward the hill. "Come on Blackie," he called to the little dog that was already beside him. Corey and Michael joined her at the fire as James left.

"We'll help George and Tom with the mules," said Corey. "Looks like James is busy."

"Thank you boys," said Olivia. "Breakfast should be ready by the time you finish."

Olivia stirred the pot of oatmeal. Like the bubbling porridge before her, visions bubbled and churned within. Thoughts of Will and Joe and the others in the prison sent such a pain that she clutched her chest and forced her attention back to the pot before her. She couldn't bear to think about Will in that dark, damp prison where she'd heard reports of more prisoners dying from exposure, malnutrition and disease than were ever shot before a firing squad. Now that she was safely out of Richmond, would he go into the army in order to get out of there? She didn't think so.

"Olivia?"

Startled, she almost dropped the long wooden spoon into the pot of bubbling oatmeal. "I'm sorry, Grandma Cooper. Did you ask me something?"

Grandma Cooper cackled her soft laughter. "You were miles away. It wasn't a look of anticipation, so you must-a been back in Richmond with Will."

Olivia nodded, sighed and stirred the porridge. "I try not to think about it, but sometimes I can't help it. If he had been with us, maybe Sarah…"

Grandma Cooper cut in with a stern voice and shook a gnarled finger at Olivia. "Will is a physician and maybe he could have talked some sense into Jeannette, but you did all you could. You saved the child's life. Her mother let her die from lack of attention. You couldn't have predicted that, much less prevented it."

"I should have taken Sarah when I took Joey."

"Olivia, none of us would ever have thought Jeannette would become so uncaring."

"She's not uncaring, Grandma Cooper. She's overwhelmed with responsibilities she doesn't know how to fulfill. She never learned to think for herself like the rest of us."

"Olivia, you're too kind to her, but perhaps you're right. Whatever her problems, you did all you could and you're not responsible for the death of that child. I imagine her guilt will be the final straw for Jeannette."

"If Will and Joe arrive soon enough, maybe…"

"Olivia Brunner, you stop that!" Grandma Cooper shook her finger at Olivia again. "As long as we have known you, you've never lived with maybes or what ifs or wishes. You'll do all you can for Jeannette until Joe arrives and that's all you can do."

"Grandma Cooper, I don't know how I would have made this trip without your encouragement. Thank you for being kind enough not to die on me." Olivia smiled at the woman who, it seemed to her, leaned more heavily on her cane each day.

"Olivia, don't depend on me to be your salvation. Look where it got Jeannette. I'm so old I don't even remember how many years I've journeyed this life – more'n eighty. I hope to make it to our new home, but if I don't, I expect you to bury me and move on." Grandma Cooper laughed that soft cackle Olivia loved to hear then added, "Course if it's easier on you just throw me in the river when you cross over the Gauley. Let me drift on forever to the ocean and beyond."

"Grandma Cooper!" Olivia gave her a horrified look that brought more laughter from her friend.

"Is that porridge ready yet? I'm starving. You don't mind if I don't wait for the rest do you? I'll bless it before I eat it." Olivia laughed with her friend and dished up a bowl of the pasty mixture.

Grandma Cooper prayed, "Lord, Thou knowest that we are near our new home. Bless this food to strengthen us for this day's journey. Lord, it's been a hard journey. It's been lonely at times, and sometimes, Lord, it's been downright difficult, but Thou hast been with us. Now, bless Olivia with the strength she'll need for whatever comes our way before she gets us home. In the name of our Lord

Jesus, we pray. Amen."

"Thank you Grandma Cooper," Olivia said.

One by one, the others arrived, rubbing sleepy eyes, stretching stiff muscles and stifling more yawns. "James and the women on the hill will be here soon."

"Let me dish it up," said Maggie reaching for the spoon. "You take yours and sit with Grandmother Cooper. The babies will be ready to eat soon. You may as well get yours first."

Olivia didn't argue. She dished herself a bowl and sat beside the older woman. Silently they ate until they heard the others coming from the hill.

As much as Olivia wanted to hurry her charges, she, like the rest, felt drained of energy. Grief lay heavily on all of them – like a dark cloud too full of unshed raindrops.

Even the children, who had been quiet and subdued since the accident, were more somber. Finally, Bobby asked, "Mrs. Brunner, why did Sarah die? Mom says God wanted her in his special garden."

"I heard someone say once that a kid only dies if God is mad at her," said Jeremiah.

"I thought only old people died, but…" Tom glanced at Grandma Cooper and blushed then ducked his head.

"Mom says we're too big to cry, but it hurts inside when we know we'll never see her again and she'll never grow up."

By then, the children had gathered before Olivia. With eyes wide, they waited for her to make everything right for them. Try as she might, Olivia could not keep her own tears at bay. She had promised herself there would be no tears until she could share them with Will. But this was different. This was not weeping in self-pity for herself and her hardships. This was for the children and her friends. This was mutual grief.

Olivia was vaguely aware of the others coming from the hill. *Perhaps the mothers should…no, they're asking me.* She took a deep breath and began.

"Sarah did not die because she was bad, or because God needed her. Sarah died because she fell in the river and her body was too small and frail to fight the pneumonia that resulted from getting so much river water in her lungs."

"Could …anyone have saved her?"

"Maybe, if we were in a city with hospitals and doctors."

"If we were still in Richmond…"

"If we were still in Richmond, she probably wouldn't have fallen in a river. But nothing is the way it was when we left Richmond. Soldiers have taken over. The Confederate Army has its headquarters there. We can only believe we are safer here."

"I don't like leaving her here all by herself," said Joey.

"She isn't alone, Joey. Remember only her body is here. She doesn't need it anymore because she's with God."

"You mean the real Sarah we knew is alive with God. Her body was a temporary home, like the wagons are our temporary homes."

"That's right, Jeremiah."

"Will anyone else die before we get to The Valley?"

"I don't know Bobby. Only God knows. All I know is that we will all do our best to keep one another safe. Accidents happen. We can't foresee them, nor can we always stop them. But we have the assurance that no matter what happens, God is here with us."

"Mrs. Brunner, will we ever see our dads again – in this life, I mean."

"Again, Bobby, only God knows. We must be diligent in our prayers and in our responsibilities to get to The Valley. Your fathers are all just as diligent in their prayers and when the opportunity arises, they will make their way to us."

"Is it all right to cry – just a little if we feel sad?"

"Of course it is," said Olivia, dabbing at her eyes with her apron.

"Mrs. Brunner, thank you for helping us to understand. We'll take memories of Sarah with us."

Olivia glanced up. Even the women were dabbing at their eyes. "Thank you, Olivia," said Tillie. "We all needed some closure for this tragic event." Tillie paused while the others nodded and murmured their thanks. Then she raised her voice a little and said, "Now, I think it's time to eat and get ready to roll out."

It was mid-morning as the last wagon left the camp, leaving behind the tiny grave on the hill. Even the mules seemed reluctant to go as they clomped along.

40 *The Great Escape*

The siren's wail from the prison gave the men a shot of adrenaline as they reached the bridge. They swam across the river, John and Joe staying on either side of Will. Robert swam ahead of him and George and Kenny stayed behind him. Jefferson swam ahead to make sure that Samuel was there.

The men neared the opposite bank of the river. A wagon waited at the edge. They could barely make out the wagon. A pile of something covered with a tarp lay on the ground beside it. Two more pieces of tarp covered the ground from the riverbank to the wagon. Two men waited – one looked like an old man with ragged clothes, the other was Samuel. The mare that pulled the wagon looked as if each step would be her last.

Reaching a hand to Jefferson Samuel pulled him up. "Stay on the covers and get to the wagon," he whispered and reached for Robert while the second man reached for Will. "Stay on the covers," they emphasized. "They be sending dogs soon."

As soon as the seven men were in the wagon, Samuel gathered the wet tarps and covered the men with them. "Fasten this so it don't come loose," he whispered. John and Jefferson grabbed the corners and pulled it down, lying on it so it wouldn't slip. Samuel pulled the other end and Kenny and Robert held the corners and end in place.

"Don't you worry none about what you feels on top," Samuel whispered as he and the other man lifted the bundles and threw them on top of the covered men. "We's got some dead slaves we going to drop in the river a little ways downstream."

"Hopefully their search lights will let them see bodies, but not be able to see who they are," said the other man. "They'll be carried downstream to the falls and out to sea."

"And it will appear we all drowned and were carried away," said Jefferson as the weight of the bodies landed on top of the tarp. "Good thinking, Matthew."

"Thanks for the compliment, sir, but it was Samuel's idea – along with the tarp to keep the dogs from picking up your odor."

The wagon began moving slowly as if the poor horse could hardly pull the weight, but Jefferson knew it was one of his mares. *Samuel was able to disguise her. She's strong and will carry us as far as needed.*

They had no idea where they were or what direction they were going, except that they must be moving back toward the prison. Suddenly someone called to them to stop.

"What be the trouble?" asked Matthew, who was disguised at the old man.

"Nothing to do with you old man, unless you're harboring escaped prisoners in that wagon."

"No sir," said Matthew. "We ain't seen no prisoners. We're just trying to earn a few dollars."

"This time of night? Where you going and what's in your wagon?" One of the soldiers asked and started toward the back of the wagon.

Parker, said in a hoarse whisper. "Dead slaves. I gets a dollar a head for getting them off the streets. The General don't like dead bodies lying in the street."

"Where you taking them?"

"The old dump west of town."

"West of town? Then why are you heading east?"

"Just picked up a load back there and looking for a place to turn Nellie around. She's a little old and set in her ways. Won't turn just anywhere. Got to have lots of turning room."

"Who's that with you?"

"Him? He's just a deaf and dumb slave I picked up to help me. Probably add him to the pile when we're finished." He forced a laugh.

One soldier checked the back of the wagon while his colleague talked to the driver. He made a gagging sound as he touched one of the bodies. "Let him go," he said. "Get those disgusting things out of town."

The other soldiers laughed. "Keep moving, old man. Get rid of that load."

"Yes sir," said Parker and started the wagon moving again.

After what seemed to be an hour or maybe even two hours, the wagon stopped. They could hear the falls. They heard a splash, then another and another – seven in all.

Samuel lifted a corner of the tarp. "Are you folks all right?"

"Yeah, is this where we get off?"

"No, we need to turn around and head west past the plantation. You'll have to stay hidden until we get out of town. We left two slaves on the tarp in case they stop us again. Hopefully, they'll think those bodies we threw in the river was you folks. They'll be gone over the falls before anyone can get them out and know it wasn't."

He dropped the cover and the wagon began moving again. When they stopped the next time, Samuel uncovered them. "This be where we get off," he said. "We'll go through the woods over there and continue west. I got some supplies hid to help us some. Won't last long, but if the women can make it, we can too."

"Thanks, Samuel. Where's Rosy?"

"She done gone. Someday we'll meet up again. Let's go. We got a couple hours before dawn. Then we'll rest. Best to travel by night."

Jefferson stepped close to Parker and spoke softly. He slipped something to the man's hand. "Thanks," he said a little louder.

Parker nodded, flicked the reins and the wagon pulled away. They were sitting ducks in the road, so they headed for the woods. Inside the cover of trees and brush, they stopped for a few minutes to get their breath and their bearings.

"This be the place I hid when Miz Olivia left and I followed her. I saw Parker's men try to stop her." Samuel chuckled. "They all had a gun ready, even the kids. But Miz Olivia talked him out of taking their animals."

Samuel chuckled again. "That Miz Olivia, she won't let nothing or no one stop her."

"Thank you, Samuel," said Will. "I needed to hear that again. Don't you think we better be moving if we want to get to The Valley before winter sets in?"

"Don't know about you, Will," said John, "but I plan to be there in time for harvest."

"What are you going to harvest?" Robert asked.

"If I know Olivia and Tillie, they'll have houses and gardens waiting for us. The least we can do is help with the harvest."

The men laughed for the first time in months. "Let's go. Lead the way, Samuel."

"Yes, sir," he said and started through a path that only he seemed to know was there.

41   Life Moves On

Except for the rattle of wagons and the squeaking of wheels, the afternoon slid by in comparative quiet. Grief hung heavily over women and children. Olivia had given Jeannette something to help her sleep and they put her in Claudia's wagon where they could watch her more closely. Tom Rayburn and Michael drove her wagon.

They rattled to a stop and made camp where the three rivers merged as the sun fell behind the mountains. James and George had scouted the area while they waited for Sarah's recovery and learned they were less than an hour from the ferry. Tomorrow they would cross the Gauley River. Excitement began to replace some of the grief.

While they settled in for the night, James approached Olivia. "I would like to ride ahead in the morning and talk to the ferryman."

"It might be a good idea if he knows five wagons are coming."

"That's what I thought."

"Me too," said Corey coming up behind his brother. "You shouldn't go alone. Right, Mom?"

Olivia laughed. "After you get the mules hitched and have your breakfast, you can both ride Beauty and prepare the way for us."

***

James and Tillie had the second watch, so James was already up and eager to go long before the rest had even opened their eyes. Olivia knew he was excited, but held him back. "You'll have to wait until the sun is up and we've had breakfast," she said.

"I don't need breakfast," said James.

"But Corey does. He's still recovering."

"You're right," said James. "Sorry, I'm just too excited, I guess."

"Why don't you and Corey feed the mules so they'll be ready to go. By the time you finish, breakfast should be ready."

"All right. Come on, Corey," said James. George Walsh joined them and they soon had the animals fed. As Olivia promised, breakfast was waiting for them when they returned.

"Why don't you and Corey go on," said George. "Tom and I can help get the mules harnessed to the wagons. Olivia smiled at James and nodded.

"Come on Corey, let's go find that ferry and see what kind of arrangements we can make."

"Okay!" Corey hopped on Beauty's back. "Bet they want lots of money and we'll have to swim across the river."

"What about the wagons?" James mounted the horse behind his brother.

"Maybe they can float," said Corey. James said something as they rode away and Corey's familiar giggle drifted back to camp. Olivia shook her head and marveled at how quickly Corey was recovering from his near-death experience, but she also felt a twinge of guilt and grief as she remembered the grave on the hill.

***

Morning was moving toward noon when the wagons pulled into the waiting area at the ferry. She saw James talking to the ferryman. He waved to them as they drove up. Corey jumped off the boat and ran to the wagon.

"Old Jake – that's the ferryman's name – wanted fifty dollars up front," he said, hardly waiting for the wagon to stop. "James told him we would give him fifteen with five up front and the rest when the last wagon is across."

Olivia smiled and waved to James. He left the man and walked to her. *He bargains better than most men I know.*

"Good job, James," she said. "Corey told me your terms. Is that satisfactory with him?"

"No, it wasn't what he wanted, but he knows if he wants the work, that's the way it will be. I told him we crossed more rivers and streams in the last two and a half months than he's seen in a lifetime and we can do it again if we have to."

"What'd he say to that?"

"He said some words we aren't supposed to hear, but James covered my ears so I wouldn't hear them." Corey put his hands over his mouth and giggled.

James punched his arm and said, "Why don't you see if Mrs. Phillips needs help?" Then he said to his mother, "The ferry can only take one wagon at a time."

"I'll take mine across first," she said. "Tillie can stay and help get the other wagons on the ferry."

"I'll take my wagon last," said Tillie, "to make sure no one panics."

"James, you can wait on the other side and get each wagon off the ferry and in line."

"Okay," he said and started moving Max and Jasper toward the ferry.

Olivia reached into her diminishing supply of coins and gave one to the ferryman. "James will have the rest when the last wagon is across," she said.

"That's one mighty fine boy, you got there ma'am. He'll do you real proud any day of the week. Sure hope the war don't take him away."

"Thank you," she said. "I'm proud of all my women and children." She could have added, "The war has already stolen their youth."

"You got much further to go?"

"A day or two – somewhere around Cabin Creek or Paint Creek."

"That's not far." The man pushed his hat back on his forehead and pocketed the money. "Good luck to you, ma'am."

Olivia thanked him, climbed back on her wagon and moved it ahead, making room for the others to fall in behind her. Several hours later, they were all across. Corey and Michael helped Jeannette, who still looked and walked like a lifeless spirit, but at least she was back in her own wagon today. As soon as Olivia saw a suitable clearing, she circled the wagons.

"We'll get an early start the next morning. One more day – maybe two – and we'll stop and wait for Uncle George to contact us."

The boys headed toward the woods and by nightfall, the savory aroma of rabbit stew sent a mouth-watering invitation into the air. Still subdued, grieving not only the loss of one of their children, but now worrying about their future, the women ate in near silence, except for the children's muted chattering. How many more times would they combine their efforts and supplies for a common meal?

***

Unable to sleep, Olivia joined Maggie and George toward the end of the second watch of the night. They had been waiting two days for Uncle George.

"Do you suppose this will this be our last morning together?" George, like James, was more man than a boy for all his twelve and a half years.

"I don't know, George," Olivia said. "Someone should come to meet us soon – if not today, possibly tomorrow."

"I hope we can live close to you folks. James and I are going to start some kind of business together some day."

Olivia was surprised, but said nothing. She knew the boys were close, but... Maggie laughed. As if reading Olivia's mind, she said, "You boys are a little young to think about a life's work."

"No, ma'am," said George. "We figure we grew past our age on this trip."

Maggie looked thoughtful, then said, "You're probably right, George. All you kids have grown away from your childhood."

Subdued voices preceded the rest as they arrived for breakfast. For almost two and a half months, they had been moving toward one destination – the Kanawha Valley. They were almost there. Gathered around the campfire, they ate one more breakfast while they waited for George Dooley to arrive. Once in a while a half/sob, half/giggle sounded above the conversations. An odd combination of fear and excitement hung in the air. They all felt it. End of the journey, but new, unknown days ahead. Olivia understood their apprehension. *I'll settle near Uncle George, but what about the rest Where will they settle?*

"Will we have to work as hard now that we're almost there?" asked Jeremiah.

"Probably harder," answered James.

"We won't have to hitch up the mules and wagons and push/pull the wagons through mud..."

"But, we'll have to build homes," said James, "unless we want to become gypsies and live on the road the rest of our lives."

"Yeah," said Corey.

"We can play music," said Michael.

"And dance," said Jeremiah.

"And tell fortunes," said Corey.

"And Grandma Cooper can tell stories," said Michael.

"What about when it rains? Or next winter when it snows?" James smiled at his brothers and their friend.

"Well, a house would be warmer," said Corey.

"And Mom could cook pies and stuff again," said Michael.

"It will be good not to feel the ground sliding under our wheels all day and maybe have some solid walls around us," said Claudia. "But...what will we do...I mean...where...?"

"Yeah, where are we going to live?" Jeremiah looked at Maggie, who looked to Olivia for an answer.

Finally, Corinne asked what they all seemed to be thinking. "How soon will we be... wherever we're going?" Her voice quivered. "Do you suppose we'll be able to settle...near each other?"

"Will Mrs. Brunner still be our leader?" Bobby's round eyes

glistened with fear.

Olivia gripped her cup in both hands and stared into the few swallows still in the bottom. Had she not been as apprehensive as the rest, she could have found the scene amusing. After all the trouble and complaining from Claudia, Corinne and Jeannette, they were now fearful and concerned about a future without her. She took a swallow of coffee, blinked and sighed.

"I don't know," Olivia said. "Uncle George should meet us soon. He'll take us to Cabin Creek Hollow, where he lives. From there I don't know what to expect, but I'm sure Uncle George will be able to help us all settle near each other. We'll just have to wait for him and..."

The sound of horses' hooves pounding the road stopped their conversation. James raised his head and listened. Blackie jumped to attention.

"Uncle George?" James shielded his eyes with his hand and looked in the direction Blackie faced. The sun, not yet completely over the horizon sent streaks of vivid colors – red, orange, purple – across the cloudy sky. Rain was possible, but that wasn't thunder.

Relaxed nerves pulled taut. Olivia nodded and turned to the others. "Might be, but we can't let down our guard yet. Betsy, Martha, get the little ones out of the way."

Being prepared for possible troubles had become second nature to the women. Tillie, shotgun in hand, ran with Olivia and James to their battle stations. Blackie stood ready to attack if ordered.

Book III

The Valley

June 1861

1   Uncle George

Two men on horseback reined to a stop, slid off their horses and approached Olivia. She gasped and almost dropped her gun. For a fleeting second, she thought her father had somehow caught up with them.

"You have to be Olivia Dooley Brunner," said the older man with his arms outstretched. "You have Jefferson's hair and eyes."

"And you have to be Uncle George. I didn't know you would look so much like Daddy." She smiled at her uncle whom she was seeing for the first time.

"He didn't tell you we were identical twins?"

"I knew you were twins, but not identical," Olivia said shaking her head.

"Well, come here girl and give your Uncle George a proper greeting."

He drew her close to him in a bear hug. Still holding her with one arm, he turned to the young man now standing beside them. "Olivia, meet your cousin, Richard."

Richard looked like a younger version of his father only taller and thinner. His hair was red-gold like her own. Grinning, he clasped her hand. "Everyone 'round here said you'd never make it," he said. "I told them, 'she's my cousin and a Dooley to boot. She'll make it in time to build a house, plant a garden and start up a business if she wants to.'"

Olivia smiled. She liked this cousin she'd never met. "Thank you, Richard, for your confidence in me. Now, come meet my family and friends. We were just finishing breakfast, but there's plenty. Nothing fancy – leftover rabbit stew or oatmeal."

"Rabbit stew? Where'd you get the rabbit?"

Olivia laughed at her uncle's surprise. "The boys – James, the twins, George Walsh and Jeremiah Cooper – mostly. All of us have done our share. Fish, rabbit, wild turkey and venison – you name it. If it can be caught and eaten, we can cook it."

Richard slapped his father on the back. "I told you. She's a Dooley all right." Richard laughed again and winked at James.

Olivia said with much more seriousness, "We're living in tough times, Richard. I regret that my children have had to become adults while they're still children. I'm also proud of all the women and children on this wagon train. We've had experiences we would never have had and seen things we never thought possible. Some we would rather forget." Her thoughts swept over the little mound of stones on a hill south of them.

"But, by the grace of God, we made it this far and look forward to settling in and waiting for the war to let go of our men folks so they can catch up with us. Sit down and tell us the news of the world and about our future."

"What do you think I am, girl, a fortune teller?" Uncle George laughed and accepted the cup of hot coffee James handed to him. He took a sip then gave James a long curious look.

"How old are you, boy? Why didn't the War take you?"

James returned his steady look, grinned and answered. "I'm too young for the army, but just old enough for the wagon train."

Uncle George burst into laughter again.

Olivia chuckled then said. "They tried, Uncle George, but he outsmarted them. James and George are the oldest children in this wagon train. According to the calendar they're twelve, but according to their ability, they are older than you."

George Dooley sipped his coffee and stared into the fire. As if musing to himself, he said, "Jefferson has every reason to be proud of his girl." He turned and smiled at her. "I used to tease him because he didn't have any boys. I have three. Richard's the youngest. The other two are in uniform. Richard would be too, except for his bum leg – accident when he was six – doc didn't set it right."

Olivia had noticed his limp, but said nothing.

Uncle George continued. "You've accomplished what many young men couldn't have done. As soon as we get home, we'll send Jefferson a wire if we can – a letter if we can't."

"What's happening with the war?" Olivia looked into her Uncle's eyes expecting the same honesty she would have gotten from her father.

"It's not good, Olivia. Virginia seceded and Richmond is the capital of the Confederate states. Where we live, folks are divided in their opinions. Most side with the North, but the South is in charge. There's talk of western Virginia pulling away from Virginia and becoming a separate state. It'll happen – just not sure how soon. Charleston is under southern government, but northerners are pushing. We have both sides slipping through the woods and valleys. We keep our guns handy in case they try to take our homes or animals."

"Where are your other sons?"

Uncle George grimaced, sighed and answered. "Mark is in the Union Army and Linsey is in a Confederate Artillery Corp."

"I'm sorry," said Olivia.

"Tell us about our new home," said James to change the subject. "Is there a house, or will we build our own?"

"Do you think you can build a house?" Uncle George looked serious and James with an astonished look, answered him with just as much seriousness.

"Of course we can build a house. Corey and Michael will help. And if there is room for two houses, George will help and then we'll help him."

Richard laughed and Uncle George shook his head. "You sound just like your grandfather. When we were kids, he would try anything. He was always getting us into trouble of some kind."

The twins giggled and Michael poked his finger at Corey. Olivia laughed because she knew Michael was right. Corey had always been the adventurous one and the instigator of trouble.

"Well, we live in Cabin Creek about a half day's journey from here by wagon. Richard and I left an hour or so before sun up and rode hard. I own several miles of land in the Cabin Creek Hollow that goes back to the mountain. There's plenty of room for new homes. There's a nice big clearing where you can camp until your homes are ready. You can take your pick. If any of the rest wants land, we'll devise a workable plan."

The others had been quietly watching with a combination of happiness, envy and curiosity. Suddenly wariness and anxiety fell like tears and smiles radiated around the fire.

"It would be wonderful to be close to Olivia since she's taken care of us for so long," Grandma Cooper said, then winked at Olivia and laughed her soft cackle. "Besides, she has to bury me when my time comes."

"Grandma Cooper!" Olivia smiled at her friend, but deep in her heart, she suddenly felt a pang of something – foreboding?

"Well, I want as far away from *her* as I can get," said Jeannette. She hadn't spoken, or even acknowledged the presence of the men. Olivia was startled, but not surprised at her tone, which was so sharp and bitter that Uncle George and Richard both turned and gave her a curious look.

Tillie explained. "Jeannette lost her little girl, who was barely four. She's not taking it well."

"Not taking it well?" Jeannette shrieked. "How would you feel if you lost one of your children? It's all her fault. She shouldn't have stopped. Her child lived. Mine died. She..." Jeannette's words ended with a sob. She ran back to her wagon.

"I'll go with her," Claudia said and followed Jeannette. Olivia sat cradling her cup in her hands staring into it while the rest told the story of Sarah's death.

When they finished, Olivia said, "Jeannette's husband is Will's best friend and medical partner. We'll build her a house at the end of the hollow."

"Do I have to live there? Can I still stay with you?" Joey's eyes were wide with fear.

Olivia smiled at the little boy who still wore the splints from his beating. The dark bruises had changed to a yellowish green in many places. "We'll work out something, Joey. Your mother will need someone to look after her, but our home will be open to you for as long as you want."

Relief spread over his face. "Thank you," he whispered.

Silence fell upon the group. Richard shook his head as if emerging from a trance. He leaped up from the stone on which he sat and said, "Let's get these buggies hitched and get this parade on the road."

The twins and Joey giggled and jumped up to follow him. "They're not buggies," the twins said together.

"They're wagons," said Joey. "And we aren't going on a parade. We don't have any drums and bugles."

"We got some harmonicas," said Corey. "We could play a marching tune and make the mules think it's a parade."

"They would probably run away and turn the wagons over. Then we'd be in trouble again." Michael shook his finger at Corey.

"Well, all right then. We'll hitch the horses to the *wagons* and take them home. Does that sound better?" Richard smiled at the boys.

"Home?" Michael and Corey looked at each other as only twins can and nodded their heads in agreement.

"But they aren't horses. We got mules," said Corey. "This is Jasper and this is Max."

Soon the wagon train was on the road for the last time.

2   Another Journey Begins

While Uncle George and Richard escorted the women to their new home, the men, who had escaped from prison, were beginning their journey. Due to the trickery of Sergeant Parker and Samuel, the authorities thought all the escapees had drowned, went over the falls and were on their way to the Atlantic Ocean.

Slowly Samuel led the men through the forest lighted by bright flashes of moonlight filtering through the trees. Ghost-like shadows created by that light retreated behind layers of trees and low brush. Stumbling and dragging themselves along the eight fugitives followed what was probably a deer path worn to bare ground over years of habitual use. Afraid to travel the road until farther from Richmond, they kept an eye on the river from the cover of the trees.

Finally, the sky began to lighten and the grayish blue tint exploded into glorious color – magenta, red and yellow. Soon the sun would pop over the eastern horizon. Samuel signaled for them to stop. No one needed to tell them twice. Some sat with backs against trees, others just slid to the ground.

Samuel waited, listening with fingers to his lips, signaling them to be silent. Satisfied no one was either following or approaching from the west, he whispered, "We should be away from any soldiers or their camps. If they fell for our trick, they won't be lookin' for you, but we has to be careful anyway. There be some caves a little further on where we can sleep. I hid some food in one o' them a few days ago. We'll eat then sleep."

The men nodded, too tired and weak to speak. Forcing reluctant muscles to move again, they followed Samuel to the cave. "This way," said Samuel and ducked into one of the caves. The rest followed. They walked slowly, feeling their way, hearing only Samuel's footsteps. A slight smell of sulfur followed by the smell of melted wax and candlelight sent shadows dancing across the top and sides of the cave.

Samuel set the candle on a stone in the center of the cave and pulled out some burlap sacks from crevices in the wall. He handed out pieces of bread and ham to each one. Mouths watering, hands trembling, the men wanted to gobble it up like hungry children, but forced themselves to wait until Will gave God thanks for the food and the freedom.

"Bless our women and children, this food, our leader and our journey. Amen."

"A little short tonight," said Robert teasing Will.

"Considering this is the first food we've tasted since night before last – and that wasn't even considered food – I think God understands. Thank you, Samuel, for taking such good care of us. We could never have done this without you."

"The good Lord done helped me," said Samuel. "He changed Sergeant Parker's mind and made him help us. And without Master Dooley's getting' hisself throwed into the jail with you, it never would a worked."

"You're right, Samuel," said Will. "Mr. Dooley, I am truly in your debt for two of the most precious gifts in this world – my wife and family and now my freedom."

"Don't get yourself worked into a sermon, Will," said Jefferson. "We have a long way to go before we reach The Valley. It's going to be a very long two to three months. We can't travel in the open road during the day the way the women did, or cook on open fires like they did or shoot game with guns. We aren't even sure how to get to where we're going."

"I have a duplicate of the map I made for Olivia," said Will. "We can follow it as much as possible, staying away from the road."

"Maybe we can use the road at night as long as we stay near the forests," said John.

"Yeah," said Robert. "We would hear the horses if soldiers rode at night. Unless they're fighting or moving to a battle, they'd be in camp at night."

"What do you think, Samuel?"

"As long as we stays close to cover, should work."

"What about food. We can fish, but can we cook?" Kenny asked.

"We can cook some things," said Samuel. "When I was a kid, an Indian tribe passed this way. One of them taught me about the wilderness and how to survive – case I ever wanted to run away."

"I'm glad you never did," said Joe.

"Yeah, me too," said Robert.

"Weren't no reason to. Had folks who was good to me."

"You can cook without fire?"

"No sir, Master Robert. Gotta have fire, but you digs a pit, builds the fire in it, lets it die down to embers then wrap your food in leaves and lay it on the coals. Cover with more leaves and dirt to keep it from smoking."

"That's right," said John. "My grandfather taught me that."

"Well, it's a start," said Kenny.

"We can catch some fish from the river early in the morning, or late at night. Let it cook all day while we sleep. We can eat before we take off for the night's travel."

"Hope we don't get tired of fish," said Joe.

"I can make a bow and arrows to catch rabbits and other small game," said Samuel. "And I bets Master John knows how to do that too."

"Yes I do," said John. "Always knew my Cherokee background would be helpful someday."

"Sounds like we have a lot of learning to do if we want to survive until we get to The Valley," said Will.

"I think the women are having just as hard a time," said Joe. "They can cook in the open, if it's not raining, but they still have to have something to cook."

"Bet the boys are pretty sure shots by now," said George.

"The women too," said Kenny.

"I was opposed to Mr. Dooley teaching our children about guns," said Will. "Looks like I was wrong. It will probably help save their lives."

"In more ways than just hunting food," said Jefferson, "if they meet up with unreasonable soldiers."

"I'm sure they've also had their share of fish," said Robert.

"God is with them, as He is with us," said Will. "But, right now, I could use a little sleep."

"We'll sleep during the day and travel at night," said Jefferson.

"Maybe we should take turns guarding while the rest sleep," said John, "at least until we are well away from Richmond."

"I'll take the first watch today," said Samuel.

"Wake me when you need to rest," said John.

"Then me," said Robert.

"In the morning, we'll organize our watches so no one will be over worked."

"This cave should be safe enough," said Samuel. "We's back aways from the road. We's far 'nough in the cave that no one should see even a tiny fire from out there. I'll sit at the cave entrance."

Within minutes, the men were lying on the ground as hard as it was, gently snoring. Samuel took his knife and some strong, straight saplings he had gathered along the way to the entrance. He sat with his back to the edge of the cave entrance and whittled arrows for the bow he had made from a strong, pliable sapling.

3   The Last Circle

Tattered and torn canvas coverings flapped and clapped, wheels squeaked and squawked and mules clip-clopped with scant enthusiasm. Like a disjointed caterpillar, the wagon train crept over the last several miles. Richard veered off to the left toward the little town of Cabin Creek. The rest followed Uncle George almost half way down the lane to a long clear valley surrounded by woods on three sides.

One by one, the wagons rolled over the lane barely the width of a wagon. Cabin Creek meandered through the lower edge of the valley and through the woods on its way to the river. Reaching the center of the meadow, a collective sigh like a breeze in the tree tops whispered through the wagons as the women circled them for the last time. This camp would be home until each family gave up their wagon for a house built on land acquired from Uncle George.

Routine had become such a habit that when the wagons stopped moving, everyone set about doing their appointed chores – unhitching the mules, putting up the cook tent, gathering wood for the circle fire and corralling the mules and horses. This stop was no different from the others – and yet it was *very* different. Questions replaced the grumbling.

"Now what do we do?"

"How long before we have homes?"

"Should we build a corral for the animals?"

"Will we be alone back here?"

Uncle George dismounted and came closer to Olivia, watching the routine unfold like a carefully rehearsed drama.

"Richard will fetch our buckboard," he said, so we can take you to meet your Aunt Molly. She's been fussing for days – cleaning and cooking. She's sure you are all starved near to death. The community and church ladies are planning a dinner at the town hall tonight for everyone. They figured you'd had enough of eating on the run and might want to sit at a table with real plates and tableware for a change."

Tillie, who had come up beside them, asked, "Do you mean the whole wagon train? Kids and all?"

"Yes, ma'am, You are all a part of our community now and you don't have to worry none about dressing up. We all go to the dinners in our everyday work clothes. Some come right from farm chores."

"Well, that's real neighborly of you," said Tillie, straightening her drooping shoulders. A smile spread across her face. "Shall I pass the word, 'Livia?"

Olivia nodded. "Thanks Tillie." Then she turned to her son. "James, you and the boys can get some water on to heat so we can all clean up a little?"

"Yes ma'am," said James. "Maybe we can scare up a couple of rabbits for stew." Not expecting, nor waiting for an answer, he ran toward the woods calling as he ran, "Corey, Michael, get Jeremiah, Joey and Bobby. Let's get that fire going."

"You mean we have to work here, too?"

"Corey, that's life," answered his brother. "We have to work every day. Tomorrow we start clearing land and cutting logs for a house – unless you want to sleep under that wagon the rest of your life."

"Clearing land? Cutting logs? Building a house?" Corey was still complaining as he followed James to the woods.

Uncle George laughed that full-bodied sound that reminded Olivia so much of her father. She felt a sudden pang of homesickness, but took a deep breath and brushed it away.

"Here comes Richard with the wagon," Uncle George said.

"We could have walked. A mile isn't far considering we've come about four hundred miles."

"Your Aunt Molly would never let me live it down if I let you walk." He laughed then said, "Come on, child. While you two visit, I'll send a telegram to Jefferson to let him know you arrived safely. Hopefully he'll find a way to let your men know."

"I have a letter to mail to Elias Harper, too," said Olivia.

His look said, "Who is Elias Harper?"

"I'll explain on the way," she said. "You don't mind if I take Betsy and the babies with us do you? They're doing well on some solid foods, but they still need to nurse a few times a day."

Uncle George gave her an odd look and she felt the old familiar anger wash over her. "You won't disown me because I'm nursing a Negro baby, will you? If it's a problem, I'll move on."

Uncle George smiled as he helped her onto the wagon. "There will always be folks who will hold it against you, Olivia – both North and

South. In Cabin Creek, we do as we please. It just caught me by surprise. I saw the baby and assumed his mother was with you somewhere."

Olivia explained how she acquired Charles, why she was sending a letter to Elias Harper, and a little about their trip. Uncle George told her about the area, his boys and Aunt Molly.

***

"There's our house," said Uncle George, pointing to a split-log house with a full front porch. The front yard was small, but covered with grass and flowers. A short, plump woman with snow-white hair, caught up in a knot on top of her head waved from the door. A broad smile spread across her face. "That's your Aunt Molly waving at us."

Uncle George jumped down and ran around to help Olivia and Betsy with the babies. Aunt Molly hurried down the step to greet them.

"Welcome home, Olivia." Her voice was soft and melodic. "Let me have that precious baby," she said reaching for Lucy. She stopped and laughed with delight when she saw Betsy with Charles. "Oh, there are two of them. Jefferson only told us about one, but two is always better. I'll have to sit to hold both." She laughed again and led the way into the living room.

"Except for their color," said Olivia, "they are almost like twins. Charles is only a week older than Lucy."

"I never had twins," she said. "Linsey and Mark are close together and act like twins – or used to." She frowned and grabbed the single tear with her handkerchief before it slid down her cheek.

"Uncle George told me they chose opposite sides in the war," said Olivia. "It must be difficult having them in the war to begin with, but fighting against each other is unthinkable."

"It is," said Aunt Molly, "but it is pretty common around here. We are so divided on what we believe. I just ask God to look after both of them."

"That's all we can do," said Olivia.

"Tell me about your other children," said Aunt Molly as they seated themselves in the living room – Molly on the couch, Olivia in a rocking chair with Lucy and Betsy on the floor with Charles. "Jefferson said you have five."

"Actually, I have six now with Charles. James, is twelve, Betsy is ten. Then I have six-year old twin boys, Corey and Michael. They aren't identical."

"Tell me about Charles. Did he belong to one of your slaves?"

"Will and I don't believe in slaves. We have a Negro couple,

371

Samuel and Rosy, who work for us and are like a part of our family. But Charles' mother is a slave on one of the plantations west of my father's. She wanted her baby to have a life of freedom, so she ran to our wagon and literally threw him at me as we were passing. Then she ran away. We would never have found her, although we did know where she lived. But time was precious and we wanted to get away before Sergeant Parker decided to send more *Volunteers* after us. So we have another baby."

"Does Will know?"

Olivia smiled. "Not yet."

Aunt Molly shook her head. "Olivia, I wish I could say all your troubles are over now that you're home, but mercy me, from what I hear about the war, our troubles are just beginning." Lucy squirmed. Olivia put her to her breast. Aunt Molly bounced Charles on her knee. He gurgled, laughed and reached for her glasses.

"Aunt Molly, I don't expect you and Uncle George to solve my problems. No one can do that. War isn't easy on anyone, least of all women and children, but we're strong. Regardless of what happens to our men, we'll survive."

Olivia smiled at her aunt and watched the weariness drain from the older woman's face. *She was worried about needing to take care of us.*

"We are all hard workers, here," said Aunt Molly, "but I'm not sure any of us could have done what you and your friends have accomplished."

Olivia smiled. "Two and a half months ago, we never would have believed it either." They were quiet for a minute or two, each lost in thought. Then Olivia asked, "Do you ever get news from Richmond?"

"We get *The Richmond Enquirer* when we can – not as often as before the war began. It's usually about a week old when we see it."

"We appreciate all that you've already done, but I would love to read a newspaper again," said Olivia. "We haven't seen one since we left in March."

"We'll make sure you get the next one. We read it then throw it away, or start a fire with it, anyway."

"Thanks, we would appreciate that. We'll give it back if you need a fire starter."

Aunt Molly laughed. "You will need it more than we do with all your outdoor cooking."

Olivia laughed with her. "How about a church? Do we have one in The Valley? Or a doctor?"

"There's a little church building up by the cemetery, but we don't have an organized church. Old Tom Hendricks, who lives on the farm the other side of the cemetery, keeps it up – just in case we ever get a preacher. Mostly we gather in the community center to sing, pray and have Bible study. When the Methodist Circuit Rider comes through, he does baptisms, marriages and serves communion. We just bury our dead and say a few words over them ourselves. We do have a doctor. Doctor Wilkerson has an office in town, but he comes to our homes if we need him."

"What about builders? We will all need homes."

"Most of the men folk are gone to war – one side or the other." Again, a tear slid down Molly's cheek, but she brushed it aside and continued. "We all pull together down here. We'll help."

"We've done more than a lot of men could do already. As I said before, our boys and women are hard workers. We can do it, but we'll accept whatever help you can give us."

"What about this dinner at the center tonight?" Olivia asked to change the subject. "Is there anything we can bring? There are a lot of us to feed." Olivia took Charles and nursed him as she talked. Betsy played with Lucy on the floor.

"We don't want any hardship on you folks," said Aunt Molly.

"If we're going to be a part of the community, we want to do our part," said Olivia. "We'll bring something."

"James and the boys probably have a half dozen rabbits, or a deer, by now," said Betsy.

Aunt Molly looked surprised. "They're good shots, are they?"

"They're the best," said Betsy.

Olivia saw a flash of fear cross her aunt's face. "Is there something wrong with a boy shooting rabbits up here?"

"No, that's all right. It's just...well...the Confederates come through here every so often looking for sharpshooters. They don't care how old they are. If they can shoot a gun, they want them. I wouldn't brag too much if I were you."

"I understand," said Olivia. "Betsy..."

"I know, Mom. I won't brag – too much."

Aunt Molly smiled at Betsy. "It's so good to have you and the children close by," said Aunt Molly. "With none of my boys married and two of them off to war, I may never have grandchildren of my own. I hope Jefferson and Elizabeth don't mind sharing theirs with us."

"I'm sure they won't mind a bit," said Olivia. "Is that Uncle

George? I hear a wagon."

She had hardly finished speaking when they heard footsteps on the porch. Uncle George stepped inside, letting the screen door bang behind him. "I sent the telegram," he said.

Olivia stood, lifting Lucy with her. Betsy stood and picked up Charles. "You don't have to leave yet," said Uncle George. "Sit a spell and relax."

"We need to get ready for our night out," said Olivia. She laughed and started toward the door. "It's the first time we've met with other people since we left Richmond."

"Well, all right," said Uncle George. "I'll bring the buckboard later," he said as he helped them into the wagon. "I won't be able to take everyone, but Grandmother Cooper and some of the children might like a ride. It's not far to the center."

"Thank you. Grandma Cooper will say she can walk or will volunteer to stay and tend the fire. She *is* getting more frail each day."

As the wagon pulled into the campsite, the sound of laughter and chatter greeted them. Months of hard travel were behind them and celebration before them. Tonight they would forget the war. Tomorrow hard work building homes would begin.

4   Cabin Creek Greeting

The sun dropped toward the horizon painting the western sky in red and gold, making a silhouette of Uncle George and his wagon as he returned to the campsite. Women and children gathered for instructions, excitement turning to squeals of delight and laughter.

"Hope you don't mind a late dinner," Uncle George said. "We try to give everyone a chance to get their chores done."

"We're used to eating late, "said Olivia. "We usually didn't stop until about this time of day. Then we had to wait for dinner to cook."

"Mom," said James, "do you suppose George and I should stay with the animals?"

"Are they tethered and corralled good?" asked Uncle George.

"Yes, sir. We don't want anyone to steal them."

"No one around here will bother them," said Uncle George. "And if soldiers from either side want them, not much you can do to stop them."

"Maybe we can leave Blackie on guard duty," said James. "He would come and get us if there was trouble."

"That sounds like a sensible solution," said Uncle George.

"We won't be staying very late," said Olivia. "The babies will get tired and I'm sure the rest of us will wear out sooner than the local folks."

"What if the townsfolk don't accept us?" Claudia pulled at her borrowed dress. She had lost so much weight on their journey that her own clothes hung like sacks on her thin shoulders.

"Yeah, we worked hard all afternoon cooking and finding clean clothes," said Corinne, "but…"

"Don't you ladies worry about a thing," said Uncle George. "These folks are all hospitable. They're as worried as you are that you won't like them."

Olivia smiled. "He's right, you know. Let's get moving. Betsy, you and Martha can ride in the wagon with the babies and Grandma Cooper."

As Olivia helped Grandma Cooper up to the seat beside Uncle

George, she couldn't help noticing a tremble in the older woman's hands.

"Are you all right, Grandma Cooper?" she asked. "I can stay here with you if you don't feel up to going."

"I'm fine, Olivia," she said. "Just a little weary, like we all are. But I didn't travel all the way from Richmond and go through hell and high water, to stay home while the rest of you celebrate the end of our journey. I'm going to have one last fling before I really go home." She laughed her soft cackle and squeezed Olivia's hand.

With Betsy, Martha, the babies and a couple other children settled in the back with the rabbit stew, Uncle George flicked the reins and they were on their way. Olivia fell in step with Maggie behind the wagon.

"She's an amazing woman," Olivia said. "I hope she has a lot more years to enjoy life."

"So do I Olivia, but I'm not very hopeful. She talks more and more of going home and I don't think she means The Valley."

"Does she have any pain – other than her normal pain?"

"I asked her and she said, 'No, but the time is drawing near. I feel it in my bones.'"

Olivia grimaced remembering the times Grandma Cooper had predicted storms and other happenings on the journey. She just attributed that to her arthritis, but this was different. "Maybe she's wrong this time," she said.

"Maybe, but she's hardly ever wrong with things like this."

***

Light from the town hall's many lamps and candles, spilled over to the approaching darkness outside the open door and windows. Inside chatter increased in volume as Olivia and her women and children joined the party. Aunt Molly met them at the door.

"Make yourselves at home," she said. "We'll wait a few more minutes while folks have a chance to greet you, then George will pray and we'll eat."

"Everything looks and smells wonderful," said Olivia.

The women and children glanced at Olivia, began to mingle, but kept glancing at Olivia. Grandma Cooper laughed. "They act like children afraid they'll lose sight of their mother."

Olivia laughed with her. "Would you like to find a place and sit until we're ready to eat?"

"No, I think I'll go mingle a little while I can. If my legs give out, I'll find a chair."

Fifteen minutes later, Aunt Molly tapped a tin cup with a fork to get everyone's attention. "Good evening, everyone," she said. "We are so glad to see so many of you here to meet our niece, Olivia Brunner and her family and friends. George is going to ask the blessing on the food and…"

Before he could speak, the door opened and everyone turned to see who was late. A tall, broad-shouldered Confederate Officer filled the doorway. Silence fell upon the room. The officer removed his hat and nodded.

"Good evening, folks," he said. "Please continue whatever you were doing. I don't intend to stay. I just heard you were having a gathering and I take every opportunity I can to scout for recruits." He smiled, glanced around the room, let his gaze linger on James and his friends then began slowly walking toward them.

Aunt Molly, flushed, cast a quick glance at the boys talking near the back wall then rushed to welcome the captain. Raising her voice more from nerves than to make herself heard in the tomb-like silence that followed his entrance, she said, "Folks, this is Captain John Marshal. His troops are camped a couple of miles back toward Charleston until time to move on to Georgia. I'm sure many of you have met Captain Marshal."

Men glowered, but said nothing. Women's faces reflected fear. Olivia's women with the subtleness of mountain cats protecting their young formed a closed circle around the boys.

"I don't remember meeting all these handsome young men?" The captain smiled patronizingly at Aunt Molly and tried to move closer to the boys.

Olivia took a step forward. "They're with me," she said.

"This is my niece, Olivia Brunner," Aunt Molly said. "She and her friends arrived from Richmond this afternoon."

"I'm glad to meet you, Mrs. Brunner. I heard about a wagon train arriving from south of here."

Olivia raised her eyebrows in question and he laughed. "Oh, I suppose everyone has heard. It is rather unusual for women to make a journey like that with no men." Captain Marshal transferred his patronizing smile to her.

Olivia said nothing. She waited for what she knew was coming.

"You must have some good marksmen in your group," he said once again letting his gaze fall on James and George.

"Why would you say that, Captain?" Olivia asked. The townspeople watched in silence, breath held.

377

"Well surely, you couldn't carry enough meat for that long a journey. Someone had to be a good shot to keep you supplied."

Olivia forced a laugh. "Captain, I can give you a hundred ways of cooking fish – and they still taste like fish. We had a lucky shot once in a while. Our dog brought in a rabbit now and then. But you're right, about sharpshooters. Every woman among us can land a shot between the eyes of any man who would dare lay a hand on one of our children." Olivia's eyes locked with his. She did not return his smile.

The captain looked surprised then exploded into laughter. "Mrs. Brunner, I was told you had boys old enough to fight and were good marksmen. If you do ma'am, I don't see any of them here, nor would I try to take them if I did. I'll pass information along that there are no eligible young men in this hollow."

"Thank you, Captain Marshal. I'm glad to see the South still has some gentlemen."

Captain Marshal bowed and said, "Good evening, Mrs. Brunner. Enjoy the dinner and the dance afterward. I would love to stay, but duty calls."

The echo of his horse's hooves died away and a collective sigh of exhaled breath whispered across the room.

"Let's pray," said Uncle George. "Lord, we give Thee thanks for so many blessings – for the safe arrival of Olivia and her friends, for the food you have so bountifully provided for us, for the hands that have prepared it and for this night of celebration. Amen."

Uncle George paused then said, "With so many good foods weighing down the tables, I don't think we'll have a hard time finding something we like. So, let's eat and enjoy."

Chatter and laughter flowed once again as people moved toward the laden tables, then found a place to sit and eat.

While Olivia watched the children fill their plates, Richard moved in beside her. "I have to say I was impressed," he said. "I was sure that captain would snatch your boys."

"Richard, we wouldn't let that happen."

"So I see."

"I promised Will I would protect our children as best I could. We've had to learn to do what we have to do to protect our kids."

***

Chairs scraped against the floor. Sighs of contentment like a summer breeze filled the room. Fiddlin' Freddie took that as a signal to strike up a tune.

"Grab your partners and let's dance," called Freddie as he pulled and pushed the bow across the strings of his shiny fiddle. Back and forth, the bow flew while the fingers on his left hand danced up and down the neck of his fiddle worn with age. It was impossible for anyone to stand still – except Jeannette. A look of wild-eyed terror spread across her face, her fingers entwined like a rambling rose. She shrank into a dark corner. The other women took turns standing near her. The community women understood and didn't insist that she join them.

"Mom, would you have this dance with me?" James grinned as he held out his hand. Surprised, Olivia looked up into her son's eyes. *When did he get so tall and handsome?*

"I would love to James. I haven't danced a square dance in years."

The next round was a slower waltz and Olivia watched as James took Grandma Cooper's hand. A broad smile covered her thin face. They glided across the floor, never missing a beat. Other dancers moved aside to watch the youth and the old woman dance as on air. A loud applause erupted when the dance ended. James blushed and bowed to Grandma Cooper, whose face glowed.

"Great to hear laughter and pleasant chatter," said Tillie as she moved beside Olivia and they watched the circle of dancers.

"Grandma Cooper really enjoyed that dance with James," said Maggie.

"She looks tired," said Olivia glancing around the room. Everyone danced, clapped their hands or stomped their feet in rhythm.

"It's good to relax and forget," said Claudia

"For a couple of hours anyway," said Olivia.

"It is," said Maggie, "but…"

"I know," said Olivia. "If everyone is as tired as I am, we better call it a night. The babies are getting cranky and Grandma Cooper looks more tired than usual."

Olivia gave an almost imperceptible nod and the women gathered the children. Music followed them out the door and drifted through the open windows.

"You can stay if you want to," Olivia said to James and George. "We need to take Grandma Cooper and the babies back to the camp."

James grinned. "The rest of you look a little tattered around the edges, too."

Olivia smiled at her son. "Maybe you're right. We're all tired."

"Actually, so are we," said James. "We'll go back now, too. Okay George?"

"Okay by me. My feet hurt. That chubby little girl in the green dress kept stepping on them."

"Course you never stepped on anyone's feet." James laughed as he and George ran down the road toward home. James called back to Olivia. "We'll get the fire going."

***

The pleasure of the evening lingered like the glow of twilight. Maggie and Olivia walked with Grandma Cooper toward her wagon.

James and George had a blazing fire in the middle of the circle.

"Thank you for the dance this evening, young man," said Grandma Cooper as she stopped for a moment beside the fire. "I haven't danced since I was a young girl. I thought for a minute I had died and gone to heaven."

"You made it a pleasure for me, Grandma Cooper," said James. "Shall I walk you to your door?" He grinned as he held out his arm for her to take. Grandma Cooper looked up to his smiling face.

"Why thank you, again," she said, taking his arm. She winked at Olivia. "You better keep an eye on this one, Olivia. All the girls will be after him."

James blushed, Grandma Cooper laughed. Olivia smiled to herself and watched them slowly make their way to the Cooper wagon. *He is becoming a handsome young man. He's grown at least six inches in stature and much more in stamina. Will would be so proud of him.*

Olivia shook her head. She wouldn't let anything ruin a perfectly wonderful evening – not even thoughts of Libby Prison.

5 Remnants of a Storm Discovered

While the women prepared for the day's end, the men began to wake and prepare for the night – their time of travel. The sun began sinking behind the western mountains and the men stretched and moved to the cave entrance. It was time to move on. John had taken the last watch while Samuel slept. He continued making arrows for the bows he and Samuel made.

"Anything happening," asked Will as he emerged from the cave and looked toward the setting sun seeing a blend of reds, reflecting on the rippling river water.

"Not much," said John, "at least not during my watch."

"Breakfast is about ready," said Samuel. "Master John and me caught a mess o' fish and put them on to cook in the pit."

"You can't even smell it cooking," said Robert.

"Wonder if the women knew about this way of cooking?" said George.

"I'm sure Tillie knows," said John, "but they traveled during the day. Didn't need to put something on the night before. They probably just cooked a pot of oatmeal over the campfire."

"Well, let's get digging. We wants to be on the road soon. I figures we can travel by road long as there is 'nough cover if we hear anyone coming."

"You sure that's a good idea? I don't want to get caught and go back to that place." Kenny rubbed the stubble on his chin.

"We either takes a chance on the road, or we takes a chance of breaking a leg or worse by running through the woods."

"Samuel's right," said John. "I think we can move faster by road. We've risked too much already to become overly cautious now."

While they were talking, George and Joe had been digging up the fish. They smelled wonderful to the men who hadn't had a hot meal in months.

"Samuel, maybe you can open a restaurant when we get to The Valley," said George.

"No sir, Master George. I just wants to find my Rosy and live out the rest o' the days the good Lord gives me."

They finished eating then poured water over the coals. They placed scraps and bones in the pit and filled it in. While John supervised the cleanup, making sure they left no sign of anyone having been there, Samuel gathered the things he'd hidden in the cave.

"I didn't have time for Rosy make proper carrying bags for our supplies. I just grabbed burlap bags and some pillowcases. We'll divide the lot so we can all carry some. Unless we hits some rain that soaks everything, we should have 'nough for a few days. Then we'll have to rely on God to provide."

"He has done that all along," said Will.

"Yes, sir, Master Will," said Samuel. "He sure 'nough has."

"I have a few gold coins," said Jefferson, "if we come to a place where we can safely buy something with them."

"That won't be for at least a couple of weeks," said Will.

"How far you suppose we can travel in a night?" Kenny asked.

"Not much more than eight or ten miles a night – as long as we use the road and the moon gives us some light."

"The wagons probably didn't move much faster," said George.

"Unless they got slowed down by rain and mud," said Robert, "they should have gone about eight miles a day."

"Well, if'n we sits here talking all night, we ain't gonna go no miles," said Samuel.

The men laughed. "You're right Samuel," said Will. "If we have the area clean, let's move out."

"We need to walk as fast as we can," said John, "run if we can. It will take us until winter if we poke along."

"Why don't we let Mr. Dooley set the pace," said Robert. "We can't afford for anyone to wear out before we even get to the bridge where we cross over."

"Didn't someone say they blowed the bridge up?" said Kenny.

"That was weeks ago. Probably been repaired by now. If not we can swim across the river if we have to. The women couldn't because of the wagons."

***

The sun rose and set blending days into weeks and still the men moved onward. They had been on the road for a little over an hour when John signaled for them the stop.

"I hear horses," he hissed. "Quick, into the woods. Take cover where you can."

They all ran and were in the meadow between the woods and the road before they heard what John had heard. Sliding behind trees and bushes they flattened themselves on the ground, waiting for the danger to pass.

Two horsemen on the road took their time. Although the men couldn't see clearly in the dark, they assumed them to be Confederate soldiers.

"Where we going?" asked one of the riders.

"Richmond, our new capital."

"How much further?"

"Maybe eighty to a hundred miles."

"Can't we move any faster? We been in the saddle all day. I'm ready for a beer and bed."

"Run your nag if you want to, but I ain't takin' a chance of my pinto breakin' a leg."

"But we got important news for that Sergeant Parker."

"Important? You think he's gonna send anyone back to Charleston for a few mules that have traveled 400 miles only to drive them back another 400 miles. They wouldn't be worth sending to the glue factory by the time they got to Richmond. That's assuming the rumors we heard were true in the first place."

"Well he'll want to know…"

"So, we'll tell him, but not immediately. It will take us close to a week to get back home. I'm stopping soon for a little sleep. You can ride your horse to the ground if you want to, but I'm in no hurry to tell him he can forget the mules."

The two soldiers continued on their way. When John no longer heard the hoof beats, he signaled for the men to return to the road.

"The wagon train mules?" Kenny asked.

"Probably," said Robert.

"Then that means they made it," said Joe.

"Sure sounds like it," said Will. "They're safe. Now we can stop worrying about them and concentrate on getting ourselves there with all our body parts."

"We'll go another hour or so then take a lunch break," said John, who had assumed the role of leader – a least for the time being. Since he and Samuel both had knowledge of wilderness survival, they took charge.

***

The rest of the night was uneventful, except for a stumble or two. They ran as much as they could and walked when they couldn't.

Finally, exhausted, they all dropped on the ground beside the river and ate their sparse lunch.

"We better get moving," said John. "Looks like a lot of river traffic – or will be when it begins to get daylight. Those steamboats don't dare move much during the night and take a chance of running aground."

The men nodded, although they could hardly see each other, much less the riverboats. Wearily, they rose and began quickly walking again. When they came to one of the clearings Will had marked on his map, the eastern sky was turning a light blue tinged with red and yellow.

"We better stop here and look for a place to hide for the day," said John.

"Looks like wagons were camped here," said Robert. "We must be on the right trail.

"The way things are crumpled, it was probably pretty wet when they stopped here – maybe that storm we had earlier in the spring."

"Probably," said Joe. "Looks like a tree was blown over or struck by lightning and had to be cut up."

"Maybe landed on a wagon."

"They was here all right," said Samuel. "Looks like they stayed several days. Probably had to wait until they could get the tree outa the way."

"Spread out and see what you can find," said John. "Maybe they left more clues to help us know they were all right."

"Over here," called Kenny. He pointed into a ditch in the woods. "Looks like the carcass of a large animal – one of the mules?"

Samuel took a closer look and shook his head. "No, sir, Master Kenny. That ain't no mule carcass. Looks like a domesticated animal. The front legs were broken. Nellie probably bolted in the storm."

"That must have devastated the children," said Will.

"At least it wasn't the mules," said Jefferson. "They would have a rough time without one of them."

"The creek runs from the woods," said George. "Maybe we can follow it a short ways and find some place to be out of sight for the day."

"Good idea," said Joe. "Maybe we can chance a small fire to boil some water to refill our jugs."

"Yes, sir," Master Joe. "We's getting mighty low on clean water. I'll take care of that while Master John starts the pit for cooking our breakfast."

"What's he going to cook?" asked George.

"Whatever we can catch," said Samuel and laughed.

"I'll help Joe gather some sticks for the fire," said Will. "I think I can tell the difference between a stick and a snake."

"You sure?" asked Joe.

"If not," said Will, "we can have roasted rattlesnake." They laughed and he and Joe started gathering firewood.

"I'll get the water," said George.

"I'll see if I can come up with something to cook," said John.

By the time the sun was coming over the horizon, boiled water was cooling, a couple of rabbits were roasting in the covered pit, and Will and Joe sat watch while the rest slept.

"How long have we been on the road?" asked Joe. "It feels like months. I can imagine how the women – especially Jeannette – must have felt in the storm."

"As near as I can calculate," said Will, "we've been on the run for about three or four weeks."

"Maybe by the end of the summer, if we don't run into trouble and can find enough food and…"

"Joe, our faith brought us this far. It will get us to The Valley."

"Thanks, Will. Can we pray while we wait – if we whisper."

"I think that's a wonderful idea."

While the sun rose higher in the sky and the others slept, Will and Joe spent their watch in prayer.

6   *Saying Goodbye*

The full moon that had lighted the way home earlier began to play hide and seek among dark clouds. Olivia crawled under her wagon and watched streaks of lightning flash in and around those clouds. A raindrop splashed across her nose, so she scooted further under the wagon, hoping the rain wouldn't soak her before morning. Bone weary, she slept soundly until Tillie's voice pulled her from the depth of slumber. Automatically, she wrapped a hand around her shotgun and lifted her head.

"Tillie? What is it? Has someone invaded the camp?"

"No, it's Grandma Cooper. Maggie thinks she's had a heart attack. You better come."

Olivia exchanged her gun for the medical bag and pulled herself out from under the wagon. James, awakened by the exchange, crawled out beside them.

"James, take Jeremiah and go to Uncle George's. Tell him we need that doctor they got in town."

"Yes, ma'am," he said and ran to the corral to get Beauty. The rain had stopped and the moon once again played hide and seek in the clouds. Olivia hurried after Tillie – dodging puddles, but not wet grass. By the time she got to the Cooper wagon, James was riding Beauty through the camp to get Jeremiah. Taking his hand, he pulled the boy up behind him.

"Stay, Blackie," he called to his dog then turned down the lane toward town.

Olivia, heart pounding, hands sweating, took in the situation at a glance. A lamp hung from the middle frame in the wagon, Grandma Cooper lay on a bed of blankets and pillows on the wagon's floor and Maggie knelt beside her. Joshua and Martha huddled together in a corner of the wagon.

"Tillie, take the children to my wagon. Wake Betsy and tell her to make room for them. I'll stay here with Maggie until the boys return with a doctor."

Tillie left with the children. Olivia climbed into the wagon and knelt on the other side of Grandma Cooper.

"Where does it hurt? Is it difficult to breathe, or talk?"

Grandma Cooper tried to smile. "Pain in chest and arm…Hurts some to breathe deep… Old ticker ready to stop ticking."

"We'll do what we can, Grandma Cooper. I've sent for the doctor in town."

"Won't do no good. You're doing all I need. Just want my friends and family here to see me out."

"Don't talk that way, Grandmother Cooper." Maggie's words sounded sharp.

Grandma Cooper smiled and patted Maggie's hand. Then she gave her attention to Olivia. "Ain't nothing you can do, 'cept sit here with me. I'm at the end of my journey."

Olivia wanted to tell her she had a lot of years left, that everything would be all right, but she thought Grandma Cooper was right. She took her hand and held it. Maggie held her other hand.

"Don't be sad for me," said Grandma Cooper. "We had a good journey. Thank you for bringing me with you…Tell James he made my last night on earth the happiest in my life –'cept of course for when I had my Albert with me. I'm going out celebrating and my Jesus will take me home celebrating."

"It was a good journey, Grandma Cooper," said Olivia. "And thank you for making it more pleasurable for me."

Grandma Cooper laughed, which sent her into a fit of coughing. When she was able to breathe again, she said between short gasps, "…not sure pleasurable…right word… Glad I could be there… when things…were rough."

Olivia smiled at her and squeezed her hand. "We'll miss you, Grandma Cooper, but you won't have to endure any more hardships."

"…always be hardships…Because you're home…don't mean easy…Still got a war…Hope it ends before our boys…" Grandma Cooper paused breathing hard and raspy. "Remember… God with you…I'll keep watch and…"

Olivia shivered, suddenly afraid for their boys. "We'll be all right, Grandma Cooper. Maybe the war won't find us back in this hollow."

"Maybe," she whispered. "Maggie…take care of the children…tell Robert…I'm all right… someday…meet again…better place."

"I'll tell him, Grandmother." Maggie squeezed her hand with one hand and dabbed at her eyes with the other. They heard footsteps.

"Sounds like Tillie," said Olivia.

Tillie held out cups of coffee for Olivia and Maggie, which they gratefully accepted. "How is she?" Tillie asked.

"Where's mine?" Grandma Cooper laughed her soft cackle, choked and went into another fit of coughing. Maggie held her until she stopped then offered her a drink from her cup. Grandma Cooper sipped the hot liquid, licked her lips, sighed, smiled and closed her eyes.

Tillie sat on the end of the wagon and the three of them waited while clouds drifted away making way for the first sunrise in their new home.

They heard horses approaching. "Sounds like the doctor is here," said Tillie. The boys rode up to the wagon with Doctor Wilkerson.

"Come on Jeremiah," said James, sliding off Beauty and helping Jeremiah down. "We'll take the horses out of the way."

"Is Grandma going to be all right?" Jeremiah looked at his mother.

Maggie, with tears standing on the brim of her eyes, shook her head. Jeremiah went to the end of the wagon. "Grandma, the doctor is here."

"Thank you, Jeremiah…be all right, son …go with James …and Jeremiah…"

"Yes ma'am?"

"Help Olivia and your mother…until your father comes."

"All right." Jeremiah climbed up in the wagon and gave his great-grandmother a hug, and left to help James with the horses.

Doctor Wilkerson stepped to the wagon when Jeremiah left. He was older than Olivia, probably in his late forties, tall and thin. He reminded her of pictures she had seen of Abe Lincoln, except he didn't wear a beard.

The women moved aside to let him examine Grandma Cooper, who had closed her eyes again. Doctor Wilkerson looked at Olivia, then Maggie. "Which one of you is related to her?"

"I am," said Maggie. "I'm Maggie Cooper."

"Then you must be Mrs. Brunner," he said to Olivia. "The boys told me a little about your trip. She was pretty old for something of that sort, don't you think?"

Grandma Cooper's eyes popped open. She squinted at the doctor. "Who you calling old, sonny? You ever ride a wagon train?...Cross a river on a barge?... Or a ferryboat?... Didn't think so…not old, Doc, body wore out…going home to get a new one."

Doctor Wilkerson looked surprised, then chuckled. He shook his head and climbed out of the wagon. "Ladies, she's right, you know.

There's nothing I can do except wait with you, give her something for pain."

"Doctor, how…?" Maggie started but the words stuck in her throat.

Grandma Cooper coughed again and whispered, "Not long, Maggie…not long."

The doctor nodded and accepted a cup of coffee that James brought to him. "Thank you young man," he said.

Together they waited with Grandma Cooper for another hour. She opened her eyes, reached heavenward and said, "He's coming for me…meet you on the other side." She closed her eyes and exhaled her last breath.

Somewhere in the mountains, the eerie howl of a wolf wavered across the valley. Blackie echoed the sound. Was he mourning the loss of one of his humans? Olivia shivered. Without turning, she knew James was near. "Would you fetch Uncle George," she said.

"I'm here, child," said her uncle. "I thought I better see if you need any help. What can we do?"

"We need to find a place to bury her," said Maggie. "She said all along that she hoped she wouldn't die before we got home. Her prayer was answered."

"There's a little cemetery up on the hill just north of town. I'll get some men and we'll dig a grave."

"We'll do it," said James. "We did it before."

"That's right," said Jeremiah. "She was my great-grandmother and my friend. I want to do it for her."

Uncle George, not yet used to children doing adult tasks, nodded. "Richard and I will help."

"What about a casket?"

"John Blake makes furniture and caskets. I'll stop by and see him," said Uncle George. "We don't have a funeral home out here. There's one in Charleston, about thirty miles away."

"Ask Mr. Blake," said Maggie. "I'm sure he'll do fine."

"Like I said before, we don't have no preacher out here. You want me to find someone to say some words?"

"Olivia will do it," said Maggie. "She's been our spiritual leader as well as our wagon master since we left Richmond. You *can* do it, can't you?" Maggie looked expectantly to her friend.

"I have Will's Book of Ritual, Maggie. I can use the same words he would use." Relief spread over Maggie's face and tears slipped down her cheeks. "Can we do the service tomorrow morning?" Maggie looked again to Olivia for help.

"If Mister Blake can build us a casket by then, I'm sure the boys can dig the grave today."

"Thank you for not leaving me alone with this," said Maggie. "I'm glad we're all here together. Even in Richmond, I'm not sure I could've coped alone."

"Let's find that cemetery and dig," said Tillie, her voice sounding a little husky.

Uncle George took Tillie and the boys to the cemetery. By mid-afternoon, they had a grave dug. Once again, James found a large flat stone and late into the night by light of the campfire, he began carving a headstone for Grandma Cooper.

7   Home at Last

Olivia pulled herself from under the wagon, stood and looked around her – the second sunrise in their new home. She moved about in a gray-blue haze toward the center fire. Tillie already had water on and coffee bubbling. James sat near the fire, hunched over a large stone.

Looking toward the red-streaked eastern mountains, Olivia said, "Looks like a promising June day."

Tillie nodded. "She would have loved it here."

Olivia knew she meant Grandma Cooper. "We'll all miss her."

"What a shame to have traveled so far and then not have a chance to enjoy the end of the journey," said George who sat beside James.

James stopped chiseling on the stone he was making for Ethel and looked up. "The journey for us hasn't ended, George. We still have work to do. Grandma Cooper ended her journey with joy. She worked hard to help us get here. Now she can rest."

"Guess you're right," said George. "I think she was one of the few who never complained about the hard work." Then he added, "I can be happy for her now. Thanks, James. I'll go feed the animals while you finish that."

George left and James went back to chiseling. Tillie and Olivia exchanged surprised glances. Then Tillie grinned and turned back to her cooking.

James finished the stone and laid it aside to follow George. Olivia and Tillie couldn't resist looking to see what he had done. A replica of the Holy City filled the top left corner with streaks like sunbeams reaching down to the words:

Ethel "Grandma" Cooper
February 28, 1770 – June 6, 1861
Worthy Traveler
Home at Last

Olivia swiped at her tears and turned toward her wagon. Tillie gave her a pat on the back and returned to her bubbling oatmeal.

***

Breakfast over, women and children hurried to wash faces, comb hair and get dressed. A mixture of grief and weariness often made voices sharp and brought tears to children's eyes. Finally, when they heard the sound of wagon wheels bumping over the uneven ground, they were ready. Uncle George had arrived with the casket.

He drove his buckboard around the circle and stopped at Maggie's wagon. Olivia went to meet him as he was helping Aunt Molly down from the wagon. Aunt Molly went to Maggie, hugged her close then turned to Olivia.

"I'll stay with the babies and any of the other children who want to stay here," she said.

"The children want to go with us," said Olivia. "Grandma Cooper was their friend. But, I do appreciate your help with the babies. Betsy and Martha are with them now." She paused and glanced at Jeannette, who watched wide-eyed from the safety of her wagon. "I hope Jeannette won't give you any trouble. She pretty much stays by herself and she's not violent, just withdrawn and…"

"I understand," said Aunt Molly. "We'll be all right. I'll just go to your wagon while you help here."

Olivia nodded and turned to help Tillie and Maggie wrap Grandma Cooper's body in a soft woolen blanket. When they finished, Richard reached for her.

"I'll carry her to the wagon," said Richard.

"Jim Blake worked overtime to have the casket ready for us this morning," said Uncle George as they slowly walked to the wagon. Carefully Richard lowered the body into the casket and Uncle George sealed it. James brought the stone he had carved and placed it on the wagon floor.

"Olivia, would you and Maggie like to ride with us?" Uncle George asked.

Olivia glanced at Maggie, who shook her head. "Thanks, but we'll walk behind the wagon with the others, if you don't mind."

Uncle George nodded, climbed to the seat and snapped the reins. The horses began to walk slowly toward Paint Creek Hollow and the cemetery on the hill. Blackie walked beside James, ears down and tail between his legs as if he knew this was not a pleasure walk. As they walked through Cabin Creek, people from the community, who had only met Grandma Cooper at the dinner and dance, fell in step with the procession.

Slowly they made their way to the white frame church beside the cemetery. As Aunt Molly had said, Old Tom Hendricks had recently – possibly yesterday – trimmed the grass. The white rail fence, while not done recently, was dazzling white. Rows of monuments faced the rising sun like soldiers standing at attention.

Olivia led the procession that snaked its way up the gravel path and around the church to the place of burial. Following close behind her, Uncle George, Richard, James, George Walsh, Tom Rayburn and Jeremiah Cooper carried the casket from the wagon to the grave. The rest of the mourners fell in step behind them.

Standing at the head of the grave, Olivia watched the men and boys lower the casket to its final resting place. James and the other pallbearers stepped to one side. Blackie lay at his feet, with his chin on his front paws. Olivia opened her Bible and Will's Book of Worship.

"The Lord is my Shepherd," she began, following with prayers for the family and friends. "Grandma Cooper often compared our journey to The Valley with Moses and his journey to the Promised Land. She was thrilled by so many new experiences. She encouraged the rest of us when we grew weary. She gave the children the gift of stories. But, unlike Moses, Grandma Cooper was given the blessing of seeing the journey's end. She was happy to go to her final home."

Olivia paused and looked around the group of mourners. "Is there anyone else who would like to say a last farewell?"

"Grandma Cooper was more than my husband's grandmother. She was my friend." Maggie dabbed at her eyes.

"She did love new experiences," said Corinne. "Remember how excited she was to help guide the riverboat?" This brought a ripple of chuckles.

Olivia waited in silence giving time for others to speak. A few more mentioned some of the highlights of their trip – when Grandma Cooper helped set broken bones, taught the boys how to dress a deer, kept the children entertained with her stories and how she had waltzed with James only hours before her death. A sense of peaceful calm settled over the mourners.

Olivia then picked up a handful of dirt and slowly let it sift through her fingers onto the casket. "Ashes to ashes, dust to dust…may the God who gave Grandma Ethel Cooper life on this earth, now grant her life eternal in His kingdom. Amen."

She closed the Book of Ritual and before anyone could move or speak, Bobby, Jeremiah, Michael and Corey stepped forward and stood like soldiers at attention beside the grave. Olivia, not sure what they were going to do, watched with some apprehension. They lifted harmonicas to their mouths and the mournful sound of *Amazing Grace* drifted across the grave and upward on the breeze. The last notes died away. Except for a few sniffs, sobs and coughs, silence followed.

The boys replaced their harmonicas in their pockets, picked up a shovel and began filling in the grave. As if on signal, everyone pitched in to fill the grave. James placed the headstone in its proper place and backed away. The children put wildflowers on top of the grave. Maggie read the words on the stone and wept. Olivia could hardly keep her own tears back, not because of her sadness, but because of pride in her children.

One by one, the mourners followed the community folks to the Community Center for a funeral dinner. In the midst of grief, life would continue. This afternoon they would finish the wooden corral they began yesterday and build a lean-to shelter for the animals. Tomorrow they would begin clearing land for homes.

***

Later that evening, although the women were still grieving, they tried to put on a stoic front for the children, who were too subdued to play. They all sat around the campfire as if hoping they were mistaken and it was all a dream. They would waken and find Grandma Cooper eager to tell a story or two. The babies were down for the night so Olivia joined the rest at the center circle. Tillie handed her a cup of fresh coffee.

Olivia took the coffee and glanced at the children. *They seem to be waiting for something, but what?*

Finally, Bobby broke the silence. "Mrs. Brunner?"

"Yes, Bobby," she tried to smile, but knew it was weak.

"Remember when Sarah died and you explained it to us?"

"Yes."

"Can you do that again? This time is different."

"Yes, Bobby, this time is different, but what is different about it?"

Jeremiah spoke with tears forming in his eyes. "This time she was family as well as friend."

"Yeah, and she was old, not a little kid like Sarah," said Joey.

"And it wasn't an accident," said Martha. "God just took her."

"Why did He do that when we just got here and she didn't have time to enjoy her new home?" asked Bobby.

Olivia looked over the children who turned to her with wide eyes. Then she glanced at the women and knew they were thinking the same things. She thought of Will in that Richmond prison. *He should be doing this.*

Taking a sip of coffee, then clearing her throat, she said, "Yes, this time is different. We all lost a dear friend, but Grandma Cooper would be the first to say, 'Don't dally mourning me. Move on. Get those houses built.' Grandma Cooper was old – older than many of her generation. She lived through wars and changes we can only read about. God gave her a special gift of enjoying whatever she did. She did love the journey, even though it was hard. She was thrilled with the dance our first night here. She loved all of us, but said many times we have more to do. Her life was over. She wanted to go home"

"You mean if we ask God to take us home, He will?"

"Not necessarily, Tom. We – and especially you children – are still young and God has work for us to finish."

"So God won't take us until we finish what He put us here to do?"

"Something like that."

"But, how will we know when our work is done?"

"As long as you are able and there is some need to be fulfilled, God will use your labors."

"Grandma Cooper won't be tired anymore will she?" Jeremiah asked.

"No, Jeremiah, she's at peace."

"And her bones don't hurt," said Martha.

"I bet she's up there telling Albert all about her journey from Richmond," said Corey who had been quietly staring into the fire.

"And singing with the angels," said Michael.

"I bet she'll help us find the right trees to build our houses," said Jeremiah.

"And chase the bears away," said Corey.

"Bears? Are there bears here, Mrs. Brunner?" Jeremiah asked.

Olivia smiled. Once given the chance to voice their fears and concerns about death, the children were ready to move on. *Oh, to have the faith of a child.*

8   Building Begins

"Looks like it's going to be a perfect day for building," said James as he crawled from under the wagon.

"How can you tell? It's still dark." Corey pulled himself out beside James, Michael right behind him.

"Look up," said James. "Clear skies. Feel that cool air – not hot, not cold."

"Smell the coffee and oatmeal," said Michael. "I'm hungry."

"So are the animals," said James. "Let's tend to them first while Mom feeds Lucy and Charles. Then we'll be all set when Richard and Uncle George get here."

Olivia smiled at her boys. Good-naturedly, Corey and Michael grumbled to George, Jeremiah and Tom who joined them as they started toward the corral.

"I'm hungry," said Corey. "Couldn't we feed the animals after we eat?"

"Maybe you can eat the grass with the mules," said George.

"Yuck! I'll take oatmeal."

"Well, horses and mules like oats," said Jeremiah.

"Maybe they'll come and eat our breakfast if we don't feed them first," said Tom.

"Well, maybe…" Corey's words faded, but Olivia heard their laughter as she joined Tillie at the cook tent.

"It is amazing how the children bounce back from grief," said Tillie. "At least the war didn't take that from them – yet."

"Maybe we should have given ourselves more time to mourn – at least until Monday. It hardly pays to begin today then stop for Sunday," said Olivia.

"Life goes on," said Tillie as she stirred the oatmeal. "Hard work is a healer of many ills and idle minds turn to worry and despair."

Maggie joined them at the tent. "That sounds like something Grandmother Cooper would say," she said.

"You're right. She did say that, or something similar, many times. We'll miss Grandma Cooper for a long time, but we are all better for having known her and having had her on this journey with us."

"I do miss her," said Maggie brushing a stray tear from her cheek. "But she would be the first to say, 'Don't wait on my account. Get those homes built and those children off the cold, wet ground.'"

"You're both right," said Olivia. "I guess I needed to be reminded of that and…"

The sound of many horses approaching interrupted her. Hoof beats grew louder then stopped. One rider moved on. The rest waited.

"It's Richard," said James shielding his eyes with his hand and peering toward the mouth of the lane. "Looks like he brought help."

Blackie yapped and ran to meet Richard and his friends.

"Morning, Olivia," said Richard drawing closer and tipping his hat to them. "Hope we didn't startle you."

"We didn't expect so many," said Olivia, "but we're glad to see all of you. You're out early. Come for breakfast?"

"Some coffee would be nice if you could handle a dozen more of my buddies. Then just tell us where to begin."

"The coffee is ready along with breakfast if they want oatmeal. They can take the horses to the corral with our mules. Last night we decided to start with the plot of land at the end of the hollow for Jeannette." She handed Richard a cup of coffee. "We'll finish her house then work our way up to mine at the other end."

"Sure you don't want yours first?" Richard gave her an inquisitive look. "I sure wouldn't go out of my way to make that woman comfortable."

"She's sick, Richard. She can't help her illness any more than a kid can help having the measles."

"If you say so, but…well, never mind. You're the boss here. Daddy told us to follow your instructions. If we don't have a lot of rain, we should be able to build six houses by the end of the summer."

"We're mighty sorry about your grandmother," said one of the men as Maggie filled his bowl. "Must be hard to grieve and still have to keep working."

Maggie smiled even though a tear slipped down her cheek. "Thank you. Grandmother Cooper was a special lady. She's in her permanent home, now we have to build our temporary ones. It's what she wanted for us."

The young man nodded and stepped aside for the next one in line. As the sun popped over the eastern mountains, they finished eating and started toward Jeannette's plot of land. Olivia watched Betsy eying the others with longing as they hurried across the field. She sighed then turned back to the babies who were both sleeping.

"Betsy," Olivia said. "Why don't you go work with them for the morning? I'll stay with the little ones. After lunch you can stay and I'll go work."

"Really? You don't mind?"

"Of course not. You need to learn more about life than just how to take care of babies."

Betsy jumped up, ran several steps, stopped and turned around to wave. "Thanks, Mom," she called and ran after the others. "Corey, Michael, wait for me."

Corey and Michael stopped to wait for her. "Hurry up," said Corey.

"Yeah, we don't want to miss any of the fun," said Michael.

Olivia smiled as the three of them ran to catch up with the rest. She knew the *fun* would turn to *work* before the day was over. Still smiling, she turned to help Tillie clean up from breakfast and begin lunch. *I wonder how we'll feed so many. They'll all be hungry when break time comes.*

"We have all that food the community sent home with us after the funeral yesterday," said Tillie. "I'll combine some of the dishes to make a chicken and vegetable stew. James and George built us another oven so we can make biscuits to go with it. Not a big variety, but should fill the empty spot and give them strength for the afternoon. We'll worry about tomorrow when it gets here."

Olivia smiled at her friend. "You're reading my mind again," she said, "but, you're right. God kept body and soul together on the journey. He'll help us now."

***

"The biscuits are ready to go in the oven and the stew just needs stirred once in a while. If you have something else you want to do, I can handle this," Tillie said.

"Thanks, Tillie. I would like to go rope off my garden spot. I'm anxious to get my fingers in the dirt and think about what we can grow to get us through the summer and put away for the winter."

"You don't have to take care of the rest of us, now, 'Livia. We're home."

"But we're still not out of danger and we're in this together until our men come home," said Olivia. She picked up the two infants, who were getting almost too big for her to carry at the same time, and walked to her chosen plot. *The men have staked out the area for the house, barn and garden, but I can't wait until they build my house before beginning my garden. That will be too late for anything to grow.*

Olivia turned over the soil with a garden spade, letting her mind wander. Libby...no, she pulled back from there. The future of her garden – fresh green beans, potatoes and tomatoes on her table. Much more pleasant thoughts. She could almost taste the vegetables with hot cornbread.

She glanced up at the sound of a horse trotting down the lane. Uncle George dismounted and walked toward her. The babies had crawled off the blanket. Uncle George picked up Charles while she got Lucy. They put them back on the blanket.

"I thought everyone was building houses," he said

Olivia brushed the sweat from her forehead with the back of her hand. "Most of them are down at Jeannette's plot of land. Someone has to watch the babies. Betsy went this morning and I'll go this afternoon. Tillie is cooking lunch, so I thought I would start digging up ground for a garden so we can have some vegetables for canning later in the summer and fall."

"Tell you what," said Uncle George. "Monday, why don't you bring the babies to our house. Your Aunt Molly would love to have them around. I'll bring the plow and we'll hook one of the mules to it and get this plowing done in no time."

"The plowing sounds good, but I don't want to impose on Aunt Molly."

"You won't be imposing. We don't have any grandkids and she's always fussing about this one or that one having little ones around and she doesn't."

"Well, maybe a couple of days a week, but not every day," said Olivia. She turned toward the camp. "It sounds like the workers are heading back. I better go help Tillie with lunch."

She reached to pick up Lucy, stopped and turned toward the mouth of the hollow. A buckboard rattled down the lane.

"Oh, I forgot to tell you," said Uncle George, "the community women will bring desserts and whatever to help with lunch today. Then they'll take turns providing a meal. That's a lot of heavy eaters for you to feed every day."

The buckboard full of women pulled up beside them. "Hi, I'm Anna. Where do we go with these desserts?" She was a big woman with a jolly smile.

"Hi Anna, I was just going back to help Tillie if you want to follow me," said Olivia, "and thanks."

"Glad to help," she answered. "Why don't you hand Susan and Josephine the babies. We can squeeze you in back there, too." She nodded at the back of the wagon where two women held out their arms to receive a baby.

"She can hop up behind me," said Uncle George.

Olivia laughed. "I could be there while we stand here talking about it. Take the babies and if you don't mind, I'll walk. Tillie – the tall one at the cooking tent – will show you where to put things."

"I'll walk with you," said Uncle George. "Oh, I almost forgot something else. Here's the latest copy of *The Richmond Enquirer*. Just came in today's mail. Haven't read it yet, but you go ahead and take it. I'll pick it up tomorrow or Monday."

"Thanks, Uncle George," said Olivia. "I'll have to save it until after lunch – probably even after supper. But James and I will enjoy reading it." She clutched the paper like a precious treasure as they walked back to camp.

9 News from Richmond

By evening, the workers had cleared the area and started digging the foundation for Jeannette's home. "Monday we'll start cutting trees and lay the foundation," said Richard. "Some of us will begin building while others clear and mark the next spot."

"Sounds like you're well organized. Uncle George said he would bring his plow and prepare ground for each one of us to plant a garden," said Olivia. "We can't thank you and your friends enough." *The future is looking better, if only our men were with us.*

"Just glad we can help," said Richard. "See you in church tomorrow?"

"In town or at the Paint Creek church?"

"We usually go to the Center."

"Our women all agreed to go to the church by the cemetery so we can be close to Grandma Cooper," she said.

"That's over a mile…"

"Richard, I think we can handle it."

Richard laughed. "I guess so, but we'll stop by with the wagon for you and the little ones."

"Thanks, but…"

"No buts. You're family. We'll all worship together."

"With no preacher?"

"The Center doesn't have a preacher either. God will be with us. That's all that matters."

"Thanks again. We'll see you in the morning."

Olivia watched Richard and his friends ride down the lane then she turned to begin the evening preparations.

***

"It didn't take the little ones long to fall asleep tonight," said Claudia.

"Don't know 'bout the rest of you," said Corinne, "but I'm about ready to crawl into my sleeping spot, too."

"Oh, I almost forgot," said Olivia. "Uncle George brought us a *Richmond Enquirer* today. It's old – at least a week – but it is news if anyone is interested." The women moved back to the fire, sleepiness and tiredness suddenly gone.

"I'll get it Mom." James jumped up and ran to the wagon. Olivia sat back on her stump and waited with the rest. He returned with the paper – handed her a section and kept one for himself.

"Read it to us Olivia," said Maggie. "What's happening in Richmond?"

Before she could hardly focus on the print, James said, "Hey, listen to this." He read, "Yesterday – that was," he looked at the date on the paper, "that was May 29, seven prisoners escaped from Libby Prison. The mayor believes they must have had help from someone inside the prison. Last seen floating down the river toward the falls, they are all believed to have drowned and been carried out to sea."

"Who were they?" Claudia's whisper was barely heard. The others nodded, waited with eyes wide, breath held.

"It doesn't say," said James turning the paper over and over trying to find more information. "Maybe it's in your section, Mom."

Olivia searched her section and suddenly stopped. The paper shook in her hands rattling as if she were crumpling it into a ball. She took a deep breath and shook her head.

"Mom?" James took the paper from her trembling hands and Maggie knelt beside her, placing a hand on Olivia's arm.

"I'm all right," she said. "What else is there?"

James continued reading, "With Richmond becoming the Confederate capital, we have seen some changes. Our new government expects every citizen to cooperate with them. We can all learn a lesson from Jefferson Dooley, who lost his plantation, his slaves and his wife to a fire that swept across his hundred acres. Mr. Dooley accused the mayor of arson and murder. He was immediately arrested and charged with treason."

James paused, gulped a swallow of air and continued. "When the jailer returned from dinner, Dooley was gone along with six other prisoners of war who have been held since early in the year. It was later reported that seven bodies were seen floating toward the falls and presumed to have gone over them. All seven prisoners are missing and presumed dead."

A stunned silence surrounded them like the evening fog. "Grandpa's plantation? Grandma dead? Moses – Mattie – Henrietta – all gone?" James stared into the fire too angry yet to even think about weeping. All of a sudden, his emotion shot forth in angry words. "Why didn't Uncle George warn us?"

"He hasn't read it yet," said Olivia swiping at her tears. "He'd just picked up the paper before he came out here at noon. Said he would read it tomorrow."

James jumped up and ran for the corral. "He needs to know – now."

"James, wait…" But he was already on Beauty and galloping up the lane.

The rest waited too stunned to even talk. Each harbored her own horrible visions of the plantation burning – the lives lost. Memories of that long ago New Year's Eve with the house aglow with so many candles flooded Olivia's mind. She remembered shivering and thinking how much it looked like the house was aflame. Had that been a warning of things to come?

Questions began to fly.

"What about our men? They had to have been the ones who escaped," said Claudia.

"Are they dead? Drowned? Carried out to sea?" Corinne shook her head in disbelief.

"Did my father even receive my telegram?" Olivia stared now dry-eyed at the dwindling fire. Tillie got up and added more branches. Flames shot skyward then settled down.

"Where is God? Doesn't He see what's happening?" Claudia covered her mouth to keep back the sob.

"How much more can we endure?" asked Corinne.

Maggie chewed her nails, while they waited. Suddenly she pounded her fist into the waiting palm of her other hand. "They can't all be dead," she said with as much spark as Grandma Cooper used to have. "*Someone* will make it. Someone *has* to make it. We did. Grandmother Cooper made it – and she was old. Surely…"

As if given a gift of hope, Olivia sat upright. A feeling of determination she'd felt often on the journey surged through her.

"What is it 'Livia?" asked Tillie. "You thought of something. I can tell by the look on your face."

"James took the paper with him, but think about what it said."

"It said they all escaped and are dead," said Claudia.

"No!" said Olivia, shaking her head. "Think. First of all, it said six prisoners and Jefferson Dooley. He's the only one named. We don't even know for sure who the others were. More than likely it's our men, but we don't know that for a fact – not yet. Second, it was thought they had inside help." Olivia ticked off the ideas on her fingers as she named them. "As much as I detested Matthew Parker, he *was* Daddy's friend at one time. That whole business of him accusing the mayor of arson and getting thrown in prison might have been a ruse."

Olivia paused watching the truth sink in. Then she continued, excitement sending a shiver across her shoulders and down her spine.

"Doesn't it seem odd that Daddy could escape on his first night in prison when the rest hadn't been able to do it in three and a half months? And third, seven bodies were seen floating down the river to the falls. The seven prisoners are *presumed* to be dead. Apparently, no bodies were recovered. But, suppose they weren't dead and they swam *up* the river before they reached the rapids. Suppose Samuel was waiting for them with our wagon. Maggie is right. We made it, they will too. They *have* to."

Olivia turned at the sound of horses galloping down the lane. "Uncle George must be with James," she said.

Uncle George, Richard and James reined to a stop. Olivia jumped up and ran to him. Uncle George slid off his horse and wrapped his arms around her. "Olivia, I'm so sorry. I would never have given you that paper if I knew what was in it."

"I know, Uncle George." She wiped her tears and once more told him what she had told the women. She waited for him to either agree or tell her she was wrong.

Richard grinned at his cousin and put his arm around her shoulders. "I think she's right, Daddy," he said.

Uncle George pulled at his chin, his brow knit in thought. Suddenly he grinned and said, "I think you're right on all counts. It makes sense that if you could do it with a wagon train, they can make it unhindered by all the excess baggage."

"But, they'll be hunted and shot," said Claudia.

"Why would they?" asked Olivia. "If the mayor thinks they're all dead, why would he even look for them? If they were seen floating downriver why would they look for them upriver?"

"But, they won't have supplies like we did and protection from the rain and cold." Corinne wanted to have hope, but their journey had been too hard and long already. She struggled with her doubts.

"The only way we got here was on hard work and prayer," said James. "We can't supply the hard work for them, but we sure can pray."

"You're right," said Uncle George. "We can hold a prayer meeting right here tonight and tomorrow I'll organize the church and community for a prayer meeting every day until they walk into our valley. And ... there is one other thing."

"What's that?" said Richard. "I thought they covered it pretty good."

"If Jefferson Dooley is with them, and it sounds like he must be, well, I always said my twin brother could do anything that can't be done. He'll get them here."

"And Samuel and Rosy," said James. "They'll be helping."

"And my John knows enough Indian ways to survive in the wilderness," said Tillie with a note of pride. It was the first time she had talked about even the possibility of Indian blood in their background.

Olivia nodded and the women, following her lead, fell to their knees and prayed until long past midnight – even Jeannette, who stayed on the fringe. Finally, giving in to exhausted bodies and hope-filled hearts, one by one each wandered back to her wagon. Richard and George returned home. James and Tillie sat guard duty and Olivia lay on the ground under the wagon, giving in to prayerful thoughts.

Have we come this far without our men, only to have them snatched away permanently? Lord, I needed courage for the journey. I need even more courage for the waiting.

10 Celebrating Progress

With homes to build and furniture to consider, there was little time for worry, except for unguarded moments. At such times, Olivia would see one of the women stare toward the mouth of the hollow, wipe a tear from her eye and fall to her knees. She, too, had her moments, but once again determined to keep her tears to share with Will.

The women worked gardens into busy schedules. Olivia's already sprouted green shoots of future vegetables. Joey spent part of each day with his mother, making sure she had food to eat. The other women and children helped him work Jeannette's garden patch.

"That's the last nail," said James, climbing down from Jeannette's roof.

"We need to celebrate," said Corey to the others who were gathering for the milestone event.

"How?" asked Michael.

"If Grandma Cooper was here," said Jeremiah, "she would sing."

"And the women would bring food," said Corey.

"Hey," said Michael. "We can play our harmonicas. And…and…I'll sing a song."

Corey laughed. "What can you sing?"

"I'll think of something," said Michael glaring at his brother.

The women, who had joined the boys unnoticed, smiled.

"Maybe you can teach us all a song," said Claudia.

The tone sounded sarcastic, but Tillie took her at her word. "That's a great idea. Michael, you write a song and I'll make some apple pudding. We'll gather for a real house warming. What do you think, Olivia?"

Olivia looked at Tillie, then Michael. His eyes were brimming with hope. "I think that's a wonderful idea," she said. "Why don't some of you start carrying things from Jeannette's wagon into her house? Michael, do you want some help?"

"No ma'am. Grandma Cooper taught me how to make up words to fit tunes I know. I could maybe use some help on writing enough copies for everyone to see."

***

Dinner was over. Michael passed out sheets of paper with the words to his song on them. Tillie carried her pot of apple pudding and others brought dishes and spoons. Uncle George, Richard and some of his friends stayed to join in the celebration. They marched to Jeannette's new house, not knowing if she would accept them or their gifts. She and Joey met them on the front porch. Joey took her hand. The other hand she pressed against her lips.

"We want to celebrate your new home with you," said Tillie.

"Tillie made apple pudding, Olivia will pray and Michael wrote a song for you," said Claudia.

Without waiting for Jeannette to accept or decline, Olivia nodded to the boys. They pulled out their harmonicas and played once through *Amazing Grace*. Then Michael sang his song to the tune of *Amazing Grace*. When he had finished, the rest joined him in singing it again:

> Bless now this house, O Lord we pray;
> Keep safe all who dwell therein;
> Keep wind and rain and snow away;
> May peace forever reign.

As the last notes faded, Olivia stepped forward and asked God's blessing on Jeannette's new home and on her as she began a new life in it. She prayed that Joe would soon join her in the joy of that new dwelling.

As soon as she said, "Amen," Tillie and Maggie began dishing up pudding. Jeannette took her bowl and sat in the chair Joey brought out for her. The rest sat on the edge of the porch or logs and stones that still scattered around the yard.

***

Once the women moved Jeannette into her house and got her mostly settled, she came out only occasionally to sit on her steps and watch the work on Claudia and Corinne's houses. Most of the time she preferred to sit alone and stare into space. Joey, who was maturing like the rest of the children, worked hard helping to clear areas for the other houses, working their garden and taking care of his mother. At meal times, he ate with the group and took a dish of food to his mother, who refused to come to the gathering.

"Do you think she is aware of the news from Richmond?" Maggie glanced toward Jeannette while she stirred the oatmeal for yet another day of building, waiting and praying.

"Claudia and Corinne told her, but I'm not sure she understood, although, she does join us in prayer."

"She's suffered a terrible tragedy – partly her own doing," said Maggie, "but maybe when Joe gets here…"

"Thank you for being so positive," said Olivia. "They *will* find us and maybe it will help Jeannette."

"Mom," said Corey plopping down beside Olivia. "How come time goes so fast and so slow at the same time?"

Olivia glanced at Maggie who grinned and turned back to the oatmeal before Corey noticed.

"Yeah," said Michael. "We just go to bed and it's time to get up again."

"And when we start working, all of a sudden it's time to quit," added Jeremiah, who joined them at the circle.

"But when we think about Dad," said Bobby, "It's been an awful long time since we saw him."

Olivia bit her lip until she could lose the rush of sorrow and compassion. While she was collecting her thoughts, James said, "Time always moves at the same rate of speed. The days seem longer or shorter because of the way the earth revolves around the sun. It takes a year…"

"We don't want…" began Michael.

"…a science lesson," finished Corey.

James grinned at his mother. She smiled at him. "Thank you James," she said, knowing he had given her time to recover. "Your brother is right. When you work hard or sleep soundly, time seems to move faster because you are so involved in what you are doing that you don't notice it. But, when you sit and think and aren't busy, you notice the time more. It has been a long time since your fathers have been with us, but if we work hard, time will seem to pass faster and we will have homes ready for them when they join us."

"Mrs. Brunner will they really be here. The paper said…"

"The paper never named your fathers, but even if they did escape, they are too smart to fall into the river and drown."

"She's right," said Maggie. "They'll be here. Now, let's eat and get to work."

"Aunt Molly is coming to be with the babies, so Betsy and I will both work today," said Olivia

"Mrs. Phillips' house is finished and Mrs. Jones' house is almost done. We should finish it and get the roof on our house today," said George Walsh.

"And we can have another celebration," said Corey.

"With music and pudding," said Michael.

"The younger kids can start clearing the fourth lot," said James. "We have it marked for the house."

"That's ours, isn't it?" Jeremiah asked.

"It sure is," said James, "so, let's go."

11   The Bear

The sun rose higher in the sky taking the temperature with it. Olivia stopped work for a minute and wiped the sweat that ran down her face and the back of her neck. *It must be a hundred degrees out here. Maybe I should have one of the boys bring a bucket of water.* Suddenly the children began screaming. She whirled around as they started to run.

A bear with a shiny black coat stood on its hind legs at the edge of the forest. Joey lay on the ground about ten yards in front of it. Between Joey and the bear were two small cubs. Blackie stood teeth bared, hair on end, a low growl in his throat.

"Stop!" Olivia said in her loud, clear voice that the children all knew they must obey. They all stopped where they were, mouths open, legs lifted to run as if they were frozen in time. Even the men stopped what they were doing and turned to her. Blackie froze ready to lunge the minute she gave the word.

"Don't anyone move," said Olivia in a voice that could be heard, but did not induce panic. "Children ease down where you are – slowly – lie on the ground face down. Slowly cover the back of your head with your hands and don't make a sound – you too, Joey. Blackie, stay."

Olivia kept her eyes on the bear but from the corner of her eye, she saw Jeanette coming down the lane and heard several guns cock, ready for use. Inch by inch she moved closer to Joey. Keeping her voice just above a whisper, she held out her hand as she moved. "James, my gun. Stop Jeanette."

Continuing to inch forward, keeping her eyes on the bear, that continued to bellow, she slipped her hand around her gun. She sensed rather than heard James move toward the lane. She moved closer to Joey. The bear bellowed, reluctant to back down, waving her paws as if to warn Olivia not to come any closer. The cubs stayed where they were, looking around them like a couple of confused children.

Finally, Olivia was directly behind Joey. The bear dropped down on all fours and began slowly moving toward the cubs. Cautiously

Olivia stepped over Joey. "Don't move and don't make a sound," she said.

Raising her voice and lifting her gun slightly, she spoke to the bear. "I know you are a wild animal and don't understand human talk, but we have the same Creator and He can tell you we don't want trouble with you. You want to protect your little ones and I want to protect mine. We don't want to hurt you or them. Take them away and no one will be hurt."

The bear stopped and stared at Olivia. Olivia and the bear kept their eyes on each other. The bear roared once again. The cubs hesitated. She roared again with more power and they took off for the woods. The big bear dropped to all fours and backed up a few steps, still keeping an eye on Olivia. Olivia lowered the barrel of her gun and backed up two steps, pointing the gun to the ground. The bear roared again then turned around and ran into the woods after her two little ones. Olivia let out the breath she realized she had been holding. Her legs began to tremble. She felt like she might even faint, but a tiny voice behind her said, "Can we move now?"

Olivia turned around, reached a hand out to Joey and pulled him to his feet. The other children began screaming again and Olivia raised her voice once more. "Stop that screaming. It's over. Get back to work."

Blackie shook himself as if he had just emerged from the creek, then he trotted off to meet James.

"Mrs. Brunner, why did that bear want to hurt us? We just wanted to pet the cute little baby bears." Joey looked at her with wide eyes, his face pale, his lower lip trembling. The other children moved in closer to hear her answer.

"Joey," she said, "what do you think I would do if one of those little bears came and tried to pet Lucy or Charles?"

Joey looked surprised, started to laugh then realized she was serious. "You would chase them off," he said.

"That's right," she answered. "And their mother would hear them crying and come to see what was wrong with them. She would think I was hurting them and come after me."

"Oh," said Joey. "We tried to pet her babies and she tried to chase us off and you came to protect us."

"That's right, Joey. Wild animals are just that. They are wild. They are to be respected for their wildness."

"But why did she listen to you? Did she understand you? Was she afraid of you?"

Olivia glanced up at the men who were grinning waiting for her answer. She laughed and said, "Joey, I have no idea whether she understood me or not. Maybe it was a mother-to-mother thing. Maybe our mutual Creator spoke her language. I don't know, but don't put me through that again." She tousled his hair. "Now everyone get back to work."

Olivia went back to her spot in clearing away the brush and weeds. She sensed someone behind her. She whirled around to see Jeanette staring at her with her vacant eyes. When she saw Olivia looking at her, she sneered, turned and walked away. Olivia shook her head and went back to work.

"She could have at least said thanks," said Richard who witnessed the exchange. "That bear could have torn Joey to pieces."

"No, Richard, she really couldn't say thanks. Her mind and heart are still frozen in that little grave along the road."

"She doesn't know what a friend she has," he said. Then he shook his head and laughed. "At least now I know how you managed to move a wagon train of women and children across the mountains. Even that bear knew better than to tangle with you."

"Richard…," Olivia had to smile at him. "Get back to work."

"Yes, ma'am." He laughed, picked up his saw and went back to his clearing.

12   Holiday

June slipped into July with hardly a notice. Almost a month had gone by since arriving in Cabin Creek. Three houses were finished, the fourth almost done and two others started. Pounding stopped and chatter began as the workers took an afternoon break. Tillie brought them cold water and sandwiches. Olivia finished the row she was weeding in her garden and joined the workers under a large oak tree they had left standing near where her house would be.

"Thank you," she said, reaching for the water and sandwich. James moved closer to her and leaned against the tree while he ate his sandwich.

"Mom," he said, "Richard said they won't be working Thursday. There's a community-wide picnic with speeches and everything. Do you think we could take a holiday and go?"

"Thursday?" Olivia frowned. "What is so different about Thursday?"

"You know, July 4. Independence Day." James laughed at her confusion.

"Oh," she said. "I forgot it was already July. Where did June go?"

"I don't know about you, but my muscles tell me where it went. We built almost four houses and are starting on the last two. Then we'll need to build a barn for the mules so they'll be out of the cold this winter. And…"

"Whoa," Olivia laughed. "Slow down. We'll get the houses built first then we'll see about other buildings. If necessary, we'll just put a lean-to against the house for Beauty and the mules. They'll be just fine where they are for now."

"Should we build on a couple of rooms for Dad's practice or wait until he gets here?" James watched her closely. She knew what he was really asking, "Is Dad going to make it?"

"We'll do the house first. I thought maybe a separate building closer to the road would give him more privacy and make it easier for people to come to him. We'll start that when we finish the house. Then we'll do the barn."

"What about a house for Rosy and Samuel?"

"Why don't we do the office first. Samuel and Rosy can live with us until their house is done."

"Mom, will Dad really make it? Have you heard anything more?"

Olivia sighed deeply. "Not a word from anyone. There's been nothing more in the paper since they named the missing prisoners."

"Aren't you scared, Mom?"

Olivia looked into the eyes of her son, who seemed years older than when they left Richmond. She couldn't lie to him. "I am terrified, James," she said, "but we can't let our fears control us. I keep countering my fears with hope. When they try to keep me awake, I recite The Lord's Prayer and the Psalms until I fall asleep. He has to come, James. He just has to."

"I know, Mom, but what if…"

"We won't think about what if's, James. But, if it should come to that, we can make it on our own. We have so far. Are you tired of being the man of the house?" She grinned and he returned her smile.

"No, but I won't mind giving it back to Dad when he gets here." He laughed and joined the others who were going back to work. Break time was over.

July 3 dawned with storm clouds threatening. "I hope the rain holds off a while longer," she said as she and Maggie finished the breakfast dishes. "I have to get those weeds out of my garden. Everything is growing so fast. Beans are already blooming. I had hoped to be in my house in time for canning.

"We could have a canning bee," said Maggie, "and do it here at the circle."

"We'll probably have to," said Olivia. "It might make it fun. But, for now I'll put the babies in their play area while I work."

"Looks like rain today," said Richard meeting them at Maggie's site. "We thought we better work fast this morning. We might not have this afternoon."

"Good thinking," said Olivia. "Maggie is here to help. I'm on my way to battle the weeds."

Richard laughed and walked with Maggie to the house, giving her instructions on what needed yet to be done. Olivia took the babies and continued on to her garden where James had put up a fenced in play area for the babies.

They were putting the last board on Maggie's roof when the first drops began to fall. Olivia had just finished the second row. She sighed, knowing that with the rain, not only would the rest grow taller,

414

but also the area she just cleared would be growing again. The workers covered Maggie's roof with tarpaper to protect the wood until they could put on roof shingles.

Since they couldn't do much on the houses or gardens in the rain, the women gathered first in Claudia's house, then Corinne's to help with the inside work. Even though Jeannette didn't ask for help, she stood by passively while the women moved her belongings from the living room to the other areas of the house. By the time they finished, the rain had stopped and Tillie was cooking at the campsite.

***

Independence Day dawned with no trace of the previous day's rain – except the weeds looked greener and bigger. Excitement and curiosity filled the children with visions of impossible and unknown activities and treats.

"How can we celebrate Independence Day, when we're at war?" Michael asked as they were eating breakfast.

"Independence Day has nothing to do with this war," said Corey. "That was the Revolutionary War when we got our independence from England."

"How do you know?" Michael gave his twin a skeptical look.

"I read it in Betsy's history book," said Corey.

"Oh. Do the North and the South both celebrate today? Will they stop fighting to celebrate? And if they do, why do they have to fight in the first place?"

"Michael, you ask the kind of questions your father needs to answer," said Olivia. "I'm sure I don't know. Why do people anywhere, or anytime, fight wars anyway? Because they can't agree on how things should be, I guess. Everyone thinks they are the only ones who are right."

"Who is right in this war, Mom? The North or the South?" The twins both waited her for her answer with eagerness in their eyes.

"I wish I knew," she answered. "When it gets right down to it, I would suspect that neither side is right and both sides are right. The problem comes when we begin to think everyone should believe and act the way we believe and act or they are wrong. They may not be wrong, only different"

"I wish we didn't have a war," said Betsy.

"Me too," answered the twins together.

"Well, we do have war and the best we can do is to keep our hope and faith until your father comes. Maybe this war won't last long." Olivia smiled at her children who had been through so much already.

415

"You mean when Dad comes we don't have to have hope and faith anymore?" Corey asked with a mischievous grin.

"Don't be silly," said Betsy, punching her brother in the arm. "We always have to have hope and faith. But when Daddy comes, we just don't have to worry about *him* anymore."

James glanced at his mother and grinned at his brothers and sister. "The war will probably last a lot longer than we want it to," he said. "George and I will probably be old enough to enlist before it ends, but until Dad arrives I'll never leave Mom and you kids alone."

Olivia, startled at the thought of him enlisting, tried to hide her emotions. "Oh, do you think I can't handle things on my own?"

James grinned. "I know you can – you did on the journey, but Dad would skin me alive if I left you."

"You might be right…" The sound of a wagon approaching stopped their conversation.

"There's Richard with the wagon," said Cory, jumping up from the rock where he was sitting.

"Finish your breakfast. He'll wait for you," said Olivia.

Richard strolled over to them. "Everyone ready to go?"

"Not 'till we clean our plates," said Cory.

"Would you like some coffee or something to eat?" Olivia asked as she lifted the coffee pot from the circle of stones containing the fire.

"Coffee will be fine," he said. "Anyone else going?" Richard asked while he sipped from the hot cup.

"I'm not sure," she said. "I know Jeannette won't be going."

"Will she be all right here alone?" he asked.

Claudia finished her coffee. "I'm not much for parades and stuff, so if you don't mind keeping up with my kids I'd rather stay here," she said.

"They'll be all right," said Richard.

"Why don't you leave the babies here," said Corinne. "I'll stay and help Claudia. We need to weed our gardens anyway."

Thanks, Corinne," said Olivia. "They are getting a little heavy to carry for any length of time."

"Okay," said Richard. "Let's move out. I think we can squeeze all of you in the wagon – kids in back, women…"

"Richard, just take the kids. We'll walk," said Olivia. "It's only a little over a mile. James you go with Richard and keep track of the kids until Maggie, Tillie and I get there."

***

Cabin Creek was bubbling with excitement. People from many of the surrounding towns milled around, ignoring signs of war and enjoying a holiday. Even so, the women had no trouble finding the children with Richard whose red hair glistened in the morning sunshine. They stood with mouths open gaping at all the sights and sounds.

"Look Mom," said Betsy. "Everything is decorated in red, white and blue."

"Even the horses have red and blue ribbons," said Michael. "We should have decorated Max and Jasper and brought them to the parade."

"The horses will pull the floats," said Richard.

"Are we going to the river?" Cory looked perplexed. Richard laughed.

"No," he said. "Floats are decorated wagons depicting something to do with the occasion. Today is Independence Day. Sometimes we have a Christmas parade with floats about Christmas."

"Why do they call them floats if they aren't on the river? Our wagons wouldn't float on the river without Captain Barnabas's barges," said Jeremiah.

"Don't know for sure why they call them floats," said Richard.

"Bet they used to float them on the river once upon a time," said Michael.

"Maybe so. After the parade we'll go to the Community Center for speeches then a picnic complete with homemade ice cream for dessert."

"Ice cream?" Cory and Michael asked together.

"They might even let you turn the crank a few times," said Richard.

"Wow! We get to help make ice cream!"

"Hey, here comes the parade," said Bobby.

"Let's follow it," said Cory as the last of the floats passed them. "Are they going to the Community Center?"

"Yes. We have to listen to political speeches first then we can eat." Richard joined the children who became a part of the parade.

"We shoulda brought our harmonicas," said Bobby.

"We could do as well as the band," said Jeremiah.

When they arrived at the Center, some men in black suits were already on the platform. After almost an hour of speeches – some for Mr. Lincoln and some against him – the mayor gave the blessing and children started running inside where a variety of food spread across the tables.

"Who provided all the food?" asked Maggie.

"Maybe we should have brought something," said Tillie.

"Richard?" Olivia looked at her cousin for answer.

"We have a community fund that buys the chicken, beef and pork. Women in town volunteer to cook them. Other communities are responsible for vegetables and desserts."

"Can we contribute to the fund?"

"Sure. There's a box inside the Center marked for donations. The money is used for various projects throughout the year.

"We didn't bring much…"

"Don't worry about it. The box is always there. We just throw something in it from time to time."

"We don't want charity," said Olivia.

"It's not," he said.

The town clock struck noon and for the next three hours people ate, rested then ate some more. Children played games, women gossiped and men speculated about the war.

Olivia, Maggie and Tillie decided it was time to leave after a couple of hours.

"Can't we stay a while longer," begged Cory.

"We need to go back and relieve Claudia and Corinne. The babies need a nap…"

"James, George and I will look after the kids and bring them home later if that's all right with you," said Richard.

Olivia looked to Tillie and Maggie. They nodded their approval. "Well, all right," she said, "but if any one of you gets in any kind of trouble, there will be no more parades."

"Okay," they all cried together. Olivia, Maggie and Tillie started walking toward home. They still had work to do before the day was ended.

13   Settling In

Two more weeks slipped by with nothing worse than a thunderstorm, a snake scare – only a harmless little, green garden reptile – and bugs of so many varieties that Corey and Michael stopped counting them. June was only a memory and July alternately ran and crawled to the center of the month. Tillie would be moving into her home soon and Olivia's house was well under way. Still they waited for word from Richmond. They'd heard nothing more, except from the following issue of *The Richmond Enquirer* that had named the escapees – Will Brunner, Joe Phillips, Robert Cooper, John Rayburn, Kenneth Jones, George Walsh and Jefferson Dooley. They were all missing and presumed dead. At least they knew for sure their men were the ones who had escaped.

One by one, each family moved into their new house leaving Olivia and her family the only ones still in the wagon. They had started hers before the holiday and now had it under roof.

The others invited her to live with them while her house was being built, but Olivia declined. "You have enough to do to get your homes in order, care for your gardens and still help with my house. You don't need extra bodies under foot."

Finally came the day when James called down to Olivia as she watched him and George lay the last shingle on the roof of her home. "That's the last nail."

"Doors are in." Richard and his friends came around the corner of the house slapping their hands together as if removing dust and dirt. Let's get your wagon unloaded and move your things into your new home."

"There's not a lot to move. I didn't bring any furniture, except one of Grandma Poff's rocking chairs. Mr. Blake is already overwhelmed with so many of us to make furniture for."

"We'll get to work on that next," said James climbing down from the roof. "We can do some beds and a table and chairs."

"Sure we can," said Corey stopping on his way to the house with a box from the wagon. "Are we going to sleep on the floor until we get some beds?"

"You can continue to sleep under the wagon if you would rather," said Olivia.

Corey screwed up his face. "It might be hard getting used to a floor without any lumps and bumps," he said, "but I think I'll stay in the house – especially if it rains." Then he giggled like the six year old he was. Michael, box in hand, elbowed his brother. They laughed and took their boxes into the house.

"We'll help with the furniture," said Richard.

"Thanks, Richard. As soon as we get settled, we'll have you and your folks over for dinner."

Later, Olivia stood in the center of the living room, feeling overwhelmed by the size of the near-empty house. But, she heard pounding and sawing out back, so she knew she would have at least a table, chairs and beds soon. Lost in her thoughts, the rattling of a wagon in front of her house startled her. She stepped out to the porch.

"Afternoon, ma'am," said the stranger. "This the Brunner place?"

"Yes," she answered.

"I got this new stove for you," he said. "Where do you want it?"

"New stove? But I didn't…"

James and Richard came around the corner of the house. "Uncle George sent it. Remember he said he'd get you one when the house was done."

"But I thought…"

The deliveryman, impatiently tapped his pencil on the order form, pushed his hat back on his head and said, "Where do you want it ma'am? I want to get back to Charleston before dark."

"Drive around back," said James. "We'll take it in the back door. Corey, go round up some help."

Corey didn't have far to go. They built the houses in such a way that each woman could see all the other homes from her front porch. No one was isolated – not even Jeannette. They all knew when something was different – especially a delivery wagon. So, everyone had come to see what the man brought. The deliveryman left and questions began flying. "What kind of stove is it Olivia? Where did it come from?"

Tillie looked at the label on the crate. "Says it was shipped from Hillside, Illinois – a Ben Franklin type cook stove."

"That the new kind that uses either wood or coal?" Claudia was impressed.

"Yes, I'll have to find out where to order coal, but in the meantime we can chop wood – right boys?" Olivia laughed at the sour expressions on the twins' faces. "Well, we can't eat hot food unless we have something to burn in the stove," she said.

"Can we have pancakes like Rosy used to make?" Corey gave her a hopeful look.

Olivia bit her lip. "Maybe not quite like Rosy made, but we'll have pancakes in the morning."

"Why not tonight for supper?" Michael's hazel eyes matched Corey's in anticipation.

"Sure, why not?" Olivia smiled at her twins – so much like young men, but yet like little boys.

"Let's go chop wood," said Michael.

"We still have a lot of dried, dead logs that we gathered for our campfire," said Corey.

Richard, James and the others removed the packing crate and moved the stove where Olivia wanted it. Making sure the vent worked and everything was as it should be, they went back to their furniture making. The women stood around and admired the stove for a while.

"Why don't we all have pancakes here tonight," said Olivia.

Maggie laughed. "I thought you'd never ask. "I'll bring some eggs."

"I've got plenty of flour," said Claudia.

"I just bought a side of bacon," said Tillie.

"I'll make the syrup," said Corinne.

"Mom just got some butter from one of the farmer's," said Joey. "I'll bring some then take some bacon and pancakes home to her."

"We'll have a pancake house-warming party," said Corey from the porch.

"We'll celebrate all the houses being done," said Maggie.

"That's a great idea, boys," said Tillie. "We'll have pancakes instead of pudding."

14   *Captain Barnabas*

While the women settled into new homes, the fugitives slowly made their way toward The Valley. A gray-dawn signaled another approaching day that promised to be a wet one from the looks of the clouds swirling above the men as they wearily climbed a small hill overlooking the river.

"That road looks like it could be a muddy trap for wagons," said Kenny. "I hope the women made it in dry weather."

"I'm sure they would figure out a way to keep the wagons moving," said Robert.

"Let's take a short rest," said John, "then spread out and look for a place to sleep for the day. It's going to be hot and muggy, especially if it rains."

"If I sit very long, I won't be able to move," said Joe. "What about you, Will?"

"I'm with you. I think once I'm down, I'm down to stay."

"Then we may as well start looking now. Will and I will go this way," Joe said taking Will's arm and leading him toward the creek.

"We'll go into the woods here," said Robert tagging George and Kenny.

"Jefferson, Samuel and I will check the other side of the woods," said John. "Whistle if you find something."

"I should have stayed in Richmond," said Will. "I'm just slowing the rest of you down."

"Don't be ridiculous," said Joe. "We're all weak and tired. Mr. Dooley's the one I'm really worried about. He's pushing himself and I don't like the grayish look around his mouth and eyes."

"Maybe we should rest for a day or two before moving on. Give him a chance to catch his breath."

"You know he wouldn't agree to that. Hey, I think I found something. Why don't you wait here a minute while I go check it out."

"What do you see?"

"A large cliff with an overhang that looks like it might be a cave. It would be protection from the rain even if it's not very deep."

"Check it out."

Will could make out the form of Joe as he climbed a small incline to the cliff's overhang.

"Perfect," Joe said. "Why don't you whistle for the rest? I'm not good at whistling."

Will signaled the others. John and Samuel checked it out. Samuel grinned. "Looks good," he said. "Looks like someone camped here not too long ago. Bet it was the boys."

"How can you tell?" asked George.

"See the dark circle in that little sunken place? They built a fire to keep animals away and stay warm. You folks get settled. We'll finish the leavin's from breakfast then I'll see if I can find us something for tomorrow."

"I'll do a little fishing," said Kenny. "I'm too tired to sleep right away. Samuel and I can take the first watch."

***

The day ended and the men rose for their next night of travel. It had indeed rained most of the day and was still raining intermitedly. Samuel and Kenny dug up the fish and rabbit that had been cooking most of the day.

"Some potatoes and bread would be good with this," said Robert.

"Wonder if the women had fish and rabbits?" said George.

"Probably. Wouldn't be surprised if the boys didn't try for a deer," said Jefferson.

"I just hope..."

"What Will?"

"Never mind. I'm sure if they ran low on supplies the women ate less so the children wouldn't go hungry."

"I gave Olivia a bag full of gold coins," said Jefferson. "When they came to a town of any size, they could replenish their supplies."

"I hope she...never mind," said George.

"Hope she what," asked Will. "Didn't flash them about and tempt strangers?" Will's voice had an angry edge to it.

George ignored the anger. "Yeah, that's what I started to say, but I remembered this was Olivia we were talking about. She would have more sense than that. She would keep them well hidden."

"I doubt if anyone on the wagon train even knew about them until there was a need for them to know," said Jefferson.

"Sorry," said Will. "Didn't mean to loose my temper."

"That's all right," said George. "We're all getting a little edgy."

"We better get movin' folks," said Samuel.

423

"Looks like we better stick closer together tonight," said John. "No moon and dark clouds with rain make it easier to trip and fall. We don't want anyone to get lost or breaking a bone."

"I still think you should leave me…"

"Don't even think about it Will," said Jefferson. "I didn't risk my neck getting you out of prison for Olivia, just to leave you behind because you think you can't make it. You might have to bury me before you get there, but I'll keep going as long as I can and I expect the rest of you to do the same."

"Mr. Dooley, are you…?"

"My heart's acting up, Joe. Nothing we can do about it, 'cept keep moving. If you can't bury me, throw me in the river, say a prayer and move on."

"Mr. Dooley, we can't…"

"You can and you will. Now let's get moving. We got a long way to go yet and like John said, the dark and mud will make it harder."

"I checked Will's map," said John. "The road veers away from the river for quite a ways – probably several days or a week for us. Won't have fish unless we find a stream with trout or bluegill."

"We'll find something," said Samuel, "even if it's only possum or raccoon."

"Maybe a turtle or… Let's go."

***

A little over a week later, as morning was beginning, the road was once again running beside the James River.

"Looks like we're back to fishing," said Kenny. "Why don't I get started while…what's that sound?"

They stopped to listen. Samuel ran down to the riverbank and returned. "It's one of those riverboats with barges. Must have been docked for the night. Sounds like it's getting ready to move out."

"Which way they going?" asked John.

"Looks like they're pushing the barges upriver." Samuel grinned. "Maybe I can see what's on board them."

"You be careful, Samuel," said Will as Samuel slipped into the river and silently swam out to the first barge. Staying in the shadows, he hoisted himself over the edge, lifted the cover, dropped it back and swam back to shore.

"Don't look like there's anything there. Maybe we can swim out and hide on that barge and hitch us a ride upriver a ways."

"Don't think that's a good idea," said a voice behind them.

The men whirled around to see a squat little man who looked

much like the fabled St. Nick. He was holding a pistol on them. "Want to tell me who you are and why you're sneaking around my boat?"

"The feeling is mutual," said Will. "It would help if we knew who we were talking to and which side of the war you represent."

Will and the stranger stared at one another. Suddenly, Jefferson Dooley slumped to his knees then to the ground. Will and Joe ran to him without a thought of the man holding the gun.

They laid him on his back and started to examine him – listening to his heart and feeling for a pulse. "Are you in pain, sir," asked Joe.

"Just get the elephant off my chest," said Jefferson, "and I'll be all right. Don't let them take me back to Richmond. Throw me in the river."

"No one's throwing you in yet," said Will.

The man with the white hair, beard and bushy eyebrows knelt beside them. "Brunner?" he asked.

"What?" Will paled and turned to him. "How…"

"I'm Captain Andrew Barnabas, owner and operator of *The Adventurer* over there. Met up with a wagon train of women and children a few months back. Lady by the name of Brunner was the wagon master. Son named James looked like you."

"You saw Olivia and the rest?"

"Were they all right?" asked the rest.

"They were fine, just stewing 'cause they couldn't cross the river. Confederate soldiers had burned the bridge earlier to keep them from crossing. Put them and their wagons on the barges and moved them upriver about fifteen miles."

"You took…?"

Captain Barnabas laughed his jolly laugh. "Promised her if I ever saw you I'd do what I could to help. I'm picking up a load of Confederate soldiers about a mile up the river to take them across. I'll let them off where I left the women off that day. They're headed for who knows where south of here."

"Then we better hole up here until they're gone," said Kenny.

"You come on board. They got no reason to come on my boat, but we'll dress you like the rest of my crew just in case. You men will stay below and my regular crew will load their artillery."

"What do you think, Will? asked Robert.

"Suppose it's a trap."

"Maybe the Confederates gave him our names."

"Why don't you talk to a couple of my men? Let them tell you something that they could only know if we really met the women. Hey

Scottie, you and Bert come down here."

The two men ran to the side of their Captain. "First Mate Scottie McDonald and Bert, best worker I've ever had."

Bert, the tall black man with bulging arm muscles said, "I been with the captain ever since I was freed. How can we help you folks."

"Tell them about the wagon train," said Captain Barnabas.

Bert and Scottie both laughed. "Never would have believed a group of women and children could do what they did. They were tired and wary, but willing to try something new if it would help them get to where they were going."

"Where was that?" asked George.

"The Valley, they called it. Said she had an uncle there who would help them get settled."

"What about her children?" Will asked.

Scottie laughed again. "That older boy – said he was twelve, but seemed much older. He sure could ask the questions. Wanted to know all about the barges, how they were propelled, how long it would take and much more."

"And the babies," laughed Bert.

"Babies? There was only one."

"No sir," said Bert. "She was caring for two about the same age – one a little black boy and the beautiful red-haired girl – both about six months old."

"Black baby?"

"Said somebody's slave tossed it to her as she rode out of town, then ran away. The good Lord helped her 'cause she helped everyone else."

"Heard enough?" asked Captain Barnabas. "We need to get loaded if you want to go with us. If not, I'll share some supplies with you and promise to have the soldiers away from here by noon."

"Mr. Dooley can't go much further until he has a few days of rest," said Joe.

"We'll ride with you as far as you can take us," said Will. "If our women trusted you, we can too."

"Which one of you is related to Grandma Cooper?"

Surprised, Robert said he was. "Was she all right?"

"She had the time of her life on the deck helping me steer the boat and push the barges. That's some lady."

"Yes, she is," said Robert swiping at his eyes.

"Let's get aboard," said John. "We'll help do whatever we can, but it would be better if we didn't come in contact with the soldiers. As far as we know, they think we're dead and I'd rather not enlighten them otherwise."

An hour later, Captain Barnabas and his crew loaded the Confederate soldiers, their artillery and animals on the barges and as promised they were on their way upriver by shortly after noon. Three hours later, he pushed the barges to the opposite side of the river and unloaded the equipment.

"Good traveling," said Captain Barnabas as he saluted the Confederate Captain.

"Same to you, Captain. If you see any Federal soldiers along the way, send one of your men after me. We're heading southwest from here toward Kentucky."

Captain Barnabas nodded and returned to his boat. Soon the putt-putt of the engine moved upriver. Three days later, he adjusted Will's map, supplied the men with food and water and sent them on their way.

"Be sure to say hello to those special woman and children," he said.

"We'll do that," said Will. They waved. Captain Barnabas turned and began moving downstream. The men started across the fields, meadows and roads on their way to The Valley. Jefferson Dooley, while not completely recovered, looked much better and felt as if he could continue the journey – at least for a while longer.

15   News of the War

Hot humid days of July melted into even hotter dog days of August. Temperatures soared. Thunder in the distance promised rain, but high rolling clouds only paused at the mountaintops then moved on, leaving that promise unfulfilled.

August was half-gone. Olivia, still marking her well-worn calendar, noted the date – Sunday, August 18. The group met for worship and Bible study as was there weekly custom since their first Sunday in The Valley. The little church on the hill became their worship center.

"Aunt Molly, Uncle George and Richard aren't here yet," said James. "Shall we wait for them, or do you want me to go see if someone is sick or something?"

Olivia thought for a minute. "I'm sure something came up. If they don't come at all, we'll stop on our way home and see if they're all right. Go ahead and ring the bell."

Up and down James pulled the heavy rope attached to the bell in the steeple tower. The pealing that sounded like, "come to church, come to church," echoed across the surrounding valley.

Uncle George and Aunt Molly arrived a half hour late. Olivia saw the pained expressions on their faces and paused in the Bible study lesson. *Something is wrong.*

"Is there something we need to stop and pray about?" She asked as they sat near Betsy.

Uncle George waved his hand as if swatting a pesky, but harmless insect and shook his head. But, he turned away and stared out the window. Aunt Molly, however, was not so willing to brush off their anxiety.

"We just learned from some friends that General J.D. Cox's forces and Lieutenant Colonel George Crohan's Cavalry Unit are headed for battle near here," she said.

"Who are they?" asked Michael.

"Cox is the Federal General and Crohan is with the Confederates," said Uncle George.

"Mark is with General Cox's army and Linsey is with Colonel Crohan," said Richard.

"You mean…they might be fighting each other?" James asked.

Aunt Molly nodded. Tears ran down her face. Uncle George, his voice more husky than usual said, "That's right, boy. I don't believe in asking God to choose sides, no more than I asked my boys to choose one side or the other. All I ask is that they don't kill each other." As if Olivia had given a signal, the group closed their Bibles and fell to the task of praying for all who were fighting – but especially for Mark and Linsey.

When worship was over and folks scattered to their many homes, Olivia said, "Why don't you come home with us?" She reached for Charles, who clung to Aunt Molly.

"Wouldn't be very good company," muttered Uncle George.

"You aren't company," said Olivia. "You're family. We need each other in times like this."

"How's that new stove working?" Richard asked, deliberately changing the subject.

"Wonderful," said Olivia. "With the table and chairs you and the boys made for the kitchen, we can all sit down to eat. The Valley folks were good enough to give me seeds and plants. Now I have fresh beans and tomatoes. The Hodges gave me some chickens so we can have chicken and dumplings. "

"Sounds good to me," said Richard. "After all, we don't even know for sure there will be a battle."

"I made some fresh berry cobbler for dessert," said Olivia.

"Keep talking, Olivia," said Richard. "I'm drooling worse than a rabid raccoon. Come on, Mom, we'll go and let Dad wallow in worry if he wants to."

"You watch your mouth, boy," said Uncle George. "I can still whup you any day of the week." Uncle George slapped Richard's back and grinned at him. He took his wife's arm to lead her to the wagon.

"We'll all worry about Mark and Linsey," said Olivia, "but we can also live as if God were still in control."

"You're right, Cousin," said Richard. "Let's go try out Olivia's chicken and dumplings.

***

Once dinner was on the table, Olivia tried to keep the conversation on other things, but worries about the war kept reappearing, grasping their attention. James and Richard listened until they were tired of hearing repeats.

"There are fish out there just begging to be caught," said James, excusing himself from the table.

"You think you can catch those trout?" Richard laughed, joining him. "They aren't like catching river fish."

***

James grabbed a couple of cane poles and handed one to Richard. Corey grabbed his pole and fell in step beside his brother.

"I'll catch them," said James.

"Me, too," said Corey.

"You got to keep quiet," said Richard. "Trout can hear if you make any kind of noise."

James called back over his shoulder. "You coming Michael? Betsy?"

"No," said Michael. "Richard brought me a new book."

"Aunt Molly is teaching me to crochet," said Betsy. "I want to practice while she's here in case I make a mistake."

The rest of the day slipped quietly away and although they were all worried about Mark and Linsey, they tried not to dwell on it.

16   *Brother against Brother*

The week continued to be cloudy and muggy. By mid-week, Olivia marched to her garden like a soldier in combat determined to attack the weeds that grew much faster than her vegetables. An hour later, she had a small pile of greens – not to be confused with edible greens – and a cleared row of tomatoes.

On her knees, she leaned back, pressing one hand into the small of her aching back, while with the other she swiped at the sweat dripping perilously close to her eyes. Once again, she felt gratitude for the women of the community who had provided her with plants. Soon she would have to think about canning. All their gardens were producing far more than they had anticipated. They would probably use the camping site for canning and all work together.

Behind the house, someone was building something. The echo of hammer hitting nails blended with sounds of the valley. *The boys are building something – a shed, or chicken coop, more furniture.*

Richard had put up a porch swing for them and Betsy enjoyed a book while she listened for any sound from the napping babies.

Swatting bugs and yanking weeds, Olivia barely noticed the sound of a galloping horse behind her. She glanced toward the lane as Richard slowed his horse and rode up beside her. Olivia stood, knowing instinctively something was wrong.

"Olivia." His voice was so taut and stressed she hardly recognized it.

"Richard?"

"They need you," he said.

She removed her apron, swiped her hands across it and dropped it at the end of the row where she had been working. "Watch the little ones if they wake before I return," she called to Betsy as she took Richard's hand and swung up behind him reaching her arms around his waist.

Richard turned the horse and galloped down the lane, through the town to Uncle George's home, stopping so suddenly that Olivia slid off. She would have fallen to her knees if she hadn't steadied herself against the side of the horse.

"Sorry about the sudden stop," Richard said as he slid down and caught her. "I wasn't thinking."

"No harm done, Richard. What is it? One of your brothers?"

"Worse," he said as he opened the screen door for her. Olivia hurried into the living room. *What could be worse than one of his brothers being hurt in the war?*

Aunt Molly sat rocking back and forth in her rocking chair, tears streaming down her face, moaning softly, her hands squeezing a handkerchief into a tight ball. Uncle George stood like a statue at the window like the father in the Gospel of Luke who waited for the return of his prodigal son. Olivia knelt beside Aunt Molly, who dropped her head on Olivia's shoulder and sobbed.

Richard handed her a copy of the *Cabin Creek News* dated that morning – August 21. She read the headline, "Skirmish at Hawk's Nest. Local Boys killed."

She glanced up at Richard, who swiped his arm across his eyes, then read further. "Yesterday General Cox met Lieutenant Colonel Crohan at Hawk's Nest. Both sides lost men. Our community lost five good men – two from one family – Private First Class Linsey James Dooley and Corporal Mark Jefferson Dooley. Our reporter, who witnessed the skirmish, said the Dooley boys tried to protect one another. Each was killed by members of opposite forces. They died in each other's arms. Others from our area killed in the skirmish were, Private Robert John Hinson, Private Samuel L. Cole, and Lieutenant James C. Berry."

Olivia dropped the paper and glanced at Uncle George with eyes blurred from unshed tears. "I'm so sorry," she whispered.

"At least the Lord answered my prayers," he said. "They didn't kill each other."

"But they are still dead," said Richard with a note of bitterness in his voice.

"Yes, they are son, but they died with honor as far as I'm concerned – family honor."

"Why don't you come home with me for the night?" said Olivia.

"I'm assuming the governments will send them home. Olivia…will you do the service…like you did for Grandma Cooper? We don't have a preacher yet, but even if we did, I want you."

"Please, Olivia," said Richard.

"I'll do what I can," she said, "but you know I'm not…" A wagon stopped in front of the house, interrupting her. Heavy boots scraped across the porch, followed by a rapid knock that rattled the screen door. Richard reached to open it.

A tall, hefty man stepped inside. "Richard, I need to talk to your dad," he said. Uncle George turned around.

"John," Uncle George acknowledged the man then turned to Olivia. "I think you've met my niece, Olivia Brunner.

"Good afternoon Miz Brunner."

"John is the father of Lieutenant Berry," said Richard, "as well as the mayor of Cabin Creek."

"Did you hear when they will send the bodies?" asked Uncle George.

A frown crossed the man's face. "I called. They informed me there were too many bodies and they couldn't send them all home. They would just bury them where they died."

Uncle George looked stunned. "They take our boys, get them killed and don't even let us have a funeral for them? Well, I don't know about you, John, but I'm going up there and get my boys if I have to fight every Yankee and Confederate soldier in sight."

"I'm with you, George. So are the others. We already got five caskets from Blake and we're riding up to Hawk's Nest. Thought you might want to ride with us. We could use another wagon."

"You bet I will. Olivia is going to do my boys' services. If you want, I'm sure she'll do them all."

"Thank you Miz Brunner. I remember the service you did for your friend. That will be a big comfort to our families."

"I'll do what I can, Mr. Berry."

Uncle George turned to tell Richard to get the wagon, but he was already running to the barn.

"I'll take Aunt Molly home with me. We'll wait there."

"Should be back sometime tomorrow – maybe do a Saturday funeral."

"The boys will start digging graves. We'll take care of things here. You ride carefully and watch for stray soldiers out to make names for themselves." Uncle George nodded.

"I'll go back and get our wagon," Olivia said to Aunt Molly as the men rode off. But before she reached the door, the sound of another wagon stopped outside. It was the mothers of the other three slain soldiers and a few friends.

"Olivia, we came to see about Molly," said Clara Berry. "Is she going with you?"

"Yes, I was just going home to get our wagon. It's too far for her to walk."

"We'll take you."

"If you want, we can all wait together," said Olivia as she helped Aunt Molly into the wagon.

The other women in the hollow had seen Olivia leave with Richard and were waiting to find out what was happening when she returned.

"We were afraid you got word…" Claudia didn't finish when she saw the tears and pallor of Aunt Molly and the other women.

Tillie helped Aunt Molly down from the wagon. "Want her to lie down on your bed?"

"Thanks, Tillie." The other women followed her into the house. "If the rest of you would like to lie down, the children's rooms are on the left."

"I've got coffee on," said Maggie. "What happened? The war?"

"Yes," said Olivia and handed her the paper she'd brought with her. Maggie gasped and read it to the others.

"They'll all stay here until the men return. They went to fetch the bodies," said Olivia.

"When…?"

"Uncle George said they should be back sometime late tomorrow afternoon."

"We'll help you with dinner," said Tillie.

"And the kids can spend the night with us," said Claudia.

"Tillie, if you would take the boys to the cemetery, we need five graves dug by Saturday morning. Some of Richard's friends will be there to help."

"Come on boys," called Tillie. 'We got our work cut out for us."

Maggie and Olivia began making dinner for a crowd. "Feels like old times," said Maggie.

Olivia smiled in spite of her grief. Silently she prayed, *O Lord, will it ever end? Did my promise to Will include burying children and youth and old friends? Comfort the grieving hearts and give me strength to do Your will.*

17   Community Funeral

Saturday morning dawned with clear skies and warm temperatures. *The day will be very hot before it's over.* James and Corey went to hitch Max and Jasper to their now coverless wagon. Even though the women from Richmond had been in The Valley only a couple of months, they already knew many of the families in Cabin Creek well enough to feel their grief. The shock of losing five young men to a war hardly in existence any longer than they had been in The Valley touched them all. Still carrying grief for Grandma Cooper and their worry for their men, the women added yet another burden to their wounded hearts.

With the heat and humidity, Olivia thought it best for them to ride in wagons rather than walk several miles. The children sat with their mothers, quiet and subdued. Maggie would remain at Olivia's with the babies and some of the younger children. They all knew Jeannette would stay in her house.

Sitting beside James, stiff-backed and stoic, Olivia stared ahead to the church in Paint Creek that stood on the hill hovering over deceased loved ones in the cemetery next to it. Behind her, a queue of mourners wound its way through the valley and up the hill.

Leaving wagons and mules at the cemetery gate, Olivia once again led the procession into the cemetery and to the gravesites. This time, however instead of six men and boys carrying the casket, many hands carried five sealed caskets. Family members and friends streamed in filling the area from fence to fence. When there was no more room inside the fence, some stood outside the fence.

Standing at the head of the center grave, Olivia lifted her voice and began, "The Lord is my Shepherd… though I walk through the valley of the shadow of death…dwell in the house of the Lord forever."

Following a prayer, Olivia spoke of the dedication and bravery of each of the young men who had given their lives for what they believed. With a mixture of tears and laughter, family members and other residents of the community shared memories and said their goodbyes.

When all was quiet once again, Olivia stepped from grave to grave, lifted a handful of dirt and let it sift through her fingers at she spoke the name of each young man. "Dust to dust and ashes to ashes. May the Lord God who gave life to – Private Robert John Hinson, Private Samuel L. Cole, Lieutenant James C. Berry, Private First Class Linsey James Dooley and Corporal Mark Jefferson Dooley – now accept these young men into His presence. May God the Father, Son and Holy Ghost, grant us peace and comfort now and always. Amen. "

Jeremiah, Bobby, Michael and Corey stepped forward with their harmonicas and once more sent the haunting strains of *Amazing Grace* across the cemetery. Many hands pitched in to help fill the graves then the hillside quickly lost its cloak of spectators and grievers. All returned to the town hall where Tillie had organized a funeral dinner.

As James drove the team to the Community Center, Olivia was lost in her internal struggles. *How many more times will I have to take on my husband's role before Will joins us? Will he and the others make it? Or will we have to raise our children alone. When...*

James had been silent since they left the cemetery, so. Olivia was startled when he spoke. "Mom?"

"Yes?" She pushed her own worries aside.

"Somehow life doesn't seem fair. Why should our community lose five good men? And...why should...Uncle George and Aunt Molly lose two sons at the same time? And why should Dad and Mr. Phillips and all the rest have to rot in prison – or be lost out there somewhere – just because they don't want to fight? Where is God? Does He really care about..." He paused and finished with, "...people?"

Olivia knew he really wanted to say, *us.* She took a deep breath and exhaled slowly. "James, after all we've been through, I can say with all assurance, yes, God cares about people – and most assuredly about us. Without His help we could never have made it this far. I don't understand why some have to bear so much suffering while others bear so little, but I do understand when men try to run things we all suffer. War brings suffering to everyone."

"Why doesn't God just stop them?"

"James, why don't I stop you, or Corey or Michael from doing some of the things you do? Not because I don't know about them, but because you learn from them. God wants us to listen to him, but when we don't, we suffer. I'm not saying it very well. Your father's the theologian. You'll have to ask him when he comes."

"I had a dream the other night. I dreamed I was someplace else – I don't know where – but I knew I would never see Dad again."

"James, it was only a dream. You'll see him. He'll be here soon." Olivia wanted to believe what she was saying, but that awful foreboding seemed to be overshadowing her. "Come on, let's hurry along. This is the last funeral dinner we'll be attending for a good long time."

"I hope you're right, Mom," said James. "Come on Max, Jasper. Move it along, now."

James looked unusually pensive. Olivia shivered, but tried to keep him from noticing how unsettled she felt. After all they had been through, what could possibly happen to them that would be any worse?

18   River Towns

Another week passed after the men left Captain Barnabas. The supplies the captain had given them were dwindling, as was their strength.

Samuel and John had the first watch, but Will joined them. The others slept as soundly as they could on the ground. The day was moving toward another very hot one.

"Mind if I join you?" asked Will as he felt his way toward where John and Samuel were sitting.

"You should be sleeping, Master Will. You needs rest."

"We all do Samuel, but I'm concerned about Mr. Dooley. I don't like the way he is coughing and wheezing."

"I've been watching him," said John. "So has Joe. You're right he's not looking good at all. The grayish tinge seems to be getting worse."

"Is there any place where we could get some medical supplies – home remedy stuff would be better than nothing."

"We've got the best in herbs and roots," said Samuel. "I been loading ya'll up with as much extra stuff as I can when I cook in the pits."

"I know you have Samuel and we certainly appreciate all that you are doing. I'm afraid Mr. Dooley needs pain medication – or will. If we can just keep him going until we reach The Valley, maybe they'll have a doctor who can…" His voice choked.

John laid a hand on his shoulder. "Maybe we can slow down a little. That won't get us there quicker, but might make it easier for him to travel. Let him sleep more."

"We would just be postponing the inevitable," said Will. "How can I tell Olivia that we lost her father on the way because I can't…"

"Will, this has nothing to do with your sight or lack of it. His heart is giving out and you are not God. You can't stop it – couldn't even if you had perfect vision. There's nothing wrong with Joe's eyes and he can't do any more than you can." John's words sounded harsh and irritable.

"They's a couple of towns near here," said Samuel. He'd been staring at the map that Captain Barnabas had revised for them. "When we gets closer, maybe we can stop early and …"

"And what? Just walk into town and go to the store like we aren't running for our lives?" It was Will's turn to express his anxiety by a harshness in his voice.

"A couple of us could go," said Samuel. "Mr. Dooley said he has some gold coins. We could buy some things to help."

"Samuel's right," said John. "We'll take an extra hour of rest tonight. Then we'll start watching for those towns."

***

Two days later, they came to Riverton. John took Samuel with him to test the atmosphere of that town. Before they had gone three yards into town, two angry-looking men stepped in front of them.

"We don't allow no niggers in Riverton," said one of the men.

"My slave and I are just passing through," said John. "Thought we'd buy a few supplies."

"Don't allow no niggers and don't sell to anyone with them," sneered the man.

"How far to the next town?"

"New River Crossing is down the road about six miles. You can go through the woods. Don't want you walking through our town."

"Thank you for your help," said John, not believing they were smart enough to catch the sarcasm. "Let's go Moses. Maybe the next town's more hospitable."

As John and Samuel turned to leave, one of the men leaped at them. John turned, whirled around, caught the man's upraised arms and flipped him over on his back before he even knew what hit him. "Anyone else want a dirt bath?" The other man stared with angry scowls.

John and Samuel returned to the others and reported the situation. "Let's find a place to rest. We'll stop near enough to New River Crossing that we can try there before many folks are up moving around," said John.

***

Taking their time, the men moved around Riverton and continued toward the next town, staying as near to the road as possible and taking longer periods to rest. They arrived at the edge of New River Crossing as the sky began to show a little blue.

"Kenny, George and I will find a place to sleep for the day," said Robert. "Looks like a cool wooded area. The way those clouds are

439

rolling we might need a sheltered place."

"I'll sit here with Mr. Dooley," said Will. "John do you want someone else to go to the town?"

"I think Moses and I can handle it," he grinned at Samuel.

"Moses?"

John laughed. "Yeah, I told them back in Riverton that he was my slave and I called him Moses in case anyone comes by and they decide to talk."

"Good thinking," said Will.

They found a place among the trees that sheltered them somewhat and Robert, George, Kenny and Jefferson Dooley were soon asleep. Will and Joe sat beside Jefferson monitoring his breathing and pulse.

"Will you be all right while we check out the town?" asked John. "Should I wake someone?"

"We'll be all right," said Will. "Joe can wake them if we need help. Just be careful."

***

A few minutes later, John and Samuel made their way down the street that stretched before them. The streets were dirt, but sidewalks of wooden planks paralleled them. Sturdy brick or log buildings stood adjacent to one another with narrow alleys in between. Halfway through town they saw The General Store, a large building of split logs with a covered porch extending the entire width of the building.

"You're out mighty early," said a man who was propping a brick against the door to hold it open. "You're strangers."

"Yes sir," John answered. "My man and I need a few supplies. The little town behind us refused to sell us anything."

"Riverton is like that," said the man who was almost as tall as John. His broad shoulders squared and he lowered his head exposing the silver white hair combed to one side. Plaid shirtsleeves were rolled halfway up his forearms. Suspenders hung across his shoulders like long fingers reaching to hold on to his pants.

"Hank Miller, here," he said extending his hand. "Don't see too many strangers in these parts since the war. Had a woman and her son here almost three months back buying supplies for a wagon train. Said they were all women and children and their men were all tied up with the war and they were taking their children up north of here."

"Olivia Brunner?"

"That was her. Nice mules she had with her."

"My name's John Rayburn," said John. "My wife was with that wagon train. We're trying to make it to our families, but we have a sick man and need something for pain as well as something simple we can fix in pit fires while we sleep."

"We'll fix you up, Mr. Rayburn. We don't have a doctor in this town, but I keep a supply of medicines on hand and do the best I can when folks are sick. What seems to be the trouble?"

"Heart," said John. "He's Mrs. Brunner's father. We're hoping he can hang on until we get there."

"Shouldn't be more'n a couple of weeks," said Hank as he moved around the store gathering supplies that the men would need – dried beef, vegetables and medicine – especially pain medication.

"God bless you," he said as they left the store. "I'll keep you all in my prayers."

"Thank you, sir," said Samuel.

"Mrs. Brunner is a special lady," said Hank. "Tell her I said hello."

19   *Maverick Soldiers*

August drifted into September, dragging with it the heat and humidity. The week after the funeral services for the Cabin Creek boys, one of the women approached Olivia after church.

"I've been watching the children in your group. I'm the teacher for the school in town and I was wondering if they would be attending and what grades they are in?"

"Is it fall already?" Olivia looked surprised. It seemed only yesterday that Corey and Michael had begged her to go to school. They weren't old enough then. Now they were too old – at least experience wise. "I'm not sure what to say, Mrs. Backus. The journey here was long and quite educational in many ways. Our children are all more advanced than most children their age. I'm not sure where, or if, they would fit."

"But they need some basics."

"I know, but we are still settling in and…"

"And you would rather wait for your husbands to help make major decisions."

"I guess that's about right."

"But, what if the men don't make it? The children will lose out on their education."

"They'll find us," Olivia answered a little too quickly. "But, you're right. The children do need an education. Maybe you, or another teacher, could come out to our valley once or twice a week, until you could decide where they belong."

Mrs. Backus smiled. "I think we could try that. How about next Saturday?"

"We'll gather all the children at my house and try half days every Saturday for a month then see where we go from there."

Mrs. Backus agreed.

***

The following Saturday Mrs. Backus and two assistants arrived early for the first day of school. Olivia greeted them, introduced them to all the children who eagerly waited in the living room, then excused herself. She returned to the kitchen where she could work and still listen to what was happening with the children. She didn't want anyone belittling them for what they didn't know. They had all been through too much for children to suffer humiliation at the hands of some teacher who didn't understand them.

As she listened, Mrs. Backus explained that she knew they had learned a lot on their journey north, so they were just going to talk about some things they learned so she would have an idea how far along they were in comparison to the other children. She heard the children tell her about how much rope it takes to corral twelve mules, two horses and one cow – until the cow bolted in a thunderstorm. They told her how to start a fire and how to measure how far it was from the creek to the fire. Bobby told them how far you can lean over the back of a wagon before you fall and break an arm. They told her about barges that can hold three full wagons at a time without sinking. They told her about how to tie a rope around a waist and save two kids from a raging river. They told her how much dirt was in a small grave. They told her how to tell time by the stars and the shadows of the day. They read to her from some books she brought along. By noon, Mrs. Backus was overwhelmed by the knowledge they had gained.

"Their reading, math and history skills far exceed the children in Cabin Creek," she said to Olivia as they walked to her wagon. "But, they need some work in writing and grammar. But you are right, they will not fit in with the other children in town, but why don't we include them in some of the social activities. They need to meet the other children – and the town's children need to get to know them. I'll have to order some different books for them."

Olivia was pleased that her children – meaning all the children of the wagon train – would not be left out of educational opportunities.

"Thank you for coming to us. We'll see you next week?"

***

Later that afternoon, as hot as it was, Olivia decided to work in her garden – especially to pick some of the vegetables for Sunday dinner. The afternoon silence was unnerving. For days – or had it been weeks – clouds came and went, promising rain, but leaving the earth dry and the air humid. Thunder rumbled in the distance now and then, but that too moved on with no hope of rain.

Olivia's inherited sixth sense prickled at the back of her neck and down her spine. It was too quiet, almost eerie. No clouds, no breeze, leaves drooped as if all life slowly ebbed away. Even the usually singing, chirping birds sat silent in the trees and bushes with heads buried under their wings as if hoping for nightfall and coolness. Insects buzzed – the only sound in The Valley until…

Gunshots from the direction of Jeannette's house shattered that silence. Olivia ignoring the heat grabbed her gun, which was propped against the nearby oak tree, and ran. *No one should be shooting. We made a rule – no shooting or hunting unless we all know about it.*

Michael and Jeremiah ran toward her from Jeannette's house as she ran down the lane toward it. "Mom," called Michael, gasping for breath, face pale, eyes wide. "Soldiers at Joey's house. Hurry! Corey and James…"

"Get Uncle George and the doctor," she yelled and each kept running in opposite directions. Maggie, hearing the shot grabbed her gun and met Olivia on the lane. Corinne, Claudia and Tillie were already there behind Jeannette's utility shed.

"Over there," said Tillie pointing toward the side of the house. "Three Confederate soldiers behind the woodpile."

Olivia stepped away from the shed and shouted, "Drop your guns and get out of here if you want to live to see another day."

The surprised men wrenched around to see who was shouting at them. "It's only more women," said one, slurring his words. "We can handle them." He laughed a nasty sounding guffaw.

"Yeah," said another and fired a shot at Olivia.

"They're drunk," said as she ducked behind the shed. Tillie returned their fire. A hat flew off one of the soldier's head.

"Hey, those little ladies can shoot," said the big, burly one who seemed to be the leader. Cover me boys, I'll take the one inside for a hostage. There's only a couple a kids in there with her." He started for the back of the house. The other two fired at the women.

The back door banged against the house. Jeannette screamed. Two shots were fired in rapid succession. Corey and Jeannette both screamed, "James!"

Heedless of the men with guns, Olivia sprinted for the house. The other women opened fire on the two remaining soldiers. Olivia's feet hit the porch as Corey pushed the front door open.

"Mom, James…" Corey, pale and shaken, was unhurt, but tears streamed down his face. Not waiting for him to finish she rushed in to find Jeannette on her knees beside James. Blood oozed from his shoulder. Crying and near hysteria, Jeannette dabbed at the blood with a cloth and chanted over and over, "James, please don't die. I didn't mean it. Please don't die."

Olivia shoved Jeannette aside and knelt beside James. One look told her the wound was bad, but not fatal if he got medical attention right away. The bullet was still in the shoulder.

"Give me a clean cloth," she commanded without turning around. With something concrete to do, Jeannette's hysteria abated and she handed Olivia the cloth, which Olivia pressed across the wound to stop the flow of blood. James groaned. Olivia was vaguely aware of the lack of gunfire outside and the soft murmuring voices of the other women.

"We need to get him back home. Michael went for the doctor," Olivia said without looking up.

"My wagon's hitched," said Jeannette. "James hitched it for me so I could go to town and get some supplies."

"I'll get it," said Corey running for the door.

"Bring it to the back door. It'll be easier..."

Corey was gone. Olivia turned to Claudia. "Send someone to Betsy. Tell her to get the fire in the stove going, put some water on to boil and clean the table."

Claudia motioned for the women to follow her and began giving orders. "Bobby, you and Joshua go help Betsy. The rest of you get buckets and go to the creek. We'll need more water than she's got on hand."

Olivia heard the rattle of the wagon and snorting of mules as Corey stopped outside the kitchen door.

"Help me carry him to the wagon," she said.

Tillie slipped her arms under one shoulder and Olivia eased hers under the hurt shoulder. Maggie took his feet. Together lifted James and carried him to the wagon where Olivia climbed in beside James. Corey waited in the wagon, brushing at the still falling tears.

Olivia noticed a red stain spread across Tillie's sleeve as her friend backed out of the way. "Tillie? Your arm. How bad?"

"Just a graze. You can patch me up while the Doc takes care of James."

Olivia nodded and said to Corey, "Take it as fast as you can without jarring him on the bumps."

Corey flipped the reins. "Come on Charlie and Zeke. Get moving there." The mules, as if sensing the urgency of the moment, moved quickly up the lane.

Corey pulled the wagon into the backyard by the porch, just as Michael and Jeremiah arrived with Uncle George and Richard. Uncle George slid off his horse and ran to the back of the wagon where the women were getting ready to move James into the house.

"Let me do that." He lifted James from the wagon and carried him into the kitchen.

"Put him on the table," Olivia said. "The bullet is still in him. Doc Wilkerson will be able to get to him easier there."

Dead silence settled behind her. Something was wrong – terribly wrong.

"Where *is* the doctor?" Olivia whirled around, taking in all the anxious faces. "He *is* coming, isn't he?" Panic edged into her voice.

"We don't have a doctor no more, Olivia," said Richard. "Confederates took Doc Wilkerson two days ago. Gave him a choice of going with them or finding his building in ashes."

For the first time in her life, Olivia wished she knew some swear words. She clenched her fists, gritted her teeth and stared at her uncle and cousin.

Jeannette stood by the door sobbing. "It's all my fault. I'm sorry, Olivia. I didn't really mean it when I said I hoped one of your kids died. Please forgive me. O God, don't let him die." With each word, her voice rose in volume and pitch.

"Someone take her out of here," said Olivia between clenched teeth. "I can't think with all that screeching." She looked from one hopeless face to another.

"The water's boiling, Mom," said Betsy. "Want me to tear a clean sheet for bandages?"

Olivia turned to lash out at her daughter. There was no need for boiling water or bandages. They had no doctor. She stopped, mouth open. Betsy's matter-of-fact expression clearly said, "You can do it, Mom."

Olivia nodded and fought back the tears that stung her eyes. She'd been strong before, she could hang on a little longer.

Betsy returned with a sheet and started tearing it into strips. Claudia and Corinne glanced at Olivia and went to help her. The look of determination they all knew so well replaced Olivia's hopelessness. She glanced first at Uncle George and then at Richard. "I'll need your help," she said.

"You've got it Cousin, but what are you going to do? Surely you aren't going to operate on him."

"Richard, what will happen if we don't get that bullet out?"

"He'll die."

"And what will happen if I operate?"

"He still might die."

"The difference between will and might is enough for me," she said and started washing her hands the way Will had taught her when she helped him.

"Michael, bring me your father's medical bag. All of you wash your hands and get over here to help me. Richard and Uncle George, I'll need you to help hold him down. Corinne, Claudia keep boiling water coming and sterilize these instruments. Someone keep Jeannette out of here unless she can control herself. Maggie, take those clean pieces of cloth and keep the blood away from the wound so I can work. Michael, Corey, take the children to the front room and watch the babies."

James groaned and tried to sit up. "Mom?"

"I'm here, James." Olivia leaned over him so he could see and hear her. "You've got a bullet in you. As soon as we get it out, you'll feel a lot better."

"Where's the doctor?"

"Not here, James. Confederates took him." Her eyes met his. She wouldn't look away.

"Dad?"

Olivia gulped back the lump in her throat. "No."

His eyes widened as he realized what she was about to do. He grinned through the pain. "Go for it, Mom." He eased back on the table.

Encouraged by her son's trust in her, Olivia said, "This is going to hurt like nothing you ever had before. Uncle George and Richard are here to help you hold still." She put a folded piece of cloth in his mouth. "We're out of pain medicine. Bite down on this when the pain gets too much. I'll try to be quick and gentle."

James took the cloth from his mouth. "Mom, I don't think you can be both gentle and quick. Don't worry. I'll be all right." He put the cloth back in his mouth, took his uncle's hands in his right hand and was ready to squeeze. Olivia strapped the left to his body.

Corinne took the tray of instruments from the boiling water to Olivia. Olivia cut away the shirt and began washing around the area. Maggie kept dabbing at the blood. Finally, sweat dripping from her brow, Olivia reached for the probe. It was still so hot she almost dropped it.

"Pour some of that alcohol over the wound," she said to Claudia. James stiffened as the burning liquid spread over his tender flesh. Olivia probed for the bullet before she lost her nerve. Luckily, it wasn't very deep, James stiffened and even with the cloth in his mouth Olivia was sure she heard his screams. She found the bullet and had it out in seconds. Pouring more alcohol in the wound, she then pressed a clean cloth over the area and began wrapping strips of cloth over the shoulder and chest to keep it in place. By the time she finished, James was unconscious.

Uncle George, unashamed of his tears, picked James up and carried him to his bed. "I'll sit with him for a while," he said.

"Thank you, Uncle George," said Olivia. A wave of dizziness swept over her. Afraid she would faint, she leaned against the table. Richard hastened around the table and wrapped his arms around her.

"You're going to be all right, Cousin," he said as her head fell against his shoulder. "You're a remarkable woman, Olivia. I'm sure glad I'm related to you."

Olivia raised her head and smiled at him. "Thank you Richard. Now I know what I missed by not having any brothers."

"Come sit for a minute to get your breath," he said leading her to the porch. "Someone want to bring her some of that coffee I smell boiling?" He called over his shoulder.

Tillie followed them to the porch with two steaming cups. "This should help calm the nerves," she said. "And we thought setting broken arms was hard!"

"I would rather stick with arms," said Olivia. Then she noticed the blood stain on Tillie's arm.

"Tillie, your arm." She started to get up.

"It was only a nick. Maggie put alcohol and a bandage on it for me. She makes a good nurse, but no one can beat you at doctoring – 'cept maybe Will and Joe."

The screen door closed again. Jeannette stood beside them, tears rolling down her cheeks – the dark, vacant stare gone. She looked at Olivia like a friend she hadn't seen for a long time.

"Olivia, can you ever forgive me? I've been such a fool, but couldn't seem to help myself. I didn't really mean it when I said what I did. I…"

"Jeannette, come and sit down," said Olivia. Richard stood, making room for her on the swing. "You don't have to go," Olivia said to him.

"I want to check on Dad," he said. "This is hard on him. He's still grieving for Mark and Linsey. He never says anything, but we know. I'm afraid to think what it would do to him if he lost James too."

Olivia nodded. She understood. James had become the grandson he may never have. She turned back to Jeannette. "Welcome back to reality," she said. "I know you didn't mean it. James isn't out of danger yet, but if he doesn't make it, it won't be because you wished him dead, or because I did something wrong. It will be because that maverick soldier shot him."

"I know, just like it was Sarah's childish curiosity and stubbornness that caused her to fall in the river. You almost lost Corey and James both and I couldn't see that. And what I did to Joey was unforgivable. Olivia one thing I said was true, though. You are stronger than I am. This journey has made you even stronger."

"It's made all of us stronger," said Olivia reaching for her friend's hand and squeezing it.

"Can I stay and help you tonight? I don't think I can bear to stay in my house not knowing how James is doing. He saved my life. That man came through the door and James jumped in front of me, knocking me to the floor, as the man fired his pistol. Corey shot the soldier."

"Thank you for telling me what happened and I'd like having someone else in the house."

"We're all staying," said Tillie from the door.

"Dad too," said Richard returning to the porch. "I'll go on home. Mom will be worried."

"I can't thank you all enough," said Olivia, rising from the swing. "I think I'll go sit with Uncle George awhile."

Olivia shuffled to the bedroom where Uncle George sat on Michael's bed, his head resting in his hands. She fell back onto Corey's bed exhaling heavily – the ache in her back almost matching the one in her heart. Except for the thrashing of James in the bed between them, all was quiet. Would the death angel pass over the Brunner house, or would he stop and take her son?

20   So Many Angels

Afternoon faded to twilight. Olivia lay motionless on Corey's bed – waiting. She closed her eyes, but sleep was out of the question. Uncle George sat on Michael's bed on the other side of James, whispering prayers and occasionally blowing his nose. James thrashed about on the bed between them. Muted voices drifted from the kitchen. There would be no trace of her latest attempt at playing doctor when the women finished cleaning.

Mingled aromas of fresh coffee and chicken cooking drifted through the open door, reminding Olivia she had babies to feed. Pulling herself up to sit on the side of the bed, she glanced at Uncle George, his face pale and tear-streaked. *James was right. Life isn't fair – two sons gone and now his nephew in the clutches of death.*

Maggie came to the door with a tray. "I brought you some soup and coffee," she said.

"I don't want anything," Olivia answered. Uncle George shook his head and waved her away.

"And just how do you think you're going to take care of James if you don't keep up your own strength?" Maggie sounded so much like Olivia during their long trek through the wilderness, that Olivia couldn't help smiling at her.

"You're right, Maggie, but first, I need to take care of the babies."

"We fed them already. They both ate a bowl of soup and you can nurse them at bedtime. Now eat – both of you."

Olivia and Uncle George reached for the bowls with reluctance, but they both knew Maggie was right. Olivia finished the soup unaware of its taste. She glanced around the room as she sipped her coffee.

"James designed and decorated this room," she said, knowing the words weren't as important as trying to focus her thoughts away from her unconscious son between them. Uncle George silently listened. There was no need for a response.

"He wanted his bed between the twin's beds so he could help curtail their bedtime games." She took a gulp of coffee.

"The walls are decorated with animal skins and other souvenirs of our journey. Richard helped him design and build the beds, with a holster on the end of the headboard for their guns – 'easy access in an emergency,' he said."

Olivia stared into her cup. Uncle George sipped from his. "In a normal world, why would children need to be concerned about such things?" she said.

"But, the world isn't normal anymore," he said. "War is not normal."

"Corey and Michael have their guns with them. Will James ever be able to shoot another deer or rabbit?"

Uncle George didn't answer. She didn't expect him to. They sat in silence except for groans and thrashing from the bed between them.

Finally, Uncle George broke his silence. "You're incredibly strong, Olivia. Jefferson has every reason to be proud of his daughter." He paused then added, nodding toward James, "You know he's not out of danger yet."

"I know," she whispered. "I did the best I could, but…" Olivia took a deep breath, feeling as though something had suddenly sucked all the oxygen from the air. She glanced at James and stated the obvious. "He's feverish, isn't he?"

Uncle George nodded. The bed creaked as he pushed himself up. "I'll get some cool water. We can bathe his face and arms. Maybe that will help bring the fever down."

Olivia waited, staring at the thrashing body and flushed cheeks. It seemed a lifetime ago when she sat with Will's face between her hands and promised him she would take care of their children if Parker ever refused to release him. Now it looked as if she might lose both her husband and her son. *I came close to losing both Corey and James once before, but this is different. How long can I continue to do the impossible?*

She chased her torturing thoughts back to their dark corner as Uncle George returned with cold water and cloths. Together they tried to cool the boy's feverish body. James thrashed even more and fought their ministering hands. He groaned and called out, "Dad, Dad where are you?"

Olivia clenched her teeth together and willed herself to keep her touch gentle. She wanted to cry out with him. *Where is Will? Why did we ever leave Richmond in the first place? Why did the war have to come and disrupt our lives?* Immediately she felt guilty for such thoughts.

We aren't the only ones suffering. The war is only a few months old and already the land is bathed in blood. Black ribbons hang on the doors of countless homes – both North and South.

"Mom!" James suddenly stopped flailing the air. His eyes flew open wide. He gazed at the ceiling lost between seeing and unseeing, between life and death.

"I'm here James," Olivia answered, dabbing at his brow again with the cool, wet cloth.

"Mom, did you ever see so many angels?" He smiled and reached an open hand toward the ceiling.

Olivia's heart skipped a beat. She glanced at Uncle George, who clutched at his chest as if his heart had stopped. She swallowed hard to push down the lump that rose in her throat and forced the words from it.

"No, James," she said. "I never did see so many. How...?" She swallowed again. "How many do you count?" Her voice sounded calm, but her hands trembled. She held them tightly together in her lap. She didn't want to alarm her son – if he were even aware enough to notice. She didn't dare look at Uncle George.

James gazed intently at the ceiling for what seemed like long, endless minutes. Finally, he said, "Oh, at least ten. They keep moving. And there's Grandma Cooper...and Grandfather!"

"James, it's the fever..." Olivia started, but her words seemed to agitate him more.

"No! They're really here. It's all right, Mom. I had a long talk with God. Everything's settled. I'm all right."

"James, please don't..." The words stuck in her throat. She didn't want to believe it was possible for him to die so young and yet, there was a child's grave on the side of a hill that would be forever etched in her memory. James had spent the night carving a marker for it – and for Grandma Cooper. Who would carve one for him?

Horrified at the direction her thoughts were going, Olivia covered her mouth with her hand lest the words escape. Uncle George didn't waste time on frivolous thoughts. He spoke with a stern harshness. James didn't seem to notice.

"Fight the fever, boy. Your mother needs you. You've got a lot of days and years ahead of you. Fight it, James. Fight it." Uncle George let his tears drop on the boy's arm as he tried to cool the burning fever.

A sudden look of disappointment spread across James' face. "Don't go," he begged and fell back to the pillow. He closed his eyes and lay so still Olivia sucked in her breath. She would almost rather watch him fight the covers and her attempts to help him than to be so near death. At least, then she knew he was alive.

"Uncle George," she said trying to keep her fears under control, "I don't know what I would do without him…especially with Will not here." She choked back the words. That dark, damp prison was too far away – too much in the past. "Will this crazy war ever end? Is any place safe for our children?"

"Olivia, war is hell, whether you're on the battlefield or at home waiting for word." Olivia winced, remembering his two sons he'd just buried. Uncle George didn't seem to notice her chagrin. "Mavericks take the law into their own hands and even women and children aren't safe anywhere. Armies take our doctors and clergymen so we can't even know health and peace of mind. All we can do is hope and pray and…"

"I know," she answered. "I know. I feel ten years older than when I left Richmond almost six months ago. Lucy will soon be walking. Will won't even know the boys or Betsy when he gets here. He has no idea we have Charles to raise." She glanced at Uncle George. He looked like he had also aged in the short time she knew him. "Have you heard any more from Richmond?"

Uncle George tried to give her an encouraging look. "Not a word," he said. He dipped the cloth into the cold water, wrung it out and placed it once more on the feverish brow of his nephew.

Blackie's barking followed by a sharp rap at the front door startled them. Both turned their heads to listen.

Without thinking, Olivia got up and left the room. Tillie had opened the screened door. They saw a man in a Confederate uniform.

Maggie came to her side. "Stay with James," Olivia whispered.

Maggie nodded and slipped into the bedroom. Olivia heard Tillie saying to the young soldier, "No one in this valley 'cept women and children."

"Sorry to intrude, ma'am. I'm not looking for new recruits. I'm Lieutenant Robert Patterson. I got word that some AWOL soldiers were in this area causing trouble. I've come to round them up. Just wondered if you folks know anything about them?"

"If you're looking for three men, Lieutenant," said Olivia, "you'll find them at the end of the lane. Two are holding down the wood pile and one is in the house – unless, of course, some hungry animal got to them."

Patterson glanced from Olivia to Tillie and back to Olivia, but before he could ask another question, Olivia continued. "I'm Olivia

Brunner. My wagon train of women and children came from Richmond a couple of months ago to settle close to my uncle."

The lieutenant glanced around the room and smiled condescendingly. Olivia stared – no smile. "Before you ask," she said, "we built our own homes with the help of some of the neighbors after we arrived around the first of June." Olivia stared at him with such intensity that he dropped his eyes to the hat in his hands. "There are six women and a number of children ranging from nine months to twelve years."

"Who killed the soldiers?" The lieutenant looked uncomfortable and changed the subject.

"We did." Olivia continued to stare at him.

"We?" He looked confused.

"Yes, sir," said Corey, who eased up beside his mother, slipping his hand in hers. "I…I killed…the one who broke into Mrs. Phillip's house and shot my brother." His voice trembled.

"And we women, all shot at the same time at the other two who shot at us first, wounding one of our women," said Claudia.

"That's right," said Tillie making a show of her arm with the bandage on it. "If you have any idea of arresting anyone for the killings, you will either have to take all of us, or fight it out like they did." Tillie didn't lower her eyes. The lieutenant squirmed.

Jeannette moved to the other side of Corey and laid a hand on his shoulder. "I was getting ready to go to the store when those three men started shouting and yelling. They sounded drunk. James said I should stay in the house. He said the other women would hear the gunfire and come to help. They did, but one of the men came into the house with a pistol in his hand. He wanted me to go with him. I said no and he grabbed my arm. James jerked me away and pushed me to the floor. The man shot him and Corey shot the man."

Tears rolled down her face and Claudia came to her side.

"They shot a boy?"

"He's back there," said Olivia. "You can see for yourself, if you want, but don't try any funny business. My friends are still agitated tonight."

The lieutenant walked back to the room and looked in at James who was thrashing around on the bed again. "Where's the doctor? Looks feverish."

"Company of Confederates forced our doctor into service a few days ago," said Uncle George. "The boy's mother removed the bullet and cleaned him up. She's taking care of him best she can."

The lieutenant jerked his head around to give Olivia an incredulous look. Without a word, he turned and started for the door with long angry strides. "We'll remove the vermin ma'am and clean up any blood stains we find. Those men were runaways. We don't condone killing children and shooting at women."

"Lieutenant Patterson," Olivia said as he opened the door. Her voice was so soft she wasn't sure he even heard her. He stopped and turned to her.

"Those men have loved ones waiting for them at home. Tell them their men were killed in battle. You don't need to specify what kind of battle."

Lieutenant Patterson stared at Olivia with his mouth open. Finally, he said, "Ma'am, you are far too generous. We'll do what we can to ease the pain of the families." Olivia watched him stride back to his horse where four other soldiers waited for him. He spoke to them briefly and they galloped down the lane toward Jeannette's house.

With slow steps, head bowed, Olivia returned to James. Throughout the rest of that night and the next, they all took turns sitting with James. The fever seemed to be easing as the first streaks of dawn broke through the window, but he was still delirious and talked to the angels that surrounded him.

Olivia watched with fear. *Will all my efforts be for naught? Will my son be in the next grave beside Grandma Cooper?* Her heart ached. *How can I tell Will?*

21 The Grave on the Hill

One more week of making little progress and Jefferson said he could go no further.

"We'll carry you if…," started Will.

"You can't carry me. Just let me rest a minute and catch my breath. The pain is getting worse and I'm feeling sick to my stomach."

Robert and Kenny had gone ahead to find a suitable place. Daylight was already making an appearance. Kenny returned alone. "There is a place just around the next curve," he said. "Sounds like the river is rushing toward a waterfall, so there won't be any river activity. The land opposite is clear and close to a creek."

Will turned to his father-in-law. "Can you…?"

"Let's go," said Jefferson. "I'll make it that far. When I quit breathing, just throw me in the river and let it take me over the falls."

The men, determination on their faces, began moving. Joe and Will helped Jefferson. They were almost there, when he could go no further. He slumped pulling Will and Joe with him.

"I can't…" Jefferson started then went into a coughing jag.

John moved the others aside and picked him up. "I'll carry him," he said.

"Lay him down near the creek, so we can get some fresh water," said Will. "We are just going to have to chance a fire and make him some hot broth or tea."

"Don't get yourselves caught…" Coughing once again took over.

"Here are some small branches," said George.

"Looks like the women might have been here for several days," said John.

"There's a circle of stone that looks like it was used for more'n just for one meal," said Samuel. "Why don't I look around and see if I can scare up a rabbit or two?"

"Kenny and I can see about catching some fish," said George.

Samuel headed toward a small hill across the creek while Kenny and George took their fishing poles to the river bank. Will and Joe sat with Jefferson, bathing his face and feeding him broth and tea.

Samuel called from the hill. "Master John. You needs to come up here, Sir."

John looked surprised. "Samuel must have snagged a bear or something if he needs my help bringing it in."

"Want one of us to go with you?" said Robert.

"No, looks like Kenny and George are bringing a mess of fish to clean and cook. Maybe you better help them."

Kenny, George and Robert began cleaning the fish and digging a pit to cook them in. John took off to the hill where Samuel waited, clearly agitated.

"What is it Samuel, you got a bear or something?"

"No sir. I thought someone ought to see this. We needs to tell Master Joe, but I don't rightly know how to do it."

"Joe?"

"Over here." Samuel led John to the small grave on the side of the hill covered with stones. The headstone indicating Sarah Phillips' grave sparkled in the morning sun.

John gasped. "You're right, Samuel. We have to tell the others. Won't be easy."

"Maybe if I goes back and sends Master Joe up here with you. I would let Master Will do it, but there's Master Jefferson. We just might have to put him beside her."

"You're right Samuel. I'll stay here. You send Joe then tell the rest when he's gone."

"Yes sir," said Samuel swiping at the tears streaming down his face. He ran back to the others as much as he could run considering the terrain and his weariness.

"Master Joe, you needs to go see Master John," he said when he got back.

"Me, but…"

"Samuel?" Will stared with half-seeing eyes.

"He needs to go, Master Will. Ain't good, but he has to go."

Joe glanced at Will, touched his arm and said, "Will…?"

"If Samuel says it's important, Joe, it is. I can take care of things here."

"I'll be all right," said Jefferson, "if you need to go with him."

Joe hurried up the hill to see John who took him to the grave and knelt with him while he wept. The others watched and saw them kneel.

"Samuel, what's up there?" asked Robert.

"It…it's…little Sarah's grave. She must a died here and someone carved a beautiful stone with angels and her name and age." Samuel swiped at his eyes again and blew his nose on the tail of his shirt.

"Sarah? But she…"

"You sure it wasn't Grandma Cooper?"

"No sir, it was Sarah."

"Go be with Joe," said Jefferson.

"I won't leave you alone," said Will.

"Can you bury me beside her? Then neither of us will be alone."

"Mr. Dooley, you aren't…"

"Yes, Will. The old ticker is giving out. I did my part in getting you back to Olivia. The rest is up to you. I'll be watching."

They had been so concerned with the grave and with Jefferson Dooley that they didn't hear the riders pull into their clearing. Too late, they heard the horses and turned to see three Federal soldiers dismounting.

"Is there a problem here?" asked the captain. "Where you folks from and more pointedly where you going?"

"I told you to leave me…" Jefferson began coughing again. Will put his arms around the man and lifted him. The captain ran over to give him a hand.

"He needs a doctor," he said.

"I am a doctor," said Will and so is my friend up there on the hill who just found his daughter's grave. We have nothing to work with."

"Wouldn't do any good," said Jefferson.

"Heart?"

Will swiped at his eyes and nodded. "It's been a long journey – too long for a man with a heart condition."

"You from Richmond?"

"Yes. How'd you know?"

"Just a guess. I'm Captain Robert Martin III with the Federal Army. You need the lady doctor I ran into a while back."

"Lady doctor?"

The captain laughed. "I expect you know her better than I do, but she sure fixed me up and helped me out of a tight spot. A half a tree fell on me and broke my arm. She set it. From what one of the kids told me she was some lady. She fixed his arm when he fell off one of the wagons."

"My Olivia?" Jefferson asked.

Will still sat holding him in a sitting position. "Sounds like our women are getting along quite well without us. You raised a considerate, self-sufficient daughter, Mr. Dooley. She's a chip off the old block."

"Thank you God, for my Olivia. Now, take me home so these men can get on with their journey."

"Mr. Dooley…"

Jefferson smiled at Will. "Thank you for bringing me this far. Lay me beside Sarah and pile some stones on top of me."

"We'll bury you properly if we have to spend the next week digging a hole by hand. When we find our women, we'll come back and get you and Sarah. We'll bury both of you near our home," said Will swiping at his tears.

"Thank …" Jefferson started coughing again. When he stopped coughing, he stopped breathing. Will eased him back to the ground, swiped his tears and murmured a prayer for him. Robert went to tell the rest.

"How we going to bury him?" asked Kenny.

"I'll see if I can find some sharp stones so we can dig," said George.

Captain Martin had left them to talk to his men. They mounted their horses and rode off and the captain returned to Will.

"I've sent my men back to our camp about five miles down the road. They'll bring shovels and some kind of box to bury him in. I promised your wife if I ever saw you, I would do anything I could to help you. This isn't much, but I'm at your service, sir."

The others returned to be with Will. He introduced them to the captain and told them what he was doing for them. While they waited, John and Samuel fixed the fish in the pits so they would be ready by late afternoon to eat.

Soon they heard the rattle of a wagon coming from the road. It turned into their clearing and a half dozen men jumped off with shovels and approached the captain. "Where do you want us to dig, Captain?"

"Up on that hill. Someone want to show them where?"

"I'll go," said Robert.

"So will I," said Joe. "At least she won't be alone anymore."

"They will be together until we can return and take them home with us," said Will.

The soldiers followed Joe and Robert to the hill and began digging. Two other soldiers began working with some planks they brought along. Soon they had, if not a proper casket, a suitable box to hold the body of Jefferson Dooley.

"We should clean him and wrap him in something," said Will. "We can wash him, but we'll just have to leave his clothes on him. I'm sure on the resurrection morning it won't matter to the Lord."

"We brought some army blankets," said one of the soldiers. "You can wrap him in them."

By late afternoon, the grave was dug, the body prepared and the casket sealed. The soldiers help carry it up the hill and lower it into the grave. They all gathered as Will did the graveside service from memory. He finished with "From ashes to ashes, dust to dust…May the Lord take the soul of Jefferson Dooley into His holy kingdom. Amen."

They all pitched in and helped the soldiers cover the grave, first with the dirt then with large stones. Robert took a sharp stone and scratched the name and date in the top stone. They would do better when they moved him.

They returned from the hill to a non-traditional funeral dinner. The fish was done to perfection and the soldiers had added some potatoes and some of their rations. No one went away hungry.

"Will you be leaving soon?" asked Captain Martin.

"We travel by night," said John. "Less chance of running into the wrong side."

Captain Martian nodded in understanding. "You heading north?"

"Yes, sir," said Will.

"My men will be moving out in a day or two. Why don't you take some time to grieve and rest? We can pick you up on our way if you don't mind traveling with Federal Soldiers."

"As long as you don't try to recruit us," said Robert. "We spent three months in prison and three months traveling at night 'cause we wouldn't fight for the other side."

"Don't expect you to fight. You can help us with cooking and washing, and things like that until we get close to Carnifex Ferry. We'll cross over there – that's where we sent the women because Galley Bridge is out. Then we'll head northeast and you'll want to go southwest."

"Thank you Captain," said Will. "I can't wait to hear Olivia's story."

"It should be a good one. I know she met up with some Confederate Soldiers. Their general was my grandfather. He gave them a note giving them safe passage through Confederate territory. I gave her one through our side."

The men spent the next two days resting, grieving and preparing for the rest of the journey. Seven days later they were once again on their own heading toward Cabin Creek.

22 The Shadow of Death Passes

Three days after Olivia took the bullet out of her son's shoulder, she leaned against the doorframe watching him. Uncle George came up behind her and laid his hands on her shoulder.

"Only six months ago he was a carefree child in Richmond," she said. "So much has happened since then."

"The world has gone crazy," said Uncle George. "Families are destroyed. Sons and fathers are killed in battle. Children have lost their childhood."

"Was I right to drag them away from Richmond? Would they have been safer there?"

"Probably not according to the newspaper."

Visions of the burning plantation pushed to the forefront of Olivia's thoughts. "You're right," she said. "Richmond would have been no safer. Will any place ever be safe again?"

"Only God knows, Olivia. You're doing the best you can."

She glanced at her son. He was quiet – too quiet. "He's so still and looks so pale." She pressed her hand to her mouth. "Is…is he…?" She couldn't bring herself to say the word.

Uncle George stepped around her. He glanced at her expression and then at James' death-like pose and rushed to the side of the bed. He lifted the boy's limp hand and felt for a pulse. His solemn face broke into a grin.

"The fever's gone, Olivia. The pulse is good. He's just sleeping." He swiped at his eyes. "He's going to make it."

Olivia stared at her uncle then at James and felt her knees begin to buckle. Uncle George jumped up and had his arms around her before she slipped to the floor. "Maggie, Tillie," he called as he picked her up and laid her on Corey's bed.

"I'm alright," said Olivia. "Just got a little weak there for a minute."

"James…?" Maggie went to the other side of James' bed. She felt his pulse then grinned. "Fever's gone, pulse normal."

Tillie left and came back with a cup of strong coffee. "Sip this," she said to Olivia.

"He's going to be all right," said Olivia as if trying to convince herself it was so.

"Mom?"

Startled by her son's voice, Olivia started to get up. Uncle George put a hand on her shoulder to keep her from getting up too fast.

"I'm here, James," she said, expecting to hear more about angels. She couldn't believe he was really getting better.

"Do you suppose I could have some of that coffee I smell and maybe a little something to go with it?"

Maggie, who had been holding her breath, let it out in a burst of laughter. "Surely, you aren't hungry. You've only been out for three days."

"Three days? Better make that a big bowl of something – soup or oatmeal. Is it breakfast, or dinner time?"

Maggie laughed again. Tillie had already gone for the tray. "It's breakfast," she said. "We'll put a chicken on to cook and have chicken soup for you for lunch." She held the tray while Uncle George helped James sit up and Olivia stacked pillows behind him.

They were silent while James ate the oatmeal and sipped the coffee. Finally, he pushed the bowl aside. "I guess I'm not as hungry as I thought I was," he said.

"It'll take a few days to get back to normal eating," said Olivia. "You can have more after that settles."

"Mom, did I give you a hard time? I sort of remember a sharp pain and angels."

"James, the only hard time you gave me was not knowing if you would live or die."

"I wanted to go with Grandfather and Grandma Cooper, but they said it wasn't time – that I was still needed here. I felt disappointed, but...I'm glad I'm still here."

"So are we, son," said Uncle George. "So are we."

"We all are," said Tillie as she took his tray.

"I think I will nap a little if you don't mind," said James and by the time Olivia took away the extra pillows and Uncle George helped him ease back on the bed, he was asleep.

"He'll be fine, now," said Uncle George. "Why don't you go sit for a while? I think I'll go home and let Aunt Molly know what's happening."

"Take Beauty," said Olivia.

"I can walk," he said, "but, if you don't mind, I will take the horse."

Corey, Michael and Betsy were waiting for her when she came out of James' room.

"Mom…" began Corey.

"Is he all right?" finished Michael.

"Did he eat enough?" asked Betsy.

Olivia knelt and drew all three children into her embrace. "James has been very close to death, but he's recovering. His fever is gone and yes, he ate enough for the time being. He's sleeping now, but he'll want more when he wakes up."

"I was scared," said Michael.

"We thought he would die," said Corey.

"I told you Mom wouldn't let that happen. She knew what she was doing," said Betsy.

Olivia smiled at her daughter. "Thank you for your confidence in me, Betsy. I don't always know how to do things, but when my children are in danger, I'll do everything I can to save them."

Michael and Corey left to tell the good news.

"Mom, can I sit with James for a while. I won't wake him or anything," said Betsy.

Olivia suddenly realized that the adults had taken turns sitting with James during the worst of his fever. She was struck with a twinge of guilt. *I should have included the children in his care.* She glanced down the hall and saw George Walsh watching them.

"Why don't you and George sit with him? When he wakens, one of you can come and get me while the other stays with him."

George smiled as he passed her to follow Betsy into James' room. "Thank you," he said.

Olivia nodded and went to check on the babies. It seemed ages since she sat with them just for the enjoyment of holding them.

By afternoon, James was improving enough to sit up for longer periods and eat a full bowl of soup with noodles.

"Looks like he's going to be fine," said Maggie.

"We need to get out of your hair so you can rest some. We'll bring dinner in, so don't you go working too hard."

"You're leaving?"

"We need to see to our homes, finish some canning and tend to our gardens," said Tillie.

"Send one of the boys after us if you need anything," said Claudia.

"Joey has done so much for me," said Jeannette. "I'm going to see if I can remember how to make a sail boat with him."

"Really?" said Joey around a broad smile. "I'm glad you're getting better, Mom. I really missed the real you."

Jeannette hugged her son and let her tears flow.

"But, first," said Joey, "we better pick the squash."

"We'll see," said Jeannette taking his hand.

"Thank you all so much for helping me through this," said Olivia. "I hope…" She didn't need to finish. They all nodded, hoping there would be no more trouble and the men would soon join them.

23   *Unexpected Visitor*

That night, everyone else was sleeping, but Olivia sat in the living room with an open book. Light from the kerosene lamp fell across it, but she hadn't turned a page in several minutes. She hadn't even read a complete sentence. Her mind whirled with questions and worries.

Lord, I don't want to worry, because I know You will take care of things. I do thank You for saving James and for the strength to do what I must. But how much longer can I be both father and mother. Somewhere along the way, what little money I have left will be gone and...

The rattle of an approaching wagon made her glance up at the mantel clock. *Almost midnight. Who...?* She hurried back to her room and for her gun, admonishing her carelessness of not having it close at hand. The boys' door was open.

"Corey," she called softly.

Instantly he was on his feet with his gun in hand. He followed her down the hall. Blackie began barking when the wagon stopped at her front porch.

"Go to the kitchen and cover me while I see who it is," she said. "If it sounds like trouble, get help."

"Okay," he said.

A short tap at the door followed unfamiliar footsteps on the porch. Olivia opened the door a couple of inches. A stranger waited.

"Yes?"

"Is this the Brunner home?"

"Who wants to know?"

The man laughed a gentle sound. "Do you have a friend named Rosy?"

"Again, who wants to know?"

"Sounds like you are a cautious person. I won't give you my name, but I'm with the Underground Railroad. We've brought Rosy to you, but wanted to make sure she wouldn't be harmed if we left her here."

"Rosy? Here?"

Stunned, Olivia opened the door wider and stared past the man to the chubby, black woman running toward her steps. She threw her gun to the couch and caught Rosy in a bear hug, tears flowing down both faces.

"Mom, is everything...Rosy!" Corey, too, ran into Rosy's arms. The man on the porch quietly closed the door and left. Corey broke away and ran down the hall shouting, "Hey, everyone! Wake up! Rosy's here."

"Corey, don't wake the babies," said Olivia.

"Babies?" Rosy raised her eyebrows.

"It's a long story," said Olivia.

The other children ran to Rosy, who caught them all in a hug, then let James go when he winced. "What done happened to you?"

"A Confederate soldier shot him...said Corey.

"And they took our doctor away..." said Michael.

"So Mom had to operate on him..."

"And he was all hot..."

"And saw angels and..."

"Boys, enough."

"When did all this happen, Miz Olivia?"

"Three, four days ago. He's getting better now."

"Umm, umm, umm. I knowed I needed to get here fast as I could."

"Where's Samuel? And..."

"Daddy," said Betsy. "Where's Daddy?"

"Like you said, Miz Olivia. It's a long story."

"Are you hungry, Rosy," asked Betsy. "I'll make you a sandwich if you want."

"Thank you child, but they fed us a while back. I am tired and that boy needs rest, but let me tell it to you short-like. The soldiers came to Richmond. They burned your daddy's plantation and..."

"We read about that in the paper. Mother was killed and all the slaves."

"Not all. Master Jefferson found Moses trying to hide Mattie in what was left of the barn. He sent them through the woods to our meeting place. Then he came to me and Samuel. He tells us to go with them and get on that Underground Railroad and head north away from there. Samuel refused to go without Master Will. But we had Noah's grandson, David 'cause the soldiers tried to take him. For David and Mattie's sake, I knowed I had to go with them. Samuel stayed to see if he and Master Jefferson could get the men out. I don't know what happened after I left."

"Where are David, Mattie and Moses?"

"Moses said he would take them North where he could get a job and look after them."

"The paper said Daddy accused the mayor of arson and murder and was thrown in prison. He escaped with six other prisoners. They saw bodies floating toward the falls and assumed they all drowned and were washed out to sea."

"And Samuel?"

"Nothing was ever said about him, but we believe he and Daddy somehow staged the escape, possibly with Matthew Parker's help. We believe they are on their way and keep hoping every day to see them coming down the lane."

"Then we need to just keep on praying for them to come to us," said Rosy.

"We built a cabin for you and Samuel, but we haven't got any furniture in it yet," said James. "I sort of got waylaid." He grinned at her.

"You sleep right here on the couch," said Olivia and tomorrow, we'll send word to the rest of the women. They were all here until this afternoon helping me with the latest crisis. They'll be back for breakfast."

"Then I better get some sleep if I gotta cook for that crowd." Rosy laughed, slipped off her shoes and stretched out on the couch.

Olivia laid an afghan over her and turned off the lamp. Tomorrow would be plenty of time to tell her about their trip – about Sarah, Grandma Cooper and about Charles.

24 Almost Home

The men left Captain Martin and started toward Cabin Creek.

"We'll stay with the daylight and the road," said John. "There's enough cover on either side if we should have to hide quick."

"We should be almost there," said Will.

"I could go ahead, Master Will, and bring back help," said Samuel.

"Might be too dangerous," said Will "We don't know how they feel about slaves or former slaves up here."

"We'll give it another day or two," said John, "then maybe... Hide, quick. I hear horses."

Joe and Robert took Will's arms and almost carried him to the woods where they pushed him down behind some scrubby pines. The others scattered and hid. They waited. Minutes later a half dozen Confederate soldiers rode past them heading toward Carnifex Ferry. They waited ten minutes more before John gave the signal for them to move.

"Confederate Soldiers? I thought we were too far north," said George.

"From what Mr. Dooley said, people up here are pretty well split. Charleston is under Confederate rule, but Federals are constantly trying to take it from them."

"Looks like we can't escape war no matter where we go," said Kenny.

"Did you really think we would?" asked Robert. "The whole nation is involved."

"I guess I knew that, but I can hope anyway."

"We better be looking for a place to stop," said Samuel to John as they moved a little ahead of the rest. "Master Will and Master Joe is dragging. Too much grief and worry."

John nodded. "Why don't you go ahead and scout out a place for us?"

"Yes sir," said Samuel and trotted off as if he were much younger than the others when in reality he was closer to the age of Jefferson

Dooley.

As the men rounded the next curve, Samuel signaled for them to follow him. He had found a small clearing surrounded by thick growth of trees and shrubs.

"We should be able to build a small fire to help keep the bobcats, wolves and other creatures away."

Two days later, they were once again on the road when John suddenly called out, "Hide."

Robert and Joe grabbed Will and ran for the woods, but the horses were galloping too fast this time. They just barely fell to the ground behind a giant oak tree when the riders stopped.

"What you stopping for?" one of the asked.

"I thought I saw someone moving in there. Maybe we can get us an AWOL soldier or runaway slave and collect the reward." He pulled his pistol and shot toward the shrubbery surrounding the tree. A small rabbit jumped straight up, then ran for the road and was across it before the man could take another shot. The two other men guffawed and slapped their thighs.

"Better get your eyes checked when we get back to camp," said one.

"Yeah, can't tell the difference between a rabbit and a man."

"Well, I just saw the bush move," said the one who had fired the shot.

"You're lucky it wasn't a bear."

"Or a polecat."

They all laughed and moved on, quickening their pace as if they were in a hurry to meet someone.

The men waited until they were gone and John and Samuel could hear no sound with their ears to the ground.

"All clear," said John. "Let's go."

"We have a problem," said Robert. "That bullet hit Joe."

"Joe? How bad?" Will sat up and reached for his friend.

"Just hit my leg, above the knee. I think the bullet is still in there. Hurts but I think I can keep going. We'll let the doc in Cabin Creek take care of it while you supervise," he said to Will.

"Let me look," said Will. "Maybe you can guide me while I remove it."

Samuel took his knife and cut away the bottom of the pant leg. "We needs to stop the bleeding," he said. "John and I will see if I can gather some wild plants to put on the wound. I saw some back there close to the trees."

"No, we have to keep going," said Joe. "We're too close to those Confederate riders. They might come back. Just wrap it and we'll see to it tonight when we stop."

***

That night they stopped beside a clear running creek and boiled water for Will to clean the wound. "I can't feel the bullet. It must be imbedded in a muscle. At least you can walk on it somewhat."

Samuel found the leaves he wanted near the camp. He wet them and placed them on the wound then wrapped it with strips torn from shirts. "He's feeling feverish," said Will.

The men took turns sitting with Joe, cooling his head with cold cloths. By morning Will told the rest, "He can't travel like this and if we don't get that bullet out, he won't travel at all."

He pounded his hand on a nearby stone then shook it.

"Did that help?" asked Robert.

"I feel so helpless. I'm a doctor. I know what to do, but I can't see to do it."

"Could you guide one of us?"

"Maybe, but...how far do you think we might be from Cabin Creek?"

"I'd say another day's travel," said John. "Why don't I leave now? I can be there by morning and bring help back by noon."

"I's goin' with you," said Samuel.

"One of us needs to stay and..."

"And what, Master John? They can take care of themselves and hide if they hear anything. Just thought one shouldn't go alone in case of trouble."

"You're right Samuel," said John. "Let's go."

"God go with you," said Will. "We need to get down to work," he said to the rest. "We need to pray for their speedy and safe return and for our women."

"That's all we can do right now," said Robert. Kenny and George nodded in agreement and the four men knelt in serious prayer while ministering to Joe as best they could.

25   Answered Prayers

In The Valley, another week had passed with little or no trouble.

"The women from town are coming out here probably Wednesday or Thursday to make apple butter," said Olivia while she and Rosy fixed breakfast on Sunday morning. "We have plenty of apple trees out here and the space where we last camped will work well for copper kettles and open fires."

"I'll make lots of bread," said Rosy then laughed. "Can't have good apple butter without good bread."

"You're right," said Olivia. She went to the end of the hall. "Breakfast is ready," she called. "We don't want to be late for church."

"We taking the wagon today?" asked James. "It looks like rain. You might not want to walk that far in the rain."

Olivia glanced at her son. He was almost back to normal, but she thought he still looked pale and he still didn't have all his energy back. "I think that might be a good idea. Eat your breakfast and while Rosy and I clean up you boys can hitch Max and Jasper to the wagon. The rest should be here soon."

The boys went out to get the wagon ready and Olivia began clearing the kitchen table when Blackie started barking – not his ordinary bark that says, 'Someone is coming,' but a more excited barking that said, 'someone important is coming.'

"Miz Olivia, that sounds like his family bark."

Olivia started for the front door with Rosy right behind her. Blackie continued to bark excitedly. Olivia grabbed her gun, started for the lane and found James right beside her. Rosy still not used to everyone having a gun handy, watched from the porch. Tillie came around the corner of the house and fell in step beside Olivia.

Blackie, tail wagging, bounced up the lane like a young pup. He stopped, body twitching and waited for Olivia's command. She stood beside him, shading her eyes from the rising sun with her hands.

Then they saw the tall, thin man turn into their lane from the main road. Tillie gasped. "That's John," she cried. Tillie, never one to show her emotions or get excited, picked up her skirts and ran up lane to meet the man who opened his arms wide to catch her.

Olivia gulped back a cry and ran toward them. Another man rounded the corner.

"Mom, it's Samuel," said James.

Blackie raced ahead of them, stopped in front of the black man and grinned as only a dog can, wagging his tail in greeting. Tears ran down the man's face as he dropped to one knee and put his arms around the dog's neck, feeling the wet tongue on his face. Samuel raised himself up to catch Olivia as she flew into his arms. Samuel held her a minute then eased her back, holding her at arm's length.

"Now, Miz Olivia, that ain't no way to greet a slave."

"Samuel Brunner, you aren't a slave and never have been for us. How are you? Where are the rest?"

"We didn't want Samuel to come looking for you by himself," said John, "not knowing what folks here think of black folks."

"Well, they is as friendly as any I've ever met," said Rosy running up behind them and into Samuel's arms. "We been prayin' real hard for you folks. What took you so long?"

"Now don't you go beatin' me up in front of these folks," said Samuel around the broad grin on his face. "We got lots of stories to tell, but right now we needs to get the rest up here."

"Where are the others?"

They're a couple miles back," said John. "Joe caught a bullet in his leg and Will …"

"What about Will? What's wrong with Will?" Olivia held her breath expecting the worst.

"He's mostly blind, Miz Olivia," said Samuel.

"But he's doing fine," said John. "Joe needs medical attention though."

Olivia sucked in her breath feeling as if an angry mule had kicked her. She would have to keep going for this new crisis. Corey drove up with the wagon and Olivia climbed in and took the reins.

"Rosy, take Samuel back to the house and feed him. John and Tillie can go with me to get the rest.

"No, Ma'am, Miz Olivia," said Samuel. "I ain't goin' to eat 'till the rest do."

"Corey, you and Michael let the others know what's happening and tell them to help Rosy prepare the kitchen for surgery again. James take Beauty to the church and let them know we won't be there. Your Uncle will be down to see what's wrong if we don't show up."

John and Tillie climbed on the back of the wagon. "Surgery

again?" John looked at Tillie raising his eyebrows in question.

"An AWOL soldier shot James. Our doctor was forced into the army. Olivia had to take the bullet out or lose her son."

Olivia called to the mules, "Let's go there Max, Jasper." She snapped the reins and they obeyed.

"They aren't too far," said John. "But Joe is having trouble walking and he's getting feverish."

"How long ago…?"

"Two days…. There's the place up there on your left. There's a small clearing where they could hide in the woods in case anyone comes by here."

Olivia pulled the wagon into the clearing and drew the team around a circle with the wagon heading out. They got down and ran toward the woods, but the men were already coming to them. Will and Robert had Joe between them. George walked beside Will and Kenny walked behind them.

Olivia ran to Will. George and Kenny took Joe, so Will could get his arms around his wife. "Will?" The lump in her throat pinched off the sound so she hardly spoke above a whisper.

"Olivia? Olivia, my darling, it's really you."

"It's really me, Will," said Olivia as she threw her arms around his neck. His arms came around her waist and they were lost in each other's embrace, tears mingling and lips connecting in welcoming kisses.

The rest moved on toward the wagon to give them a moment of privacy. Finally, Olivia said, "We need to get Joe back to the house for treatment."

"We have a house?"

"We all do – and barns and a house for Samuel and Rosy."

"Rosy. Have you heard…?"

"She's here. Got here a little over a week ago."

They reached the wagon and Olivia greeted all the rest. "Robert! Your face! What happened?"

"Ran into a low limb. Will didn't tell me it was there." He grinned

"Are all of our women and children all right?" asked Kenny.

"Let's talk on the way back. It'll take us months to catch up. The women and children are all doing fine, except…" Olivia bit her lip and Tillie continued.

"Sarah fell in the river and took pneumonia. We had to leave a grave on the side of the hill."

"We saw it," said Robert, "when we…" It was his turn to bite his lip and pause.

"Your father got us out of prison and came with us, Olivia," said John, "but his heart gave out. We buried him next to Sarah. Some Union soldiers helped us dig the grave. As soon as we can, we'll bring both of them home."

"Grandma Cooper made it to The Valley," said Tillie. "She enjoyed the square dance the community held as a welcome for us. She died later that night."

"Is Maggie…?"

"Maggie is fine. We have all helped each other."

"We're home folks," said Olivia, "at least to my home. You can see the rest of the houses down the lane. We arranged the houses so we could all see one another in case of trouble."

Robert, George and Kenny fell off the wagon into the arms of their waiting wives. Jeannette climbed into the wagon beside Joe sobbing. "Oh, Joe, our little Sarah is gone. Olivia did what she could, but I let her get pneumonia. I hurt Joey and I was out of my mind and…" Jeannette stopped, realizing that Joe was in so much pain he wasn't hearing half of what she was saying.

"Someone help him to the kitchen," she said. "Will can…"

"Will can't see, Jeannette," said Tillie.

"But who…? Olivia?" She gave Olivia a pleading look.

Oh, Lord, I'm not a doctor. Why do You keep sending these people to me?

26   Another Emergency

Olivia returned to her wagon master role and began giving orders. "Get Joe to the kitchen," she said. "Is the water hot? Is the table clean? Betsy, get a clean sheet and prepare bandages. Corey, give that bag to Maggie, then you and Michael put the mules in the corral."

"Is your wife always this bossy?" John laid his hand on Will's shoulder.

"I think she's acquired a new note of authority," said Will. He couldn't help smiling.

Tillie smiled at her husband. John was used to women being more aggressive than *polite society* allowed. "None of us would have made it out of Richmond, much less through the summer, without her," she said.

Olivia ignored them and started for the kitchen to prepare for another round of playing doctor. She turned at the sound of a horse galloping down the lane.

"It's James," said Corey.

"Uncle George is with him," said Michael.

"You folks take care of the introductions. I have work to do," said Olivia and continued to the kitchen to make sure that everything was ready for surgery again. She heard Uncle George greet the men, James introducing him to everyone and comments about how much he looked like Jefferson. She paused on the porch and turned to see Samuel reach for Joe to carry him into the house. Uncle George ran to him and said, "Let me do that."

"Yes sir, Master George. You sure do look like Master Jefferson."

Uncle George laughed as he carried Joe to the house. Olivia held the screen door and he followed him to the kitchen.

"Put him on the table, so I can take a look," said Olivia and Uncle George placed Joe where Olivia could reach him then moved back out of her way.

Joe clenched his teeth to hold back the groan as Olivia touched his leg. "John said the bullet is still in there," she said. "I noticed you can't stand on it. Do you think a bone is broken?"

"I don't think so."

"What did you eat?"

"Whatever we could find. Mostly Samuel and John were our cooks. Both were excellent shots with a bow and arrow. They both knew how to cook without creating a lot of smoke. A riverboat captain and some Union soldiers gave us some food. We didn't take much with us because we left in rather a hurry when we escaped from Libby. And I don't really care if I never see another rabbit or fish."

Olivia listened more interested in keeping his mind off what she was doing than what he was saying. She cut the ragged pant leg off as high as she could. The wound was just above the knee and looked red and swollen. Forgetting for the moment that Will and Joe were both doctors, Olivia automatically took charge.

"Betsy, bring a wash basin of hot water and soap over here so I can wash the area. Corinne, either wash your hands to help me, or move aside and let Maggie help."

"I'll let Maggie help. I can't do that kind of stuff."

"Neither can I Corinne," said Olivia as she scrubbed the flesh around the wound.

Joe's eyes widened as he eased up on his elbows. Olivia smiled at him. Jeannette hovered next to him with her arms on his shoulders.

"I've learned to do a lot of things I didn't think I could do," said Olivia. "On the journey, we had no doctor and now the war has taken Cabin Creek's doctor, so it's me or no one. I don't have pain medication left. All we have is a clean cloth to bite down on. You're welcome to scream if you would rather. It's your leg."

"It's all right, Joe," said Jeannette. "She took a bullet out of James. She set broken arms, took care of snakebites, near drownings and deaths. She protected us from Confederate and Union soldiers, helped build our houses and still has time to tend her garden and put away vegetables for coming winter."

"Sounds like you've all got a lot of stories to tell."

"We do have a lot of stories and so do you. We'll get you patched up and all of you fed, then we'll begin to catch up.

"John, don't we have some pain medication left?" Will asked.

"It's right here," said John, "in my pocket." He handed the bottle to Olivia. "We travel light."

"We bought that in New River Crossing for your father," said Will.

"From Hank Miller," said Olivia. She took the liquid and gave some to Joe. "This will help some," she said.

"Rosy and Maggie will help me here. Tillie, you can keep the water boiling and the instruments ready for use. The rest of you clear the kitchen so I can breathe. Will, you and Uncle George hold Joe – don't need any involuntary jerks."

While the rest retreated to the living room, Tillie held the pan of sterilized instruments ready for Olivia's use.

"Maggie hand me the prob. Rosy swab the blood away while I work." As with James, once again she probed for the bullet and got it out. "Wasn't in there too deep," she said. "Didn't touch the bone."

Half an hour later, she was tying the bandage in place. Joe was groggy.

"Shall I take him to the boy's room?" asked Uncle George.

Joe mumbled, "Help me to the living room. I don't want to miss all these stories we have to tell."

"Mom," called Corey. "Aunt Mollie and Richard are here."

"Make sure they are introduced to everyone," she called back to him then turned to Uncle George. "Take him to the boys' room." She looked at Joe who was about to protest. "You need to rest. We'll hold the stories until later – after dinner. I promise I won't let them tell a single story until you are awake."

"All right," he said. "Always trust Olivia to keep her word." His last words faded as he slipped into sleep.

Uncle George carried him to Michael's bed. Jeannette and Joey had been hovering near the door. They followed and sat with him.

As Uncle George left with Joe, Olivia glanced at Rosy who grinned from ear to ear. Rosy loved fixing meals for large families.

"The men needs food now," said Rosy. "Betsy and I made sandwiches. The other women can help her carry them while I cleans up my kitchen. Then I'll put three chickens in the oven and potatoes and beans on the stove to cook."

"Claudia, Corinne and I will help clean up," said Tillie.

Olivia leaned against the table for a minute feeling more than a little weary. "Will, did…"

Before she could say anymore, Will had his arms around her. "You did just fine, Dr. Olivia," he whispered.

"Will, I'm not…"

"Yes, you are. Let's go sit. You're trembling."

"I'll bring her some coffee," said Tillie. "Take her to the porch where she can get some air."

Tillie brought the coffee to the porch. Corey and Michael followed.

"You all right, Mom?" asked Michael.

"I'm fine," she said from the safety of Will's arms.

"When we going to hear the stories?" asked Corey

"Yeah, we want to know how they escaped..." said Michael.

"And survived their journey..."

"And how Mr. Phillips got shot..."

"And..."

Will laughed. "And we want to know all about your journey."

"But I think we all need to catch our breath," said Olivia. "Joe needs to sleep a couple of hours. Why don't we just let everyone get acquainted with Uncle George and the family. We'll tell stories after dinner."

"Okay," said Michael and Corey together.

27   *The Stories are Told*

Dinner was over and everyone gathered in the living room – some standing, some sitting on the floor and some bringing chairs from the kitchen.

"You left first," said George Walsh turning to Olivia. "You start."

"We left early in the morning of the 20th of March," said Olivia. "I can't say how glad I was to see five covered wagons waiting for me at the churchyard. James and I both sensed that someone was following us and thought it must be Samuel since Blackie, too, seemed to sense his presence."

Samuel laughed. "Yes'em. I did follow so I could let the men know you got off safely. I saw Mary toss something to you. Didn't know it was her baby."

Charles crawled to Samuel, pulled himself up to Samuel's knees and lifted his arms to be picked up. Samuel smiled and held the baby close.

"Miz Olivia, did you know Mary was my sister's child? That makes this little fellow related to me."

"I didn't know that Samuel. I'm glad. He's really a good baby."

"I wondered how we acquired twins since we only had one baby when I was imprisoned." Will grinned at his wife.

"Let me introduce you to our little black son." Olivia laughed.

"Olivia, it's so good to hear laughter. The remembrance of our happy families is all that kept us going when despair crept into that dingy room."

Charles decided he would try Will's lap for a while and crawled over to him, pulled himself up to Will's knees. Will picked him up and held him close, running his fingers over the baby's smooth skin. Charles chuckled when Will's beard rubbed his face. His chubby hands patted Will's face. He gurgled then said, "Dada."

Betsy laughed and the twins giggled. Olivia said, "How do you like that? I caught him when Mary threw him at me from the side of the road. I bathed him, fed him, protected him from harm and the first word he speaks is *Dada* to a man he's never seen." Olivia tried to sound indignant, but even Will heard the joy and pride in her voice.

As if the baby understood her complaint, he reached to pat her face and said, "Mama." Lucy not to be outdone said, "Dada, Mama," then clapped her hands and laughed.

Charles crawled back to Samuel and Rosy. Rosy, grinning hugged the baby to her while Samuel went back to his story. "I was mighty scared for you when Parker's men stopped you. I almost ran down to help, but was afraid that would cause you more trouble."

"What did you say to make them give up so quickly," asked Robert.

The women all laughed and Tillie said, "She told them they would have to kill every woman and child in the wagon train in order to take the mules. Then she said he could have all the mules, horses and the cow as soon as we got to The Valley. Said she'd send word and Parker could come and get them all if he still wanted them."

They all laughed and Olivia said, "Well, it worked – that time."

"When did you start playing doctor?" asked Joe.

"Our second day out."

"Yeah, I was leaning over the back of the wagon to see how far I could go without falling," said Bobby.

"Did you find out?" asked his father trying not to laugh.

"That's what Mrs. Brunner asked me, too," he said. "I did – and I broke my arm."

"You had good weather for about three weeks – at least I'm assuming you had the same as what we had in Richmond," said George Walsh.

"We did," said Olivia, "and we made pretty good time. Then the rains came and slowed us down considerably."

"We had a real bad storm," said Jeannette. "The thunder and lightning was really scary. A tree fell on my wagon."

"Were you in the wagon?" asked Joe. "We saw the evidence of a tree cut in pieces and knew something like that must have happened."

"No," said Jeannette looking sheepish. "I was so scared, I took the kids to Olivia, hoping she would make it stop."

"And she didn't?" asked Will.

"I'm not God," said Olivia.

They all laughed – the women because they were there and had heard her say that often, the men because they knew the incredible journey she'd led.

"Parker hauled me off to his office often at first," said Will. "Then he said he was through. When I changed my mind, I could let him know. He told me he had sent a recruit out to steal your mules. We worried about how you would get to The Valley without them."

"Oh, we would have gotten here," said Claudia.

"Olivia would have made us pull the wagons ourselves," said Corinne.

"As it was, we had to help the mules through the mud and up the hills," said Maggie.

"Parker did send a green recruit – promised to make him a Lieutenant, or something," said James, "but Blackie caught him in the act of trying to cut the corral rope. We sent him back to Parker, empty-handed, with rope around his wrists."

"What happened to Sarah," asked Joe gulping back the lump in his throat.

"We were going to fish at the river," said Corey.

"Joey tried to make Sarah go back to the wagon," said Michael.

"And she fought him and got too close to the river bank," said Corey.

"She fell in," said Michael.

"Corey jumped in to get her," said Joey, "but she fought him and they were carried down the river toward the falls."

"James rode Beauty and got ahead of them," said Tillie. "He tied a rope around his waist and the other end around a tree. He jumped in and swam toward them to catch them before they went over the falls."

"I knew the rope was going to be short, so I took the rope off the tree and put it around my waist, stood in the water as far as I could, holding on to Tillie. It gave him the extra length he needed to catch them."

"Sarah got more water in her than Corey. She took pneumonia. We tried, but we couldn't save her," said Maggie.

"They're all being too kind," said Jeannette, tears streaming down her face. "I was out of my mind with fear from the time I left Richmond. Something snapped. I just couldn't do anything and I couldn't ask for, or accept, help. If I had let Olivia care for her…"

"We don't know that, Jeannette," said Olivia. "It was hard for everyone."

"We found the grave, when Jefferson died," said Kenny,

"What happened to him," asked Uncle George.

"He got real sick," said Will. "Joe and I took take care of him as best we could. Captain Barnabas gave us food and took us up river a couple days' journey, but his heart couldn't take any more grief and running. A scouting party of Union soldiers came upon us as he was dying. We told them who we were and where we were going. They helped us dig a grave next to Sarah's."

"Captain Barnabas," said Maggie smiling.

"That was some trip on the river," said Claudia. "I never thought he would get all those wagons on the barge."

"I was sure we would sink," said Jeannette.

"Grandma Cooper loved it. He gave her a captain's cap and let her steer the barge up river."

"And the Union Soldiers? Their Captain said to say hello to the *woman doctor.* He said you helped him in a tight spot."

Again the women laughed. "Captain Robert Martin – His grandfather is General Robert Martin of the Confederate Army. We met both. A large tree limb fell on him in his sleep. His men came looking for men to help lift it off. The boys, with the help of Max and Jasper, got it off and I set his arm."

"Now tell us about your escape," said Corey.

"Why did the paper report you as drowning and going over the falls?" asked Maggie.

"There were fires all over Richmond when the Confederate's moved their headquarters there. The general ordered our homes burned and slaves killed. He didn't even know we don't have slaves. The renegades included extended families. They burned Mr. Dooley's plantation, slaughtered his animals and killed the slaves and Mrs. Dooley while he was in town trying to help us. They planned to parade us down Main Street the next day then shoot us." John stared into the distance as he spoke as if he were reading a script of some kind.

"Mr. Dooley went to the mayor's office and accused him of arson and murder. Mayor Nelson told Parker to take him to Libby. But before he did, he placed the master key to the prison on his desk and turned his back so Mr. Dooley could pick it up. As Parker walked him to the prison, he made arrangements to help." Kenny, too, spoke as if reciting a ritual of some kind.

Robert picked up the story. "We swam across the river where Parker waited with a wagon. We got in the wagon and Samuel threw a tarp over us then piled the bodies of dead slaves on top of us. They threw seven bodies in the river where they would be seen going over the falls. Then Parker took us west. We got out of the wagon and headed for the woods."

"Samuel and John both know a lot about camping," said Joe, "so they got us through the long days and nights. We tried to stay close to the river, but we didn't dare let anyone see us. Even if they weren't looking for us, which we figured they wouldn't if they thought we were dead, they would take Samuel as a run-away slave."

"It has been a long, hard journey for all of us," said Olivia. "What we did as women was difficult and much against customs, but when you are surrounded by God's grace and the loving arms of friends you can do far more than you ever thought possible."

"You're right," said Robert. "We couldn't have made it out of prison, much less the journey to The Valley without each other's help. Samuel, we will be forever in your debt."

"Now, Master Robert, I just do what the Good Lord tells me I should do. I promised Miz Olivia I would get you folks here and I keeps my promises."

28   *Promises Fulfilled*

Much later – the neighborhood quiet for the night except for the call of mountain wolves and owls nearby – Will and Olivia, wrapped in each other's arms, shed the tears they had saved for each other. They shared fears and hardships of the last six months, as well as the joys and hopes for the future.

"Will, what happened to your eyes? Did they…?"

"No, 'Livia. The only torture I received was not knowing where you and the children were and if you were safe. I was having problems earlier this year and intended to see an ophthalmologist in Washington, but never had the chance to go."

"And you didn't tell me?"

"Didn't want you to worry. When I made the appointment, I would have taken you with me. I didn't intend to keep it from you, but circumstances got in the way. There was nothing you could do – unless you have taken up ophthalmology along with your medical practice."

"Will!"

Will laughed and pulled her close to him. He was silent for a minute or two – so long that she thought he had fallen asleep. Then he sighed and said, "Olivia, how will I ever support my family? It's all well and good talking about keeping my partnership with Joe, but we both know a blind doctor isn't the norm."

"Whoever said we were a normal family?"

He laughed again. "Do you really think I can still help Joe?"

"Of course you can, and besides that we have a little church in The Valley that needs a pastor. You don't have to see to preach. You always were good at remembering. Either I, or one of the children, will read the scriptures and anything else you need to hear. You can do it."

"Would they accept a blind pastor?"

"Will, they have no one except me and I'm not a preacher. I don't even try. I manage some Bible studies, prayer meetings and did a few funerals, but only because they were friends and family. You can do it darling. I know you can. We'll still find an eye doctor and see what he has to say."

"Olivia, when I asked for your promise to take our children to safety, never in my wildest imaginations would I have seen so much hard work and sorrow. And yet, God has truly blessed each one of you. I hear the difference in the voice of each of my children and friends. You're right. The children have all grown far beyond their years."

"Will, had I known the hardships, I still would have promised. I did everything in my power to keep them safe, but…"

"'Livia, you kept your promise. It was hard knowing you were gone and not knowing if you were really safe, but it was easier than it would have been knowing you were in Richmond when the invasions came."

"And you kept your promise to come to us when you could. You're here. You and the other men had a harder time than we did. At least we had food to eat and fire to cook —most of the time." She smiled remembering the times the stew was semi-done because of the wet wood and rain. "We have all bonded into a friendship that will never be broken. Any one of us can protect our children, hunt for food or pick up at a moment's notice and move again if we have to."

"Oh, really?" he said. "I heard about a little place about three hundred miles north of here on the Ohio River…"

"Will Brunner, I said if we have to. We don't. Now, go to sleep and get some rest. Who knows what tomorrow will bring?"

ABOUT THE AUTHOR

Mary Lu (Pennock) Warstler was born in Oak Hill, West Virginia. She is a 1956 graduate of Collins High School.

In September 1957, Mary Lu married Rodney J. Warstler and became a full time Minister's wife. They have four children, nine grandchildren, and five great-grandchildren.

In 1980, Mary Lu received her B. S. in Education with a minor in music from the University of Akron. After teaching learning disabled children for two years, she enrolled at Methodist Theological School in Ohio and received a Master of Divinity in Theology in 1985.

Mary Lu and her husband, Rodney, are both ordained United Methodist Ministers. On July 1, 2000, she joined her husband in retirement where she pursues other areas of ministry – primarily writing. They live in Copeland Oaks Retirement Community at Sebring, Ohio.

Mary Lu loves animals, especially cats. After the death of her two Siamese (Nicholas and Sugar Plum) and her "British Blue Wanabe" (Michael), she decided not to have another pet. However, Katie (a three-year old part Siamese) and Charlie (a six-month old gray female) have stolen her heart.

Mary Lu has written numerous worship resources, plays, sermons and novels. In her *spare* time, she enjoys reading, writing, painting, music and needlework of all kinds,

www.ingramcontent.com/pod-product-compliance
Lightning Source LLC
Chambersburg PA
CBHW060757030726
47503CB00002B/279